Perfect Playbook

A Small Town, Second Chance, Marriage of Convenience

Starlight Canyon

Sienna Judd

PERFECT
Playbook

STARLIGHT CANYON SERIES
SIENNA JUDD

To everyone who has set aside their own dreams to lift others up, I see you.

Chapter One

Logan

SIXTEEN YEARS AGO

I STARE at the sign on the door and read words that make the death of my father even harder to accept. As if it wasn't already a suffocating reality, now, I promised my coach I'd attend at least one session and give this a chance. I need to talk about my father out loud, in front of strangers. Pretending it isn't real by ignoring this harsh reality is about to come to an end.

I've been lucky to be in another town and not have to pass his armchair at home, the one where he used to pluck his guitar strings, yet never failed to glance up to ask how

I'm doing. I'm lucky to not roam the hallways where we used to get hurt playing tag. Away at college, I don't sleep in my childhood bed where he'd come and sit on the edge and talk to me with his cup of hot cocoa just before hitting the hay. His presence isn't here at Golden Sierra. I'm not Billy's son to everyone who passes by. I'm just Logan Hunter. Number Nine.

But I have to face the truth if I'm ever to get my strength back. He's gone, and it's time to deal with the aftermath of chaos in my mind that's led me to lose my nerve in games. An NHL team has been in contact with my coach, and I'll be able to leave my college team soon. I'd be feeling over-joyed if my secret weapon hadn't become unreliable since my dad passed. My aim and fail-proof penalties were my superpower, and now, they're average at best.

After our last game, Coach took me aside and put his hand on my shoulder as we walked behind the others toward the dressing room. "Hunter, I know what it's like to lose someone. Let's get you some counseling. Get you back on track. It works. Trust me on this."

I choke up at the memory of the conversation that led me here. It was a vulnerable moment I shared with a man I constantly tried to impress. It took everything not to cry then and there, having him know I'm weak but believing in me all the same. I hope I'll offer the same grace to someone else someday.

I read the sign on the door again, and it might as well be glowing neon. Why do I feel so uncomfortable? Surely, it's normal to need to talk it out after someone as close as a father dies? But being from a small town where a man isn't meant to show emotion means there's an uncomfortable tug of war at play in my gut. I know I should talk, but I've been taught to suck things down.

I heard confidentiality is a big thing in support groups, and I wasn't required to put my last name down to sign up for today, but I'm not exactly anonymous all the same. I'm a high-profile athlete, and much as I don't like it, I get stared at everywhere I go. I already feel eyeballs on me right through the door. I scrub my hand over my face with a balmy palm and check my watch.

I'm late.

Come on, Logan. Just do what you gotta do.

When I push open the door, the person I suspect is the counselor is already speaking to a group of six other people, introducing herself.

Her gentle gaze lands on me. "Hi. Come on in."

I'm paralyzed staring into her eyes; my mouth is dry. What am I going to say? I can't seriously be considering telling all these strangers about my absolute darkest moment when I've hardly even spoken about it with my siblings and Mom.

"I'm Fiona. Please, take a seat."

I don't want to draw any more attention to myself than I already have so I take the nearest spot in the circle of chairs where four other students fill some of them.

She resumes her introduction. "My office is in the health services building, and there are counselors on call twenty-four seven with the Samaritan line. So don't hesitate to reach out. Now let's talk about our current session. You can tell people who you are. You can talk about your loved ones who are still with us and the ones who are not. You share anything that comes to your mind really. It might be about how your day went or something that seemingly has nothing to do with your grief. There's no specific format about what you should share or how to share it. Grief manifests in lots of different ways. You might be sad. You could

3

be angry. Fearful. This group isn't therapy. It's camaraderie. Here you'll find out, you're not alone."

I lean my elbow on my knee and put my chin on my fist. The movement shifts me closer inside the circle, and that's when I feel it. Eyes on me. I haven't wanted to actually see the faces of my fellow grievers. But I glance to my left where my senses tell me someone is having a good look at me. I'm brief. Discreet. I don't want to make full-on eye contact with whoever it is. But it doesn't take more than a glance at the woman to impact me. Her pert nose, glossy black bob, and two irises to match smack into me like I just ran into a brick wall.

She's pretty.

Is it inappropriate to think that? Here? Probably. I should be more focused, especially on what I will be saying when it's my turn to talk. But my mind works hard to allow the distraction of this pretty girl and her haunting stare because distractions are my coping mechanism.

Running.

Avoidance.

It's what I do.

So I can't help another quick glance to see if she's still staring at me, but she's moved her gaze elsewhere, which means I can rest mine on her for longer. She seems familiar.

I swear I know her.

Her eyes flick to me unexpectedly, and I quickly dart mine away, self-conscious on every level. I don't want to hold anyone's gaze, least of all someone who has piqued my curiosity. I should be formulating the words I'll say when the circle comes around to me.

The guy to the mystery woman's left introduces himself. "I'm Casey, uh..."

His nervous pause has my underarms prickling.

The deep plunge his Adam's apple takes while he considers his next words makes me even more aware of the stone in my throat.

Casey manages a little more about himself. "It was my brother. He got in a car accident. So..." He clears his throat harshly and completes his words with glassy eyes. "Yeah, he didn't make it. He was twenty-five."

My heart hammers. I can't even fucking imagine losing one of my brothers or my sister. *So young. His brother was only a few years older than I am.* I try not to think about what he just said too deeply, but his pain emanates right across the circle and lands on my lap like a roasting coal. It's hot as hell in here. Couldn't Fiona have cracked a window?

Casey manages to tell us how long ago it happened and how he's not been able to concentrate on his exams.

I get it, Casey. I feel you.

My mystery woman listens respectfully, and even though she does, and maybe I'm projecting, I suspect she's thinking about how she's next in the circle.

I feel my own turn coming on like a final countdown.

Just her left to talk.

Then me.

She heaves a silent sigh, perhaps trying to steady herself, keep herself from passing out in this inferno. Her chest moves up and down. Inhale, one, two, three. Exhale, one, two, three. It's like she's doing box breathing like Coach taught us when I was a freshman. Watching her breathe lowers my heart rate and reminds me to do the same.

I glance back down at my legs and am surprised to find them bouncing up and down. I'm usually so composed, but a self-conscious panic consumes me.

I raise my gaze just enough for it to rest on her lap where the woman nervously runs her index finger under the band of a bracelet. A bracelet I recognize. It's the graduation bracelet all seniors get from Starlight Canyon High School.

Casey finishes his confession, and Fiona thanks him for his words.

Mystery woman is next. *The bracelet.* Now that it's her turn to speak, it's more appropriate for me to take a better peek. Is she the girl who always headed up the bake sale fundraisers?

Her voice is mellow and mature, on the low side compared with the voice I'd have expected from a woman I can only describe as some sort of pixie. She has light-brown glass skin, her black bob is so carefree compared with her serious features. She's a tiny thing, and her voice is much more womanly than her face.

She continues to run her finger under the bracelet as she talks. "I lost my mom. It just happened two weeks ago so it's still fresh." Her eyes dart to mine but not long enough to see if I'm looking back. "Cancer." Her throat dips and she stares into the distance at nothing in particular but then briefly to me.

She pauses, and the room is silent. You could hear a pin drop. Nobody is eager to push in.

"To be honest, I don't feel ready to talk about it. I mostly feel numb right now. But I promised my dad and brothers I'd come here."

She wrings her hands for a moment and seems to focus on nothing in particular across the room, but her dark eyes flick to me.

Brothers. Mom. Cancer... Shay Mendez? Shay's hair was long in high school, and she's lost some weight, revealing cheekbones I don't remember her having. But it's her all right.

Shay. She was the cake-baking phenomenon who raised tons of money for sports at our school. Shay and I never ran in the same circles. She's a year younger for one, and unlike me, into artsy stuff and, of course, baking. And some baking it was. We all lined up for a taste of her cupcakes and a lick of that icing that was not too sweet, not too buttery. It was perfect. I can still taste it now if I think about it hard enough. Vanilla cupcakes with chocolate frosting. Classic perfection.

Last time I was home for a night Colt spoke about lending Luis Mendez some ranch hands so he could be with his wife during her treatment and recovery.

That stone gathers weight in my throat. *She didn't make it.*

Why didn't Mom or Colt, or anyone really, tell me Carmen died? I guess it was very recent. I suppose they'll mention it next time I go home. Maybe they figured I'd had enough bad news; they know I've been having trouble performing already. Some of the hockey games are televised, and I choked on national TV more than once. Maybe they were protecting me from hearing any more about death.

Shay shrugs like she's finished and turns her head to the right where her gaze, and everyone else's, lands on me.

It's showtime. My body is a furnace. I'm used to being stared at. I'm used to people watching my every move. Sometimes on the ice. Sometimes fans or puck bunnies. I'm used to attention. It's often unwanted, but it doesn't usually make the hair on my arms rise. But this sends me into a spiral. My mouth goes dry, and I'm dizzy as if dehydrated.

So I anchor myself. Shay, like all the others, waits patiently for me to speak, and I look her straight in her eyes. I connect with the familiar memory of sliding coins into her hand in high school and picking up one of her cupcakes to devour immediately then choosing a few other treats to take home. Dad liked her brownies best.

"Take your time, Logan," Fiona encourages me.

I don't want to take any more time. I just want to get this part over and done with.

"My dad died a couple months ago. He had a heart condition for years. We all knew about it but thought he managed it all right. Then, one day he had a heart attack. It was hardest on my brother, who found him."

Still now, months later, I wish it was me instead of Dash who dragged Dad out of Mustang Valley. Dash has always been closed and guarded; this trauma will certainly make a hermit out of him. I feel for the kid. He's still so young. I don't know how he did what he had to do. It's painful on a mythical level.

"I... Dad was a real rock for me and for everyone in the family really." My lips form a tight line.

Shay's gaze is caring and kindred. Fiona said we're here for camaraderie, and I feel that from Shay. Maybe I feel even more than that because she knew the exact man I'm talking about. He went to her ranch more times than I can remember; our parents even traded cattle. She's met him. She knows my whole family and I know hers. Something about having permission to open up to this circle and having someone like Shay to do it with helps the words flow more easily.

"I think the thing affecting me a lot right now is the guilt. Everyone back home is dealing with the loss firsthand. They have to have his things all around and be reminded of him in a way I don't being away. It feels like I get a vacation from it or something and I'm getting some unfair advantage. It's complicated to explain why, but I know I feel guilty."

Shay nods compassionately, and that's when Casey speaks up.

"I really get that. Like it's not fair that you get to run away to some adult playground while they're working in the trenches. Or something like that."

I nod. "Yeah. Something like that. Don't get me wrong, I think about Dad constantly, but when I somehow manage to have a good time, it makes me feel bad. Like I shouldn't be having any fun at all when they have to deal with the suffering more than I do."

The woman to my right with bright-blue dyed hair chimes in. "I think that's totally normal. I did this." She points to her cobalt locks. "I just did it for fun, to do something young and dumb like a person my age might do, and my sister said I was attention-seeking. I'm thinking, gosh, I'm just trying to be a normal college freshman and do stupid things like everyone else, but because my cousin died, should I not? How long do I have to wait before I can live my life again?"

The room comes more alive with allied nods, and it's like suddenly, we're in a house of mirrors.

I let others take over the conversation, but Shay and I continue ours across the room. A silent knowing, more powerful than any spoken language could communicate, travels across the space between us.

Coach was right. Coming here was good for me. The energy in this room right now could never take away the ache. But knowing others are going through the same thing, and with Shay sending me a subtle smile across the circle, everything feels less daunting. It's a bittersweet realization that sharing tragedy can somehow transform us. I don't want any of these people hurting, and yet, because they do it makes me feel better. I don't know if a problem shared is a problem halved but a spoonful of life pours back into me as the session progresses.

When the hour is up, Shay moves quickly, shoving the business card Fiona gave us in her backpack and making a beeline for the door.

I catch her up and gently grab her arm. "Hey."

She's startled.

"You're Shay, right? Shay Mendez?"

She pulls her lips into a thin line and hugs her backpack. "Yeah. Logan, right?"

"Yeah... from..."

We both say it at the same time. "Starlight Canyon."

"Sorry to hear about your mom. I knew Carmen was sick but I had no idea it was that..."

"Terminal? Yeah. It was." Her eyes grow glassy, but she quickly blinks away the film. "Sorry about your dad, too. Billy used to really make me laugh when he'd come over. He had that dad joke book..."

I nod, and my heart winces, recalling that book. He got it for Christmas just the year before. I didn't know he ever used those terrible jokes on anybody but us.

She adds, "He was a really nice guy."

A metallic feeling builds behind my eyes. I'm grateful that she knew him. "My dad loved your cupcakes. But he did support the conspiracy theory that there was something addictive sprinkled in them."

She blows a laugh out of her nose and quirks the corner of her mouth. I'd love another one of those.

"The MSG scandal? That kind of thing would only make headlines in a small town."

Some parents thought Carmen and Shay Mendez used either additives or voodoo to win the bake sales year after year.

"Hey," I bump her arm, "MSG or not, I'd give anything for another one of those cupcakes."

She purses her lips and nods. "Thanks." She tucks hair behind her ear and heads to leave. "Well, I guess I'll see you next week."

"Wait..." The word and my hand on her arm extend involuntarily. I don't want her to go. Not without me, anyway.

She flicks her eyes to my hand on her arm, and I remove it.

"I have to eat like six or seven times a day..." *Why on earth am I divulging this?* Nerves. That's why. *Real slick, Logan.* "For sports... anyway, do you want to get something to eat? It's that time of day."

"I would, but to tell you the truth, I haven't been hungry for like, a month now."

I claw up her honesty, and sad as her loss of appetite is, how raw and real life has been for the past hour. I want more. The pit of my stomach tells me not to let her leave.

"Well, the other thing I really should be doing six or seven times a day is study. Library?"

I'm probably coming across as desperate. I never really wanted to hang out with a woman before who I wasn't damn sure wanted to hang out with me, too. All in all, I don't hang out with women much. I went to dances with some girls in high school and had pizza with a few cheerleaders. I did the make-out sessions behind the stands but I don't recall ever making a first move. Hockey has always been the only thing I invited into my heart, but something tugs at me to be by Shay's side tonight.

I'm working overtime for the possibility of a few more minutes. What does that mean?

She lifts her eyebrow, so nonplussed I'm not sure if she's saying yes for me or for her.

"Sure. Why not."

We walk down the hallway, talking about our old high school. We step out of the health center, and I ask about what her brother from my year is doing now. Conversation flows freely, we even laugh a few times. I'm enveloped in her comforting presence that seems to make all else disappear.

We wind through the paths of Golden Sierra, lined with fallen leaves and an autumn breeze nipping at our edges. By the time we reach the library, I don't mention we should head inside. I don't want to go anywhere where we aren't supposed to talk. She tells me about this year on her dad's ranch and her brothers wanting to be tech entrepreneurs. I tell her about how my brother, Colt, is dating a French woman. Our words, some special, some meaningless but still full of simple pleasure, power our feet all the way to the river's edge where there's no more path, just a quiet bench. And we talk until the sun goes down.

But we don't just watch *that* sunset. We watch it the next night and every night after. And before much time passes at all, Shay becomes everything I never knew I was missing. She becomes the glue that puts me back together. She becomes my moon, and she calls me her sun, and with the collision of me and Shay Mendez, a brand-new universe is born.

Chapter Two

Logan

I STAND in a VIP check-in line for my mid-tier Vegas hotel. I don't like staying at the Firenze. It's dated now compared to a lot of the newer places, and the room service is slow. But an old high school hockey buddy is getting married on a gondola on the river, and I'm motivated to go straight upstairs to my room after the reception. I don't need the temptation of the Las Vegas strip after a few drinks. I promised myself I'd be good. Well, better.

Next to the VIP check-in is the general public, standing in a line the size of the Great Wall of China. Somehow it still seems to be moving faster than mine. I tap my foot. The man in front of me is angrily telling the newbie at the front desk about his frequent gambler reward points. He wants to use them for an upgrade. I watch the boy stand nervously and run through the back door, probably hoping to grab ahold of his manager.

I stop short of a sigh when he disappears, and my attention wanders behind me to a lobby full of eager energy. I've been to Vegas a thousand times, or at least it seems, and the buzz never fades, though it's true, this crowd looks a lot like the one I saw a few weeks ago when I snuck to the Strip for an appearance between hockey matches. Just when I'm about to turn back to the desk, a more unusual sight enters the foyer.

There's a stack of white boxes that seem to have sprouted tiny legs in skin tight jeans. Two young guys don't notice the Tower of Pisa and nearly collide with them, but the person carrying the stack deftly rolls, like some quarterback dodging a tackle. Somehow, barely, she manages to keep the boxes upright. Now, with her back to me, I have a view of a curvy ass below a curtain of long, black hair.

"Watch where you're going," the woman says, and it's a voice I'd recognize anywhere.

It's smooth and mature with a dusting of *don't mess with me*. I don't hear this voice often any more, but it once meant so much to me, I'd know it even across the foyer of a busy Vegas hotel. Shay Mendez.

Nearly any time I catch Shay in Starlight Canyon she's juggling boxes, carrying around something special she's baked, and those boxes always make my stomach drop, reminding me of the last day she was mine. I bet she's the one who brought the wedding cake for tonight. She knows the couple as well as I do.

The top box slides ever so slightly to the left, and I bail

on the line to hustle over and help. They're stacked so high they practically engulf her. She can hardly see a thing.

I slide up next to her. "Need a hand?"

Her brown eyes light up with surprise, but I hardly see it on the rest of her steady features.

"Logan. Hey... You're here for the wedding?"

"Yeah." I point to the box. "Did you make the cake?"

"I did."

I cross my shoulder bag around my body and make a move to grab the box out of her hands. "Let me help."

She takes a step back. "No. It's really fragile."

"I can be careful."

It's clear from her raised eyebrow she doesn't believe me. Trust doesn't come easy to this woman, but I've always liked that about her. It's all the more precious when you've earned it.

"Come on, Shay. There are too many drunk assholes around here. I balance blades on ice for a living. I'm pretty sure-footed."

She draws her lips into a thin line and nods. "Okay. But these cakes are like babies to me."

"Trust me... I'm eating this thing later, so it's in my best interests to protect it, too."

She gives me a reluctant but grateful smile, and my heart thunders like a kid with a crush.

I used to chase those demure and subtle Mona Lisa smiles of hers in all my free hours back at Golden Sierra. Sometimes, when I run into her in the Canyon and she smiles like this, it's hard to remember we aren't those in-love college kids anymore. But we aren't.

Shay and I have both lived a lot of life between now and then. Hell, she's a mom now. And me? I'm barely even in Starlight Canyon anymore, haven't been since we parted ways in college and I moved from city to city playing for various teams in the NHL. No, we aren't those same in-love college kids we once were.

That seems like a lifetime ago.

But even after all those years, her rare smiles still cause the most insane high before crashing down and crushing me with the weight of the impossible. Shay and I were in the wrong place at the wrong time back then, and I knew I wouldn't even be able to try my chances with her until I ended up back on the team in New Mexico. By then, she had a baby and never seems to take one of my flirtatious moves to run with it.

She's over it. I count myself grateful to still see her smile.

"Come on," I reassure her. "Hand 'em over."

"Okay, but..."

"It goes without saying." I take the boxes as if there are explosives inside instead of cake.

The boxes are a lot heavier than I expected, and the strength in her frame is impressive. I remember one time we had a family arm wrestling competition when I was younger, and my own mom, who though a lot taller than Shay is slight, was strong as fuck. I guess mothers carry things in their arms and on their shoulders their whole lives. It builds strength, for sure.

We walk along the elaborate patterned rug toward the ballroom where the Grishams are having their reception.

"So you're doing weddings now?" I ask.

"It's actually my first one. But that's the plan." She patters along in quick, small steps next to me. She's a good foot below, but her presence has always been bigger than her stature.

"I'm happy for you. You always wanted to be an entrepreneur like your brothers."

"Yeah. I've had a few detours," she offers, humble as ever. "But there's no time like the present, I guess. We'll see."

"Your *Sugar Shay* social does well. You must have good exposure?"

A whisper of doubt spreads across her features. "*You* follow *me* on social?"

"Course I do. I'm kind of hurt you didn't know that. Guess I'm just one of many fans," I tease. "Just one of the minions now that you're famous."

A sarcastic laugh rushes out. "Lush coming from you."

If Shay is comparing herself to my fans, there really is no comparison. I've never forgotten one damn inch of this woman, inside or out, in sixteen years. But I don't want to think about that. Not right now. In fact, I promise myself not to think about it every time I do run into her. Which is more often than I want and not enough at the same time. No one can make me uncertain like this woman.

I search for small talk to dampen what feels like the return of a young man's crush in my chest. *It happens every damn time.* "Are you staying for the reception tonight?"

It's a hope to change the subject, but it only makes me wonder what she'd be wearing, and it spins me in a circle right back where I started. She used to look so cute in my jersey.

"Yeah, that's the plan."

"Where is Antonio tonight? With your dad?"

"Yup. I've never left him overnight; even though we live with Dad, it makes me anxious to leave him. I'm one of those overprotective helicopter parents."

I bet she outright smothers that little boy in the best possible way. And Luis, too.

"No such thing as overprotective, is there?"

She rewards me with a grateful smile, the second in a short space of time, so I must be doing well.

"I guess I'll find out when and if Nino ends up in therapy."

I let out a rough laugh. "Yeah."

We're nearing the hall where the Grishams' reception will be. Even though I've briefly run into Shay many times over the years since college, we never really talked much. Everyday *how is the weather* kind of conversation was about as deep as it's gotten. Yet being from the same small town, I somehow knew most of her business, which means she knows most of mine.

That same sick bile I've tasted more than once over the years creeps up when I think again of what transpired with her son's dad. Anytime I've run into Shay in the Canyon and we're making conversation I want to ask more. What kind of man would do that to her? Are they on good terms or complete strangers? Has she ever seen anyone since? I know some of her business but I never know enough to truly satiate my appetite.

She opens the door of the ballroom for me since my hands are full. We enter an enormous hall where staff sets up tables and chairs for the party in a few hours. When I set down the cake, I let out a stale breath. It's hard to believe that I have men with sticks and blades attacking me for a living and carrying a cake for Shay Mendez is what gets me worked up.

I rub my hands together. "See?" I point to the cake. "Told you you could trust me."

She tilts her head, and the way her hair drips down her

shoulder is a sight to die for. She grew it out after we dated. I never got a chance to run my fingers through it.

"Thanks for helping. Not gonna lie, it was a close call out there." She rolls her lips.

I mirror her. It's time to get back in that check-in line, but I really don't want to. "Is there anything else I can help with?"

She shrugs. "No. All good."

Neither of us leave. It occurs to me it's the first time we've been alone together since she broke up with me. It's been sixteen years. Not that I'm counting.

"Well," she smooths hair behind her ears, "I better get this all set up and get ready. See you at the reception?"

"Yeah. See you later." I half turn to leave but can't help myself. There's no harm in asking. "Did you... do you have a plus-one?"

She laughs. "Yeah, right." Her sarcasm melts away, replaced by something harder to read. She runs a finger along the box's edge. "What about you?"

That box sure is interesting.

Her sarcasm returns. "I suppose they had to offer you a plus-two or three?" She glances up from under her eyelashes, and the corner of her mouth dips in with a reluctant smile.

I take a step closer. Her sweet perfume encircles me. Her pink lips shine with alluring gloss.

I tap her nose. "I came for the cake."

Chapter Three

Shay

SIXTEEN YEARS AGO

I LIE on my dorm room floor with the poster for the Equal Pay march tomorrow. I color in the black Sharpie outline, slowly brushing the felt tip up and down over the same ever-wetter, ever-darkening orange spot. I'm distracted. I check my alarm clock. Logan is late, but then again, he always is.

How on earth did I get to the point where I can't think about anything but that man? It's worked almost as if by magic, like I'm under some spell that binds my common sense. Logan completely disarmed me that night, and we took drinks to the bench where our friendship began. We wandered down with a beer for him, a wine cooler for me, and he kissed me. I let him. When his lips touched mine, everything inside me exploded and blazed. I came alive as if I never even knew what it was like to live before.

I shouldn't have done it without knowing where we stand, but life isn't always linear. Lust rages inside me every time Logan is near. I get why people don't wait for marriage much these days.

I'm falling hard. Occasionally, since being with Logan I wish I wasn't such a lone wolf, and it makes me miss my mother even more, having this thing, no matter what it is, with Logan. She'd be asking about Logan every day if she knew I was with him. Or friends with him. Or whatever this is. She'd be curious, and though I'd probably never confess just how far I've fallen, at least I'd be able to explore some of these feelings. I've always been introverted and cautious. Without her support, I'm downright terrified of how much a man like Logan could hurt me.

But I take the risk because no matter what happens, I guess it's better to have loved and lost than to never have loved at all.

Somehow this quote makes me think of my mom all over again.

I turn my head slightly to catch sight of a small care package under my bed, the one my mom made for me before she died. I slide it out and lean against the side of my bed and place it on my lap. I haven't looked at it since I met Logan, even though for the first weeks of her passing it was in my hands every day. My mom wrapped it with heavy-weight, beautiful paper in pink, and she wrote in her most elegant script: Shaylita.

I've seen the contents many times before, they still seem

a surprise, and I imagine her fingertips are still warm on the items—recipes she previously guarded, including her *abuela's* secret *caldo* ingredients on a yellowing note card, and photos of me and her throughout the years are scattered inside. I already took out the ruby ring she left in there and gave it to my dad for safekeeping, but the gold rosary I still risk leaving under my bed. I couldn't store it back in Starlight Canyon, it somehow feels like her protection over me.

In addition to these items is a CD with a recording of her singing 'Cielito Lindo.' I never noticed she sang off-key until she made this recording, but I treasure it even more for it being so raw. You never realize a person's voice is so unique to them until it's gone. If I ever am blessed with children, I will make sure to sing them songs.

I come across the last item I brought with me here to college. Her letter. I'm sure she wrote one to every one of us children. I unfold the weighty, official embossed stationery and smooth it in my fingers, trying to feel remnants of her spirit. We don't write notes to each other nearly enough these days.

Mi cielito,

I want you to remember every time you read this I am looking down on you. I made sure to say my prayers and have Jesus in my heart. So I promise I am here, in the sky, raining love down on my one and only daughter every single day. I am proud of the person you've become. I loved you from the moment I first laid my gaze on your ebony eyes and I will think of them in Heaven.

I cannot teach your brothers how to be men, but I've always seen it as my biggest duty to show you how to become a woman. It hasn't always been easy to find the sweet spot between respecting our culture and at the same time defying things that have no place in this modern world. I hope I've been an example to you of a strong, capable, and independent woman. I see this spirit in you.

I have wrung my heart out, giving you every last drop for your life, mija. My heart, I leave on Earth with you, your father, and your brothers, I take only my soul to Heaven. It will be hard for Papá. Please promise me you will all look after each other always.

I wish I had time to teach you a hundred more lessons, but I leave you with five. I hope they guide your spirit to true happiness in this world.

Put your family first.

You do not become a woman by becoming someone's wife.

Always stand up for yourself.

If you fail, don't give up.

Be gracious for the small things and all

God gives you and be generous with what you have.

    Con todo mi cariño,

    Mamá

These life lessons were things she repeated often, even before this letter. It says so much and not enough at the same time. Am I woman enough now not to lose myself in a relationship? Or did she mean just don't define yourself by one?

Logan and I have been in a situationship for two months. Maybe it's dating, but we aren't official. Despite the fact I don't hold the title of girlfriend, he sure as hell treats me like one. He knows my schedule and meets me after lectures to carry my backpack. He leaves notes for me anywhere and everywhere with inspirational quotes or jokes to make me laugh. And he doesn't take no for an answer when I don't feel like eating. I've gained every ounce back in relationship weight. Late-night pizza is a staple of our diet. I don't know if we're hungry at that time of night or if it just gives us an excuse to stay up talking.

Never in a million years did I think I'd lay down my guard, but Logan disarms me like a ninja. I never see it coming. Mr. Popular from Starlight Canyon High seems to have chosen me, and every time I tell myself to be careful, somehow I still end the night in his embrace. Has he cast a spell on me? Or is he earning my trust?

Just then, there's a musical knock on my door. It's him. Logan, helpful and involved as ever, offered to help with the posters.

I fold up my mom's letter, place it in the box, and slide the entire thing back under the bed. "Come in."

He steps in, tall and sexy with his backward baseball cap on. He throws his jacket on the end of my bed and exposes a fitted Henley and the broad shoulders and biceps that are also a source of this problem. Why didn't I ever experience this hormonal rage in high school? It was easier to stay away from boys then. Maybe that's just it. Logan isn't a boy. He's a man.

It's not just his body either. He's more mature and deeper than I ever would have given him credit for. It's been a beautiful surprise. Our conversations about our grief have shown a compassion I've not really seen in a man before. He's supportive with other topics, too—my career aspirations, my studies here at college, and how much of a struggle it is with my dyslexia, my worries about dad back home. I've inched closer and closer to Logan, letting the drawbridge down inch by inch, and he seems so... safe.

"Hey," he says, crouching. He kisses me then throws himself on his belly and grabs the orange marker to finish the job I started. "Sorry I'm late. I..." He seems to choose his words carefully. "I had some conference calls, and they ran longer than expected."

Do I want to ask, or don't I? My stomach twists in knots every time I know he's having these discussions, and I say a silent prayer that he'll get signed by the Santa Fe Scorpions and stay in state.

He's more than strong enough. More than ready.

But I'm not.

Still, I won't chase him or make him claustrophobic. There's no point in discussing it because it's out of our hands.

Anyway, the idea of being clumped in with the pretty

cheerleaders and campus beauties who bounce up to him with perky breasts and Hollywood smiles chasing his tail gives me the ick. I'm sure all the women in Logan's life have chased him, but that will not be me. I saw how the girls were in high school. They swooned by his side while he practically ignored them, chatting with his hockey buddies, laughing, throwing back his head with wide, pearly-toothed smiles framed by the sexiest dimples of an all-American hunk.

Not that I was watching him.

Maybe just a couple of times.

I take a red marker and start on another letter, giving myself an inner eye roll. If I'm holding back and making him come to me, I sure do let his tongue dive deep inside my mouth. It's not exactly giving the milk for free, but he knows the cow is ready.

I focus on the letter and draw long colored lines in the white space.

Scribbling more orange, he slows his marker down around the lined edge. "You need to come to the game tonight."

I chuckle. "Oh, you're telling me what to do now?"

Logan and I spend just about all my free time together, but I have never gone to one of his games. No way I'm going to be another one of his midriff-bearing fans and puck bunnies in waiting.

"You think you can boss me around after two months of kissing me?" I keep my gaze fixed on the poster and my red letter A. I might manage to keep steady but I have to work hard to hold back the pleasure his invitation gives me.

I care about Logan, so I'd love to go to a game and actually watch him do his thing live, in the flesh. I'd love to scream my head off when he scores instead of holding it in with balled fists so people don't think I'm being murdered in my dorm room while watching him on TV or online. I should support him as a friend, anyway, I shouldn't care what other people think, but I just don't want to be labeled as one of those girls.

The tip of Logan's tongue rests on his lip, and he's deep in concentration, as if he's painting a masterpiece for the Louvre. His features stir that warm space between my legs that never cools when I'm around him. The heat between us when we actually do touch makes me think about my virginity all the time. It's never been such a big thing until now.

I stare at his profile out of the corner of my eye, and that strong jaw of his clenches with focus, his hand grips the marker firmly, and he strokes the paper with its tip so damn smoothly. *If I give it to anyone...*

His gaze flicks up, and I fix mine back on the paper, but I feel his dirty-boy smile throbbing in the space between us and I have a feeling I was caught red-handed admiring him.

He shuffles over to me on his elbows until he's less than an inch from me. Brown eyes sink into me. A subtle wave of dark hair falls over his forehead, and the shape of his lips is too much sometimes. I can't even look at the man without bursting into flames. He's so damn beautiful.

"You asked if I'm telling you what to do?" He cocks an eyebrow. "I guess the answer is yes." He presses his lips into mine. They're warm and soft and caring.

It's like I've been waiting all my life for that kiss, and despite my mind constantly telling me to slow down, my body rages forward. I part my lips to give him access, and he sinks his tongue inside my mouth. The next thing I know, he's lowering me to the floor, or maybe I pulled him on top of me. It's hard to tell who's initiating when it comes to us because it's all so natural, so organic.

He writhes on top of me, rubbing himself on my thigh, and I raise my hips up into him in sync, grinding as hard as I can. My jeans are too damn thick to give the relief I need, but I know I'm wet enough to soak right through them. My nipples are diamond-hard when he laces his hands through my hair, plunging his tongue in further, lapping me up like a hungry man.

I want him inside me, and not just in my mouth.

But just as he has every other time, somehow, just as I'm about to shove my hand down his pants, he eases back and slows us down, prying himself off with a devilish laugh that somehow says, *not yet*. It's good he has self-control. This whole thing between us is confusing as hell; crossing that line isn't wise until we figure this out. Then again, does anybody really know what they're doing that first time? Surely, it always happens something like this? People take it a little further each time until the wildfire gets out of control?

He snatches the marker back in his hand and taps it against his palm, staring at me cool as ever. "You coming to the game is a fair exchange, *pastelito*."

I could melt at the sound of his term of endearment, and in Spanish, no less. *Little cake*. The choice couldn't make me feel more special.

I laugh. "Oh, you speak Spanish now?"

"I got an app on my cell. It's pretty good actually. But don't deflect, *bonita*." He quirks that playful eyebrow of his. "I'm going to the equal pay rally, you come to the game." He taps my nose.

He always says how cute my nose is. He likes my nose.

My *nose*. I like his, too. I worship every inch of the way he looks.

This is the third time he's asked, and we're friends. At some point, I need to drop the ego. He's dropped his to come with me.

I pretend to be aloof. "Fine. I'll come." Really, I can't wait to see him play in person.

"Good." He pops off the floor and rushes to his backpack. "Because I bought you a jersey."

My heart flutters. "You bought me a jersey?"

He pulls it out. It's not just any jersey. He stretches out the fabric to show me the back.

Hunter. Number 9.

His strong frame saunters over to me and puts the fabric flush over my body, smoothing his hand along the shiny polyester, and one of my pebbled nipples sends a flood of wanting to my core. His hands wrap around my hips and pull them in close. The top falls and crumples, held up by our kissed hips.

"You'll look so good in this." His voice is gravel.

I can't wear this. "You should have saved your money. I can't wear the shirt, Logan."

"Wear the jersey, Shay." Something in his gaze tells me he's not taking no for an answer. "I'll go insane if you wear anything else."

I walk up what feels like hundreds of concrete steps to get to the top of the stands. Just because Logan is on the team doesn't mean he has endless access to free tickets. It means a lot to me that he bought one for me. Apparently, I'm sitting with the right winger's girlfriend who has two season tickets, and Logan scored her second. I don't know her but as I ascend the stands, a girl with long red hair and a Golden Sierra Wolverines jersey is standing waving at me.

It must be Kelly.

"Shay! Up here!"

She's so very much my opposite and waves her arm wildly in the air, long red curls fling from side to side like she's in a shampoo commercial.

I climb the rest of the way up, trying not to give in to vertigo with a soda in one hand, so big I can hardly wrap my fingers around it. Who needs this much soda? But it was the only size option.

I shuffle through the row to the seat next to her.

She points to my drink. "Careful with that. You'll spend half the game in the bathroom."

I like this girl. We clearly both worry about lines in the ladies' room.

I put down my drink, and she hugs me. It surprises me, and for a moment I'm stiff but manage to hug her back.

"Thanks for letting me have your second ticket."

"Logan asked to buy it from me weeks ago. He said you've never been to a game in the stadium?"

"No." I take off my jacket and become instantly self-conscious. I'm wearing his jersey.

Kelly is hardly discreet. She winks. "Cute top. All the girlfriends wear their man's jersey. And if you want to make them jealous or go absolutely feral, put a different name on your back."

"Oh, Logan and I are just..." I hate belittling who he is to me but I can't let her think we're official. "We're..." I don't know what to call it. I keep it simple. "I'm not his girlfriend."

I can't read her rosy smile and cheeky expression. I don't know her well enough to understand what the twinkle in her eye is saying. Does she think I'm just another puck bunny?

I drive my point home. "I'm cool with that. It is what it is." I mean to sound blasé, but since it's insincere, there are burnt, bitter edges on my words.

Thankfully the music blares, saving me from any more small talk.

She tugs my sleeve. "Oh. It's gonna start."

The boys head onto the ice for warm-ups, and instantly I'm flooded with heat and that overfilled sensation I get when Logan's anywhere within a two-mile radius. I watch the drills. I recognize Ashton Dane, too. He's also from Starlight Canyon, and because he's super tall he stands out on the ice. And when the warm-ups are over, my gaze tracks every deft and agile move Logan makes. He skates backward to the side of the rink and lifts his stick in the air, pointing right at me.

Kelly leans into my side. "Someone is happy you're here."

Yeah. I let out a satisfied breath.

That someone is me.

The Wolverines play a blinding first third. Logan is on fire, assisting a goal and narrowly missing out on one of his own due to a damn good keep on the other side. Then the buzzer goes, signaling the end of the period.

I get up. "I have to pee..."

Kelly pulls me back down to my seat. "Not yet."

And just as I ask myself why this chick is being weird about my potty break, the loudspeaker in the stadium goes.

"And now, ladies and gentlemen, please turn your attention to a very special announcement on the JumboTron from our very own Wolverines forward, Logan Hunter..."

Kelly squeezes her fists into tight balls, bites her lip, then whips her head around to look at the JumboTron. "I wonder what Logan's message is?" She squeaks.

There, the screen shows digital fireworks exploding and somehow turning into a bouquet of roses. And then, words that will forever remain etched on my soul appear.

Shay Mendez: Will you be my girlfriend?

My jaw drops. Breath gets trapped in my lungs, and I dart my eyes to Kelly who clearly knew about this all along, and then let my gaze drop a hundred yards away to the Wolverines on the rink's side.

Whether Logan and I are ten feet apart or ten thousand, there's something tangible, connected, and so real about when our gazes find each other. From across an entire stadium, his eyes still reach right inside me and encircle my heart with warmth.

I think he tilts his head, like he's asking for my answer.

I hope he sees me nod.

But if he doesn't, he'll have no doubts about it later when I have him in my bed.

Chapter Four

Shay

I TAKE a moment to flop down on the bed in my room at the Firenze. I've never had a California King before. Not only is my bed big, I have a suite. When I checked in earlier downstairs, the receptionist asked if I was okay. Was it the hard lines between my eyebrows so deep I felt them in my brain? I was worried about Antonio. Nino and I have never been apart for a single day since he was born. Hours, yes. A night, no.

So at check-in, when the receptionist asked if I was okay, I blurted that I was missing my boy. He asked what his name was, and it turned out his brother is named Antonio, too. So he upgraded me. I'd say I wish everything in life was that easy, but if I had to choose between this room and being with Nino, I'd take my boy every day of the week. Being away is a necessary evil of my career, a sacrifice I must be willing to make.

I get up and head over to the window, snatch open the curtains, and laugh to myself. Yes, I may have a California King and a jacuzzi tub, but the bland view of the taupe hotel next door has nothing on the Starlight Canyon mountains.

It's still an hour to the reception, which isn't enough time to wash and style my long hair and more time than I need to tie it up. I'm useless when it comes to makeup so I probably won't try anything special. Though I bought a pair of fake eyelashes at the pharmacy before I left, I throw myself down on my bed rather than search around for useless accessories. Fuck it. I'd rather relax than fiddle with those right now.

I close my eyes and suck in the perfume-laced air. This air smells faintly like my grandmother, and after a few more breaths, my muscles finally release and melt into the bed underneath me.

Getting that cake here was one of the most stressful things I've ever done, which is saying a lot because I've been through a few tough things in my day. In the last decade I've had two cheating exes, one who regularly "borrowed" my car and forgot to return it on more than one occasion, and one who ditched me when he found out I was pregnant. I've been through so many rock bottoms I've gone through one side of the earth to the other. And still, the stress of getting that cake here was up at the top of the list.

It represents something more important to me than finding love anymore; no, I've long since given up on that. The cake represents hope.

I can't believe I let Logan carry it for me.

And I can't believe he's here. I figured he'd be invited, but the celebrity hockey player has time for an old hockey buddy's reception? I thought he'd be too busy. Not that I wondered if he'd come.

You wondered if he'd come.

After all these years, fireflies explode in my belly every time I see him. It's a mystery because with the man he's become I'd rather he wasn't my type. In fact, I've now, in my mid-thirties, finally learned to avoid that kind of heartache.

But I'm just a woman. Yes, I'm a strong-as-fuck woman, but a woman nevertheless. And Logan is *bring you to your knees* gorgeous, and it's undeniable. He's attractive to any woman with eyes. On the backs of my lids I catch a glimpse of his dimples again, the way he licks his lips and wets them. His amber eyes, now framed by crinkles of a man who's aged like fine wine, still mesmerize despite his boy-next-door ways.

I open my eyes and stare at the textured ceiling. I know he's changed so much, but every time we see each other, he really feels like the same guy I fell for.

You let him carry the cake, for God's sake.

I sit up and glimpse myself in a mirror above the adjacent desk. The back of my hair is a tangled bird's nest, and my earring is upside down. Did I look like this down in the lobby? Logan is always so well put together. I'm going to see him later all dressed up in a suit. The man is insanely attractive in formalwear. I know because the paparazzi just love Logan Hunter. Unfortunately, they love all the women dripping off his arm, too, and those are his go-to accessory these days.

I get up and head to the mirror, bracing my hands on the desk and leaning over, closer to my reflection. No one would ever believe it. No normal American citizen would ever believe that this curvy, cellulite-laden single mom with tiger claw stretch marks once had the dashing playboy. I'm fine with that because I'm not sure I'd want to be seen as just another tire track in the wake of Logan's dust. But most of the guests at the party tonight know about us, and it makes me feel funny.

Maybe I should have a go with those eyelashes, after all.

No. There is no reason I need to impress him. Or anyone else. My inner matriarch crosses her arms and nods in approval, refusing to play that game. I have bigger plans than that now. A recent study told me women spend on average three hundred and fifty-five hours on their hair and makeup every year. Yet another reason why we have less time to get ahead.

Which makes me think of work again, so I grab my cell from my purse, slip off my shoes, and snuggle up against the plush assortment of pillows to see if Dad left me any messages.

There's one. It's a goodie. It's a photo of him and my little boy. They're in one of the tractors, and it appears they're mucking out the cow barns. Nino loves anything to do with cleaning and putting things in order. It's not a typical five-year-old going-on-six hobby. But the smile on Nino's face is one of sheer delight, and his beloved Papá Luis is just as happy.

It's hard to believe I ever had to endure my father's one-hour rant in almost unintelligible warp-speed Spanish, swearing to the end of the earth about how disappointed he was that I got pregnant out of wedlock. He threw his arm in the air until I thought it might launch off into the sky as he lectured me on the contradictory Catholic view he himself didn't seem to understand.

"It's a sin," he shouted. "But the baby isn't a sin..."

When wedlock wasn't an option—shit, even if the guy stuck around, I knew better than to bind myself to that one by marriage—Dad became slightly more sympathetic to me becoming a single mom. My new reality sank into his psyche, and he waited out the nine months mostly in silence. But then, our brilliant, unique little Antonio entered the world, and now this baby is the favorite of all he's ever had in his life. It was as if something magical happened the day Antonio was born, and since, Dad's always treated Nino like he was always meant to enter this world in exactly the way he did.

Satisfied that my men are alive and well, I switch screens to check my email for any new enquiries. It's become my obsession since launching my new brand, Shino Cakes. Shay and Nino. By me. For my son. It's time to elevate our lives. Not only do I want to offer Nino chances I never had, and all the gifts I got, too, I need to show him that no matter who you are, you can make something out of nothing. I want Nino to have a boss lady mom who leads by example, a mentor for his own life.

It's the biggest financial risk I've ever taken since Nino was born, or even before it. But since my brothers ventured out years ago to Silicon Valley, determined to be tech entrepreneurs, they convinced me that time, belief and sweat is all it takes.

They still haven't quite moved their business out of the red, but when it goes, it's going to explode. And they are very, very close. If I can look up to them even though their business is technically still in debt, I can teach Nino a lesson or two with my tenacity alone.

I hope.

Sadly, my Shino Cakes' inbox is empty, and there's no

dopamine hit waiting for me there. I switch over to my personal mails and scroll through the usual suspects. Credit card bills. Marketing from face cream and nutrition blogs. Then there, nested amongst the noise, is another email I've been waiting for. The principal from Nino's school.

Dear Ms. Mendez (when the hell did I become a Ms,?)**,**

We received Antonio's test results back, and I must say, this is unprecedented. In all my years as an administrator and as a teacher, I've never experienced a moment like this. Antonio is very intellectually advanced, like nothing I've ever seen in all my days of working in education. Below you'll see his math, memory, spatial perception, and linguistic scores compared to that of a twelve-year-old child of average ability. He is well beyond his years in capability.

In light of this news, I'd like to discuss options for his schooling and suggest Longbrook Academy. I can make a call on your behalf to get the ball rolling...

I continue reading, and the strangest combination of elation, relief, and guilt mix in my gut and it churns into nausea. The letter includes his off-the-charts scores. I read the email over and over, my phone getting closer and closer to my nose until the blue light sends me dizzy.

My son is a genius. In any given world it's a miracle.

But it's an expensive miracle.

I had a gut feeling that taking my savings down to zero

was a bad idea, especially when, not that I'd ever want to take his money, Dad had disease hit the cows this year and our ranch isn't having a good season. My brothers have everything tied up in a property they're developing and their tech business.

I thought I was doing the right thing, finally taking a risk to do something special, to pursue success for the family on the back of my parents' sacrifices. But I had to make my own as well to start Shino Cakes. I have a very expensive website, kitchen rental, branding, artwork, and a stock of boxes and ribbons just waiting to wrap up those wedding cakes... I have no answer for the principal.

I'm paralyzed; the bridge of my nose stings. If I'm breathing, the rise and fall of my chest is imperceptible. A sort of numbness finds a home inside me, and I stare out at the opposite wall in my hotel room, but my eyes don't focus on anything.

I fucked up. Big time. All these years I should have given up the cake dream and gotten a so-called real job. I should have a pension plan and insurance paid for by a company and paid time off and a boss who's been giving me raises every so often. I should have just followed the pack. I'm sure there's not one single baker paying Longbrook tuition out there.

Tears sting the backs of my eyes, but I blink them away fiercely. I have to find an answer. Thinking like this, looking back? It won't give Nino what he needs.

I ruminate for what seems an eternity more, but eventually, my faraway thoughts return to the room I'm in.

Maybe now isn't the time for such answers. It's been a grueling day of driving. I don't think I spent a second on the road without adrenaline humming in my veins. I'm exhausted, and exhaustion leads to bad decisions and self-loathing. I can do this. I *will* figure this out. When the sun comes up, I'll return to my seemingly impossible problem.

But right now, there's a casino bar calling my name.

I sure as hell need a drink.

I wander down in my jeans and t-shirt, not even bothering to change. They probably smell like sweat, and I know there's at least one blob of frosting somewhere, but I just don't give a shit.

I pass the blinking lights of slot machines, considering where I'll spend the few bucks I shouldn't, and a wave of guilt washes through me for spending even a dime on drinks tonight. But thirty bucks isn't going to solve this problem. I need more like thirty thousand.

This place is too hectic, so I read the sign above that spells out my options. *Ciao Mario Restaurant, Capri Lounge, La Liga Sportsbooks, Firenze Reception Rooms...*

The reception rooms. Logan. He's probably in there now in that dapper suit, dancing with some bridesmaid who will spread her legs for him tonight. No way I'm headed there tonight.

I consider the options on the sign again. Not hungry. Not dressed for Prosecco. Not rubbing shoulders with my ex.

Sportsbooks it is.

Chapter Five

Logan

I MIGHT HAVE PLAYED coy with Shay when I left her in this room earlier today, but now that I've had a drink or two, and inhibitions are at bay, it's evident I *didn't* come for the cake. I didn't come for the cake, the YMCA, or the brides-maids asking for a quickie in the bathroom.

I didn't come here for Shay either, since I had no idea she'd be here, but it's as though that's the reason. Every shot I take is a hope to dull my curiosity, but my gaze continues to slide over the heads of my fellow revelers. With every bite of steak, I glance around looking for her at the table where I spied her name card. My heart stutters with every empty glance.

She's not here.

The disappointment is heavier than appropriate and, try as I might, I can't get my skin to stop searching for her even when my back is turned to the entryway. My muscles tingle with the kind of anticipation that arises when she's anywhere near.

Sometimes I wonder if settling in Starlight Canyon is the right thing. I can't even get through this party. What would happen if Shay actually did move on with someone and I had to run into her and her new husband at CCs and pretend I care what the fuck his name is while we wait for our lattes? I still can't handle a casual conversation without all of that.

But she sure seems to have taken being a mom in her stride. The few times I saw her with Antonio, he seemed like a bright boy. Not that I could be sure. She only introduced me to him once in town and another time at the Danes' Fright Night. Other times, she'd stand there with him holding her hand, while we'd have a polite catch-up. He was pushing up his little glasses, peering up at my direction while we made stupid everyday chat like I was a nobody to her. Not that it would have made any sense to introduce me as her ex-boyfriend to her five-year-old son.

The groom taps my arm. "You all right, man? You need another shot?"

I don't need any more alcohol, but I buy another round for any takers. I try to sink into the festivities and enjoy the nostalgic banter, but as if my mind wasn't completely fucked enough by thinking about Shay, I get a text.

REGGIE

Your PA said you're in Vegas at the Firenze?

What's my agent chasing me for?
I text back.

> Yeah. What's up?

REGGIE

> I'll be in the VIP bar nearest the entrance in twenty. Can you meet me?

Before texting back, I take one more hard scan of the room. It's full but still so empty.

> Yup. See you then.

When I arrive in the VIP bar, impressively on time, sadly, Reggie doesn't look like he's here for any sort of celebration. For the past three years, the only news Reggie has shared with me is good news, but his strained features are as if he's in the process of getting a colonic.

"Were you already in Vegas, or do you just miss me?" I greet him. Maybe I can lighten the mood. Hopefully his tense expression isn't because of me.

"I thought we better talk about this one in person." He shifts in his seat and takes a sip of the drink he got while waiting for me.

Oh, it's me, all right. It wouldn't be the first time.

"You came all this way to talk?" I ask casually.

"Not really. I'm watching Carl's fight at MGM tonight so I thought I could kill two birds with one stone." He sits back and throws his foot over his knee. "But Carl will win, which leaves me with only one bird to kill tonight."

I glance around for a server so I can grab a drink, but a nearby guest is flirting with her. I only have a few minutes with Reggie anyway. I should get back to the wedding reception.

I stroke my top lip. "Judging by the fact you look constipated, I guess you're not about to have me sign another million-dollar endorsement offer?"

A sarcastic laugh leaves his lips along with an equally cutting comment. "You're lucky you do have your face, Logan, because that's the only thing I can count on these days."

If anyone else would have suggested I'm prettier than I am talented, I'd have taken offense. But Reggie and I have been working together since I first got drafted to the NHL. We're not friends, but we're straight. So this can only mean something has gone south.

He perches elbows on his knees, leaning over toward me. "Logan, I told you over a year ago to clean up your act."

"You're the one getting me these gigs in Vegas." Are we seriously regurgitating this conversation? He didn't have to talk to me face to face for this. "If Coach is banging on about these appearances again, you're as much to blame. My image is your doing."

"Me?" His eyes light up with surprise.

"Yes, you. I get the publicity is good but I told you a year ago these hired hands and fake dates needed to stop."

He's flabbergasted. "You think having a new woman on your arm every day is the problem? My job is to make you money. Not be your moral compass. The ladies and resulting publicity aren't the problem, Logan. Shutting down clubs every time you're out is your problem."

I check my watch.

The smallest amount of pink shows under his light-brown skin, and I'm not sure it's from the vodka tonic. I annoyed him.

His nostrils flare when he speaks. "Are you checking your watch because you're busy? You won't be so busy if you get traded and find yourself playing third string on some shitty team."

My hand lowers slowly to the armrest, and I grip the leather. "Traded?"

The word liquifies my stomach, and I guess my response is visible because Reggie clears his throat and composes himself almost apologetically. "Yeah, man. That's the rumor."

Traded?

The NHL is a professional league where trading can happen nearly anywhere, anytime, even mid-season. There are only a few freezes in an entire year, on or off-season. Rumors are common, and it's part of the fun and games our sport has to offer... for management anyway. Most managers have a ruthless approach. They are *grass is always greener* types, and it can make the life of a hockey player highly unpredictable.

But I've been playing for the Scorpions for three solid years, and never once did something like this come up. I have Reggie to thank for that. The first year was tough, but after that, me and my best friend, Ashton, playing together has brought some good revenue to the club with small-town hero stories. The past two years I haven't lived with the nearly daily question of a trade taking place and the prospect of leaving my home state again.

"It's just a rumor?" I'm on edge.

Reggie knows how much I want to stay in New Mexico with Ashton this season.

He shakes his head. "A little more than a rumor. Your coach has been considering options with Scorpions management."

More desperation creeps into my voice than I'd like, but I need this man to get me out of this. "I can't get traded, bro. Not this season. *After* this season..." I let out a stale breath. "Fuck... you got to do something."

"No. *You* got to do something."

I hang my head. This can't be happening. Reggie's voice wafts into my ears.

"Look. Everyone loves the story of two small-town boys playing together and possibly winning the Cup this year. With Ashton's retirement announcement, the marketing department will be all over trying to keep you guys together for Ashton's last season. Dollars talk."

I lift my head to see if there's as much hope in his eyes as there is in his words. This is a fucking knife in the gut.

He continues. "But your coach is done with the party-ing. He sees it in your play."

"He fucking doesn't," I defend, but my underarms prickle like it's a lie.

"That's not for me to determine. But if you want to stay on this team... I know how important it is to you to play out Ashton's last season with him. To have a chance at the championship together."

Reggie is Ashton's agent, too. I'm sure my friend had a mini breakdown when he told Reg he was leaving the game. I bet I'll have one, too, when the day comes.

"Clean up your act, Logan. Just... do something to show your coach you've changed. And I highly suggest we stop booking appearances here in Vegas this season. If you want to resume that shit when the season is over we can have a look at it, but I think you need the integrity more than you need the money right now."

I don't even need the money anymore. I was in it for the escapism.

I swipe a palm down my stubble. "Yeah. Good idea."

"Stay in Starlight Canyon whenever possible."

I nod.

"And..." He pushes fingers into his eye sockets as though they're communicating with his brain. "I've been thinking. Pulling away from this image is one thing. Pushing toward another would be..."

"What are you saying? Pushing toward another? Like what? You want me to become a bead mumbler or something?"

At that, he finally lets a laugh out of his nose. "You don't need to become a man of the cloth, bro. Just. You know, something to convince Coach that you're committed to small-town life and not big-city hustling. Something that will erase any ounce of doubt that man has in you."

It's an idea. But one that doesn't exactly light up the bulb. Still, I can stay away from Vegas after tonight. That's an easy change, and I can only hope it's enough.

Reggie finishes his drink then rises, yanks down an incredibly expensive blazer to smooth himself out and I follow suit.

He pats my arm. "Take this seriously. There's a lot at stake here, both personally and financially. Trust me, Lo, third string doesn't earn your current salary. I'll do what I can behind the scenes. You play the part on stage, and hope-fully this noise will fade."

I watch Reggie's back sway away from me, both my attacker and my savior. I finally grab the attention of the server and sit with a bourbon I don't need but really feel like having. Reggie's news weighs heavily on my mind, and as I sip the firewater I decide only one of two things will help me calm down—I can go out tonight and get annihilated, if any of my Vegas contacts are around. Or I can knock myself out with a sleeping pill.

My family has always said I'm extreme. I'm an adrenaline junkie, and as such, I've never been good at calming myself down. My mind flashes back to Shay earlier today. I hate to admit it, but I've never been so level-headed since I was in college during those months with her. She had a way with me. I don't know why, but for some reason, the way she'd talk to me just made me stop spinning. She was such a straight-shooter and called my bullshit, told me when I was being stupid.

I wonder why she didn't come tonight?

I've been coming to Vegas for years now, and it's usually pretty easy for me to make a night out of nothing. All I'd have to do is buzz the VIP hosts at Taj Mahal and I'd have a party on demand.

It reminds me of the party I ditched. The one where Shay was not.

Where did she go?

I shake my head of the thoughts. I've come to expect these kinds of questions because every time I see Shay it's like I've walked through a cobweb and it just takes a while to unstick myself. Being around other people will help me get out of it. It'll help me forget Reggie's news.

One more night. That's all I have before I really need to make a change, and I'll be damned if I spend tonight with a sleeping pill.

The server comes over, asking me if I want another drink. Since my texts need more correcting than usual, I pass and head out into the circus-like gurgle of the casino, staring at my cell as I walk, scrolling through a hefty address book of Vegas contacts.

A woman wobbling along in stilettos, drunk as a skunk, bumps into me. Or maybe I bump into her.

"Sorry," I say, looking up, but she's already passed.

I stop walking and scan the crowd. Is Shay out tonight? It would be nice to catch up with her some more; I'd rather that than anything. Then again, if she wanted to see me, too, she would have come to the reception, and it's hard to accept, but I've given us chances to reconnect since moving back to the Canyon. The RSVP never came.

I squint. There's a sports betting bar which will be quieter. I can make some more calls or texts from there. I'll drown this trade news for a few more hours under the thump of bass, behind the sparklers of two waitresses delivering a bottle of Moët to my table. It's a bandage at best, but one I won't be allowed in the months to come as I live in constant fear of being traded.

The crowd thins as my feet take me deeper into the casino. The hum of exciting energy becomes lighter on my skin because the sports bar is in the recesses of the building and it's more for the end of the night than the start of it.

I approach a long, horseshoe-shaped bar with big screens in front. There aren't many people here this time of night, but one catches my eye. Silky dark hair drips down the shoulder of a woman wearing a t-shirt and jeans. There's nothing particularly special about a pair of high-top Converse in a casino full of miniskirts. And though my conscious mind swears finding Shay here wasn't intentional, the way every inch of my skin illuminates with triumph upon finding her here has me questioning how well I know myself.

Chapter Six

Logan

SIXTEEN YEARS AGO

AFTER MY SUCCESSFUL JumboTron girlfriend proposal, we head back to the dorms. Shay unlocks her room while staring at me, kitten-like, seductive. I've never seen her like this before.

My girlfriend.

She's mine. All mine. *Only mine.*

I know a man could never truly possess a woman like Shay and shouldn't even try. She's independent, and more than happy in her own company. She's strong, and I'm not surprised because I remember being intimidated by her mom. Shay appears to have inherited that dry, quick wit, gives zero fucks, and has no need to please.

I like the challenge and I'm glad I won. We both did, because this is the beginning of something special for both of us. I won't stop until she sees it that way, too.

Shay leads me into the dark dorm room by the hand, bypassing the overhead light switch. She heads to her nightstand and clicks on the table lamp, casting a more gentle mood into the stark surroundings.

The air around us is charged with anticipation, crackling with an unspoken tension. Her eyes, pools of deep, inviting brown, hold mine in a mesmerizing gaze, drawing me closer with each heartbeat. I've been in her room many times but never with *this* Shay. This is a side she's never let me see before.

I have to work not to let my voice waver, unsettled by the increasing voltage between us, unready for the surge I'm pretty sure will burn me this time. I've held my resolve previously, somehow summoning control to stop me ripping her clothes off like a heathen and taking her. But it's too big a deal to not be intentional.

It wasn't my intention tonight, but Shay's wild eyes tell me it's hers.

She walks backward with my two hands in hers, leading me to the bed with the wanting of a greedy, stalking tigress. It's never been like this. Usually, it's me making the moves. And me stopping things before we get ahead of ourselves... My pulse quickens. Intuition weighs heavy in my stomach. The dynamic between us has changed. The way she gazes at me has changed. The way she lures me into the darkness of her room has changed.

I've been in this situation before and I know what it means.

Even though it would take a lifetime to discover this woman, there's nothing mysterious about the impossible darkening of her nearly pitch-black gaze and the way she lowers one knee onto her mattress to pull me into her sacred space. I never dared let us kiss here on this small single bed made smaller by clouds of blankets and pillows. She lays her head down on a cushion that looks like a donut with sprinkles, then tugs me forward until our bodies are pressed together.

It's both paradise and terrifying, knowing what she brought me here for. The soft warmth of her body and the gentle rolling of her hips steals my self-control. I run my hands along her curvy waist, now healthier and more womanly than when we first met. I revel in her health. In her healing. In both our healing.

I press a soft touch against her lips with my own. At the faint brush of my tongue she gives me permission to enter, our tongues dance and my involuntary groan falls into her mouth. We stroke each other, long and unhurried. But then she moans, and it vibrates through my core, quickening my heartbeat.

She raises her thigh to massage my growing shaft, already hard with anticipation. Her pace is hasty, and that feral, manly need I've felt so many times before and easily resisted rises like a fucking warrior inside me. My kiss morphs into a full-on devour, and I wrap my hand around her throat, her pulse races under my palm.

She spreads her legs wider so I can nestle between them, and even through the heavy fabric of my jeans, the heat of her core sends sparks to mine. I want more. I always stopped myself before, wanting more, but now... I want it all. I fucking want it all and I want to give it all to her.

It's all I can do to lace my fingers through her hair, grip her skull, and hold on for dear life, because though her body says yes, uncertainty is still there, too. Is it coming from me? Or her? Every nerve inside me begs to rip her clothes off, pleads to be skin to skin while my mind strains to remind myself this is a big fucking deal... And then it happens... she unbuttons my pants.

Her dainty hand shoves inside them, wiggles underneath the fabric of my boxers, and when she grips my cock with those soft fingers of hers, I have to bite my lip to not explode then and there. I've never had her on that bare sensitive skin. I purposely stopped it to respect her, to force her to take the time to consider what this means. I know she's a virgin.

"Do you like that?" Rarely is there so much uncertainty in her questions.

I want to fucking praise her till the end of the earth; her touch is divine. "I'm on fucking fire. You want to keep touching me like that?"

I need to know.

"Mmm-hmm..." she mewls and pumps harder.

With her every movement, my breath becomes more ragged. "You know exactly how to touch me..." I groan, my voice not even my own. "Do you want me to touch you? Do you want my hands between your legs, *pastelito*?"

Her gaze is deep and all-consuming. And her words... unexpected.

"I have a condom."

Just like that, the dizzying world stops turning. I stop writhing. I stop fucking breathing. We stare at one another as her strokes become slower and slower until she stops but keeps her hand down the front of my jeans, and her tiny fingers wrapped around my cock.

Her confidence fades, her words are exposed and tender. "I'm ready."

At that, I drop my body to her side. As if it's a cue, she pulls her hand out of my pants and lays it on my hip. Instant dejection slaps her across the face. It's not what I mean her to feel but I can't... *we* can't keep going without talking.

I trace her jawline and drop my forehead to her hair and breathe in her vanilla sugar scent. "Shay, you don't have to have sex with me just because I asked you to be my girlfriend. I need you to know that... I'll wait till you're ready."

She traces the shell of my ear with her finger. "I want to, Logan. I didn't just decide tonight." The soft light of the lamp casts romantic shadows like those of a sunset all over her features.

"Are you sure?" I smooth my hand over that beautiful curve on the side of her hip.

"Never been more sure." She smirks. "My hand down your pants was a cordial invitation."

I mean for my laugh to be more subtle than it is, less throaty and a lot less dark, but fuck me if I can stay composed knowing what's about to happen.

I kiss her lips and stare in her eyes, where I find something that's never been there before and may never be there again. I never want to forget the way she looks right now.

Shay's skin is soft as powder under my fingertips as I slide my hands up her shirt and behind her back to unclasp her bra. Her breath hitches when I do, anticipation mounts, and I bury my face in her neck, breathing in her perfume and the faint scent of her body heat. Feeling her breast, firm, full, nipple tight, pointy. My shaft surges painfully against my zipper.

She pulls her shirt off, exposing herself and the breasts I only dreamed of before. I pepper kisses down her neck in a trail leading to her stiff peaks and suck one into my mouth, swirling my tongue around.

"Mmm. That's so good, Logan..." Her hands slide down the ridges of my hips, and she tugs at the waistline of my pants, urging me to take them off. "I want to feel you, too."

I sit up and rip off my shirt. Instantly, her hands are on my abs. She feels up and down my torso until I lie back down and connect us skin to skin for the very first time. Her breasts push against me, her fingernails gently scratch my back, and my skin explodes with tiny fireworks everywhere it touches her.

I gently bite her neck, my teeth scraping her perfect skin and she arches her back, her body making more connection with mine.

"Lose the pants, Hunter..."

She doesn't have to ask me twice, and I take hers down along with mine, aligning our two bodies for the very first time. I already felt connected to Shay without this. *With* this? I'm fucking done.

I part her pussy lips, she's already soaked. I circle my fingers around her nub, and she sucks her teeth. I open my eyes again to find hers closed, her lids squeezed so tightly together they crinkle along with her eyebrows.

"You like that?"

"So much." She chokes out her words. "I want you inside me."

Her impatience brings out the devil in me, and the corner of my mouth lifts. There's no way I'm doing that before she comes. I dip my fingers inside her tight, textured insides and start to wonder how much it will hurt. I don't want to hurt her.

She spreads her legs wider to give me better access, and I smooth my fingers around her clit. It grows harder and harder. Following the lead of her breath, my movements become firmer and faster until she bites her lip and releases a whimper, pulsing under my touch.

She whispers, more to herself than to me. "Oh God, Logan... shit..." she can't string together a sentence but manages to reach her hand out, eyes still firmly shuttered. She taps the bedside table. "Condom."

It's the only thing in her nightstand apart from a book and some hand cream. There are three. I tear one off and roll it on. By now, she stares at my dick and worry tangles with desire.

"I'll be gentle..." I notch my cock at her entrance. With both hands braced on either side of her, I sink in, inch by inch... slowly, carefully. I take my time, clenching my biceps until they almost shake not to put any more pressure inside her than I have to.

The room grows quiet and still. I can't even tell if she's breathing, and it pains me to know no matter how much I pleasured her beforehand, no matter how soaked she is right now, this will never feel as good for her as it does for me.

Still, she's giving. Still, she opens herself to me, and I'll never take this for granted. I'll never forget for as long as I live how it feels to be inside Shay Mendez, to have her endure this ache so we can share this once-in-a-lifetime moment.

My arms burn trying to keep my weight off her. I want her to be comfortable even though her furrowed eyebrows and tightly closed eyes make it clear she's not.

Her core clenches around me. She's so tight. Not only is she a virgin but she's so much smaller than I am. Does that make a difference? Maybe I'm too big for her.

"Are you okay? I can stop. We can try another time."

Her eyelashes flutter open. "I'm okay, Logan. I want this. It's just... not that I have anything to compare it to, but you're really big."

"Try to relax. Breathe, baby..." I sink in another inch, and I have to clench my ass to stabilize myself, working hard to be careful.

She reaches up, lacing her fingers through my hair. I know men are supposed to last as long as they can, but a combination of not wanting her to hurt too long and a solid inability to hold back from the ecstasy building has me dragging in and out of her only a few times before every muscle in me coils.

"Shay..." Her name escapes me in a choked exhale as I release inside her.

Stars explode over my vision, and my balls clench. I worry I'm burying myself too deeply. Her body is taut, too... I jerk inside her. My ecstasy somehow finds space inside her tight insides, and I come undone.

But as soon as I can see again, I pull my dick out and wish her features didn't fill with relief. What kind of cruel creation has God conjured that this feels so good for me and hurts so much for her?

I peel off the condom and toss it in the garbage can, not sure where I should wipe off, if not her sheets. Then again, they won't survive a second night because there's blood on me and surely on them, too. Shay is eager to cover herself with the duvet, maybe bashful from the spots of blood. I make a note to help her with her laundry tomorrow.

We lie down. Our bodies naturally find a comfortable crescent shape for both of us, and I spoon her until she falls asleep in my arms.

But I'm wide awake. I've always had trouble sleeping,

but it's no surprise insomnia finds me tonight. Even in the darkness, every feature of this room is remarkable, crisp and etched into my mind. I'll never forget this donut pillow or the cable-knit blanket at the end. I'll never forget the way she breathes when she sleeps, a silent inhale and an exhale that huffs out with exasperation so similar to her peppery nature. I'll never forget the fragrant scent of her silky black bob or the way her eyelashes nearly touch the apples of her cheeks.

I found it at the most unlikely time. I never thought in the wake of my father's death such a beautiful thing would come of it. I can't help but ask myself if Dad didn't die, would Shay and I have ever come together? Does Shay ask herself the same question? I hate thinking about it and gather her more tightly against me, spooning her firmly from behind. No. Shay is my fate.

I can't believe all the times I passed her in the hallways in high school, ate her sweet treats, and stood in line with her at CCs, not realizing she was my person. It makes me laugh, how blind we are.

When I open my eyes in the morning, I dread the thought of her roommate being in the bed next door. How on earth did I not think of it when falling asleep naked as the day I was born?

Shay reads my tug of the sheets over my ass and my rigid body perfectly.

"Do you really think I'd let us have sex and sleep in here

if my roommate was going to be around? She went home for the weekend. Left yesterday afternoon."

I instantly melt back into her. "Why don't we do that, too?"

"What?" Her voice is muffled against my chest.

"Let's go home. Together." Shay and I sure as hell would give my mom something better to think about than the booze. "Mom can always use good news. I can check on Dash, and if your dad needs any help, I can roll up my sleeves."

She peeps up from my chest. There's crust in the corner of her eye and mascara flakes on her cheek, and still she's the cutest thing ever.

"Are you sure you want to do the family thing already?" Her voice is raspy.

"They already know you. It's not like I'm bringing home a stranger. Besides, we've been together a couple months. I didn't meet you yesterday."

Shay hesitates. "Really? You're ready for all that?"

"Are you?" *Please say yes.*

"You don't know what Mexican families are like, Logan. If word gets out there's a man in my life, I'll be taking calls from Oaxaca every day. I have more aunts down there than there are days of the week."

"You don't want to be that popular?" I already know the answer.

"No thank you." She kisses my nose. "I'll save the blinding blaze of the spotlight for you."

I hoist her naked body on top of mine, my dick instantly growing between her thighs. "Is that a no?"

She scrunches her nose. "Are you sure you're ready for that?"

"I'm ready as hell. I wanted to ask you to be my girlfriend after we got bagels before our second support session."

She tilts her head, disbelieving. "After one week?"

"Yeah. Or you can calculate it as seven days if that sounds more appropriate."

She slaps my chest playfully. "Shut up."

"I did," I laugh, but there's nothing funny about how quickly and deeply I tumbled. It's actually scary, but my mom did tell us all, when you know, you know. It takes but a moment.

"If you were so into me, why did you wait two whole months to ask me to be exclusive?"

I grip her hips in my palms and rub her core softly over me. Jesus, it's going to take Herculean strength to rip my body from hers today, now that I know what it's like to be inside her.

She circles her hips, teasing me. "Well? Why did you wait?"

I'm more serious than I've ever been. "I waited because a man shouldn't enter a relationship unless they have every intention of staying."

Chapter Seven

Logan

Why is Shay at the sportsbooks? She came to this grubby bar instead of the reception?

Her eyes peel off her drink slowly, reflexes clearly a bit numb from whatever she's been shooting. Those dark-as-night brown eyes of hers sink into me. Her lids are heavy; it's clear to see she's been drinking.

"Logan?"

I glance around at the empty stool behind her, just to be sure there isn't a coat slung over it or a half-drunk glass waiting for a friend to come back from the bathroom. Nothing. An echo of concern ricochets in my belly. Shay is drinking alone in Vegas, and even though I've done it more than a few times myself, it's sad to see her in that position.

She skipped the reception. There is an empty shot glass, an empty highball, and a half-drunk clear beverage on the bar in front of her, so she's here to blow something off. One drink alone is a wind down. Three is a wish to forget.

"Hey." I slide into the space next to her. "Fancy seeing you here."

She pops off her stool but she's petite so she's still the same height as she was sitting down. Her arms wrap around me, and those luscious breasts I can still sometimes see in my mind's eye press against my stomach. We've hugged before. We usually hug when we see each other in the Canyon, and every time I wonder if I should have extended a hand between us instead because it feels too damn good. She slides her hands into her back pockets, pushing those round tits out toward me. I really wish I didn't know what they felt like.

"Why aren't you at the reception?" she asks.

"I could ask you the same thing."

She perches back on her stool, and I lean on the bar next to her. I wait to see if she'll answer, even though I don't expect her to. Shay is comfortable with silence, more at ease with it than I am. I take the moment to scan her features.

Every time I see her face there's something new and captivating. She has a few smile lines that weren't there when we were younger. What's made her so happy all these years? Her son? In any case, those sweet, delicate lines aren't filled with happiness now. They are simply a frame for two hollow eyes focused on an idea so far away from here, she's clearly turned to the sauce to keep it there for a while. A lot of time has passed between me and Shay, but she hasn't changed very much from what I can tell. I read her like a book.

Apparently, she can still read me, too, and knows I'm wary.

She raises the pitch of her voice to sound cheerful, which of course only makes me more suspicious.

"Did you stay for the cake? Tell me Ethan and Natalie liked it."

"I doubt there will be any left over."

I pull out my cell and lean in to show her a picture of the happy couple smashing cake into each other's mouths, as is tradition.

Our arms, both perched on the bar, collide with one another, and her touch sends a shiver right through me.

We admire the newlywed moment, but I'm hardly focused on my screen. There's electricity in the air now. I'll talk about the wedding if it's what keeps us here a little longer.

I slide my cell in my pocket. "The cake was..." I search for the perfect word because I know how important baked goods are to her. "Remarkable."

Her eyebrow quirks. "Remarkable?" She scrunches her nose in some sort of scrutiny over my word choice, but there's amusement there, too.

"Yeah. As in worth remarking on. Outstanding works, too. As in it stood out."

She beams at me for a beat until her smile fades and her eyes mist over. She turns away. The sudden gush of emotion has me even more concerned than the drink.

"Hey..." I touch her arm, beckoning her to come back to me.

She whips her head around only to look at my hand on

her arm with an unreadable expression. Does she want me to pull it away or keep it there?

"Are you okay?" I ask again.

Shay and I aren't close anymore, but we have history, and if she needs to talk, I'm probably better than the ruddy-faced man with a suspicious backpack who just sat three stools down. A lot has passed between the Shay I had in college and the one now. I'm sure she's changed. Hell, she has a kid. But drinking alone in Vegas isn't usually a good sign, especially when old high school friends from your small town are around the corner waiting for you to join the electric slide.

Maybe I've got it wrong. Sometimes a stiff drink makes me bleary-eyed, too.

"There's nothing I want to talk about, Logan." She slips her arm from under my touch. "But thanks for asking." She throws back her drink and drains what's remaining. "Why aren't you at the reception? It's probably kicking off."

"I'm having a weird night." I consider telling her about the meeting with my agent. This news is the third worst thing to happen to me in my life. Shay, despite not being close anymore, knows as well as anyone how big a deal it is to me to play with Ashton this season. Everyone in Starlight Canyon knows. Our dads' rancher friends used to call us peanut butter and jelly.

My mind wanders to my best friend retiring and the thought of me not receiving his passes, checking an opponent for him, giving each other shit-eating grins when the game is ours. It would kill for us to have to play on the opposite side during Ashton's last season and never wear the same jersey again. We did that for years in the NHL before finally landing on the Scorpions together back in our home state.

To top off my friend leaving the game soon, Ashton's announcement to retire has mortality creeping up my spine and gripping my throat. We're getting older. I'm *old*.

Shay always knew how to listen. She knew how to give an honest opinion, and very often, she was right. She was good to talk to and had a way of putting me in my place when I needed it, and I feel like getting my ass kicked right now. Reggie has too much faith in me fixing this, and in a rare moment of self-flagellation, I just want a punishment. Landing myself on the trade list was a massive fuck-up. Maybe I should tell her about it.

She lifts her eyebrows. "Weird day? You and me both."

I'm back in her cobweb. My mind is stuck on the burning need to know what a weird day means in her world.

"Why didn't you go to the reception?" It's likely the reason she's diving into the booze. I want to give her a chance to talk. Sometimes you need to ask people more than once about their troubles before they realize you truly intend to listen.

"Because..." She drops her head, and that beautiful hair of hers makes a veil between us, hiding why she's solo drinking. She didn't have this hair when she was mine. It was short and spunky, but just as shiny, raven silk. I used to love how it bounced around her jawline when we walked around campus together.

She composes a careful explanation. "I checked my email."

It's hard to imagine anything rattling Shay. Every time I see her, she seems cool, calm, and collected. Ever since that day in college, she's taken the reins of her wild destiny. She chose to leave school because it was best for her and her family, staying true to the daughter she needed and wanted to be. She makes being a single mom look like the best thing that ever happened to her. But Shay is only human, so I'm sure *email* isn't the whole story.

I slide into the space next to her and lean my elbow on the bar and try some humor. "Do you want to talk about it? I know all about emails. Get them all the time. Contracts. Spam. Inappropriate jokes from my teammates. I have a lot of experience."

Her laugh is more like an exhale. "You can't help me with this one. And frankly," her words are something of a command, "I came to this bar to forget about it." She wraps her fingers around her glass.

I lean closer as if sharing a secret. "I know as much about that as I do emails."

She chuckles again, and it's more genuine this time. Making her feel better makes me feel better, too, and the balm washing over me urges me to keep her talking, to keep *us* talking.

I bring up a character from Starlight Canyon High who everyone knows and the best story from tonight's wedding slash reunion. "Finchley was at the reception."

It only takes a beat for her to remember the guy. "Stoner Finchley? Doesn't he live in Colorado now? No surprise he moved somewhere where weed is legal."

"Yeah. He lives near Telluride. He's a teacher."

"He's a teacher?" She narrows her eyes. "No way."

Her thoughts surely replicate my own when I heard. Finchley could barely be in charge of himself back in the day.

"Sorry, I'm telling the story wrong. Finchley *was* a teacher." I recall the tale that had as all in fits of laughter, hoping it earns me another smile. "Apparently, he was an English teacher at some private high school. Just a normal stoner teacher offering up a lit class until they came to *Lord of the Flies* in the syllabus. You know the book?"

"Is that the story where the boys get stranded on an island and turn all wild and violent? With the poor kid named Piggy?"

"Yeah. Piggy. Well, Finchley, who by the look of his bloodshot eyes tonight still smokes, decided it would be good immersive work if the kids had a *Lord of the Flies* experience in the woods behind his school."

"No..." She braces herself to hear the result of his very bad idea.

"Apparently, these private school kids brought spray perfume and pillowcases filled with sand and flour to throw at each other's eyes." I let out a low chuckle at the thought. "It got dirty..."

Shay throws her hands over her mouth, trying to stop herself laughing at something so inappropriate. "No way... I shouldn't be laughing..." But she does anyway, and the sound dances in my heart.

"I hope nobody got hurt."

"Just Finch. Got fired, and some kid took the chance to pants him."

She giggles again. "Oh my God. Stoner Finchley..."

She shakes her head, imagining it, but as the image fades, so too does her enchanting smile. My story is a temporary fix. The only thing that would truly help her right now would be to get things off her chest, but maybe she thinks too many years have passed for that. Maybe it's about another man; I guess it would be weird for her to confide in me if it was. My stomach twists.

I offer another bandage and point to her drink. "Can I get you a...?"

Amusement puffs out of her nose and lifts her shoulders. She tips her drink and nods. "Gin and tonic."

I call the bartender over. "Two Sapphire and tonics."

She rolls her eyes and stops shy of smirking, the way she used to in college when she thought I was being cute but worked hard not to let me know. I must be seeing this all through rose-tinted specs, but once my beer goggles are on, they typically don't come off till morning. So Shay is looking more attractive than ever. I'd love to lean in closer and get a whiff of that frosting smudge on her thigh.

I have a lot more restraint than people think I do, but Shay's personality is my kryptonite. When a tempered and in-control woman like Shay offers you any sort of approval, it's like oil slipping into the dry cracks of life.

I crave more because it's massaging the ache of Reggie's news. So when the bartender brings our drinks, I sip alcohol I do not need. I watch her lips on the glass and stare at the faint coral stain they leave behind, then raise my eyes to hers, firmly fixed on my gaze.

We're drunk. We're not in good places. I'm reminiscing. *The cobwebs are very sticky tonight.*

We get to talking more about mutual classmates and things going on back in the Canyon. I should make sure she gets to her room safely and then find that dark nightclub I intended to lose myself in. I should not cave in to the soothing feeling of being next to Shay and having an actual conversation like we did in the old days. I should not let my mind wander to the stretched AC/DC logo hanging on for dear life to either side of her voluptuous breasts. I shouldn't wonder what kind of advice she'd give me about my Ashton dilemma or how good it would feel for her to pull my head against those soft, sexy pillows, run her fingers through my hair, and tell me I've got this like she used to.

My cell interrupts my train of thought. I pull it out of my pocket and swipe.

KRISTA VEGAS TAJ

> Hey! Toby told me you're in Vegas, handsome. Are you down for a little mayhem?

I stare at the invitation I *thought* I was waiting for, and when I glance up, Shay's beautiful round eyes are half-mast, just like her bedroom eyes years ago. Peaceful. Relaxed... but that's not what she's feeling right now. These are *get drunk and forget it* eyes.

She flicks her gaze to my phone and back up, and her cocked eyebrow says she knows I've been summoned. It's like a goodbye. "Thanks for the drink, Logan."

I give my cell one last glance but don't reply and slip it in my pocket.

It's a greedy thought that I might be able to go out with Shay tonight instead, but we can't help the ones that come to us, especially after countless shots into a Vegas evening. I'm not surprised I'm sitting here still feeling attracted to the only woman I ever loved. I'm not surprised by the urge commanding me to whisk this raven-haired beauty from that stool and off for a night drowning our sorrows in a town that makes drowning feel like the best way in the world to go down. I've had whimsical impulses to ask Shay out again even when I was sober.

Shay traces the rim of her glass. She's written me off and expects me to leave. Her eyelashes flutter, delicate and pretty like a moth's wings. If she needs a light to make her flicker and fly again, well, why not me? Am I really going to leave her with dubious backpack man? It's an act of chivalry and friendship to make sure she's safe and has a damn good time tonight.

She can read her email tomorrow.

My phone vibrates in my pocket, but I ignore it.

"Are you planning on staying here all night?" I ask, gesturing to the bar.

She shakes her head, staring at her drink. "I really don't know."

I don't know either. I don't know what the hell I'm thinking. If the point is to forget about my problems, spending time with her and resurrecting the biggest one I've ever had isn't going to give me relief.

But my judgment clouds with alcohol. It clouds with the sweet smell of either perfume or frosting emanating from her hair. It clouds from the depth of her eyes where some of my own past is still hidden, the part when I was a man with so much less, but so much more.

Yeah, I'm not leaving without asking. "Do you want to get out of here and find somewhere worth our time?"

Chapter Eight

Shay

I DID NOT EXPECT THAT.

His question doesn't immediately translate, and I blink. One. Two. Three times. And then I can't help it, but I let out a thick, amused, and somewhat wild laugh that doesn't belong to me, but I love just the same. It's the laugh of someone tipsy, free and fun. It's a laugh of someone hiding inside me I never let out.

Or haven't since college.

Logan Hunter.

Of course the man with the confidence of ten and never a hair out of place would come across me swimming at the bottom of a gin and tonic with fondant icing smeared on my jeans. The one moment I let my shield fall, I run into Alexander the Great, who proposes my inner war can be solved with a night out.

"Us?" I say. The smile I released while laughing still dances on my lips. I lick them and swallow it down, urging myself to conjure up the maturity required for this situation. "Me and you? Go out?"

Is this a good idea or a bad one? Logan and I haven't done much more than exchange pleasantries over the years and somehow kept in touch through the thriving grapevine in Starlight Canyon. I knew some of his business. I'm sure he knew mine. We aren't close anymore but we're hardly strangers.

Tonight is not my finest hour, and I'm not sure if our history is a reason to stay away or if it means he's exactly who I should be with tonight.

He loosens his tie then leans in closer. His broad chest is on display, and manly heat radiates on my bare bicep under the sleeve of my vintage t-shirt. The way it sends my core all heavy has me landing back on this being a bad idea. I've sworn off men like Logan Hunter.

"Why is that funny?" he asks, leaning in even closer. All six-three of him gobbles up my personal space and warms the atmosphere around me like a humid, exotic vacation. "Maybe we didn't manage to stay in touch with me being away, but I recall you once saying we should be friends."

It's such a benign but loaded statement, because it reminds us both of when we were more.

Nothing could quite make me stop caring about him, not even me being angry with him for turning into this caricature he is now. He used to be better than this. He used to respect himself. He used to respect me. I've had nothing but the most complicated feelings for Logan since that day he left. Sometimes I'm angry he's not become the man I thought he was, sometimes I'm glad he didn't, because he surely would have found someone else.

It's such a problem, missing someone so much you can't forget them.

Our past is still there, now, as it is every time I see him, our story swirls in his whiskey eyes. He's seen parts of me I've hidden since the moment we parted.

I'm sure he's not the same guy.

We've *both* changed.

Logan doesn't seem to have any of the same reservations. Our guards are down in this adult playground with spirits in our veins.

He runs his knuckle gently along my cheek. "I'll get you home safe."

Heat blossoms under the trail of his fingers. Unfortunately, blood isn't rushing simply to my face. It rushes everywhere else, too. I've often wondered how on earth Logan could woo so many women. I don't wonder anymore. I'm quickly finding reasons to say yes.

As much as I know Logan would attentively listen to my woes, staying here with him tonight could create a whole other set of them, because now that he's touched me, a lust ignites in the small space between us. I have been off games for far too long. No sex since Nino's father. Almost six years. *Six years.* I didn't even know I still worked down there till now. My core screams for me to accept this invitation.

I shake my head. "No. But thank you..." It's the right thing, and yet as soon as I say the words I regret them.

My Lord is this confusing.

What's the alternative to going out tonight anyway? My hotel room, an overpriced minibar, and *Grey's* reruns? Do I really want to do that more than hang out with Logan? I'm so used to responding negatively to men now, I can't even tell if I want to do this or not.

He's probably just being nice anyway. I doubt he wants to go out with me tonight when he can have the pick of nearly any woman in this state. Country. Hell, universe.

"I'm not dressed for it," I add.

He lets his head flop to the side. Maybe he's had too much to drink as well because he says, so naturally, as if it was yesterday, "You look good in everything, *pastelito*."

His compliment sends sparks right through me, and a girly giggle bubbles in my tummy. Thank God I don't let it out.

He waits for my answer with one of his patient, charming grins. I wait for more excuses to come, but the only thing that exits is an exasperated breath. Let's face it, if I didn't want to be with him tonight, I'm not too polite to show someone my back. I'd already be upstairs. *I want to do this.* I know I do from my toes right to the one pesky gray hair I have to pluck out when it grows out and sticks up straight.

He pops a shoulder. "Don't let a dress code stop you. No club will care what you're wearing. Tables cost too much to turn us down on account of a pair of Converse." His gaze tracks down my body and up again, connecting cozily with mine. "Which are stylish and cute by the way."

I almost smile and have to crinkle my nose to stop the bashfulness from bursting to life and giving him the wrong idea.

He jokes, "Or are you resisting because you still have no rhythm and don't want me to see you dancing? I won't judge. Promise." He crosses his heart.

I narrow my eyes. "As a matter of fact, my two-step is much improved."

"Okay. Just making sure you didn't think I was going to write to the *Canyon Express* about it. What happens in Vegas and all..."

I really should say no. I am rock bottom and probably looking a hot mess. I nearly cried when he paid me a compliment earlier about my cake, the cake I thought would be the start of my new business venture but won't make me money fast enough.

But no matter what I do tonight, tomorrow will still come. The escapism Logan offers is a circular road and will only lead me right back to where I am. The symphony of promises in Logan's amber eyes is damn tempting. His dimples are tempting. Forgetting my responsibilities and the weight of the world for just one night is tempting.

One night to just breathe and dance... to maybe hear that wild laugh burst out of my throat again.... Logan, unlike me, has never been good alone. I stare deep into his brown eyes and I know we're not close anymore but I recognize the familiar glint of vulnerability. What happened to *him* tonight? I haven't even asked. It's kind of shitty of me.

My hesitation is starting to seem like an answer.

He peers down. "I don't want to make you feel awkward, so if you say no again, I'll step away."

His gaze somehow makes me feel like the most gorgeous woman in the room despite how I see myself in this moment. Logan's stare is always admiring and reassuring. It's also devilish, coy, flirty, and... panty-dropping.

I'm not really seeing him as a friend right now. The drinks sink into my brain, and I search for boundaries and definitions to ground me. I don't know what the heck this guy is to me. An ex? A handsome coincidence? A night to remember waiting to happen? All I know is here and now, Logan proposes we go out as friends, and that's the last word my libido would use to describe him.

But for just one night, don't I deserve to let my hair down? Don't I deserve to relax? Why can everyone else run away to this adult playground and enjoy some reckless behavior?

I remember the text he received.

"Why don't you just take..." I point to his cell that beeped only moments ago, likely from someone with no cellulite and stretch marks.

He shrugs as if the answer is simple. "I'd rather be with someone I like."

A flattered laugh escapes. But I have to admit, it's my sentiment exactly, too. I don't want to be alone. I definitely don't want to stay down here with that man at the end of the bar carrying a backpack. This is starting to sound like the best worst idea I've heard in a long time.

Logan is safe. He would never hurt me. No matter how many years have passed between then and now, I know that statement is as true as the sky is blue. Plus he's handsome as hell and probably knows all the best places to go. He's a gentleman and was raised right by his mama so he will make sure I end up back in that suite in one piece.

Fuck it.

I throw my hands in the air. "I'll hang out with you." I have no idea why I add, "But it's not a date."

He opens his mouth, but the laugh that comes out is silent. Nothing unnerves this man. "Fine. Will you escort me?"

"Escort is yet another word I'd rather not use. Especially in Vegas."

He laughs this time out loud, and it's magnetic. So

magnetic it latches on to the *fuck it* moment I'm having and reels it in with his flirtatious lips.

He taps my nose. "We used to be pretty good at having fun together."

We'll drink. We'll dance. If I want to let loose in Vegas it's best to do it with him than on my own in this crazy place.

What's the worst thing that can happen?

Chapter Nine

Shay

Music gobbles up the air around me, and my vision is filled with darkness, smoke, and flashing lights in some club called the Taj Mahal. We've been here for what seems about an hour, but it could be way more, or maybe less.

We've had shots. We laughed about old classmates and Starlight Canyon gossip with me lying on the sofa, legs sprawled over his lap in drunken delight. Scantily clad waitresses have come and gone with a tacky firework display presenting us with overpriced champagne, but I'm so drunk I can't even taste it, I merely feel the bubbles on my tongue.

And we dance.

Now, my back is against the wall in the space between two plush couches in our VIP area big enough for about ten people, occupied by two. I've completely forgotten myself, today, tomorrow, and even how to move my feet in time to the beat in the music. Not that I've ever been that good to begin with.

Now, I stand with my shoulders against a wall and roll them sexily; they don't even feel like they belong to me. The DJ drops a bass beat, and euphoria pounds through the club. Logan sways in front of me. His cool, subtle dance moves become more animated; he throws his hand in the air with youthful abandon to celebrate the rhythm wrapping us in the all-consuming rapture of this sound. The DJ controls us with a baseline that vibrates the heart and rattles the rib cage as if nothing else in the world matters. I close my eyes and tip my head upward. Blinking lights make their way to the backs of my eyelids and party with me. The music takes a turn, and a diva-like female voice on the DJ's track bellows into the space.

Throw yo' hands up in the air...

I do as my girl commands and throw my hands up along the back wall. A few droplets of champagne spill out of the flute onto my head, but I have no control over my body, my mind. I'm floating away...

Until the pressure of Logan's pants zipper pushes into the softness of my tummy and my breasts are suddenly sensitive, nipples peaked beneath my t-shirt. Logan's eyes are trained on me, and his hips undulate in tandem with my torso.

I'm exposed with my arms still in the air. He wraps his giant hand around my waist and places it on the small of my back. He leans in to say something that sounds like: *Are you getting dumb?*

My loud, drunk shout searches for his ear. "I can't hear you."

He repeats himself, but I just point to my ear, hopeful he didn't actually ask if I'm getting dumb, because let's be honest, I am. I am very dumb right now. My brain has been drowned in at least three different kinds of spirits.

He shakes his head, places our drinks down on the nearby table. As if I weigh nothing, he grips the sides of my waist, fingers sinking into my flesh with a delicious sort of pressure. My feet land on one of the couches, and the uneven, soft surface isn't great for my lack of balance. I throw my hands around his neck to stop myself from falling.

We're face to face now. A strobe light illuminates his already gorgeous eyes.

"I asked if you're having fun?" He still has to talk loudly for me to understand.

My lips are so close to his. His secure grip around my waist is hot as hell. His scent roams around me like some enchanting fog, a spell so alluring I want to fall under it. This is fun all right. Drunk, idiotic fun but I can't deny it's a good time.

I'm wasted and I'll pay for it tomorrow. But for now, the alcohol resurrects that familiar bond between us, that magnetic comfort that we always had, and the ease... it doesn't feel like it's been sixteen years since our bodies collided like this.

"This..." I start to shout over the small expanse between us but then close the space and find his ear. The potion that is his cologne is even more potent this close to his thick, muscular neck. *Maybe I should just sink my teeth into it now for a taste.*

"This place is amazing. Thanks for bringing me here. I needed it."

I'm finished talking but I don't ease back. I like it here with our waists connected, his hands somehow both splayed over the humps of my ass, and his thumbs so close to either side of my zipper.

What big hands you have, Logan Hunter...

"Why did you need it?" His voice is low in my ear, and his nose clips my lobe.

My eyelids flutter shut at the flick of his nose on such a sensitive spot, and an inaudible purr races through me.

"What happened today?" he asks again.

I lean back and quirk my eyebrow. "I told you. I got an email."

He bites his lip and nods. His gaze is intense in the short beat that passes, and I think he's going to press.

I turn the tables. "What happened to you?"

His confession comes easy. "My agent told me the Scorpions are thinking of trading me."

I swear the record scratches. That's the worst thing that could happen to Logan. Leaving his best friend when Ashton's retiring? No wonder he wanted to get messed up tonight. I would, too. Hell, I did.

I fold my arms more deeply around his neck and pull him against my chest for a hug. My nipples rasp against my bra, and I'm not sure if it's the bassline or his heart I feel through my t-shirt.

"Sorry, Lo. I know you want to play with Ashton."

Our hips are connected.

"That must sting. No pun intended. Because of the Scorpions. Sorry. I'm not trying to be funny."

"I know. Don't worry about it. It sucks." For the first time tonight, something other than sensual charm plays on his features; a sincere disappointment weighs on the corners of his mouth.

He strokes his fingers along my hip bones absentmindedly as if we're still in college when we used to talk like this. Sometimes we were as drunk as this when we did, then, our guards were fully down just as they seem to be now.

"I fucked up, Shay. All I care about is playing this last season with Ash and I fucked it up."

I let my forehead fall to his, and it clunks against his skull because my head seems to weigh more than usual, but he doesn't flinch.

"Logan, you can fix this. If anyone can, it's you. Turn it around. Pull your head out of your ass and show everyone you belong there. Score like you've never before. Train harder. You're not going to give up easily, are you?"

His eyes are hollow with dejection and too much to drink. This news must have been agonizing. The friendship between Ashton and Logan is brotherhood. Even in college they talked about being on the same team in the NHL, winning a Stanley Cup together and bringing it home to Starlight Canyon. They said they'd throw a party with the whole town invited. They talked about decorating the Danes' barn, having an open bar, something at the time as poor college kids seemed like the most luxurious thing to offer.

I cup the sides of his face with my hands. "Hey, it isn't over till the buzzer goes off. You're good under pressure, Logan. This is pressure. Rise. Yeah?"

A sparkle of life comes back into his gaze, or maybe it's the strobe lights.

"All right, it's your turn, Mendez."

The words come easier this time because I can't let him feel alone. "I fucked up, too. My son is a genius. That's what was in the email. His test results."

Logan's head falls back, and his mouth drops open with a silent laugh. His neck is on full display again.

He jostles my hips playfully, and in a flirty move I didn't expect locks our zippers together. There's as much sarcasm as there is sincerity in his question. "Fuck, *pastelito*... You messed up because your kid is a genius?"

Even though hours ago this was serious, inhibitions are dead. I slap his chest like he just said something funny.

"Yeah, Logan. I fucked up because I'm just some baker, and Nino needs... private school."

His brown gaze dives into me. "Do you need some help?"

Did he just offer to help me? I'm not sure I like that. Or maybe somewhere inside I do, because even though I'd never let him help me, it's nice to know he would. Maybe. Kind of... *I've had too much to drink.*

I nestle into the crook of his neck. "I'd never take money from anyone."

He turns his head to the side, and his stubble skims my cheek. I think he hums his response. I can't hear it over the pounding music but his chest vibrates against mine because we're pressed together tightly. His neck is hot, humid, and slightly scratchy. His breath tumbles with a warm, sensual mist over my ear. My lips are so achingly close to his balmy, musk scented skin, with less than the flap of a butterfly's wing I could touch him.

"I know you don't like help...."

His words tingle on my neck. I'm so close I feel the muscles of his throat flex and swallow, and then his words come out a restrained, husky whisper.

"But I'd give you anything you ask right now."

My breath hitches. Self-control has clearly checked itself at the door. The anonymity of this heaving, dark nightclub entices lust to the surface. My mind races back to when we were in our twenties, college kids needing each other so badly... lush memories of late-night chats ending in him between my legs, my hands scratching at his ass, him stretching me. And how he would always tell me I could take it, telling me what a good girl I was.

It should have been demeaning, but I gobbled that shit up. I'd eat it now and I'm overcome with an impulsive need for him to dish it up again.

"You want to help?" I ask.

"I do."

"Then make me forget about it."

His lips are so close, they touch mine as he speaks. "I'd beg for the opportunity."

I want to ravage him. He has me wrapped around his finger. It doesn't take even a second more and we crash our lips together. He meets my kiss with such hunger, I question which one of us moved first.

Chapter Ten

Shay

NEED WATER... *need water... need...*

I let my hand flop to the side, and it hits a firm, balmy, naked chest next to me.

A low voice grumbles. "Ow..."

My head snaps to the source of the grumble, and there he is... *Logan.*

I sit up in bed and snatch the crisp white bed sheet around my bare chest.

Oh. My. God.

I vaguely remember telling myself it would be okay to have sex with him last night. Being honest? I think I might have even thrown myself at him. I barely remember anything after Taj Mahal, but I do remember not coming up for air all the way from that VIP table, through a throng of clubbers, and into the carnival sounds of the casino. I'm not going to play innocent, I let this happen, but... *shit*.

Logan raises his eyebrows and smiles, not at all sheepish. Of course, this is probably normal for him.

I clutch the covers a little tighter.

"Shay..."

"Shh..." I don't want to hear it. He probably has a speech planned for just this occasion. "We're cool. It's fine."

He tosses me a look that tells me he doesn't believe I am but that he wants me to be. I might not do this every day like him, but I'm a grown-ass woman, and one who refuses to shame myself or any of my own. That's not to say this wasn't an error of judgment...

"Logan, we're two consenting adults having fun in Vegas. We'll go home and leave this here and chalk it up to us both being emotional."

He runs his hand through a gorgeous head of hair and sighs out his words. "It was definitely emotional."

I can barely swallow. I'm so thirsty and I remember he let out a groan. "Are you okay?"

"Yeah." He clears his throat. "Why?"

"You said ow."

He rubs his pec. "You scraped me with your rock."

I circle my neck, trying to ease some of the knots out. "My rock?" What kind of sex did we have? I feel like I've been railed by a Mack truck down there.

He points to my hand. "Your ring."

He pushes himself up to sitting, not even caring that he's sliding his dewy torso out from under the sheet. It rests precariously above his dick, over his manly smattering of hair. Exposed now are two of the reasons I caved to my desire last night—the cut edges of his hip bones are just as alluring now as they were so many years ago.

He asks as if he doesn't want to know the answer. "Were you wearing that last night? I feel like I would have noticed a diamond on your ring finger."

I rub my temples. *God, it sounds like a toilet is being flushed over and over inside my head.*

Just then, a cloud shifts and mid-morning sun glimmers through the curtains we never bothered closing. Something shimmers through the tiny slit in my left hand's fingers and catches my eye.

I whip my hand in front of my face. "Shit. What is this?"

"Your ring. The one I said you smacked me with." He lowers his eyes and scratches his forearm. "Who gave it to you?"

Panic replaces every other feeling I had a few moments ago. "Nobody gave this to me. Did I buy it last night?" I dread the answer to the question. Surely I didn't blow my life savings on jewelry last night.

He digs inside his eye sockets with his fingers for an answer, but not much pays him a visit. "Maybe we got it at the pawnshop?"

Pawnshop? Oh, please let it be a cheapie. Is it real? I dissect its surface up close as if I know anything about gems and fine jewelry. *God, don't tell me I used my credit card...*

"Do you remember how much I paid for it?"

"I don't even know for sure you got it there, I just remember you wanting to go. After the slot machines, it's pretty much a blur, but I remember you saying you wanted to visit a pawnshop from some show you watch on TV."

I contemplate the beautiful sparkling object on my ring finger. My stomach drops for so many reasons, the money, but also a twang of regret that I've never had one on this finger before. It is a lot like my mom's, a ring I wanted but that she gave to my eldest brother for his wife one day.

No matter how much it was, I shouldn't have bought it. "I need to take this back." I tug it, but my fingers are swollen from drinking so much.

He chuckles lightly but not at me, just in general, so much more comfortable with this kind of moment than I am, which is a fact that dredges up all sorts of discomfort. I'm sure this is commonplace for this dirty little playboy. The memories from years of seeing gorgeous women on his arm has me pulling at the ring harder. I'll flay myself in a moment if I don't stop. I'm going to need Vaseline or a health spa to get this off.

He hands me a bottle of water from the bedside table. "Here. You're dehydrated." He grabs another bottle for himself and slugs more than half of it before stopping abruptly. He pulls the bottle away from his lips in slow motion, staring at the back of his hand gripping the plastic.

I trace his gaze, and it lands on his ring finger, wrapped in a circle of platinum. He caps the bottle, hypnotized by the ring.

I tread lightly with my words. "I didn't notice that last night."

"I..." He can't even finish his sentence. The man is in shock.

"Why are we both wearing rings, Logan?"

He lists off what he remembers, and it sounds like we took psychedelics.

"Slot machines. Roller coaster. The pawnshop. And after..." He furrows his brow in concentration. "I kind of remember us seeing Elvis."

There are only two kinds of Elvises in this town. My

heart thumps. "Elvis, as in an impersonator?" It's not a question, but more a warning that I need the right answer or I'll pop.

He shakes his head as he tries to remember. "There was confetti..."

"Confetti?" Is there confetti in the stage shows?

He stares at his ring again, and it doesn't feel like he's really talking to me. "Do you like Elvis? I've never really thought about seeing Elvis before."

I whip up and out of bed, securing the sheet to my body in the hopes of finding clues. Receipts. Accounting is my second religion. I wouldn't throw out the receipt if I'd bought this ring.

I bury my hand in my purse, and there are a lot of tiny pieces of paper. It's like a trashcan in there. I pull one out, and it's from the club. I feel a heart attack coming on.

"Oh shit..." If I had any water left in my body, I might just cry. My voice is high and squeaky. "I spent three thousand dollars at that club last night?" I have to put my hand in front of my mouth. I swear vomit is on the way. "I don't even have that limit on my credit card."

"That was me."

I turn my head toward Logan who is now on the bed with a pillow over his dick since I whisked the sheet off.

"You insisted I start filing my receipts and keeping track of expenses." He points to my handbag. "You said you'd store them for me."

This man lives on a whole different planet. I lift another wadded-up paper snowball between two fingers. "You're a bookkeeper's dream."

I smooth and read out the tiny white slips one by one. *We won some money on the slots. We got some fries at the MGM hotel bar...*

He waves his hands as if urging clarity to come to him on a breeze. "I remember being in some... some office we were in?" He turns his head to me sharply. "Did we get arrested?"

I roll my eyes. I would *never* get arrested. I snatch out another wad. Smooth it. Read it. Read it again. And have to read it a third time because I cannot believe what I'm seeing. This can't be. *It's just not possible...*

"What's that one?" he asks from behind me.

I turn around to show him, but his eyes are closed, with no idea I'm about to give him a nightmare. His nonchalance disappears in an instant when my words drop like a bomb.

"We bought a marriage license, Logan."

He lets out a disbelieving laugh, one I've never heard before because I'm sure Logan typically believes all the other shit he gets up to. He shakes his head, jaw slack, eyes full of disbelief. "I'd never..."

My eyes narrow temporarily, and I wonder if he means he'd never marry *me* or marry at all. I throw the paper onto the bed over his bare legs, and he picks it up while I dive back into my purse, my stomach sloshing with dread.

"Maybe we just got the license. Maybe we didn't actually..."

Tiny balled-up pieces of paper and the evidence of our sordid night seem to go on for days.

His deep, reassuring voice reaches me from behind. "Honestly, Shay, *neither* of us would do this..."

I keep digging. It's mostly food and gambling, and somewhere in this room is a teddy from a lingerie shop. Just when I think we might have gotten away with the worst, that maybe we just got a license but didn't get married, I pull out the last slip of paper.

Hunka Hunka Burning Love Chapel.

"Oh God..." I let my head fall into my palm and rub my temples again. "This is madness, Logan." I could cry.

I turn around and raise the paper into the still sordid, humid air in front of us. "Why would you let us get married?"

"Me!" His eyebrows shoot to the ceiling. "I wouldn't..."

"This paper says we're married, Logan!"

He throws the pillow aside and jumps up to snatch the paper from my hand. "No way in hell..."

I try not to be distracted by his swinging cock. "Why did you let us do this?"

"I'm pretty sure you've always thought *you're* the responsible one between us. What's your excuse, *boss?*"

I grab a discarded towel from the floor and shove it in his direction. "For goodness sakes, Logan, put some clothes on."

"Clothes aren't going to fix this..." But he wraps the towel around him.

I throw myself back into the bed and stare at the opposite wall. "I hope this is your first time." I bite, regretting my attack instantly because I know I'm as much to blame.

"Of course it's my first time," he says, offended. "Jesus, Shay, what kind of degenerate do you think I am?"

I should back down but don't because it's not like his reputation doesn't precede him. "The one portrayed in *Snowed* magazine. The one everyone knows is a..."

He cuts me off. "I'm not that kind of guy. It's... never mind." He contemplates the paper again. A line forms between his brows, then he sits next to me and stares at the same wall I do.

"Trust me, *this?*" He waves the paper like it proves something it doesn't. "God, we must have been off our rockers."

"We screwed up." I take a few calming breaths. Blaming Logan wasn't fair. "Sorry I said that about you doing it before. I shouldn't have said what I said. We both did this. I'm just..."

"We're just... shocked."

I clutch the sheet like a lifeline. "We need to fix this. I have a son, Logan. I can't just do things like this. I shouldn't have even gotten that drunk. Antonio counts on me..." My heart races thinking of Nino. This was so irresponsible. I could have gotten hurt last night.

I'm weak. Weak from an entire night out. Weak from nausea. Weak between my legs, probably from riding this man. The shock slowly fades, and a dull ache of shame settles behind my eyes. I let my head fall to the mattress and find a pillow to cover my face.

Silence surrounds me, and I breathe hard against the feathers until it almost feels like I'll suffocate under here. How could I have been so irresponsible drinking that much in this crazy town? Nino counts on me. A single tear escapes out of the corner of my eye, and I refuse to let Logan see me if another is to fall, so I sweat under the Egyptian cotton.

It's crazy enough I got accidentally drunk-married at all, but to Logan? I have to think it's the best worst-case on some level because I know we'll be able to sort it out. I know he's become an idiot over the years we've been apart but he's not an asshole, we'll be civil about it. Still, it skewers my self-esteem. Logan must have a thousand secret women. I'm just another notch.

Logan aside, even when we sort this, I'll carry this boulder of guilt forever.

The pillow mutes my pathetic words. "I'm a terrible mom."

Logan breaks his silence by placing his hand on mine on top of the pillow. His hand is an affection I don't deserve right now but tenderness that's a balm for my shame. He strokes his thumb over my sensitive skin, and slowly, his caring caress convinces my heart rate to come back to normal.

"You could never be a terrible mom."

I throw the pillow off my face and onto the side of the bed with a dull thump. "How would you know?"

"Shay..." He shakes his head.

I know he's wanting to be nice, but a defiance churns inside. He has no idea what kind of mom I am, and unless Jesus walks in here and tells me otherwise, Nino deserves more from me.

He shrugs. "You're right. I guess I don't really know, but all I have to go on is how good I thought you'd be when I used to think about things like that."

I hate thinking about our past. I hate thinking about how Logan Hunter once used to cherish me. How he made me feel seen, heard, and valued in the worst moment of my life, but it turned out I wasn't really special. No. I've seen over the years *everyone* is special to Logan, which technically means nobody is.

"We need to get a divorce." I tug at the ring on my finger again, but they're still sausages. They're holding on to every ounce of moisture available.

He's deep in thought. I'm not sure he even heard what I said until impossible words leave his lips.

He places his hand on mine again to stop me from tugging. "What if we don't?"

"Don't what?"

"Don't get divorced."

I don't know if I should laugh or cry. "Logan..."

"No... let me talk first. What if..." He drops a look into my eyes like he knows I'll want to stop him from talking but warns me not to. "What if last night was fate in disguise? Both of us ran into each other lower than low. Of all the days we could have been in the same place at the same time..."

I roll my eyes. "We ran into each other after a friend's wedding. That's not fate, that's a very likely coincidence."

He ignores me. "We're both going through shit and somehow we landed in the same place at the same time. Maybe we can help each other."

My brain is messed up from last night. Maybe I'm still drunk. Maybe he is, too, if he's thinking there's any reason in the world we should stay married.

His wheels turn inside that pretty head at a million miles an hour. "I hated seeing you like that last night at the sportsbooks."

"I was fine," I interrupt, coming to my defense as if there's something wrong with being upset.

"Woman. You weren't fine. You weren't anywhere close to fine when I found you at that bar."

I want to resist again but I don't because Logan can still see right through me. I wasn't fine. I'm not fine *now*. Not being able to provide for Nino is just about the most heart-wrenching thought I could think. I'd rather go to Hell than not give that boy what he needs.

My eyes sting thinking of it. They nearly burst when Logan's familiar, intense gaze sinks into me like lying to him again is futile. He's accepting me for all the ugly I'm trying to push away. Just like he always used to. Just like he did the moment I fell in love with him.

"You said last night Antonio is gifted. That he needs to go to that school in Longbrook."

It was like scanning some Wikipedia page about some other person's child when I read that email yesterday. I've always known Nino wasn't like other kids. He could read when he was two. He could do times tables well past what I can do in my head by three. I knew it was wildly unusual but just nurtured it the best I could until he went to school. Then the principal and the test came into the picture. My kid is a genius. He's gifted as can be, and I am so damn normal I can't help him.

I close my eyes briefly. The gas money alone to commute Nino to a school feels like more than we can bear. And the tuition? A cool thirty-five thousand a year and the fees go up in high school. His principal mentioned in the email that Longbrook would enter him into sixth grade. He's five. He'll likely move through those years quickly and right into high school.

I sank everything into my rebranding, my website, a rental space in town that had a food-grade service kitchen so I could make wedding cakes and not drive my dad wild in the kitchen. I can't say yes to Logan. But can I really say no? What's the alternative? Saying no to Nino?

Logan envelops my hand. His long fingers grip my palm. The comfort of his touch worries me. It shouldn't feel this natural after so many years.

"Giving back to you and Antonio would be karma. I've never forgotten my roots, Shay. You know how much help I got from everyone in Starlight Canyon growing up. Financially. And more."

The Hunters weren't always wealthy. They only really came into their money when I was in middle school. Hockey is an expensive sport, and he received a lot of gifts from our town. It's nice this man can spend thousands like it's nothing now, but he still appreciates where it started. Maybe he hasn't become a total egomaniac after all.

I want everything for Antonio, and yet my own ego is ringing alarm bells. The whole reason I wanted to start this wedding cake business was to provide and also show Antonio what the Mendez family can do. Logan seems to be suggesting a handout.

But he said we can help each other?

"It doesn't take a genius to know how you can help me, but..." I let my lips flap with an exhausted breath. "How could I even help you? Seriously?"

"You know about the trade. You know how much it means to me to stay on the Scorpions for Ashton's last season. It might sound small to someone else, but..."

It's not small. Never in this history of time has such a bromance existed. "I know how much it means to you boys to play together. It isn't silly."

His eyes soften in appreciation. "You get it. I know it's my fault I landed in this situation but I'd die a little inside if I had to tell Ashton I fucked this up. That our last chance just went up in smoke. I *need* to stay on the Scorpions. Just for this season. I need my coach to believe I'm a changed man. And becoming a family man couldn't be more convincing."

It sounds so sensible when he says it, but this really is madness. I need to get real. Staying married to Logan has some fantastic side effects, but there could be consequences I'm not sure I could bear a second time around if...

I pull my hand out from his grasp. "Just stop right there, Logan. I want you to play with Ash..." I let out a breath. "I know you two never got that Stanley Cup together and that's always been your dream since you were kids. So let me start off by validating that."

"Thank you..."

"But me and Nino are not up for grabs. I'm not saying I don't want the best for you. I do. But that is just a step too far." Maybe it's ethics, maybe it's pride, but I can't do something so... well, something meant for movies and books.

I fix my gaze on an armchair in the corner with my everyday cotton panties strewn over it. Ugh.

"Do you have another plan?" he asks.

His words are a knife in my gut. What *is* my plan? I can't even ask my brothers to help with money because they've done the same thing I have. They've sunk every penny into a years-long business venture and developing The Compound where we'll all live together again. And my dad has always been a rancher, he hardly makes more than I do.

"How on earth would that even work out? It's not just *us*, Logan. I can't lie to Antonio about being married."

"Even though it's for his own good? Tell me you've never lied to him. Just white lies to make him do what you want or keep him out of trouble?" He lies down on his side. "It's such a mom thing to lie. Mine used to tell me ghosts came out on the pond after dark so Ashton and I wouldn't sneak out there after sunset when we were little."

I cross my arms. "You're comparing telling my kid we're married to a lie that kept you from falling through thin ice?"

His gaze deepens, and a serious cloud darkens his amber eyes. "She told me bigger ones."

"Like what?"

"Like my dog went off to live a wild life with the wolves when he actually got run over by a car."

I let out a slightly sympathetic sigh, but he knows I'm not convinced.

He stares me dead in the eyes, and his usually friendly

97

glint fades. "Like my dad was looking down from Heaven and was proud of me and my hockey achievements." There's such an ache in his voice.

I soften instantly. Logan's biggest pain was his father never seeing him make it. He only ever wanted his father to feel the satisfaction of all the sacrifices he made for his son. Logan talked about it frequently when we were together in college.

By the looks of it, he's been haunted by the thought for years.

I want to reach out for his hand to comfort him but don't. "Logan, what she said is true. He would have been proud."

"Shay." Now he talks to me like I'm the one being silly. "He was not looking down on me. He was not rooting for me from up in the clouds. She said it so I didn't self-destruct and ruin my chance with hockey due to grief. I'm not a parent but I understand they don't always tell the truth. When shit hits the fan they'll do whatever it takes to soothe and heal their kid's pain. They'll cheat, lie, and steal to give their kid the best shot. So I don't know what kind of mom you are, but if I were a dad? I'll be damned if I let a white lie get in the way of my kid's destiny. Anyway, it's not even a lie." He raises his left hand. "We *are* married."

This was a completely unexpected and epic speech. And I'm left with two unbelievable feelings. One, he's right. And two...

Logan would be a wonderful father.

It goes quiet between us. Enough time passes with us staring at each other. His dark past passes like a brief storm, and the daylight returns to his eyes.

The adrenaline of the situation seems to have cured my

headache. I can't believe it but I feel completely sober when
I say, "How would we do this?"

Chapter Eleven

Logan

D<small>ID SHE ACTUALLY SAY YES</small>?

She stares at me with those dark, pensive eyes of hers, waiting for my next move, waiting for me to tell her this is going to work. Because it was my idea... is it actually a good one or another case of me diving in headfirst?

Sure. I'd like to convince Coach. But even when I said it to her moments ago, I knew this isn't the kind of arrangement I need to make the coach happy. Shay doesn't know it, but I've had hundreds of fake dates and girlfriends over the years to keep my playboy image alive. Reggie could probably find me a fake wife easily enough, too, if that's what I decided to do.

No. Much as I need what I need, the first spark to alight was that I never, ever want to see Shay that low again. She might have broken my heart but she's a good, honest person with so much determination. She deserves to win.

And of course there's Antonio. He deserves more, too. Thinking that a little boy might grow up without a father, even without this other issue, is an ice pick to the chest. I'd hate it even if I didn't lose my own father; I hate it more because I did. Every boy needs a dad, and I was lucky to have my older brother and coaches who stepped in. They never could replace Billy Hunter, but they sure as hell tried.

In some ways, Antonio and I are kindred spirits. Like him, I had a talent I wouldn't have been able to nurture without the goodness of a few kind neighbors. Helping him would be a fulfilling experience for me in this otherwise empty personal life of mine. Paying it back would be a full circle gesture that will add some wholeness to my life I badly need. I'm over everything but my family and hockey.

Shay needs details. "So we'll tell everyone in Starlight Canyon we got married last night? Just like that?"

I didn't become a winner following rules. I've always been instinctive on the ice. But if Shay and I are to come out of this unscathed, we'll need some moves. It has to be flawless. Start to finish. For this to work, we need the perfect playbook.

"Yeah. We'll just say we're married. It's the truth."

"The truth?" She laughs. "That's a funny word to use for what's happening."

"But we *are* married, Shay. It's not a lie."

"No. But it's a *dirty* truth."

The way the word *dirty* falls from her puffy pink lips makes me feel like I'm in trouble. Like living together isn't going to be easy.

She taps her lips in thought. "Do you really think your mom would believe this? I mean, my dad is a total romantic, sucker-for-love type who secretly watches romcoms, but Joy?"

I stroke my chin. "Yeah. She's a reality TV type."

Shay lets out an airy laugh.

"She probably won't believe it but what is she going to do? Ask for CCTV footage from the casinos? She'll accept it. She always loved you."

"She did?"

I nod.

Shay's gaze lowers; she tucks hair behind her ears. I've always loved her cheeks. Her jawline. That tiny nose in her pixie profile. I wish I could remember more about last night. How she might have looked with her tits bouncing, her heart-shaped lips parted...

She snaps me out of it. "At least our families know each other. That's helpful. It's not like we're strangers," she reasons.

"Yeah, you know how the Hunters are. If I'm happy, they'll be happy for me and go with it. They'd never expect me to get married, but if I did, it would probably be like this."

She laughs. "I guess." She makes pensive circles on the sheet with her index finger.

"Story-wise, I think we should tell people we've been talking for a while. We can say I found out you were doing the cake for the Grishams and we decided to go out a few times, have been texting and calling each other for a while, then... this."

Her eyelashes flutter upward, and our gaze connects.

"This?" she almost whispers.

"Yeah." I sigh back at her.

A thick storm looms in the space between us. The way she's staring at me conjures up all sorts of emotion that has no business in this transaction.

I find focus in my haze. "It's very believable."

She pretends to care about that spot on the sheet again. "Yeah. My family can buy that, too. It's still extreme but also... not out of the realm of the possible."

She lets out a sharp breath. "September fifth."

"What?"

"Let's say that was the day we started talking. We saw each other at the tack shop? CCs is too obvious."

"I thought your horse, Daisy, went over the rainbow bridge?"

She nods. "I get cat food there."

"You have a cat. Okay... Cat's name?"

"Cayenne."

"Like the pepper?"

"Like the capital of French Guiana."

I scratch my head, wondering how all these things happened and I didn't know it. "That's out there as a capital city."

"Not for Nino, it isn't. It's his favorite capital from the South American countries."

"Right." I remind myself I'm dealing with a prodigy. "Little genius. Any other favorite-sounding cities? Or things Nino likes or doesn't like that I should know about?"

"He hates cheese." She scrunches her nose almost apologetically.

"That's unlucky."

"Tell me about it."

I've never been intimidated in life apart from in all things Shay. Everything is daunting when you so badly want to do it right.

But I can deal. I just hope Shay can.

"Are you going to be okay?" I need some reassurance she isn't going to bail. "Telling your dad and Antonio? I know what I said earlier about parents lying and I didn't mean to act like just because they do that it's easy. I'm sure it isn't."

"It'll be weird. But you were right. I lied to Antonio before." Her eyes widen. "But he's not that easy to fool. Then again, he's also only five, and even though he's very intelligent, he's still his age emotionally. He'll like you."

"I hope he does."

She looks at me like I'm silly. "Everybody does, Logan. My dad will be over the moon. You know how old-fashioned he is and ... he compared everyone who came after. No one ever measured up."

How many more were there after me? *I hate them all.*

"Bearing in mind he's not impressed by your current reputation." She rolls her neck around in circles. "Thankfully, my brothers don't live in the Canyon anymore."

The Mendez boys. I might need my gear on for them. I shift in the bed thinking of it, and the towel around me loosens.

She yanks it back over me tightly. "We're going to need some rules, too. First, no being naked in front of each other."

"Wow, that's rule number one? That really says something, Shay..." I tease.

She gives me one of her famous head wobbles. "They're in no particular order."

Little does she know, I need that rule as much as she apparently does. When she rubs the back of her neck, all I want to do is throw her down on her stomach, cover her in oil, and work those kinks out from the top down.

Last night proved the attraction is still there. We need to

limit that. I guess I won't be visiting the kitchen naked for my midnight snacks like I usually do.

I sigh. "Reluctantly agreed. What else you got?"

"Two, I need to feel a part of paying Antonio's tuition. So you can help me build my business. Maybe I can take some contacts to help build my business as a token of friendship. I would do the same for anyone from our town or a friend. But anything you pay for outright, like fees or uniforms or whatever private school stuff Nino needs, will be carefully tallied. It's a loan."

"I'm not *loaning* my wife money," I say, borderline disgusted by the thought.

"I'm not your wife."

"You *are*. And not even for fake but technically. It's against my principles, Shay. Strike the rule."

She lets out a laugh, a little like the gorgeous, naughty laugh she let out last night when she was sipping gin and tonic. "So getting married drunk is okay but lending money to your accidental wife isn't? I'll never understand you."

"Fine, let's make it easier to understand then. Think of it as money for Antonio. I'm not loaning money to a child. Not a single person in Starlight Canyon came knocking on my door asking for repayment for my hockey gear and coaching when I was a kid, not even when I got signed to the NHL. You need to let me do this, Shay."

Her expression still doesn't agree, but she moves on. "Three. No touching."

These rules are getting ridiculous. "No can do, *pastelito*."

She throws her hands to her hips. "You really do hate rules, don't you, Logan?"

"Come on, Shay, zero people would believe I wouldn't be all over my wife, especially if she looks like you."

Something uncomfortable and pleasant at the same time overcomes Shay. She doesn't know what to do with what I just said, and neither do I. But it's a fact, and one we can't ignore.

"Our love and me going home to it every night has to be convincing to the people around us. Staying on the team means showing the coach and anyone who talks to him that I got a woman I'm desperate to be with and a kid who makes me a contented man."

She draws her lips into a thin line. "Fine. We touch but we have to plan what we're doing ahead of time. No... spontaneity."

I burst out laughing.

"Why are you laughing?"

"You really can't handle touching me? What are you so worried about?"

She narrows her eyes.

I dart my gaze to the ceiling. "No touching unless it's pre-agreed and perfectly choreographed."

"Thank you."

I watch her process, and finally she stares me dead in the eye.

"No other women. I mean, if you have anything going with anyone right now, I'm sorry, but..."

"Stop." It doesn't sit well that my behavior over the past years makes her think she even needs to make this a rule. "This goes without saying, Shay."

Drinking me in with an inquisitive chocolate stare, she searches for more than my answer. Something inside me goes sour knowing this rule has even entered the discussion. But now isn't the time to talk about what sent me off the rails, how I stopped believing in love a long time ago, how greed was a great distraction from heartache. Despite being a serial dater, I'm not a cheater.

"Stop looking at me like that, Shay, I'm not a traitor and I'd never humiliate you. If it's us, it's us and only us."

Her face twists with something I can't read, but she lowers her gaze so I can't investigate any further. Finally, she huffs out her last commandment.

"There's one more rule. One thing that might sound like a lot to ask, but if we can't agree, it's... well, it's a deal-breaker, Logan. When this is all over. When our rings are off and we're both where we need to be, you don't have to be my friend, but you do have to be Antonio's."

We share a moment that belongs more in the past than in this agreement. I let the words slip that are both the truth and too much to bear.

"I'll be there for both of you."

"As friends." She nods and speaks as though it's more to herself than to me. "We're doing this as friends."

I put out my hand as if shaking on it will make it less emotional, more businesslike, but when her palm hits mine, it has the opposite effect.

Not the word friend. Not the rules and play by play of our unromantic agreement. None of this stops me from feeling that spark when her skin hits mine.

No touching is a good rule.

She slips her hand out of mine and rubs her fingers over her own palm. I wonder if she still feels me there like I can feel her in my hand.

She lets out a sharp breath. "Wow. So we go home together, today, and say we're married. And where will we live?"

It's cute she asks. As if I'm moving into her dad's house. I don't need to answer.

She does it for me. "Right. We'll live with you."

I nod. "We can go see the school soon with Antonio if you get an appointment."

"*We...*" She lets the thought of me joining her sink in.

I see she wants to refute the idea of me coming, but in our arrangement, it only makes sense I'd be there.

She doesn't dwell on it. "Let's go through your home game schedule and see what games I can attend. I'll have to arrange for Dad to babysit, of course."

"Why wouldn't you bring Antonio to games?"

She opens her mouth as though she has a reason, but nothing comes out. Eventually, she asks, "You want him there?"

"Why wouldn't I want my kid to come to games? But aside from me, the last thing Nino needs is you away from him with so much change happening. There's me, moving house, and if he starts at this new school he'll be needing his mom more than usual. You being away at night isn't the best for him. You know?"

Shay smiles almost slyly, giving me a side-eye. "That's very *daddy* of you, Logan Hunter."

"Hey, I get kids."

"Why? Because you're just a big one?"

I take a pillow from alongside me and smack her on the tummy with it gently.

She groans but through a weak chuckle. "Careful with the stomach right now."

"Sorry." To be fair, mine is queasy as ever, and I'm not entirely sure it's the hangover. "Any more rules?"

She shrugs. "I think we just need to leap now."

"Yeah."

A moment of silence passes between us. It's not uncomfortable, but my curiosity fills the empty space with questions I can't ask aloud and only time will answer. Will Antonio like me? Will Shay's brothers test me? Will I manage to not think she's the most beautiful woman in the world every morning? Because right now, her mascara is flaked, her lipstick is gone, and her eyes are purple-rimmed, and still... I've never seen anything more stunning.

But I've been friends with lots of beautiful women. I have to believe I can do it with this one.

She stares into space and bites her nail. "How are you feeling?"

"Confident we can pull this off and both get what we need. What we want. And I'm looking forward to balancing out that karma finally after years of debauchery and sin." I joke but her body tells me humor is the last thing she needs.

I know the stakes are high for her. Higher even than they are for me. She has to trust me with her son. It's huge, and I won't take the responsibility lightly. In fact, though it's the weight of the world, I'm not Atlas, condemned to hold up Earth. No, it's different.

It's as though the whole universe shifts in this moment when I realize I *want* this. I'm ready to be something more for somebody, and Antonio deserves to take full advantage of his gifts.

"How are *you* feeling?" I ask.

A tired breath huffs into the space. "I'm kind of scared."

I want to reach out and grab her hand, but it's against the rules. I want to tell her I won't stop until Antonio is living his best life, and her, too. I want to hold a part of her so she can feel how sincere my words are, but all I can do is hope she believes them.

"I got you."

Chapter Twelve

Shay

SIXTEEN YEARS AGO

My arm is draped over the naked, chiseled torso of a hockey god; it's hard to believe this body belongs to my *boyfriend*. These muscles. This smooth skin with the perfect smattering of chest hair. And underneath it all... this heart, the one so full of anguish when we met, yet somehow capable of bringing me peace.

Since my roommate has a boyfriend of her own, Logan and I often have my dorm room to ourselves, and boy do we use it. I had no clue what dam I was breaking when I started having sex. We can't keep our hands and mouths off each other.

I lift his hand laced in mine and stare at it like it's a miracle; maybe he is. My miracle. The way he arrived. The way he stayed. He spun a warm, much-needed cocoon around me, sheltering me from the world, and I healed in there. But I'm not sure I've quite turned into a butterfly.

For the first time in my life, I want to fly. But Logan soon entering the NHL is less like soaring and more like floating in deep space. It's terrifying. We're anchored to nothing. The mere thought of it leaves me with no oxygen. It's likely he'll move away. There's one home state team, but I know how often NHL players can be traded, usually at a moment's notice. I Googled it.

Logan isn't afraid of leaving, or at least it doesn't seem like it. He always alludes to us staying together. Sometimes he talks about how we'd see each other and make it work, and I hang on by one measly thread of hope that he gets signed by the Scorpions. There's no topic, including my mom, that makes me feel more vulnerable than Logan entering the NHL, so I make sure we talk about it as little as we can without hiding it.

He traces the humps of my knuckles with his finger, focused on my skin as though he's memorizing every contour. "Have you always loved baking?"

"Baking?" The question feels out of the blue here in my bed, especially when it's a million miles away from where my head is at. But I sure as hell am not going to talk about what's really on my mind.

I welcome the segue.

I don't have to think about it for long, though, because baking has been in my life since for what feels forever. The turning point with me and putting things in the oven is still clear as day.

"I started out making bread when I was about six, I think? Yeah, I must have been about six."

I recall the moment so many years ago back home, when my mom had long, untamed hair. The kitchen then sported the seventies look with pine cupboards and mustard-yellow walls. Sometimes I miss that kitchen now because in my mind, so many of my best memories were in that harvest-colored room where my mom and I put things into an oven I called green and she lovingly referred to as avocado.

She didn't want to redo the kitchen two years ago; my dad did. After he renovated it, we all loved the fresh, sleek modern look that brought our humble home into the twenty-first century. But now... I'd give anything to run my fingers along the patterned tiled counter with my mom next to me. I'd give anything to have it back even without her because her soul was in the cracks of it. I used to complain, but now, I'd even enjoy scrubbing the flour out of the grout just to see her close her eyes and inhale the scent of our sweet creations. It's funny the small things you miss about a person, they're the things you remember when they're not with you anymore.

Logan reads my silence. "Are you thinking about your mom? You can tell me."

Fully attentive as always, he puts me at ease so effortlessly, just by being him.

"Did she teach you to bake?"

He holds me more tightly, and I roll over onto his body a little more, my weight falling onto him.

Here, in his arms, I'm safe.

"One day, I was really annoyed with one of my brothers one day. I don't even remember which one now. I went into the kitchen in a huff, and Mom was making tortillas. She pulled a chair up next to her and told me to climb up. She was kneading the dough."

If I close my eyes, I can still feel her tall, slender body slide in behind me. "She stood behind me and told me to ball up my fists. She was trying to make me laugh when she told me to punch the dough and pretend it was my stinky brother. She used to call them stinky to make me laugh." I still feel her hands wrapped over my fists. "She said, my secret when your dad is being stinky? I punch the dough, *mi ángel*. Eventually, I feel better."

I laugh to myself, but not because it was funny, rather because at the time, I had no idea pulverizing that dough would change the course of my life. "I loved punching that dough. But not because I was angry, it just felt so good on my hands. The texture of it was so... calming. It was smooth and sticky and crumbly all at the same time, and I just loved it. Some kids like Play-Doh, I loved real dough. After that day, I asked her to show me how to do it like her and learned how to knead."

Logan listens with a soft smile and offers me space.

"We did that a lot. Eventually, as I grew older and it became a bit harder to tell her everything I was thinking, you know how it is when puberty hits, we used dough to communicate. My mom wasn't like my dad. She was a lot more guarded."

He nods knowingly, getting where my introverted nature comes from.

"The dough kind of got us moving and gave us a focus other than our words. It made conversations easier."

Logan hums a wordless reply that says he's right there with me.

My thoughts float far away to the cinnamon-scented

moment when she promised me she wouldn't die. My words are still agonizing to say. "She told me about her cancer while making churros." She couldn't admit how bad it was back then. Heck, I'm not sure she ever did. One day she just said goodbye.

"Anyway, it evolved from tortillas into cakes and other things, mostly because I loved talking to my mom in the kitchen. But I don't take my anger out on the food anymore." I let out a half-hearted chuckle.

He toes the cushion at the end of my bed with his bare foot. "Does that explain the donut pillow?"

I squeeze his broad torso hard, affectionately. "Nothing gets past you, does it, Logan Hunter?"

My leg is wrapped over his, and I run my inner thigh up and down his steely skating muscles. My knee catches on his dick.

"Careful under the covers, *pastelito*. I have essential reading to complete before heading to your dad's today." He reaches down and rustles in his bag, pulling out *Farming Weekly*.

I thought he was kidding when he told me.

"Did you seriously get a subscription?"

"I'm brushing up on the latest calving techniques." He winks.

"You don't need to do that to impress my dad."

It's true, and yet my heart nearly explodes watching his gaze drop to the pages and his eyebrows pinch together.

He snaps open the pages of the sparse publication. "I'm not trying to impress him. I'm trying to bond. It's how men do it." He holds me against him tighter. "It'll be our baking."

Later that day, we're in Starlight Canyon for dinner with my dad and aunt, Rita, who has been staying since not too long after Mom died. She made a veritable feast, which means she wants to impress Logan and make me proud to be a Mendez. Our family doesn't have much, but there are a lot of culinary skill in our genes, and if the way to a man's heart is through his stomach, well, I might lose Logan to Tía Rita tonight.

My dad is laughing at our dining room table. He only laughs when Logan is home with me, and I'm not sure if he thinks my boyfriend is truly funny or simply escapes into something new for a momentary break from the painful past. Either way, I love seeing his eyes come alive just a little bit when Logan is here.

Mostly, when I talk to Dad, he's speechless. Not flabbergasted speechless but zero energy, total depression speechless. It's scary seeing my dad that way, and it makes me want to bring Logan around all the time. I can't wish for that, though, because more likely than not, Logan could be gone all of the time. I should pray for strength equal to my task and learn to make my dad laugh the way Logan does. But I just wasn't born with his magic.

Rita and I listen to their conversation, Logan's jaw moves confidently, his eyes sparkling with every word he says. His hands tell stories like they're tales, and watching Logan's body as he speaks is as much a show as the words themselves.

He and my father have been discussing electric fencing

and the solar-powered energizers he read about in his magazine. He's like the captain of his ship, feast laid out in front of him, ready to change the world.

"Luis, you should really try them. They're just as strong, they can do five miles of tape and they never run out of charge. Imagine not having to check your batteries and having to recharge them."

I know my dad is old-fashioned and would normally swat an idea like solar-powered fencing to the side, but with Logan, his chin is perched on a fist, and he listens.

Logan goes on. "I used to think it was such an annoying job having to go around and swap out the batteries, especially since most horses don't even go through the electric fencing if it's not on."

My dad interjects with a wagging finger. "But you see, cows do. Cows do. They will charge right through that fence if they can't hear the ticking sound of the electric going through."

Logan should be a salesperson for these things. "Then all the more reason to try one of these. Imagine that. Free power. From the sun. It never needs recharging. No weekly checks just to swap out batteries around the ranch. No cows loose when a battery dies..." He sits back and delivers his final point. "It's good for the environment."

My dad taps his lips thoughtfully, like Logan is talking about something far more compelling than electric fencing.

My man is utterly captivating. It's not just me. It's not just my dad. Or aunt. It's everyone... because he has genuine interest, and everyone wants that. Every single person on this planet wants someone to care about their *why*. That's Logan's beauty. Whether you like hockey or ranching or baking... he validates. He's curious. Logan is capable of so much more outward affection than I am. He oozes it unconditionally, like it's the most natural thing in the world, like he doesn't even need it in return, an endless well I want to drink from forever.

Unfortunately, Logan's dashing, charming nature is a quality I both admire and cherish, but one I find gives rise to jealousy, too. I want it all for myself. I fear him growing bored of me. Or finding someone more like him. Sometimes I wonder how he can want a woman like me. I'm practically his polar opposite. Logan is warm. I'm a tad bit frosty. Logan is tall, I'm short. He's impulsive, I'm careful. He's an athletic hockey god, and I can't even throw a baseball without it landing behind me.

Still, everything inside me screams he's my perfect match. I guess puzzle pieces don't fit together with straight lines either. He's good with my family, loves animals, wants children one day, is compassionate, is outgoing enough for two people, and damn is he hardworking. If there's one thing my mom told me it was to never marry a lazy man.

He's even from my own small town.

After Mom died, most of my hope went along with her, and I use my last thread to cling to Logan getting on the Scorpions.

The four of us have finished eating my aunt's famous tamales, which, knowing how much time it takes to make them, shows she adores Logan as much as my dad does. She would have been in the kitchen hours today before we arrived.

Logan sits back, having taken thirds, which pleased my aunt to no end.

"You're an incredible cook, ma'am. Thank you so much for going through all the trouble. This seems like a lot of work. It must have taken you hours."

Logan's country boy manners are as perfect as the rest.

She flutters her eyelashes down bashfully, and I can't help but notice that even though she's forty-three, this college boy makes her blush. He's just one of those guys. The kind of attention he serves is slightly on the hot side and makes every single woman's cheeks go red. I notice it with Tía Rita and every girl who crosses our paths on campus, too.

I like it with my aunt. With the other college girls? *Not so much.*

Rita raises her glass of lemonade to take a sip and eyes me over the rim. She wiggles her eyebrows because I'm not the only one sitting here with an internal monologue all about Logan Hunter.

The way Logan slips into my element like he's always been here makes me lose my mind, and it quickly wanders down the aisle. It's madness. I've only been connected with Logan for a few months, and my heart already begs to hang on to him forever. I'm probably super hormonal. And I'm also not in a place to make these kinds of calls so soon after the tragedy. But we can't help what our hearts feel.

My dad raises his glass to his sister, to thank her for the dinner, bringing me back to the table and out of the gutter.

"*Delicioso.*" Then he turns to Logan and continues their conversation about electric fencing. "Well, even a solar energizer can't solve some problems today. I need to check the line."

He refers back to his initial reason they started talking about electric fencing in the first place, the cows breaking loose today. When these things happen, I wish my brothers were still here. I wish *I* was still here. I know my dad has some ranch hands, but I imagine him being in the middle of cooking for himself and having to drop everything and leaving a gas burner on. There's no one here to be his partner when shit hits the fan. Ranching is a twenty-four seven gig, and to top off not having my mom for support anymore... he's not getting any younger.

"There must be some growth or loose leaves, branches somewhere. Hopefully it's just the connection gone, but it could be something else."

Logan, still talking to my father about finding an electric fence fault, wraps his hand around my thigh under the table and gives me a gentle squeeze. It's meant to be innocent, I think, but now I'm the one who's charged. I'm buzzing, hot and ready to head back to my bedroom. Or the bathroom. Or a shed. Anywhere my dad and aunt aren't. Dad snaps me out of it.

"You don't mind if Logan and I go out to the fields, *mija*?"

I hope he can't read my thoughts.

"Dad, you can't put Lo to work every time he comes over."

Logan rubs my thigh. "I like helping."

Oh Lord, he can help me.

I see in his eyes that he wants to help my dad. And much as my core is tingling right now with his fingers splayed across my thigh, I want him out in those fields with my dad even more. Logan and my dad are similar men, both warm and outgoing. Maybe being around Logan will remind my dad he is a man and wasn't just Carmen's husband. He needs something, someone to help him find his way out from under that shroud of grief.

If Logan did it for me, maybe he can do it for Dad.

Logan gets up with his plate in hand, takes mine from in front of me to bring to the kitchen. "I'll just do the dishes and then head out."

"No, no," my aunt insists, "Go. We'll do these."

119

Logan heads toward the kitchen with the plates, so natural, like he's always been part of the family. "You sure?"

"Yes, of course," she insists, getting some of the dishes herself.

He places the plates next to the sink and swipes a hand around my waist. Logan doesn't mind public affection. His hand is polite on my back, a gentleman with my family here, but no matter how he touches me, I rage like a bonfire.

"Be back in thirty."

"Maybe an hour, *mija*," Dad corrects.

The door clicks shut behind the men when they leave. My aunt and I clear the rest of the table and take piles of dishes to the kitchen counter.

"You're done for, Shaylita." She purrs.

I barely suppress my smile. "What are you talking about?"

"That boy. *Dios mío*. He ticks all the boxes. Handsome. Talented. Kind. Good appetite." She begins to fill the sink, squirts in dish soap, and a mound of white suds begin to rise. "Have you two... you know... ?"

My aunt, unlike most of the women in my family, knows not many women my age save it for marriage anymore. It's a well-known fact but still taboo in my still quite traditional family. I'm caught off guard.

Since I lost my virginity to Logan, I've missed my mom more than ever. It's not the kind of thing I would have run to her and talked about. I probably wouldn't have mentioned it at all and just let her assume, maybe allowing a simple knowing nod to pass between us. But I miss Mom so much now that somehow, I pretend I would have shared it all with her while cooking here in this kitchen.

"Well?" She puts her hand on her hip.

I pop a shoulder.

She whips me with the towel. "*Órale!*"

Instantly I freak out that I confessed this. "Don't tell Dad..."

"Like I'd ever." She turns off the faucet and puts plates in the bubbles. "Do you love him?"

I put the remains of the meal into plastic containers. "He's the best thing in my life right now."

"Mmm." She whooshes her hands around in the water, cleaning as she thinks about what I said, then rinses some dishes, puts them in the drying rack. "He said he loves you?"

"Yes." I pick up a towel and dry a plate. "Many times."

"But you've not said it to him?"

"I'm... worried about what it will do to me. It just feels risky, you know?"

"Risky?" She says the word like I misused it. Or like she suddenly doesn't understand its meaning.

"He's... Logan might not be here in New Mexico for much longer. He's going to be signed soon. To the NHL."

Her mouth opens with understanding. "Oh. So you think it will hurt less when he has to leave if you don't tell him you love him, even though you do?" She winks.

"I don't know if I do." I haven't even convinced myself with these words.

She puts a wet, foamy hand on her hip. "Shaylita? Seriously?"

I dry a plate. *Of course I love him.* But sometimes I don't want to. I don't want to love him when I think of him possibly going out of state.

I'm trying desperately to pretend his leaving won't hurt if I hold back. But the truth is, Logan already has my heart. He was the one who found it, hiding in the darkness of my grief, so holding back is pointless. I might as well be concentrating my power on trying to levitate.

I don't realize I've been drying the same dish for the past few minutes, mind far away in the distant future where more heartache finds me.

My aunt's voice is an echo in my mind. "Shay?"

I snap back to reality and reach up to put away the dry plate into a cupboard.

"Have you talked to him about your worries? Do you know what he wants?"

I tilt my head. "Not really."

"Why haven't you talked about it?"

I take up another dish to dry it. "I'm too... paranoid."

She laughs dryly. "Jealous, too, I suspect."

"Gee, thanks, *tía*. Makes me feel better."

She dives her hands back into the suds, searching blindly for cutlery at the bottom. "You know I'm not the softly softly type, so here are my words for this. You either figure it out because it's worth it. Or you let go because it's too hard."

She wraps her arm around me, wetting my shoulder. "I'm a good judge of character. I'm not worried about him. I'm worried about you."

Chapter Thirteen

Logan

SHAY HAD to drive her car home from Vegas. I didn't tell her I abandoned my chartered jet back in order to ride with her and talk. Suddenly, private jets, something that for years has felt so normal, seemed ostentatious. So I climbed into her Honda Civic coupe, put the seat back as far as it could go, and spent the nine-hour drive downing water because the air-con wasn't very cool, or powerful. Or maybe it works just fine and I'm incredibly hungover.

It gives us time to catch up and formulate plans that need formulating. We called Luis from the car and told him what happened. We called my mom and all our other family members. Surprisingly, most of them, apart from her brothers, of course, squealed with what sounded a lot more like delight than suspicion. I suppose the shock will wear off and the questions will come in thick and fast at some point. Or maybe not. After all, I know my mom gave up on me settling down. I doubt she'll want to do anything to put the brakes on me being married.

Plus, it's done. What are they going to do? Tell us to split up and divorce?

Between calling her four brothers, dad, my three siblings, and Ashton, the car journey goes quickly. And I even feel grateful to be in her car instead, especially when we get greasy fast food which goes down so much better today than whatever five-star gourmet meal they would have served on the plane.

Eating junk food with Shay driving reminds me of old times. We drove back quite a number of times from college. I shouldn't let old feelings creep in, but I spend the entire car journey looking out her side of the windshield and have the worst crick in my neck admiring how age has been so good to her.

And, moreover, how confident she's been in allowing it to happen. Shay is thirty-six and still plenty youthful. But she's definitely not a college kid anymore, and I really like that. I've never been one of those guys chasing girls half my age. Shay is more stunning than she was at twenty. Her whole body is fuller and curvier than it was when we were younger, and I only wish I was a hell of a lot more sober last night to fully remember it. The few strands of silver woven into the darkness of her locks only serve to enhance her allure, adding a touch of sophistication to her appearance. Her smile lines are delicate etchings, evidence of joy having visited her in these past sixteen years without me.

My heart thunders thinking of these other men. I tried

to bring it up, we've had plenty of hours, but we're not there yet with each other, and Shay is tight-lipped. We have plenty of time for me to ask again and receive the words like I'm their whipping boy.

We pass Blackrock; we're close to Starlight Canyon. In thirty minutes, this whole deal of ours will be truer than it has ever been, and there's one big thing we haven't fully discussed—Antonio.

Shay has been silent for the past twenty minutes, maybe listening to music, but I doubt it by the tension in her jaw.

The clock is ticking, and we'll be at her dad's house soon, so I guess it's up to me to serve up the topic. "We should talk about Antonio again."

"You're right. I've been thinking about what to say." She turns down the radio that's barely audible anyway.

"So the silence wasn't your hangover getting the best of you? I could have driven."

She deadpans, "Insurance. Plus, since you have had drivers pretty much since college, I'm guessing you haven't improved behind the wheel."

I *have* improved.

"How do you know I've had drivers? Have you been following me, Shana Mendez?"

She rolls her eyes. "Don't flatter yourself."

"Thinking about insurance reminds me. We should make a list of admin for my PA. Do you and Antonio have health insurance?"

"We do but it's expensive and shitty since I'm self-employed." She cocks her head. "Wait, your PA is a guy?"

"Yeah. Why?"

"I just thought you would have hired a woman. It seems like unless a person skates for a living, you only hang out with ladies."

It would be a dig if not for the truth attached to the statement. I have been around a lot of women. I went through a phase of intense escapism and partying, and where there is booze and Vegas, there are women. Sometimes they were just around, and paparazzi got photos of me with somebody I didn't even know was near me. Now and then, it was me trying with someone who seemed nice enough. Other times, it was just an orchestrated media charade Reggie put together to keep me in the public eye. It was exhausting and kind of sad.

It never would have happened if me and Shay had stayed together. They say life comes full circle. Now here I am with the very woman with whom I wanted a family and kids. She's also the reason I had neither of those things.

I'm not getting into that right now any more than she'll tell me about her men in between.

"You'll like Tom. I'm always shocked how quickly he can get things done. He stays one step ahead of me even. I told him about us, so I'll give you his number and you can call him day or night."

She nods but she's still thinking about the same thing I am, and it isn't Tom. "I know I told you that I have lied to Nino before."

Her features contort as if she's convincing herself of something.

"But it really has been about the smallest things. I tried to give him tacos with a little bit of cheese once to trick him into saying he liked it. And there are the obvious stories like Santa and the tooth fairy... not that he's lost any teeth yet, but one of his classmates got one knocked out, so we talked about that. So I have lied. *Tiny* lies. And I don't think there's any right or wrong answer here, it just depends on what kind of parent you are, and every parent does things good and not so good but..."

I know where she's going. "You're still happy about telling Nino we're married..."

"Well, yeah..." Her knuckles go white. "Also, you need to know, just because Nino has a really high IQ, it doesn't mean he's any more mature than a normal five year old. He isn't. I mean, he can remember people's names and pays more attention to his surroundings maybe than some other kid, and of course there's the math... but he's still just a baby. And impressionable and..."

She's working out mom shit inside. I've watched a lot of my teammates become parents; spoken to them about raising children. It's tough, even just hearing about it I sometimes get stressed. It's the biggest gift but also seems like the most enormous responsibility in the world.

What Shay says next tells me she's really damn good at it. Just like I thought she'd be.

"I want him to view relationships in a healthy way. Like, even when I was going on a date I'd tell Nino about it. Inform him what I was doing that night and never pretended otherwise. I explained how people meet others and can fall in love..."

Who were these guys? Are they in Starlight Canyon? My stomach curdles thinking about Shay on a date.

"Did he actually understand what you were saying? When I think back to my five-year-old self, if kissing was involved or the thought of anything like that, I pretty much tuned out."

She laughs. "I don't think he really took it in. But I always told myself I would teach him not to have a toxic view of relationships. I want him to know that sometimes people are together and then they aren't and it's okay. The end doesn't mean failure. I think it's such a shame-based lie —that two people deciding they aren't healthy for each other anymore, or aren't a match, is some sort of failure. Failed relationship. Failed marriage. It's such bullshit."

Shay has always had a mind of fairness and she's that girl in college with the rally posters all over again.

"Yeah. That makes sense." I laugh quietly to myself.

"What's so funny?"

"Nothing. I was just wondering if you still go to marches and rallies."

"I do as a matter of fact."

"I always liked that about you."

Her lips curve upward for the slightest moment. "Thanks."

I stare at the road ahead. A green sign with distances tells me we don't have much longer until we're at the Mendez ranch, and we don't need to talk about politics right now. "So you don't want to tell Nino I'm your special friend?"

"Telling him you're my special friend is belittling. He's five, and I know he really doesn't understand marriage because he's never seen me, my dad, or my brothers married..." She sighs. "Gosh, we're an independent bunch..." She shakes her head. "So it's not like he'll really get it, but equally I don't ever want to treat him like a fool."

"Unless it's for the sake of cheese?"

She scoffs. "I'm over that, too, now. It's a lost cause. I don't try getting that under the radar anymore."

Thinking about the little guy I've only unofficially met a few times in a coffee shop, who I'm suddenly responsible for, has a world of other questions coming to mind.

"Will Nino be okay living with me? Moving out from your dad's and the only home he's known?"

"Again, Lo, he's only five, so it's harder for me if anything."

I check her face for signs of concern, but she simply turns on her indicator and takes the county road leading to the Canyon.

"As long as Nino is with me, he'll be fine. He might wake up in the night to come to my room..." She squints an eye. "I *will* have my own room, won't I?"

"We can't sleep in different rooms, Shay. I'd never. This town is too small. I have a housekeeper and a pool cleaner, separate rooms can't happen."

"Shit..." she says, as if realizing she's made a big error. "Can we at least get two single beds, like push them together and leave a crack?"

"Don't worry, Virgin Mary, my bed is huge."

Concerns start to build up behind her furrowed brow.

"Nino is a bit of a character. Loves to talk."

I offer an appreciative look. "Great. You know I love the banter."

"And he has a very unusual, well, blankie? Or stuffy. Anyway, his comfort toy is... a bit different, and please don't mention it."

"Like what?"

"Oven mitts."

"Oven mitts?" I can't help the amusement that slips from my mouth.

"I guess he saw me with them over my shoulder all the time and one day he grabbed a set off a chair where I left them and refused to let them go. He sleeps with them every night. So you can't say anything about it. I don't want him getting self-conscious."

I cross my heart and smirk. "And how do I not make *you* self-conscious?"

"Please. You have no such effect on me," she deadpans.

I can't tell if she's serious or playing a game.

"Living with you will be fine. Being in front of other people all the time *would* make me self-conscious." She turns onto the long single-track road leading to the Mendez ranch. "We'd have to break the no-touching rule way too much."

Chapter Fourteen

Logan

It's dark and late when we park up at Shay's house. The moon and a few dim porch lights barely illuminate the path of what feels like a thousand steps to her front door. Memories flood back like an unstoppable tide, and nostalgia crashes through me.

I really liked Luis and our times out in the pastures on this ranch.

He was a kind but tortured man, and in those hours we mended fences, wrangled cattle and bulldozed manure, mostly silence passed between us. Still, we somehow felt comfortable in each other's presence. I knew he missed his wife soul-deep, and once, in a rare moment of him talking instead of me, he told me he wasn't sure he'd last long without her.

I thought at the time how tragically sad it was and yet how similarly I felt about his daughter. But he managed. And so did I. Though it wasn't without so much change, some might say I left behind the old me altogether. Has Luis had to change, too, in order to survive the heartbreak?

The curtains from the living room snap aside, a tuft of hair appears before they shut again.

"Looks like Nino's still up." Shay glows.

With a mere glimpse of her child, Shay radiates with something beautiful I haven't ever seen before.

Tiny footsteps thud softly toward the front door. But it's Luis who opens it.

"Logan!" He throws the door open and pushes himself out, embracing me, slapping me on the back. He pulls back with my arms in his hands. "*Dios mío*... what news! I have another son!"

It looks like he hasn't changed. His embrace is the same welcoming temperature as the first time I walked into his home. While still wrapped in Luis' arms, the door cracks open more, and there, hidden behind the limbs of his grandfather, Antonio peeps up.

Shay crouches. "Baby... you're up so late!"

Antonio rushes through and into his mom's open embrace. His voice is high and raspy and so damn adorable. "I missed you."

Shay holds him like she's been gone for longer than a day. She holds him like she didn't breathe that entire time. She holds him like I want to hold a kid someday.

Luis and I stare at the beautiful sight until Nino draws back from the hug and looks up at me, curiosity beaming right through his tiny round glasses.

"You're the man from the coffee shop and you play on the Scorpions."

I crouch down to his level. "How did you know? Are you a mind reader? That's some superpower."

Nino giggles, and it's a sound that tickles my heart. "I can't read minds! I saw you at CCs and Fright Night! Mom makes us watch all the Scorpions games even if there are better things to do."

I glance up at Shay. "You do?"

She says it a bit too quickly: "Everyone watches the Scorpions."

Her dad, clueless on what I was really asking Shay, jumps in. "Tell me one person in Starlight Canyon who doesn't want to see you win. Am I right?"

I hold out my hand for Antonio. "I'm Logan. Nice to meet you."

He laughs again, maybe at the formality of my offered hand, maybe just because he seems like an incredibly happy kid. Either way, he takes my hand and squeezes it pretty damn hard for a five-year old.

I flick my hand as if it hurts. "Wow. Firm grip."

"Papá Luis says there's nothing worse than a wet fish handshake," he says, matter of fact.

I remember Shay's brother, Santi, nearly crushing my palm with a shake. The Mendez family takes greetings seriously. "Your grandpa is a wise man."

Shay scoops Nino up into her arms, standing at the same time, and kisses his cheek. "You, mister, are going to be very tired tomorrow if you stay up any later. It's nearly ten o'clock."

She carries him inside. Luis ushers me in and closes the door behind us.

Antonio protests. "But I went to bed for two hours

before and then got back up to see you. So if I go to bed at eleven then I'll still get ten hours of sleep which means I can stay up one more hour." He turns his wrist around to read a tiny watch. "One more hour and eighteen minutes with you. And Logan. He's the one you used to be in love with but now you're friends. Right?"

There's a touch of embarrassment hidden in her laugh, but her eyes shimmer with affection. She explains to me why she spoke to her son about me. "He asked who you were after one of the times we ran into each other."

And that's how she explained who I am? A rush of tenderness warms my chest, but I catch it before it runs away with me.

"I told you I like to be honest with him," she qualifies the situation but quickly escapes any touch with the past by whisking Nino over to the living room.

She shuffles over to the couch with Nino still in her arms, and they plop down together. In a deft move, she swoops Nino onto her lap and snuffles his neck with her nose. His giggle releases a magical, joyful energy into the room, the kind only children have.

"I missed you, baby." She gives him a hundred kisses, and he laughs with every one.

Luis gestures for me to sit. We both take armchairs to either side of the couch where Shay seems like she would gladly stay hugging Nino for the rest of her life.

But to my surprise, she says, "I need to get you to bed, my gorgeous young man. We have a lot of things to talk about tomorrow."

"Like how you and Logan got married?"

Shay impulsively whips her gaze to her father. "Dad!"

"I..." He throws his hands up in defeat. "I have a big

134

mouth. It's hard to keep news like that." His shoulders are at his ears. "I mean, it's not exactly a secret!"

Nino looks confused. "Is it a secret that you're married?"

"No, baby. No. Of course not. I just wanted to be the one to tell you."

"So you and Logan love each other again?"

Her jaw drops, and her face freezes, but instead of saying yes she simply nods, not really up and down, but kind of in a circle, and I think she's about as good at hiding what she thinks from this little guy as her dad is.

Clearly, this is a tough moment for her. Harder for her than for me, so I come to the rescue. "I care about your mom, Antonio. Would it be okay with you if we care for her together?"

His smile fades, and for a beat I'm worried I went too far.

His nod is almost somber. "That would be great, Logan, because she is very messy in the bathroom."

Shay's jaw really drops now. "I am not." She tickles his tummy, and the sound of wind chimes fills the room.

I hope it's like this every day. Though I have laughs in my life, there isn't laughter. Not like this. Innocent. Simple. Fireflies sparking in the middle of a pitch-black night. This is special. This is something I've never had.

Shay stands and pulls Nino up with her in one fell swoop.

"I'm taking you to bed. We'll talk about everything else tomorrow. Say goodnight to Papá Luis and Logan."

She turns to leave, and he waves over her shoulder.

"*Buenas noches, Abuelo y Logan.*"

"*Buenas noches,*" I say in my best accent possible but I

haven't used my language app since college. I should get one fired up again.

She takes the munchkin down the hall, leaving me with Luis. Just when I'm thinking that went well, the temperature in the room changes.

Luis gets up from his spot opposite me and takes the seat nearest to mine, leaning against the armrest to get as close as he can. "Shay said you've been talking for a while. Resurrecting your past..."

I draw my lips into a thin line. *Here we go...*

"You know I always liked you, Logan. And still do. I work with your sister, Jolie, now here on the ranch. I do deals with Colt. You're from a good family."

"Thank you."

"But... Do I need to show you the size of my shotgun?" He's serious for all but a moment, but one of his eyebrows gives away the bluff.

Gosh, Luis is one hell of a man.

"No, sir. I'm pretty sure your daughter has plenty good aim for the both of us."

"That she does." His gaze lowers. "Never thought I'd see the day."

"Do you mean Shay getting married or me being the one to marry her?" I ask, but I'm not sure I want the answer.

He scratches his chin. "Maybe both. She's allergic to hope, and you... well... you haven't exactly been searching for a bride from what I've heard."

It stings. Luis knows what I've been up to? I hide behind humor. "Are you telling me you read more than *Farmers Weekly* now?"

He chuckles. "Nope. That's all I read, but this is a small town, and... people talk."

That they do. There were times I didn't want to move

back to the Canyon because everyone knows everyone's business and there are a few somebodies around these parts happy to profit from a snapped pic or a sold story. It happened to Jolie and Ashton not too long ago.

Shay emerges from the hallway, and boy do I welcome back my wife. She saves me from Luis' interrogation.

"Hey. I'll stay here tonight with Nino," she says, hands in those back pockets and her breasts stretched out. She adds, "Like we talked about."

We didn't discuss tonight, but I'm on her wavelength.

I stand. "It's been a long twenty-four hours. I'll let you get him settled."

Luis stands, too, and smacks his hands against his jeans. "I'm going to throw a party to celebrate."

"No, Dad. We don't need that," Shay interjects.

"Shh. I won't have it. I only have one daughter, and the father of the bride is supposed to throw the reception."

"Dad, that's old-fashioned. Anyway, we're already married. We already celebrated."

Too bad I can't remember that part.

He won't be deterred. "We must unite the families." He laces his fingers together.

Neither of us bargained for this.

"Truly, Luis." I come up with a halfway point that supports my wife but satisfies my father-in-law, too. "We could all just get together for dinner."

He slaps me on the arm. "I insist. Give me time to prepare. And I suppose I'll need your hockey schedule."

I don't do meek smiles, but it's the best kind of one I can conjure. I'm damn exhausted, and I didn't expect this to feel so good being back in the Mendez house and meeting Antonio. The kid is special, Luis is as warm as ever, and it was all far too comfortable. It seems to me this might be the beginning of an era requiring herculean self-control. The thought of rekindling something with Shay crossed my mind more than once since landing a place at the Scorpions, and yet, she shot down any and every first move I ever made.

Plus, we made rules.

But rules are meant to be broken.

Shay ushers me to the door. "Okay, Dad, Logan and I are tired, so I'm going to say goodbye. We have a lot to do tomorrow."

She waits for her dad to give us privacy, which he doesn't do, so she shoves me out the door and into the darkness of the night. Crickets chirp. The mountain air is cold and sharp.

Shay wraps her arms around herself to stay warm. "That went well."

"Yeah." I scratch the back of my head. *Too well.*

She rubs her arms. I take off my blazer and throw it around her shoulders.

Immediately, she starts taking it off. "I'm going inside in a sec."

"You're cold."

"I'm fine," she insists.

But I stand there like a board, not giving her an option to hand it back.

Eventually, she sighs and puts it back on like a cape. "So tomorrow we'll move some things into yours while you're at practice? I don't have that much since most everything here belongs to Dad. Just my room and Nino's to pack up."

"I'll get Tom to arrange a van."

She darts her eyes to the curtain, and it closes quickly. Luis is anything but subtle.

Shay keeps her voice low. "I hope it's not too hard on Dad."

Her concern is knitted together with the same beautiful loyalty that tore us apart. But I could never fault her for it.

"You can invite him to ours anytime."

"*Ours.*" She tucks hair behind her ear. "That sounds weird."

I personally like the sound of it, but I don't tell her that. An awkward silence lingers on the visible breaths passing between us in the frosty air. I'm not sure what else to say, but it doesn't feel right to say goodbye just yet either. There is a mix of uncertainty and familiarity, and I can't help but think all the best moments of my life can be described the same way.

It's cold and late, and I'm depleted from last night, but when the cab I ordered pulls up, I have no desire to crawl into it.

She shoves those tiny hands of hers into her back pockets. "Okay, well, see you tomorrow when you get back from practice?"

"Yeah. See you then."

How exactly do we part? She's my wife, for God's sake, I should kiss her.

The air crackles with tension. Damn, she's still so radiant, her eyes pools of deep brown, and in them, there's mystery. I read her better when we were younger, and yet her gaze is just as mesmerizing, inviting me into their depths. The shadow of a moth trapped in her father's porch light dances on the delicate curve of her cheek. Amber light falls on her lips, drawing me in.

The cab driver beeps.

Without a word, I close the distance between us. My heart pounds with each step, even though my only intention is to give her a simple hug goodbye. But when my arms envelop her petite, curvy frame, it's both achingly familiar and entirely new. She wraps her arms around me to embrace me back. I breathe in the sweet scent of her hair and really wish that cab wasn't here yet.

Just then, her dad whips the curtain aside, allowing a sliver of light to become our spotlight. I see his creased face out of the corner of my eye. I know we didn't plan it, but Shay is my wife, and I'm not about to let her dad think she's living a life without passion, so I enclose my hands around her more firmly... and kiss her.

I catch her sharp breath in my mouth but I can hardly hold on to it because my lungs stutter, too. In a split second her lips feel like home. Everything in my head screams to be careful, to not go too far, to press my lips against her just enough to prove a point to the man behind the curtain. But connecting with her like this rips through my system, burning me in the sensation of our past and present colliding. My intention was for show, but the way my heart thunders against my rib cage speaks to a level of intimacy we never agreed on.

My body begs me to inch my hands up her waist, to take her harder and crush her into me, to slide my tongue inside her mouth... but I don't.

A brief moment later, I pull back, and sharp air cools the hot space between our mouths.

I drop my forehead to hers, her waist still soft and womanly in my grip. I whisper against her cheek, "Sorry, but your dad is watching."

I don't even know if Luis is still looking.

She seems almost in a trance. Did I go too far?

The cab beeps again, and she jerks at the sound, breaking her out of the hypnosis.

I rub the side of her arm. "Are we good?"

She stares past me, into the darkness. "Yeah. Of course. It was fine. Go. Sleep."

As I amble down the stone path toward the taxi in the darkness, I know I overstepped the mark, but it sure as hell didn't feel like I was doing anything wrong. Quite the opposite. Shay's lips pressed against mine felt so right I want to do it a million times over.

A voice of caution tells me we were right to make the no-touching rule. Still, I now know, no contract will protect me from the tornado that rips through me when I touch that woman.

Chapter Fifteen

Shay

I'm so glad Dad had a vet check, Nino had school, and Logan had practice, because at every empty moment I come across thoughts of Logan's lips lurking in my mind. I try to keep busy, but along with the inability to think of anything but Logan is the stereotypical array of desire-related symptoms—butterflies, unexpected hot flushes, and way too much wondering when we will do it again.

Damn it. I knew this might happen. Not because it's Logan. I'm over that. I really, really am... or at least I want to be. A sigh makes its way from my throat. Sadly, I'm wise enough now to know this isn't the whole story, though whatever the tale is, it's written in some other language. My heart speaks one way, my head another, and the truth lies in the translation which is in a mysterious tongue I've never learned.

I need therapy. I know I do. I've needed it for a very long time. But I'm not sure even a doctor could crack this nut. I was taught from day one to be strong. The high expectations of my immigrant parents and four older brothers are the source of my toughness. Those childhood lessons learned through survival of a five-sibling household morphed into me thinking strength was a lack of vulnerability. Only when I met Logan did I realize it takes a hell of a lot more courage to be vulnerable than it does to grit your teeth.

Back then, he made exposing myself bearable, a relief even. With him, showing him the girl behind the armor was putting down its heavy weight, and so many times in my life, so many moments in the years we parted I craved that safe space. I've had to be strong, all on my own, more times than I could count.

Now, in his presence again, I wonder if the same respite he gave me in the wake of my mom's death could happen with all my new everyday struggles. Would I feel better admitting to him I don't know if I'm any good at this mom thing? Would he want to hear about how even though I know I'm a hell of a baker, I really struggle with social media and even though my dyslexia isn't as bad as some, it makes me so nervous about writing pitch emails. Would he still offer me that judgment-free, totally validating and compassionate gaze he did when our problem was the same? Or was that a once-in-a-lifetime crossroads?

We've gone in different directions. We're not the same anymore. I try to even tell myself we never were the same, though it feels like a lie. Even with Logan becoming America's most wanted playboy, when I tried my hardest to convince myself our college relationship was some illusion, those months are the least fleeting memory in my mind. Some memories cling like icing to a cake. You can try to take it off, but crumbs of your wholeness will go along with it.

I fall into my dad's overstuffed sofa, with forty brown packing boxes stacked all around me, and hope mindless scrolling provides a distraction until the moving van gets here. I don't like the idea of a stranger moving my boxes; few of them are important, but some of them are priceless.

I check emails, as is my new obsession. There's one from Logan.

From: loganhunter@purplemountainresort.com
To: shanamendez@shinocakes.com
Subject: Contacts

Morning, Wife,
You might have guessed my contacts are a goddamn mess and my phone and inbox are about as organized as those wadded-up receipts in Vegas. I asked Tom to sift through my contacts today and make a spreadsheet of anyone who might want to hear about your cakes.

Once I have it, I'll drop everyone a text or email and tell them about your business. You can work your magic after that, but at least they'll be expecting you to contact them.

I'll be home as soon as I can get there after practice. I hope Tom and I were able to get the place up to your standard (which apparently isn't very high according to the little man).

We got this, pastelito.

Lo

"Wow, you got this done fast."

I jump and clutch my chest, not realizing my dad entered the room. He has on his dirty jeans and Carhartt coat that he swears still keeps out the rain even though it's threadbare. But I know better than to wish for upgrades. This is the dad I know and remember. The one I cannot believe I have lived with for all but almost two years of college. This man and I have been roomies for thirty-four years.

He sits on the couch with me and puts his hand on my thigh, giving it three affectionate taps, and with each one he says my name. "Shaylita. Shaylita. Shaylita."

I drop my head to his shoulder. "I'm finally a grown-up, Dad. Moving out."

"Oh, *mija*... you've done me proud."

My heart withers when he says those words. Do I deserve them?

He snuggles his arm around me, and I keep my head on his shoulder, staring at the place where Nino used a magic marker on the skirting board.

He sighs. "You have your own business, you're a wonderful daughter and a mother. And now... you're a wife."

He reaches a finger up to his eye and swipes away a tear.

"Dad... Are you getting sentimental on me?"

"You know I'm a crier."

"We aren't far away. You can come any time, and we'll be here, too."

He pats my leg again, but I'm not sure if he's reassuring me or himself.

"Trust me, this is a dream come true. The first time I thought you'd marry Logan, I imagined you having to live across the country, wherever he had to play."

My withered heart is now completely dehydrated and crumpled into flower crumbs. Dad imagined Logan and me getting married? He's always been sappy and sentimental and even an unrealistic romantic at times. I never could have left with Logan.

He wipes his eyes with his fingers, drying them completely. "What did Nino say this morning when you spoke to him about moving?"

Over breakfast this morning, I told Nino about our new adventure living at Logan's, and it never ceases to amaze me how much that little boy trusts me. "I told him we were going to live with Logan today, and he said he had three questions."

I count with my fingers for each question. "Will I have my own room? Will we still see Papá Luis? And can I take cookies to school instead of cake today?"

My dad chuckles in his deep, throaty way. "Kids are resilient."

"Yeah."

"As long as they have a parent, they can be anywhere. And now, Nino has two." Dad beams with a joy I didn't expect him to feel when I told him Logan and I got married.

Two parents.

Though the process thus far in terms of considering Antonio has been seamless, the weight of this responsibility, the enormous sense of duty to guide us in the right direction, has a gravity so immense it can be crushing. Sometimes I think being a single mom is easier than having another person to deal with. Negotiating all the discipline and the values I instill in Nino isn't something I really want to argue with some man about. But other times, having another voice of reason around would be wonderful.

When Logan talked about lying to children in Vegas... I kind of liked it. It was a touchy topic, but hearing his experience with his own mom gave me a perspective I don't have in this parent of one.

Just then, there's a knock on the door. *Movers.*

I rush over and when I open it, there's a tall, slender blond man with impeccably coiffed hair. He's wearing a starched salmon-colored button-down shirt.

He shoots his hand out sharply. "I'm Tom!" he says brightly, beaming ear to ear with the most pearly-white, straight-toothed smile I've ever seen.

He tries to contain his excitement, but his shoulders shimmy just a little. He throws two fists up to his chin when he asks, "Can I hug you? I just have to hug you. I'm so happy for you and Logan."

I hesitate, but Logan told me Tom is his right-hand and is, next to his family and Ashton, the most trustworthy person he's ever met. But aside from the glowing comments Logan has about him, there's something warm in his smile that puts me instantly at ease.

"Sure, Tom. Hug away."

He wraps his arms around me, towering over. The guy is a virtual giant.

He says somewhere over my hair, "I'm so glad Logan finally found someone."

Finally? It didn't seem like he was looking very hard if I'm to believe social media.

He pulls back and slaps his hands together. "Right. You have to get Antonio from school in an hour and a half, so we better get cracking."

"You're moving me?" I ask.

"Since Logan couldn't be there to welcome you and Antonio, he asked me to roll out the carpet. And you don't have much. Logan said you only requested forty boxes."

Dad pops up from the couch. "Well, let me help, too." He introduces himself. "I'm Luis."

"Tom. Logan's PA. And now all of yours, too. If any of you need anything, just shout. But yes, for now, Luis, a little help would be great. Shay, you can't be late picking up the boy."

Two hours later, Nino and I pull up in front of Logan's house, both crouching to peer up at our new home out of the windshield. But there's not much of a view from the end of the drive, just wrought-iron gates and some excellently pruned landscaping of flowers and palm trees. It's all so domestic from the outside, and nothing about the street level appearance screams bachelor pad.

The gates groan, and the other side of the boundary reveals just the same. Logan's front yard is an oasis. We walk hand in hand up a tiled path with beautiful manicured lawns and shrubs to either side, and it all leads to an unexpected sight. Logan's house is one of the most beautiful adobe structures I've ever seen. It's not at all the house I expected Logan to have. It's as traditional-looking as can be in New Mexico, with smooth terra-cotta-colored exterior. I expected Logan to have some sleek, ultra-modern home.

I love it.

Nino and I wander up the long path to the front door, holding hands, silently taking in our surroundings, but when we arrive at the entrance, Nino tugs my arm.

"This is a mansion."

"I told you you'd have your own room."

His eyes are wide. "Maybe I'll have two!"

We stand at the front door, and I reach in my bag to find the papers Tom gave me that included key codes for the alarm and the door itself, which doesn't use a key either. Traditional as the structure is, Logan has built in the latest tech. But before I scan the document for the codes, the door swings open, and it's Tom, shining just as much as when I left him, despite having moved the forty boxes into the house himself.

"Welcoooome!" he sings.

Nino's response is equally as excitable. "Thank yooooou!" he sings back.

Tom crouches. "You must be the formidable Antonio. I'm Tom. Logan told me about your amazing memory, but he didn't say you were an opera singer."

"You're funny." Nino giggles.

"Come in..." Tom ushers us inside.

I have to hide my awe. The interior somehow morphs from traditional to contemporary without losing the charm of the earthy exterior. Windows line the entirety of the back of the home, stunning views of the mountains painted in every direction. The wood-beamed ceiling is a warm and cozy honey color, somehow making the cavernous space and modern decor feel snug.

We follow Tom through the large open-plan living room, through a dining room with an enormous oak table, and into a kitchen the size of my entire home. My heart flutters, and I swear I'm about to swoon and pass out like a Victorian lady. There is counter space for miles. A total canvas. There isn't a single set of tractor keys or leather work gloves or loose nuts and bolts cluttering the white marble runways.

It's clean and yearning for flour and sugar and whisks to get it nice and dirty.

Tom stops our tour briefly. "There is still one small problem with the kitchen." He takes two strides to a nearby cupboard and opens it. It's as empty as the counters. "I did manage to buy enough plates and cups for everyone, but there isn't anything to cook with. Logan instructed me to focus on Antonio's room first."

Tom moves deeper into the house. We follow him and make it to the end of a hallway leading to bedrooms.

Tom opens one door. "Here's your room, Antonio. I hope you like it. It's not finished yet, but we'll need your help because Logan thought you'd like to choose some of your own things."

Tom opens the door to a little boy wonderland. At least one for *my* boy. The room has neutral, earthy-toned bedding. In one corner, there is a teepee with fairy lights strewn around it and pillows inside for chilling. I wander over to the snug den and catch a glimpse of two books—*Gulliver's Travels* and *Around the World in Eighty Days*. Travel. Geography.

Thoughtful. My mention of Nino liking geography was subtle in our conversation about our cat and world capitals, but Logan remembered, and in doing so, touched on one of my son's passions with this space. What really catches my son's eye is the wall. One entire wall has a huge world map on it, and he launches himself toward it.

"A map!"

Nino jumps onto the bed, flattening himself against the giant poster to read all the fine print and explore the tiny lines and dots and borders.

Tom puts his hands together in a prayer position in front of his mouth. "It's the best Logan and I could do with so little time. Logan mentioned Antonio is good at geography, so this decor seemed a good place to start?"

I point to Nino. "I think you have your evidence of a job well done."

Tom heads to the foot of the bed and leans his tall frame against Africa. "Now where is Cayenne?"

My heart flutters knowing Logan imparted all of this information to Tom.

Nino asks. "My cat or the city?"

"Both."

"The city is here." He taps his hand on the exact location. "In South America is French Guiana, and there's a space center there, too."

Tom appears genuinely interested. Maybe he is. He seems like the kind of guy who would be, even if just for his general sunny nature.

"Wow. That's a cool fact. I'm ashamed to say I couldn't have told you where on the map it was let alone any facts. Though I might have guessed they speak French there."

"The clue is in the name," Nino says, matter-of-factly.

"Any other interesting facts? It might come up in a Trivial Pursuit game or something." Tom makes an invisible notebook out of his hand and holds an imaginary pencil, ready to learn.

That Logan has chosen this man as his PA is telling. Maybe somewhere under that beautifully starched Gucci shirt there's still the down-to-earth man I fell for. It's not that I need him to be that man for this arrangement to work. Still, sometimes I miss that twenty-one-year-old Hunter boy from a cattle ranch, the one who dreamed on a dinky pond at the far end of town.

Nino draws his lips into a thin line, digging deep for a good factoid. "Oh! France used to send their prisoners there."

Tom scribbles on his hand. "To say I'm impressed with your knowledge is an understatement, Antonio." He glances around the room. "To circle back to Cayenne the cat, will he be coming here today? We've gotten a number of scratching posts and some beds for him..."

Nino laughs. "Cats don't need their own beds! Cayenne sleeps wherever he wants. Usually on someone's face."

Tom darts his eyes to me. "Yeah?"

It's a shameful truth Logan might soon find out. Our cat is the love of our life, but I wouldn't say he's anyone else's. It will be harder for Logan to win over Cayenne than Nino.

I sit on the edge of Nino's bed. "I thought we'd bring Cayenne in a week or so. He's not really fond of new people."

Tom considers what I've said, gaze on the ceiling. "I've been warned. Well, I need to return the van before the rental place closes. I'll leave you two to settle in, and Logan should be home for six. He has weekly meals delivered, so food will arrive at four-thirty, but I put some nibbles in the fridge, minus cheese." He winks at Nino.

Nino says, "Thank you. Cheese is evil."

"But do they like it in French Guiana?" He points at Nino.

My son simply scrunches his nose as if he really hopes they don't.

His condemnation amuses Tom. "Noted, Antonio. I'll do my best to keep cheese out of the house. Shay, please call if you need anything at all. Twenty-four seven."

Tom leaves, and when his footsteps fade to nothing, Nino starts jumping on the bed. "Woo-hoo! This room is awesome."

Before I can tell him to stop bouncing on the mattress, he plops down on his butt.

I scoop him onto my lap and kiss his dark hair. "This bedroom is pretty cool."

"It's perfect." His voice has that wonderful touch of whimsy that only happens at Christmas and birthdays.

Logan thought of everything for my little boy. I should be thinking about what a good job he's done being a friend to Antonio. I should appreciate what a good friend he's being to *me* with all these gestures. But instead, I stare over Nino's head across the hall at the door to our bedroom.

Our bedroom.

Do we really need to sleep together? It does seem as though Tom could drop in day or night when things are needed. And Logan is right, whoever the cleaner is, it's someone from this town. And this town talks. But I could just sleep on the couch and sneak back in the morning. After that kiss it's going to be very, very hard to fall asleep at night.

But then there's Antonio... he's probably more meddlesome than Joy Hunter and Monica Dane combined, and those ladies know everyone's business. No, Nino would know if I slept on the couch and could drop something into conversation that doesn't belong there.

Anyway, what on earth am I so worried about? I can resist a good-looking man.

Nino dives into his tent and opens one of the books.

But a man who does all this for my son has a whole other kind of appeal.

Just then, my phone beeps with a text. I pull it out of my back pocket.

LOGAN

> I hope Antonio was happy with his room.
> I'll finish off yours tonight.

I have to work hard to stop my mind racing and reading into this text with my now activated libido. *Oh God, save me from myself.*

Chapter Sixteen

Logan

I'M GEARED up and on the ice before Ashton. I had to be.

Of course he knows about me and Shay. I called him just like everyone else. He's married to my sister, for God's sake. I can't avoid the guy, I've known him as long as I've known myself. But the fact that I talked to him almost every single day in the week that followed my breakup with Shay means he knows how much this woman means to me.

I expect a grilling; he'll expect details.

He must be at physical therapy this morning because there are only twenty minutes left of optional skate time when his tall ass steps onto the ice. He barrels toward me, as

I knew he would, comes at me like I'm in trouble and shoves me playfully into the plexiglass with a fake check.

"Congratulations, Mrs. Mendez."

I push myself up properly. "Thanks." I start skating off so I don't have to look him in the eye, but it's what we're supposed to be doing, so there's no shade.

He skates alongside. "Fuck, man... I had no idea you were talking to Shay for a while. Why didn't you tell me?"

"Payback." I punch his shoulder. It's a blow-off answer but a solid one, too, since he had his secret relationship with my sister not too long ago.

My best friend isn't one to talk without thinking, so he holds on to my answer, and I'm sure once the initial humor wears off, he'll be thinking about why Shay and I would be a secret. After all, *he* had a good reason to stay private when it came to Jolie.

Ashton will not think of me and Shay the same way everyone else will. I was able to hide a lot of my heartache back then from my family, but from Ashton? It was impossible, because once I decided the dark place I was in was too scary to be alone, that week at Golden Sierra, Ashton made me get out of bed every day. That might have been over a decade ago, but Ashton still refers to my life as *Before Shay* and *After Shay*, because much as I don't want it to be true, our breakup was a major demarcation in my life.

I changed a lot. I changed to survive.

So I find the most plausible explanation to our low-key dating. "Shay has Antonio. Out of respect for her privacy and giving her time to tell him on her own, I kept us quiet."

"Well, you couldn't have had a louder marriage in the end. Everyone is talking about it. It's all over social media already, and I'm guessing you've been offered a mag spread?"

I hope Coach has social media.

"Yeah. We were already papped in Vegas, but Reggie told me two magazines want multi-page stories and photos."

"I can't see Shay being up to that." He remembers her precisely.

"Nope. I'm not even going to ask."

I focus on the ice ahead, but it doesn't stop me knowing Ashton is staring right at me.

"What was it like being with the love of your life after a year-long dry spell? You must have sucked."

I wish I could remember. "I've got a lifetime to make up for it."

I round the bend in the rink and head down center ice for a more active skate and to make a temporary break from his scrutiny. I glide a drill down the middle. *Three right. Three left. Quick feet.* Ashton follows me and pushes himself hard to blow past me, then skates backward to capture my gaze.

He breathes heavily. "You know I'm really happy for you, right?"

"What else would you be?"

"Suspicious."

I manage a staccato laugh because he's far too close to the bullseye, as always.

But he's kidding, thank God. "Seriously, Lo? Maybe now we'll get some of that true you back."

Sincerity fills the space. Sometimes I miss the old me, too. Apart from hockey, the life I've been leading has been like a skipping record, repetitive, boring despite the vast variety in it. For the past years I've barely slept in the same place twice in a row. Women's names are like an alphabet I've been through front to back more than a few times.

Even sex, which I didn't do nearly as often as people

thought, lost its appeal. I stopped chasing for meaning in it over a year ago. That's when I told Reggie to stop setting me up, but he convinced me it was still a wise idea to maintain my public persona.

It's been a long dry spell indeed. I probably blew my wad in a millisecond with Shay just like Ashton suggested. I'm surprised I managed to get a condom on with a woman like Shay under me.

In all the years gone by, I never found a woman who excited me quite like she can. She's the kind of woman who doesn't take shit and keeps you on your toes. She's a woman you can confide it and get the truth, even if it hurts. She was everything a guy like me needed back then and probably still does. There are few people in my life who don't blow smoke up my ass. It's boring, and there's nothing worse for your life than people puffing up your ego with thin air.

As a man who's always been at the top of his game, people remarking on my God-given talent, I've had a huge amount of attention. Whenever I'd puff my chest, my dad would warn me, "Ego is like fire. Your servant if kept under control. Your master if you let it rage."

Shay kept me in check from the minute I first spoke to her. It's amazing how easy and uncomplicated love is when you drop your ego.

But this isn't a conversation I'm down to have right now. Dredging up the past will muddy our vision. Reflecting on how she's the only woman I ever loved is reckless.

Thankfully, Ashton shifts the narrative to Antonio. "How's the kid dealing? Jolie said he's a little Einstein. Antonio, right?"

"We call him Nino. Damn, news travels fast. Shay only got the results of his tests this weekend."

"Yeah, the principal told Sam, and Sam told Joey."

Of course, my sister-in-law is a teacher...

"Don't principals have some sort of teacher-student privilege or something? Ever heard of confidentiality?"

Ashton slows us down by doing some lunge and drags. "Why should good news be confidential? She's proud to have a kid like Antonio at her school. We're all stoked to have a genius come out of this town. It's mostly been jocks doing well."

I forgot just how fast gossip and news spreads in Starlight Canyon. People are supportive at best and meddlesome at worst.

We're lunging in sync now. "We're taking him to the private school in Longbrook."

"The Academy?"

"Yeah, Longbrook Academy has a much lower teacher-to-student ratio so they can give him more attention. Apparently, he's going to be in high school when he's nine or ten if things keep moving like they are."

Ashton teases, "Shit, man. He'll be smarter than you when he's a teenager."

"Smarter than you, too, asshole." I smirk. "I..." I think of Antonio's tiny glasses and his adorable baby-toothed grin and how he remembered my name, and it makes my heart glow. "It's going well so far. They're moving in today. I see a bit of myself in Antonio."

"What? You're both male?"

"Suck it, Dane." I dig my blades in intentionally, with some of the passion I'm feeling now, remembering how important that special boy is in all of this. "He's got a gift. I might be getting old now, but once upon a time I was the shit. Antonio is destined for greatness. I can tell you that."

"You still *are* the shit, bro. This team is the goddamn shit." He says it with his chest, like a chant. My friend's impending retirement will be heavy on his mind this season, and being reminded of that now shores up this decision.

I can't let him down. I have to stay on this team.

Ashton taps the side of my arm. "You'll be a great dad to him." He carves into the ice and with a burst of speed pulls away from me.

We are here to skate after all. But his words only slow me down.

Dad.

Shay and I talked about being Nino's friend, but... I watch my teammate, now thirty feet in the distance, his back still to me when he steps off the ice.

Will I be a good dad? Am I supposed to be a dad?

I always wanted to be one.

I hope I got his room right. After work, I'll finish off Shay's.

The timer hits zero, and I get off the ice, joining Ashton on the bench to take off our skates. It's briefing time, but I have a five-minute meeting with the coach. Since Ashton is defense and I'm offense, we normally separate now anyway, but I've got nerves about this trade and need a little more reassurance.

"I'm meeting with Coach now." Thankfully, my words don't sound as heavy as they feel on my shoulders.

"Are you in trouble again?" Ashton tugs off his huge skate. "Hopefully Coach will cool down about things. I'm guessing Vegas is a thing of the past now you're hitched? Joey showed me a newborn's sleep schedule, and we'll be in bed at six p.m. come next summer, so I don't think I'll be up very late any more when I retire."

"Yeah. Early nights will be good for me, too." I shove my foot into one of my shoes. "I just want to ask Coach if I can go to the Longbrook appointment for Nino tomorrow.

Otherwise we need to wait another two weeks for the admissions officer to come back from vacation. The appointment would be during optional skate in the morning, so hopefully he'll let me stay later to finish training."

"Good fucking luck. I'm surprised you're asking. I already told Joey she needs to hold little Fletch until the season is over."

I laugh lightly. "Yeah. We'll see." I tie on my sneakers and start the march over to the coach's office. This is supposed to mostly be for show. Me asking for a morning off optional skate, which is really only optional if you have physical therapy, is a smokescreen.

I expect Coach to say no, which should be fine because then at least he knows about Shay and Nino. But my gut wants a yes. I want to be there for the appointment. I want to support them. I want to ask questions and scrutinize this place where Nino will be spending all his time.

We know people in the Canyon. Six degrees of separation is probably more like one in our small town. Longbrook will be full of strangers, and a protective urge bubbles inside me to check for signs of danger before sending the five-year-old off all day, every day amongst much older kids and a bunch of teachers I've never met.

I knock on the coach's cracked door; he glances up, and through the gap he waves me in.

"Take a seat." He points to the chair with his pen then throws it down, sits back, and presses his fingertips together.

"I came to ask for a few hours off tomorrow morning. Just during optional skate, and I'll make up the workout after briefings instead."

His expression is unimpressed.

I rush out the words. "I got married. And I have a little boy now."

Coach scratches his stubble. "*You* got married?"

I need to sell this. "And we have a kid."

He's thunderstruck, I'm sure, but has a great poker face. I let him digest my words. I let him make a move.

"Guys don't even get off for births, Hunter."

I'm not sure if this is actually true because I've never seen it come up.

"I've never asked for a single minute off. My kid is... I don't know how else to say this, but he's a genius, and we need to check out a more appropriate school for him. It's going to be a massive change and a huge move for our family."

By the way Coach's features twist, he thinks the genius story is even less plausible than my marriage.

"I know it sounds wild, but he's one of those kids who gets into Mensa at five. It's not skip-a-grade level. It's like high school at ten years old. College when he's thirteen. It's a big deal to put him in school with much older kids and to trust the staff we've never met. He might be really smart but he's still just an ordinary five-year-old, and we need to be sure. I don't want my kid going away to some place that I haven't seen with my own eyes."

My request comes from a more meaningful place than I thought it would. I really don't want Nino somewhere I haven't inspected.

Coach scratches his head. "Well, I didn't expect *that* from this meeting."

"We got married quickly and on an off day just so it didn't disturb my play. I'm really committed to this team. I want to play hard this season. For you. For Ashton. Now for my family. But having a few hours off just this once..."

How hard am I going to beg? I want this more than I thought I did.

He flicks his hand like some mob boss. "Go. Have the appointment."

I swallow down my surprise. "Thanks."

I get up to leave, but before I'm fully out the door, he catches me.

"Hunter?"

"Yeah?"

"I hope this is the beginning of better things for you."

Chapter Seventeen

Logan

AFTER A QUICK STOP TO pick up some packages from a home store in Santa Fe, I head back home for our first night as a three. Tom already told me Shay and Antonio seemed happy with the house and assured me the only thing I might have to worry about is the cat. As a ranch boy, I've always been pretty good with animals, but Tom said by the way Shay spoke about him, Cayenne might live up to his fiery name and be the hardest one to please. Nobody knows Shay like I do, so he couldn't be more wrong, but I didn't correct him.

Still, I allow designs of befriending the cat to consume most of the drive home because it's easier to think about picking up a robo mouse or some fresh fish from the Super-Mart than it is to worry about Nino being homesick or Shay not liking my house. It's easier to worry about getting the cat to purr under my touch than to think about how nice it was when Shay did. And I've thought of that more than I should lately.

A dirty thought about Shay can be triggered by just about anything since that kiss.

When my mind weakens and loses focus on the cat, sleeping together in my room tonight is the first thing that comes to mind. It seemed like a sensible thing to agree to at the time. This town is way too small with an overgrown grapevine. One slip up, and my housekeeper, or Antonio saying something to Luis, would have news of us not sharing a bed traveling fast. Also, thinking about how Shay wants to raise Nino with healthy views on relationships, I'm not sure if sleeping in the guest room, which as a gentleman I would have done, would serve to give the little man a positive view on marriage.

Still, Shay disarms me. Putting distance between myself and women has always come with ease, but with her? The connection is just different. It would be enough to still think the world of this woman, I admire her grit and dedication to her family so damn much, but the fact that she's only become more attractive since college doesn't help matters. It's a lot for me to adjust to, but I will.

When I pull into the drive and my heart skips at seeing another car parked there and warm lights on to greet me, all I can think is that it might not take me so long to get used to this.

I throw my i7 into park, grab the packages from my trunk, and in a moment I'm heading through the front door.

"Hey, gang..." I greet them.

The TV plays some mystery-looking show, but the minute the door clicks shut behind me they turn around.

"Logan!" Nino jumps up and over the back of the couch and comes pattering over to me. "Thanks for my room!"

He wraps his tiny arms around my thigh, and a warmth so pure melts my heart.

He glances up at me. "I already started reading *Around the World in Eighty Days*. I wonder if Phileas Fogg will win the bet?"

I dart my eyes between them. "Wow, I didn't know you'd be able to read that already. I thought it would be a good bedtime story. I loved it when I was, well, I read it when I was twelve?"

The kid will be reading *me* bedtime stories this time next year.

Antonio takes my hand that isn't holding a shopping bag and leads me deeper in the house. I try to quickly shed my shoes near the door while walking with him.

"Fogg's bet was for forty thousand pounds, and that's fifty thousand four hundred and six dollars! But Mom said it would be way more in today's money."

Shay has now made her way in front of me and shoves her hands in her back pockets. There's something about this pose that gets me every time.

"I had to help with a few words in the book, but his reading is..." She ruffles his hair. "It gets better every day, doesn't it, *mijo*?"

He nods so hard his glasses slip down his nose. He pushes them up with his finger. An urge to bend down and gather him up into my arms to hug him hello overwhelms me. I just met the kid, but he feels right here. And, man, I love his enthusiasm. When I was younger, my dad used to say I was like a puppy. Throw me something and I just had to go see what it was. Antonio and I have that in common. Curiosity.

Shay tosses a glance toward the kitchen, hands still bashfully in her pockets. Breasts still full and inviting me inside my own home that never felt like one before they were here.

"I heated up the dinner Tom sent. He said you'd be home at six, so it might be cold now."

We head deeper into the house.

"Sorry I was late, I had to get some things at a shop."

I follow Shay with my shopping bags in one hand, Nino leading by the other.

She leans toward me ever so slightly and mumbles quietly, "Nino is a hugger. Hope that's okay."

"You kidding? Love it. I'm one, too."

We reach the kitchen. She hurries over to the oven and reaches inside with a towel to get the hot foil meal out for me.

"It's still pretty warm actually." She removes the card lid from my ready meal.

I melt inside. Nobody's ever made dinner for me apart from my family.

It's not that Shay cooked this, but it feels like it. She thought of me. She tried to time supper just right. Shay isn't the type of woman who is out to please. Being considerate is her idea of decency, but when she pulls her hand away quickly so as to not let the steam burn her, I fire up inside like this ready meal means more than it does. Until now, it never quite hit me how the simple things can be the ones to make a person feel thought about.

Antonio climbs up on a stool and sits at the counter. "I had the meatballs, but they had spaghetti sauce on them. My mom makes them in soup. *Albondigas*. Mom's taste better, but I like the containers the food comes in. It's cool like a drive-thru. So it was fun even though it didn't taste as nice."

"Nino..." Shay buries her face in her hand.

"I'm sure your mom's meatballs are a million times better. She's a good cook." I place the large plastic bag in my hand on the counter. "Which is why I had to buy her this."

Shay's eyes dance with confusion. "What's that?"

"I said I'd finish your room off."

She suppresses a smile, but her gaze flickers, and her cheeks flush like maybe she didn't think I meant the kitchen.

Nino crawls along the counter and peeks into the bag. "Boxes of stuff."

I slide them toward Shay. "Hope I picked well."

She skims the plastic down the sides of one of the boxes in the bag and immediately gasps. "Oh my gosh. Copper pots. I..." She puts her hand in front of her mouth but calms down before she orgasms. "I always wanted copper pots and pans." She points behind her but still stares at the top of the closed lid. "They match your..." She shakes her hands as though her excitement is hurting them. "They'll match your gorgeous sink."

"*Our* gorgeous sink."

Her gaze meets mine. An electricity runs between us; a familiar feeling exchanges on the current, sending shivers through my spine. But she soon lowers her eyes back to the box.

"*Our* sink and pots match." She runs her finger along the writing on the side, still admiring just the exterior of the box.

A warm feeling rises in my chest.

"Logan. These must have cost a fortune..."

Nino leans toward me and talks behind his hand but doesn't whisper. "One time, Mom told me about a new whisk for hours."

She pretends to be offended, throwing a sassy hand on her hip. "Hey, it wasn't *hours*, and it was the first time I tried a silicone one over a metal one. It was a big deal, and I swear my meringue wasn't the same."

Nino shakes his head and laughs behind his hand. Shay reaches over the island, her scoop-neck t-shirt falling to reveal the most luscious cleavage. Then, she tickles Nino under the armpit as punishment for the burn, and I don't think I've ever felt so many conflicting feelings at once. I want to dive inside that shadow between her breasts and at the same time be part of this joyous innocence visiting my house for the first time.

"Mercy!" Nino yells through his laughter.

"Okay. Just remember this isn't a roast fest." Her gaze shimmers with an affectionate joke. "Roasts are on Sundays."

Nino catches his breath after a few more giggles, and the infectious sound echoes through my body. I'm not around kids much anymore. Eve is my only niece. Though she still giggles and jokes plenty, she's a teenager now, with a boyfriend and everything. It makes me miss when we used to joke around like this. I always used to think I'd have a few kids by my mid-thirties. That such a common wish was less likely than being a top player in the NHL is baffling. I'm sure I fucked up somewhere along the way. Probably starting with the woman right in front of me.

Shay makes prayer hands and tips her head. "I really, really appreciate the cookware. You didn't have to."

"There's more stuff in the car. I'll bring it in later. I

wanted you to be able to cook. Not for me, of course. Just that you like it."

She throws me a sassy look, the one she used to give me when I toed the line between the perfect level of dominance and being a pig. "I'm happy to cook for all of us, Logan. Provided you like Mexican food and can live without cheese."

I take a moment to connect with Nino through my intel from Tom. "Cheese is evil, right?"

Nino's smile fades, and he could be a superhero talking about his archenemy. "Evil to the max."

I go around to Shay's side of the counter to find a plate for my dinner, easing into a small space behind her, and suddenly, in my kitchen, there's a whole new atmosphere. It's ten degrees warmer next to this woman and much harder to breathe. I'm not one to seize up next to anyone. There's something different happening here. It's all so familiar in that I know the feeling of Shay, we know each other intimately, but with Nino here, and this entirely new domestic situation, I ask myself. How the hell do I fit into this place I clearly belong?

I want to slide my body flush with hers, wrap my hands around her from behind, and pull her in to smell the sugar scent of her neck.

But Shay awkwardly dances away from me. "I'm in the way."

I lift my eyebrows. "I wouldn't say that."

Her laugh is delicate and breathy. She brushes off what I've said by tucking it behind her ear along with some of that shiny, long hair of hers. Her cheeks glow with that terra-cotta warmth I used to see when I managed to make her blush. She lowers her gaze, swallows thickly.

What I wouldn't give to flirt a little more, but she quickly gives her attention back to her son.

"Well, *mijo*, we need to get you off to bed. We have a big day tomorrow."

Nino jumps down off the stool, and I can only see his tufts of hair over the counter. "Are you coming, Logan? To my new school?"

"Of course. I wouldn't miss it for the world. I love new beginnings and big adventures. New school is one of the best ones."

Shay tosses me a grateful look mixed with a trepidation I guess every parent feels sending their kid off somewhere new. "Well, night."

"*Buenas noches, Logan.*" Nino waves me goodnight.

"*Dulces sueños,*" I practiced how to say *sweet dreams* and a few other basic things on some language app, hoping to keep the Spanish going. The Mendezes would always speak English in front of non-Spanish speakers, but I know their language is important to them. I don't want Nino getting rusty just because of me.

Shay is impressed. I see the sparkle in her eyes, but her voice is deadpan.

"Decent accent."

She heads down the hallway holding the tiny hand of a human she created at some point in all those years without me.

I should have known she'd be able to grow a kid that wonderful.

How did I end up without one?

I take my fork between my fingers and twirl it, her sugar scent still succulent in my kitchen.

How did I end up without her?

I'm not used to going to bed at nine-thirty p.m. But after staring blankly at the TV for an hour, I figure out of respect for Shay, I should try to slip into bed now and not disturb her sleep in the middle of the night. I pad in my socks quietly on the wood floor up the hallway, stopping to peek in Nino's room where the door is cracked.

He's not in the bed but curled up in the teepee. The fairy lights illuminate his precious features. His thick, long eyelashes rest peacefully on his cheeks, and he hugs his oven mitts. It's just about the cutest and funniest damn thing I've ever seen.

Our bedroom door is closed. I turn the handle carefully, not wanting to wake Shay. A sliver of light from the hallway illuminates her face. Her hair cascades down bare shoulders, covered by nothing apart from two slinky, vulnerable spaghetti straps.

I slip inside and shut the door, quietly taking myself to the bathroom, worrying about every sound I make in there. I brush my teeth with only two spurts of water. My shower is fucking loud; I never noticed before. And then, I wonder if I should wear boxers or something to bed. I should. But I'm doing my best to make this place comfortable for Nino and Shay. Some things I gotta keep for me, and after being in sweaty pads all day, my dick just needs the air. It's not like we're going to touch each other.

I flick off the light to the bathroom and tiptoe to the bed with a hand towel over my dick, drop it, then slide under the sheets. Shay has put a pillow in the middle of the bed like some sort of boundary but she's always been wise beyond her years, so I accept she made a good decision.

I let out a long, quiet breath. I'm not tired. My skin is sensitive to everything. Even the sheets feel weighty and, dare I say, sensual tonight. I run my fingers through my hair. I need a fucking sleeping pill or something.

"Logan?" Shay whispers.

"Yeah?" I whisper back.

She turns from her one side away and onto the one facing me and hugs the pillow between us. Her hand is so close to my chest. Her warm body is now impossible to ignore.

She doesn't say any more, but I feel her gaze on me right through the darkness.

"Are you okay?" I ask.

There's something both dangerous and safe about this bed. Here, I smell her. From inches away. Just over the pillow, I can feel her breath. Her lips are one small dip away from mine.

"I'm okay," she answers.

But the way she says it, I don't think she is. I don't know if inside this woman is the same Shay I knew from college, but if it is, getting her to talk is an art form. It takes finesse. Delicate stroking and a soft brush adding a thin veneer one layer at a time until we both see the picture.

I offer a topic that's surely far away from whatever she's thinking about. "I heard the cat will hate me."

"Mmm. Likely."

I put my hand on the pillow just under hers. She shifts as if getting more comfortable, and her body inches closer. I don't want it to, but my dick thickens. My thoughts wander to what she's wearing, if her bottoms are as skimpy as the top.

I wait for her to offer more, but she doesn't. So I keep talking. This was how we did it. I talked and talked until she said what she needed to, maybe thinking her words would get lost in mine. But I never missed a single one of them. When Shay uses words, each one counts.

I search for more of the mundane. "Tom sorted out the credit cards and bank so you're on my account now."

"Why did you do that?"

"We're married, Shay. It's what people do. You want me to leave cash on the nightstand for my wife and kid?"

She scoffs.

I thought she'd protest more and make a feminist comment, but she doesn't. Her thoughts are tangible in the air, I can feel them heavy and present, but I'm no expert at braille. I search for more unrelated topics to fill the space for her.

"Nino seems happy. Tomorrow I'll read..."

"Logan I'm scared," she blurts.

"Scared?" I instinctively take her hand; she doesn't pull it away.

"Not scared. Just worried. Am I really letting that little boy be around kids twice his age all day? They're going to be talking about sex when he's like seven. And... he's so innocent, Logan. I don't want him to lose that."

I reach my arm around her back and rub her soft skin, trying to soothe her. The pillow presses between us, and my dick sinks into the soft feathers.

"It's a big deal. It's normal you'd be worried about these things."

I can't tell her it's going to be okay and I don't want to. Validating her is the best way to be her friend, though urging my hips deeper against the pillow is not. Am I a scumbag for having this kind of reaction while she's worried about Antonio? I take my hand back and lay it on our line of demarcation. It doesn't feel right not to hold her when she's down, to gather her up in my arms and make her feel safe. But no touching is a rule that's good for both of us. My senses are on fire being this close to her in bed, and she needs me in every way but the way my groin is telling me.

She swallows thickly. "I don't know any of these adults promising to take care of him. It was hard enough taking him to school in Starlight Canyon where I know some of the teachers and so many of the other parents. It's predictable here."

What can I give her that will help? I've never been a parent. I don't know what it's like to have this level of intense worry and responsibility over someone. The Shay I know has always been more of a homebody than a party girl. More movie nights than two for ones at Slys. And that's where I shine. I'm a chameleon. I'm adaptable. I can bring her to the shoreline on this wild sea.

"If there's one thing I know about, it's how to cope with life changing way too fast. When I was a kid, I was constantly being put into new situations. It's a lot, but I can tell you from experience, Nino is more resilient than you think, especially because this change will feed his passion. He'll be excited, I can see that in him. From what I see, you have great communication with Nino, so all these concerns that you see coming from a mile away, you'll be there for him. He'll be okay. Not only okay, but I'd be surprised if he doesn't have the time of his life."

"Mmm." Her tiny hum is a loaded response. "Yeah, that's what my dad said. That Nino is resilient."

"As long as he has you." I tap her nose.

She laughs lightly. "My dad said that, too. Except he said as long as he has *us*."

The darkness is a space for such words, but with my dick still full only inches from her thigh, I'd rather not consider them.

"I'm pretty sure how you're feeling right now is all part of what makes you a loving mom, *pastelito*. Let yourself worry. But let yourself think it's going to be okay, too."

If I thought my words would shift my attention to Nino, they've had no such effect because it's my exact state of mind when it comes to this raven-haired beauty on the other side of the pillow. Why does she hold back from me so hard now? And why, despite that, do I think I can still have her as mine?

She shuffles her face closer; if she only knew what it was doing to me and how much I want to shred this pillow right now. The only thing I want to do is take her in my arms and kiss her all better. My pulse races, whooshing in my ears.

"Thanks for listening, Logan. Sorry to bother you with my bullshit. Especially after you've had your own long day."

I hum a response. Maybe I am just tired, but the thought of saying goodnight and rolling over without her in my arms burns a searing loneliness through my body.

I take one last touch for my dreams and trace her jaw with my thumb to make sure she's paying attention. "We're in this together."

She places her hand on mine. The weight of it presses my palm deeper onto her cheek, but it doesn't take long before she lifts my hand off and back onto the pillow. Then the room goes silent, and we both decide to keep it that way.

Chapter Eighteen

Shay

Thank God I prepared a list of questions to ask the admissions officer at Longbrook Academy, because walking next to Logan on this tour, him glancing at me and Nino like some proud husband and father, playing the part like an Oscar winner, almost has me believing it, too.

I cannot talk to him like I did last night. He was so sweet coming home with those pots and pans. So generous doing up Nino's room. So alluring in bed with what I just *know* was no clothes on. *That was hard to ignore.*

He listened to me right through the darkness like he always used to, wholeheartedly, with an addictive empathy. I hungered for that comfort all over again this morning, as soon as I woke up and my mind started reeling about Nino and this school again.

I can't talk to Logan like that. I can't go to Logan for reassurance. I can't let him touch me with his hands or his words; one is just as strong as the other when it comes to tugging at my heartstrings. After all these years, and me really being frustrated by the man he's become, the way he disarms me is like no other. In his presence, I'm both exposed and invincible at the same time, and if it's not confusing enough to be still wildly turned on by the man, well, him reaching into my soul is not going to help things.

I will not fall for Logan Hunter again. Not now. Not when I know better. After years of lying men, tearstained nights, and enough streaked pillows for a lifetime, I've sworn off men. Certainly ones like Logan who think women are some game.

Having Nino has been the best thing to happen to me. It's allowed me a place to house my love. Unconditional love suits me because it's not loving that causes heartache. Things don't ever go wrong when you're *giving* love, they go wrong when you don't get it in return. With motherhood, Nino doesn't have to love me back for me to feel fulfilled. I don't hold my breath hoping he says it back every time I whisper it in his ear at night. Saying that, when I pray with my dad on the Sundays we go to mass together, I sure as heck thank God he does.

After our hour-long tour of a sprawling campus, the admissions officer, Kaylin, has done an amazing job catering to my and Logan's questions, but mostly speaks directly to Antonio. This is something I appreciate and watch with what is probably an unhealthy attachment.

Kaylin is about my age, though doesn't have a single white hair or line on her face. I only feel she is the same age due to maturity. She's dressed elegantly in a color-block sheath dress that fits her slender frame like a glove. It's not revealing, but her figure was made for a dress like that, and every time we follow her up a staircase, I glance over to see if Logan notices how nicely her ass sways in it.

He doesn't. All he has eyes for today is Antonio and this amazing school which, quite frankly, is an academic, sports, music, and artistic paradise. Who even knew an academy like this existed? It's as nice as our college was.

Walking around the labyrinth of paths, through brick buildings and quads, around a hushed library of studious youth... It brings back memories. When I catch a glimpse of Logan eyeing some ivy or running his finger along an etching in a bench, I see that youthful, sexy jock of mine all over again and the ache inside returns. It's a dull throb that visits me every so often and wishes he was the same guy I once knew. Where did he go? Did he ever really exist in the first place?

Logan and I walked for hours sometimes, and he'd always stop to notice anything out of place. He'd carry my backpack. He'd make me bend down to see ladybugs on top of each other and ask if they were having sex. God, he made me laugh like nobody else.

I put that all away because it was too painful to keep it out in the daylight. But I broke the airtight seal on our past by confiding in him last night. I should have kept my feelings to myself. Lord knows I'm capable. I passed plenty of years, alone in my bed at night, worrying about my son... I don't need Logan's comfort. *But I wanted it.*

I woke up this morning facing the door away from him, determined to keep said distance, but when I sat up, a whole other feeling tugged at my insides. There he was, dawn slipping through the curtains casting an ethereal veil on his bare skin. He was still sleeping, buck naked on his stomach, steely glutes of a Greek god and a back so broad with skin delicious and inviting. The man isn't hot. He's beautiful. Sexy. There are no words really for a man like Logan, but I can say, he's a rare specimen and I could not take my eyes off him as I sat there staring, my heart racing like someone about to be caught doing something downright sinful.

I snuck off to the bathroom, managing not to wake him, and stared at myself in the mirror for a good five minutes. I told myself not to, but the next thing I knew I was touching myself in the shower to relieve the wanting between my thighs. Afterward, I argued with the woman berating me in the mirror that it helped tone down the tension I was having over this Longbrook tour. She didn't believe a goddamn word, and eventually, my reflection simply shrugged. I'm only a woman after all.

And so is Kaylin, who I can tell is trying very, very hard not to care who Logan is or what he looks like, but I've seen the exact shade of casual she's trying to portray so many times in college. I know she wishes she could just have a good hard stare. I know she's going to go home and tell her friends about it and name drop for life. Goddamn it.

I'm still jealous.

Kaylin brings us full circle, the tour stopping where we started in front of the dean's building. "So now that you've seen the labs, art room, gym, and music building, Antonio, which do you like best?"

"The room with the Bunsen burners is cool." He takes my hand. "But I don't think my mom will want me playing with fire."

I bite my lip. "Not especially."

"You have to get a 'fire license.'" She makes air quotations, "to use the Bunsen burners, and that's not allowed until seventh grade. So there's time..." Her words trail off as she comes to the same realization I do.

He'll be six years old when he's allowed to use combustible gas.

"Do you have any questions?" she asks Nino, dropping the subject because it's too complicated to broach in the next five minutes.

Nino puts his finger on his cheek to think about it. "Do you have a playground?"

My stomach flips. Yes, Nino loves learning. Yes, his true potential is likely to solve cerebral problems rather than practical ones like a rancher or a lumberjack. Yes, I want to accelerate his growth, have staff around who actually know what quantum means when he asks and give him a chance to save the planet.

But he's still just a kid. Much as the gym we saw was fully equipped with state-of-the-art rowing machines and squash courts (a sport I forgot existed until now), all my little boy wants is to learn new things and climb around on a jungle gym in between classes.

Kaylin laughs lightly, and I'm not sure if that's her answer or she's thinking of one.

I take Nino's question and run with it. "When Antonio isn't in class, how will he be cared for? Every kid needs downtime during a school day, and being five, he only just started school. I'm not sure I'd count lunch hour as down-time for a five-year-old and..." I say one word that encompasses my biggest concern of all. "Friends?"

Kaylin flicks her gaze between me and Logan with an empathetic expression. "Mr. and Mrs. Hunter..."

I don't correct her that I'm still Mendez... Mrs. Mendez? Am I a Mrs. if I still have my last name?

"... a gift like Antonio's doesn't come to this campus

every day. In fact, we've never had a child working beyond two additional grade levels. I think this is going to be a learning experience for all of us. But we have hired a new support staff with a degree in child psychology whose sole purpose is to support Antonio. We have a peer-to-peer support program that will ensure Antonio always has a student dedicated to listening; even if they're not his age, they're also not an adult. I think we need to observe Antonio's needs as he grows and adjust to them accordingly. So what I can tell you is that Longbrook is very committed to supporting your son. It would be an honor to have him here and graduate him as an alum."

Nino taps Kaylin's hand. "You didn't answer the question about the playground."

"Sorry, Antonio. Of course. There isn't a playground on campus, but we have trees to climb in, and if a jungle gym is of interest, Mrs. Hansen, your staff support, could drive you to a local park during break times, if your parents give permission."

Parents.

She sells it hard. "You could also have swimming lessons, tennis lessons, soccer, baseball, paint in the art room... we have lots of coaches here who would love to introduce you to a new sport and can offer one-on-one lessons. Or teach you a new instrument? We'll make sure you have lots of fun. Work hard, play hard." She punches her fist in the air.

Logan smirks. "Don't tell me that's your school motto?"

Kaylin tries not to totally ogle Logan, so she answers facing me as if I asked the question. "It's not our motto, no. But I think we can all agree it would be a good one."

Logan has been respectfully quiet for most of the tour, allowing me to ask questions, but he just can't resist his own pitch to Nino in an effort to focus on the positives. "Did you see the two hockey rinks? I had a frozen pond growing up. This place would have been a dream for me."

Kaylin has mostly avoided eye contact with my insanely hot, famous husband, but she allows herself a bashful glance, almost blushing at his humility. He's oblivious because Logan doesn't take much notice of admiration. It must be nice to get so much you can take it for granted.

Logan continues. "You have a special gift to grow, Nino. This sure looks like a sunny spot to me."

Nino gazes up at him. There's something in his expression I only see when he's speaking with my dad or my brothers. Affinity. My son is young, but he's fully aware of his boy-ness and reiterates frequently how he thinks makeup is for clowns. Once he learned what a period was by walking in on me in the bathroom. He now tells me how glad he is to never have one, every time I buy tampons at the SuperMart, typically right when the checkout person scans them.

Nino and I are bonded, truly close, but he also knows we're different.

He's a boy. Logan is a man. And they're having a moment.

Kaylin interrupts the affectionate exchange, not picking up on the significance. "Mr. Hunter, it would have been an honor to have you as an alum, too. I'm sure the hockey team would love to get your skates on that ice."

She's being nice. Not flirting. But I don't like it anyway.

Logan doesn't reply to her. He still only has eyes for my son. "What do you say?"

"About hockey?" Antonio scrunches his nose, unsure. "You think I should try hockey? I play football." He gazes up at Kaylin briefly. "Known as soccer only to Americans."

Logan crouches to be on a level with Antonio and grabs

his little hands. "Yeah, I mean, getting you a pair of skates would be awesome, but I'm talking about the school. It's pretty incredible, isn't it? I can really see you having a great time here. Learning lots and never being bored."

My heart pangs seeing Logan be such a... dad. That's not his position in all of this. This is my job.

I slide up next to Nino and crouch as well, taking one of his hands from Logan. I search for something equally as encouraging to say, but when I gaze into my Nino's big brown eyes, I see it. A flicker of excitement. A desire for this new adventure. No. I don't need to convince him this is the place for him.

"You like this school?" I smile.

"It's really cool. But really big."

"It is big." Instead of saying, but there will always be people to help you, I wait for Nino to say more. He's heard enough adult voices, it's time we heard his.

He considers for a beat. "But the library is huge. And they have lots of pianos and..." He glances at Logan with a smile. "I could try hockey if a coach will help me."

I watch my son exchange another man moment with Logan, perhaps trying to please him. I thought I'd have until Nino's teen years before he really needed a father figure. But something is starting to happen here between Logan and my son, and I know it's a good thing, but apprehension buzzes through my veins nonetheless. He's better at being Nino's friend than I thought he'd be.

Nino grins from ear to ear and asks me, "You two really want me to go to this school, huh?"

Logan doesn't answer, glancing at me for guidance. But before I do, Nino laughs.

"I wanted to come here before we got in the car. I watched the campus tour on YouTube."

Logan and I gaze at each other. Soft laughs leave our lips. A shared relief passes in the mere inches between us, along with something else. Is it appreciation? Is it triumph? I can't tell, but whatever it is, it washes over me with the warmest sensation. This is going well. We're getting along great. Almost too great, especially when I know that later today part two of the day's plan will unfold.

Logan is playing his part, and soon, I'll have to play mine.

Our first public kiss.

In less than one hour, his lips will be on mine. Mine will be on his. Our bodies will touch. His hands will hold me. And I will try like hell to erase the memory of his body in bed this morning. I swallow hard, thinking about how he reached over the pillow for me last night, infusing me with that special touch of his, and then I woke up weak in the knees for the man, circling my clit in the shower like some teenager.

I recite about twenty thousand prayers in my head all the way to the hockey arena in hopes of getting some help from *El Señor*.

Our Father, lead us not into temptation...

Chapter Nineteen

Shay

I DO a good job occupying myself with normal driver activities nearly the whole way to the Scorpions' arena. I pretend to concentrate on directions, fiddle with the sun visor, and change the radio station to look as though the car is very, very important to me.

Thankfully, Nino can't stop talking about his new school, or at all, because of the excitement it's all caused, so my passenger has had plenty of entertainment without me, and the latest conversation takes my mind off kissing Logan for twenty minutes as well.

"Do you think Phileas Fogg would have had a better

chance getting around the world in eighty days if he went through Europe and Asia instead of by sea?"

"Hmmm." Logan nods next to me, considering the premise. "I guess it was the most direct route, if you draw a line on a map?"

"Exactly. Plus when he took trains, those days were shorter trips."

"We could try the math out later." Logan indulges Nino's theory.

"It's a lot of countries to go through. France, Germany, Austria, Slovakia... um... Ukraine..."

I'd rather talk about geography forever than face this kiss, but there's no more delaying the inevitable. I park my modest car in a team space amongst the Audis and Porsches and Mercedes.

I'm going to kiss Logan.

Sure, we had the one on the porch, and Lord did it take my breath away. But it was also rushed and the shock element makes it seem like a dream. This kiss? It has me shaking in my boots.

We all tumble out of the car, and Logan opens an inconspicuous side door leading into the facility. We enter a very long, stark hallway. Having been on a tour and in the car all day, Nino sees the hallway as a tarmac and races ahead pretending to be an airplane.

His voice echoes behind him. "Neeeeaaaawwwww..."

Soon he's off in the distance.

Logan takes my hand, lacing his fingers through mine. We're about to be rink side where we discussed him having his arm around me. Holding my hand. And... sharing this kiss. I'm sure the kiss won't be anything too dramatic. That would be weird. Too much PDA. Right?

I slide my hand out of his grasp. "Nobody's here so the no-touching rule is in effect."

He's exasperated. "Seriously, Shay?"

I take one more step, faster, in front of him, when he grabs my wrist and pulls me toward him. I didn't expect it so I nearly bump right into his rock-hard frame. He wears that crooked, dimpled smile of his, and I'm close enough to smell him now. Logan's cologne isn't like a lot of men. It's not sharp and fresh. It's a sensual trail of sandalwood and jasmine laced with spicy black pepper. It's comforting, alluring and edible. His scent is hypnotic, and the only explanation for why I haven't pulled my wrist back.

But I find my tongue. "Seriously what? Those are the rules."

He tilts his head to the side, so adorable. "If you can't even hold my hand leading up to our performance, we might have problems."

"I can hold your hand, I just don't want to." It's a lie. This morning I would have held his hand and every other bit of naked skin hanging out from the covers. Happily. I add, "It's just better if we don't."

He sinks his teeth into his bottom lip, considers me with his boyish amber eyes. His thumb circles over the thin tender skin on the underside of my wrist. The space between us grows heavy and humid.

Mischief dances on his features. "Do we need to practice, Wife?"

His words caress me like foreplay. I yank my hand away, but his touch still lives there. I tug my sleeve down over the spot in hopes of being able to ignore the electric warmth still tangible on my skin.

"Practice holding hands? I think I can manage holding your hand later, Logan."

His manly hands grip my waist and he walks me back as if we're dancing. One step. Two steps. Three... my back is against the wall, and my hips are owned by his firm grasp.

There's a twinkle in his eye, and his lips quirk with amusement. He taunts me. "If you can't even hold my hand down the hallway, you might have trouble pulling off a convincing kiss."

I roll my eyes. "Seriously? Get over yourself."

With him so close my knees nearly buckle, and I'll never admit it, but he's right. I'm nervous about this kiss. But out there, in public, it will be... quick.

I remind him. "We agreed on a low-level lingering peck with no tongue. It's not that big of a deal."

His gaze becomes more weighty, just staring, waiting, but not for words. He listens to my body, and she betrays me by buzzing in high frequency. He can probably hear my heart throb against my rib cage. He probably smells that my perfume has become more fragrant as my temperature rises. Cool as I think I am, Logan's dimpled smirk tells me he read me as perfectly as a predator reads its prey.

He smirks. "You are so transparent."

"What's that supposed to mean?" *I know exactly what he means.*

He rubs his thumb along the front of my hip bone. The movement sends sparks the rest of the way down the crease, right down into my panties.

"It means either you forgot how to kiss a man," he wiggles my hips with his flirty grip, "or this particular one is making you sweat. I see it, *pastelito*. You're nervous."

I exhale sharply. "I'm fine. I'm sure if I can manage to forget sex with you in Vegas, I can get through an equally forgettable kiss."

He releases a low, throaty laugh. "You're still so savage."

He holds me more tightly, though not too firmly. Not softly either. Just right. I should ease myself away from his hands. I should shove some personal space between us, but it will only prove his point. Then again, my heart races so fast, the dramatic pulse in my neck is all the evidence he needs. I am liquifying right on this very spot.

But I'm the kind of person who would die before backing down. "Fine. Let's practice if you need to."

Stepping his feet on either side of mine, he's taken the challenge. We're closer than ever. "Me? This practice is about *me*, is it?"

He lowers himself nearer to my face. His lips hover just over my nose and lustfully within reach. His eyes lock with mine. A rush of anticipation floods my senses. His smell is divine. His breath cascades over my mouth. His presence envelops me, and a potent cocktail of emotions swirls inside, making me feel absolutely drunk with uncertainty.

His gaze blazes into me, intense and unwavering, and whether he intends it or not, threatens to ignite a fire to consume all reason.

"Trust me, Wife, *I* can handle it."

My voice is quieter and less sure than I want it to be. "You're the one who needs to convince your coach right now."

His fingers lace through my hair. His thumb teases the line of my jaw. He lowers further, so close his lips are feath-erlight on mine when his minty breath tumbles all over my mouth. "Which is why I want to make sure you can do this."

My thoughts are all over the place. He was once every-thing to me, then nothing, and now... I find myself relying on him all over again, and the trust I don't give freely surrenders to him with ease when he touches me.

My mind tells me I'm strong and resolute, but my body tells another story. My body wants to hitch a leg around his middle and heave his chest against my rock-hard nipples for relief.

His thumb swipes along my lip. "Are you okay with this?" He grips the base of my skull possessively. "I'm not sure your idea of a lingering peck is the same as mine."

Fear mingles with desire, indecision tangles with longing.

I swallow hard. The only words that escape are a meek dare. "Do it."

When his lips press to mine, it's a gentle caress. A soft embrace. And surprisingly, in the wild whipping storm of emotions brewing inside, Logan offers me the calm I've been wanting all these years.

He closes his eyes. I close mine. His palm cups my head. My senses are on fire. I almost completely lose myself in the security of his arms, the perfect pressure of his full lips and even the delicate warm draft of his breath... the tip of his nose on my cheek. Time warps, and I'm back on campus. Back in my bed. Back on that bench riverside where we used to kiss until we were too cold to sit there anymore.

I don't even hear my son's footsteps coming toward us and only know he's arrived when he says, "Ew."

I draw in a sharp breath at the very needed interruption.

Logan lifts his lips off mine, but his forehead connects with the hot, bothered skin of my certainly flushed face.

He asks quietly, "That wasn't so bad. Was it?"

It wasn't bad.

It was worse.

I loved it.

Nino is clueless apart from thinking kissing is yucky and pushes himself between us. The magnetic connection breaks; it's a sharp, abrupt jerk in my chest.

"Mom, I really want to see the ice rink."

Logan glances at his watch, his nonchalance the complete opposite of the inferno inside me.

"Are you going to stay and watch me play for a bit?" He places his hand on Antonio's shoulder.

"Yes!" Nino grabs his hand. "Let's go!" He tugs at Logan's hand to follow him the rest of the way down the long hallway.

I follow Logan and Nino, attempting to cool off, breathing deeply. I smooth my fingers through my hair as if it's tousled, and I'm sure it isn't, but that experience, Logan's body close to mine, his mouth so warm and delicious, so...

I was worried about wanting to have sex with Logan. The impulsive desire from this morning was cured only by my own ravaging fingers. But that kiss? Yes, it set my core on fire. Yes, my nipples ached. They were so hard they could have fallen off. But, his lips... they were still tender, still caring. It was worse than lust. A foolish woman would believe there was much more there than simple desire.

No, I can't think there are still feelings like that here. That Logan is gone, swallowed up under the sheets he shared with a thousand women between what we once were and what we are now.

And yet my feet move as if they don't even belong to me. My soul has teleported to some other world at that moment, and I struggle to come back to where I am.

As we get to the end of the hallway, I realize I'm about

to time travel all over again. Here, we did his version of a lingering peck. Next time, we'll have to do mine.

Chapter Twenty

Logan

I DIDN'T NOTICE one single step of getting from that kiss in the hallway to rink side. I'm basically fucked. I'm a college kid all over again who just wants to crawl back onto her skin and dive into her aura.

I should have been able to shake it with the long walk down the hall but I'm still floating like I've had an out-of-body experience, heart still pounding so hard it's drowning out all logic. If Antonio wasn't holding my hand, I'm not sure I'd be able to control them. I want Shay's soft, womanly waist on my palms. I'm burning to touch her again.

Only the sound of blades digging into the ice starts bringing me out of my haze, and then, the coach's shrill whistle yanks me back to reality, snapping my head in his direction where he salutes me in a way of greeting.

He knows we're here.

Nino has been patiently waiting for me and his mom to get through our *practice* session and to be entertained. His forehead is now plastered against the plexiglass, but he can barely see over the boards, so I hoist him up in my arms for a better view of the plays.

"Right now, they're practicing a move called *hitting the trailer*. It starts with a rusher, that's an offensive player. Wait, you know about offense and defense from soccer, right?"

"Yeah. I play in the defense, but my coach just tells me not to move. So I mostly just stand there."

Not move? My gut gets heavy, instincts setting off. Why can't the little man move?

Antonio asks. "What position are you?"

"I'm a forward for the offense."

"Are you good?"

So innocent. "I'm all right."

"You have to be really good to be a professional, right? The chances are really, really low in soccer."

I don't like the way Nino reveals the odds. It sounds almost as though he thinks the statistics mean it's impossible.

Shay leans up against the boards and plexiglass on the other side of Nino in my arms. She rubs his back, caring, but mindless, while watching the guys play. Her gesture is that of every mom in the world, an instinctive touch, a reach out to reassure her cub. Pride swells in my chest with this boy in my arms. His beautiful mom, and my wife, frames the picture of a real, actual family.

"So what are the chances in hockey to be a professional?" Nino asks.

I'm still watching Shay, who's watching the team.

"I don't know. I never once thought to look, because if you want something badly enough..."

Shay swipes hair behind her ear. She's flawless...

"If you want something badly enough, you need to ignore the odds."

Shay tilts her head, and her dark eyes connect with mine. The corner of my mouth pulls up in a half-smile. She offers a tight one in return. Fuck, I want to kiss those lips until they're soft again, until they're plump and swollen and... *mine*.

They are mine. *Mine for now.* All of this is mine. Antonio perched on my forearm is mine to support, to nurture. Shay is mine to do the same. It's her hour as much as his to get what she wants out of this life, for her to succeed in her business and reach her true potential, too. I won't stop until I give it to them.

My heart aches with something deeper than happiness. A sense of contentedness washes through me, like this is what life is all about and I was somehow able to finally manifest it. A good woman. A wonderful child. And, of course... hockey. If you'd asked me what my holy trinity was when I was twenty years old, that would be it.

I'm never short of wild ideas, but dangerous ones are paying me a visit now. Shay is volatile. I couldn't pick a more explosive stick of dynamite to set a match to. The reason we couldn't stay together hasn't exactly changed, and something about the way she treats me now has me thinking there's another one I don't know about.

Her hips, thighs, lips, and pebbled nipples say yes. But

her words tell another story, always working overtime, ripping apart the clear magnetism.

Nino snaps me back to reality. "My coach says the odds are zero."

"He said what now?"

"He said the odds are zero." He shrugs. "To become a pro."

My jaw tics. So his coach has this eager child standing on the spot, not allowed to move, and tells him making the pros is impossible? My fist curls and I'm a few degrees hotter.

Shay wraps her arm around her son, brows furrowed. "When did he say that?"

"Last practice. At the end I told him the odds of being a professional were less than one percent, I found it online, and he said for some people the odds are zero."

I am instantly seeing red. I don't give a shit if this coach thinks Nino has God-given talent or not. A coach's job is to help kids thrive. To develop what they have and spit a kid out to the next level better than he was when he came in. One thing that's not in the coach description is dashing people's hopes and dreams when they're five fucking years old.

I'm seething.

Shay's features tell me a concoction of something similar brews behind her eyes, too.

But just then, someone joins us on the other side of the plexiglass.

My coach.

Even though we haven't always seen eye to eye, he doesn't feel like an enemy, and even less so now thinking about how not once, even when totally frustrated with me, did he cave in to the kind of things Nino's coach does. A sudden appreciation for him surges through me. Deep down, and in my more mature moments, I know he's annoyed with me because he doesn't want me or anyone on this team to squander their opportunity. When I came to the Scorpions, I noticed he's a father-like figure to a lot of the guys.

Maybe I resisted him being one to me because it reminds me just how far away my own is.

Coach wears a soft smile I've never seen before. It's grandfatherly.

"Well, hello there, little guy. What's your name?"

"I'm Antonio. But you can call me Nino."

Coach nods. "Nino. I like that. It sounds like something the crowds would be chanting."

I bounce Antonio in my arms and cheer. "Ni-no. Ni-no. Ni-no."

He giggles.

When I consider Coach's expression, eyes gazing at a kid and not my own face, there's encouragement there. As much as he can chew our asses, get angry until his face is beet red and spit when he's shouting, never once has he said this team isn't capable of a Stanley Cup. I look at him differently now. Especially with the twinkle in his eye staring at Antonio.

I stop bouncing Nino. "I can hear your name in the stands already."

"You ever skate, Nino?" Coach asks.

He tips his head down, gazing at Coach from under his eyebrows, seriously. "I don't have very good balance."

"Well, I'm sure your pops will be a good teacher. He's a decent guy when he puts his mind to it." Coach gives me a side-eye.

I know Coach won't stay here at the boards long so I introduce Shay. "Coach, this is my beautiful wife, Shay."

My wife. My God does that feel good to say that about such a golden woman.

She waves. "I'd love to shake your hand, but you'll have to settle for the thought of it today."

"It's what counts." He tips his head cordially.

She shoves her hands into those back pockets of her jeans, and it takes me back into the hallway.

"I know you're busy," she says graciously, "so thanks for coming to say hi to us. And thanks so, so much for the morning off for Logan. It means a lot to us. Especially Nino."

Something akin to a satisfied smile tugs at the corner of Coach's mouth. I'm not sure, but I think he's happy for me.

Pride swells for the second time.

"I'm glad it worked out." He shakes his finger at her playfully. "But no more family emergencies until postseason."

She laughs lightly. "Trust me. I get it. My dad's a rancher, so our activities were strictly controlled. He had five summer babies." She winks.

It takes Coach a moment to realize her parents only tried to make children that would be born when cows weren't.

He shakes his head, and a laugh blows out of his nose when he gets it. "Your dad sounds like a dedicated man. I respect that." He lifts his hand to wave us off and turns to skate away. "Time to gear up, Hunter."

"Well," I wiggle Antonio, "gotta go, little man."

I place him down, and with him no longer between us, that magnetic force strong enough to rip my soul straight out of my skin is back. I'm not sure if I were to touch her now

I'd be able to contain it. A lingering peck, her style or mine, isn't in the cards, because frankly, I want to throw her against the plexi and absolutely devour her.

"That went well?" she asks.

"Very natural."

She draws in a deep breath, and her full breasts rise up and down invitingly. "Showtime, eh?"

She means it's time to kiss like we planned.

Fuck do I want to. I want to for real. Which is why it's better we leave it.

"I think we're good. Coach came over to say hi, which is, you know, even better than showtime. If you catch my drift."

We have to speak in code around Antonio.

She nods quickly. "Yeah. I was thinking the same thing. Job done. Right?" She seems hassled, all of a sudden in some sort of hurry. "Well, we'll leave you to it." She takes Antonio's hand.

It would probably be better if she left so I can gather my thoughts or rather lose them on the ice. But instead I say, "Stay. I'd love for you to watch. You and Nino."

Antonio instantly tugs at Shay's pocket. "Yeah, Mom! Let's stay!"

She eyes me and speaks more carefully than she needs to. "Okay. Guess we're staying."

"Grab yourselves a snack in the cafeteria. I'll be on the ice in thirty."

Half an hour later, I'm warmed up and doing drills with my teammates. Nino sits on the side with Shay, and they both eat a sandwich. How on earth can I see a mom and her kid eating a sandwich and think it's the most touching sight in the world? There's something magical in the ordinary. Something pure. Anchoring. Primitive.

The only other place I feel so calm is on the ice. It's time to focus.

I step onto the rink. Crisp air fills my lungs, and the familiar sound of blades slicing against the smooth surface echoes in my ears. The rink is alive with energy; teammates zip across the ice, each one focused and determined.

I join the circle of players gathered around our coach. His voice booms over the noise of our skates. He outlines the next set of today's drills, emphasizing precision and speed, the keys to success. I glance around at my teammates. There is a sea of nods. Understanding. Faith in Coach as a leader.

It brings back thoughts of the dickhead managing Nino's soccer team. I don't even know for sure he's a dick. Nino is only five and maybe misunderstood, but in my opinion, kids are often smarter than we give them credit for.

I glide effortlessly on the ice. The puck dances at the end of my stick as I weave through cones, sharp turns testing my agility. Around me, my teammates mirror my movements, the rhythm of our strides syncing in perfect harmony, which is a miracle because the exertion it takes to fuel this fast-paced agility test is grueling and you'd think someone would drop.

But no one does, and a lot of that has to do with Coach. A strange sense of shame floats around me. That man has believed in me, and I haven't taken it seriously. Maybe I took it for granted. Or maybe there's something deeper going on like when my mom suggested I needed Vegas and women because I was afraid to sleep.

I am afraid to sleep. I don't know exactly when it started, only recall the punctuated moments when it got worse. When the town got funds together to buy my first set of gear was when I had my first sleepless nights. That kit in the corner of my room stared at me through the night, a ghost with high expectations. Not long after Dad was sick and we found out he had a heart condition, I struggled again. Even though he promised us all it would be fine, I still had late-night Google sessions worrying about cardiomyopathy. When I got scouted in high school, when I almost didn't pass chemistry, when our dog died... and when my dad did. Well, they all stole one more wink of sleep at a time.

Laughing off my insomnia seemed easier when I became a party animal. So did not having a relationship or taking myself too seriously. My persona protected me from people talking about therapy with me too much, all but my big brother, Colt, and my mom, that is. They never stopped suggesting it, but therapy? It reminded me too much of Shay, the only other time I took myself into a professional setting for mental help. Instead I hid my problems under a shiny playboy reputation, and sometimes, even I didn't realize my sleep issue was there.

I work harder on the ice, pushing my muscles to the limit, digging my blades in deeply, furiously... pushing away thoughts of the past. When I take my slap shot at the end of the cones, I whack it right into the top corner and can't help but glance over to Nino and Shay. Nino jumps up and down. Shay has put her sandwich down to give me two thumbs-up.

It's a silent cheer from just two people, and I've never

felt better with a whole crowd on their feet and a stadium filled to the brim with thundering roars. It was the same in college. I only cared about Shay's hands clapping. Shay's cheers. Shay's tits bouncing up and down with encouragement.

When a woman doesn't love freely, it's the best thing in the world when she gives it to you.

The whistle blows, signaling the end of the drill, and I pause to catch my breath. The burn of exertion tingles through my muscles. We all step off for a quick power-up of energy drink.

I squirt my Gatorade into my mouth next to Ashton.

"How did the school trip go?" he asks.

"The place is insane. It's as nice as Golden Sierra. Save your pennies. Two hockey rinks for little Fletcher. Grandstands on either side of them. I'm telling you, the place is out of this world."

"Did you get skates for Antonio yet?"

"Nah. But I should. I wanted to respectfully let his interest in soccer ride out, but I have a feeling his coach is a prick, so maybe I'll see if I can encourage him to play a better sport."

Ashton draws his lips into a thin line, a sort of smirk I can't read.

"What?"

He cocks a brow. "You're protective."

"Hell yeah, I am."

The whistle blows, signaling our next drill.

Ashton shoves his big hand into his glove then pats me on the shoulder. "It's nice to see you care about something this much."

My friend steps onto the ice, but his words don't skate off with him, and I kind of wish they would.

How do I care for, protect, and fulfill my end of the bargain for Shay and not fall totally back into the addictive need for her love? How can I kiss her, sleep next to her, even eat her goddamn mouth-watering food without memories creeping back in to remind me how perfect she was for me? How much more perfect she seems now.

I broke so hard after Shay. I couldn't trust anyone. For over a year, I lost interest in socializing. Eating. If it wasn't for my professional contract I might have withered away.

I met the woman of my dreams in college, and my NHL contract came around with bad timing. Impossible timing. I needed to become an entirely new man to live again at all. It took ages to get over her.

Maybe I never did.

Chapter Twenty-One

Shay

THE NIGHT AFTER THE KISS, thank goodness Antonio asked me if I'd have a sleepover in his room. I put his mattress on his floor, and he piled up loads of pillows in his teepee. Since Logan had to stay later than usual at practice last night to make up for his morning off, I was safe behind the oak door of Nino's room, pretending to sleep off how disturbing this all is.

Logan wasn't supposed to be so good with Antonio.

He wasn't supposed to be so good with *me*.

Over all these years, I've been able to morph my Logan from college into the man I see on magazine spreads, in the newspaper, and all over the shameful puck bunny websites

I sometimes frequent when I'm having a particularly bad bout of late-night anxiety. I wasn't pining for him, just curious. I wondered how a man who healed me could also become such a heartbreaker.

But now that we're together again, all I see is college Logan. College Logan was a giver. He didn't take himself too seriously apart from his appearance and had surprisingly little ego for a guy with his talent, body, and face cut from the gods. That's the guy I've been seeing now. I saw him in Vegas. I saw him at Longbrook. With my dad... even his choices of the people he surrounds himself with show his character. Ashton was always aloof but so mature; the pair never communicated like apes the way other jocks did. Tom, his PA, is a gem of a human. And, of course, the whole Hunter family is full of golden people. Logan is genetically inclined to be decent.

So why hasn't Logan ever settled down? Why has he become such a womanizer?

That question blows through my mind all night until the morning when I wake up with hair like tumbleweed, my eyes sticky with crust that I have no idea how it got there because I don't remember sleeping.

I'm a veritable zombie but somehow wake up my baby and get the morning routine going. I stare out the back window at a cactus in the garden, hot coffee getting cold in my hand. Nino eats his breakfast, and I have no idea how much time passes, but I finally look at the clock. I need to get back to my work, and Dad has offered to bring Cayenne over this morning and take Nino to school.

"*Mijo*, turn off the iPad now and focus on your breakfast. You need to get out the door in fifteen minutes. Papá Luis will be here soon."

"It's soggy." He lifts his spoon and lets sloppy cereal plop back down in a sea of milk.

"That's because you were watching cartoons instead of eating. You need to focus when you have cereal or it gets soggy."

It's my fault for not reminding him. For letting my mind wander. For being in a haze.

But one thing I can't stand is food waste, so he'll have to suck it up. "Baby. You just need to eat it. You need your energy for the day."

"It's yucky," he protests, tapping his spoon into the bowl and making a sloppy sound, that I admit, doesn't sound particularly appetizing.

And so it begins. A morning food war.

I glance into his bowl. "Looks like only five bites of torture left in there." I try a joke to lighten the mood, but Antonio's face is gloomy.

Just then, Logan's footsteps come down the hall. When he comes around the corner, I nearly lose my shit. He has no shirt on, no socks, and a pair of gray sweatpants with... no boxers. It's downright sinful. His skin is the perfect shade of golden, and I try to convince myself his hue is from a bottle because manicured men are a turn-off. But my gaze trails down his six-pack and settle on a naughty, sizable bulge, and I know... absolutely *nothing* about Logan is a turn-off.

My nipples are instantly hard. I cross my arms. "Morning."

He combs his fingers through wet hair then scratches his flawless taut skin just above the waistline of his pants. The gesture attracts my gaze down to the ridges of his hip bones, the slung cotton fabric and the outline of a thick, juicy...

"Let me get you a coffee." I spin around and step to his fancy machine. "What do you take?"

"Thanks. Just black."

I open the drawer of perfectly organized coffee pods. "You have this fancy machine and you drink black coffee?"

"You can take the boy out of the ranch but not the ranch out of the boy."

I smile to myself, absolutely loving that answer way too much. I take up and *original* pod and place it in the machine.

A chair rumbles across the floor behind me. Thank the Lord he is going to sit and hide his indecency.

He speaks to my son. "My dad used to say if you can't drink coffee black, you shouldn't drink it at all."

I flip on the machine. It whirrs. "My mom used to say you just shouldn't drink coffee at all." The small cup fills quickly. "She said bitterness is a sign of the Devil."

His laugh rushes over my shoulder. The mug finishes filling, and I hand him his drink. It's easier to face him now that his cock lines aren't on display.

"What are you eating?" he asks Nino.

"Slop," he complains, still putting up resistance to finishing his breakfast.

"You're going to finish that cereal," I say, meaning it. I hate throwing out food. We grew up with very little, so to me, it's a deadly sin.

Logan peeks in the bowl. "Oooh. I love slop." He snorts dramatically.

Nino giggles.

Logan changes his voice to sound like what I presume is his pig impression. *Snort. Snort.* "Feed me, boy."

Antonio is amused and scoops a spoonful up to Logan's mouth, which he chews then says in his pig voice, "Deeelicious." He takes the spoon from Nino's hand. "Come on, piggy, try some."

Nino snorts. Giggles. Then opens his mouth and Logan feeds him the slop. Nino chews loudly, with his mouth open, because how else would a pig eat?

Suddenly my son finds the food irresistible. "Yummy."

I roll my eyes. Of course it's yummy for someone else. And of course it's easy for Logan to saunter in with fresh energy and new ideas when he's not a parent day in and day out. When he didn't swap a mattress for a few rogue pillows on the carpet in the middle of the night because a kid kept kicking him.

Nino finishes the bowl like it's a fresh one and he's starving.

Just then, the doorbell rings. Logan gets up to answer it. His dick sways heavy and long as he rushes out of the room. *Holy hell.*

"Time to grab your backpack, baby. That's Papá Luis."

He hops off the chair and gets his backpack off the one opposite when Dad and Logan's full frontal come back into the room.

What is it about sweatpants?

My dad lifts the cat carrier. "Cayenne missed you."

Nino rushes to hug my dad who bends down and sets the cat carrier on the floor. My dad embraces Nino with warmth painted on his face.

"Let's get him out!" Nino reaches for the latch.

"*Un momento.*" Dad, stops Antonio then glances at Logan. "You might want to back up first."

An incredulous laugh leaves Logan's boyish lips. But my dad's expression is dead serious, so Logan takes a few steps back.

"Do you have a cat or a tiger in there?" he jokes.

I rub my hands together, ready to snatch Cayenne up if he decides to go for Logan.

"He's just not a people person. Well, he loves us, but..." I bite my lip. "I'm sure it will be fine."

Nino unlocks the door and pulls out our very round cat, the one who allows my little boy all leeway. Cayenne wears his permanently bored and bothered expression, but I've never been sure if it's just his unusual and patchy markings that make one of his eyes look skeptical.

Nino kisses his face while the rest of Cayenne's body hangs in a long line to Nino's knees. "You're going to love our teepee."

He puts Cayenne down who immediately rushes behind him and toward Logan, bounding in long aggressive strides. Meowing loudly, he makes his subtle attack, hissing and swiping for Logan's leg.

Logan doesn't move from the spot but puts his hands in the air. "Whoa. This one is feisty."

I rush over and snatch Cayenne up before he has another go. "Sorry about that."

"No problem. Guess we have a guard cat now. I just didn't think I'd want one that protected my own house from me."

"He'll calm down." I say the words but I'm not so sure.

At least Logan isn't fazed. I swear Cayenne was the cause of the longest string of first dates with no seconds I ever had. He specifically hates men. I stroke my cat's belly in his special spot until he purrs then put him back down. He walks off toward the back of the house, eyeing Logan suspiciously the entire way.

Dad puts his hands on his hips. "That went well." He claps his hands together. "Let's get you to school, *gordito*."

Nino takes my father's hand but turns back to Logan. "Are you going to be home when I'm back from school?"

"Sorry, little man. I'm in Canada for three days. Calgary then Vancouver."

"Those are in the west."

"That's right."

My son takes his time with a thought then offers what he believes to be an objective assessment of Logan's chances. "I think you'll win because you were really, really good yesterday. I can't believe anyone is better than you."

Logan's body melts under the warm compliment, and it melts me, too, thinking how much my boy's opinion impacts him.

"Thanks, bud. That's encouraging. I'll be back in a few days. I'm sure you'll have a lot of stories to tell."

Nino waves. "Bye."

Soon enough, Logan and I are alone. We are alone and he's half naked. Interesting how I can't force my mind to think he's half-clothed instead. I've never been the glass-half-full type, but never have I thought of that as a weakness before. But now, keeping my gaze fixed on his gray sweat-pants instead of his cut abs is as silly a choice as the water in a cup. There's the same amount of water no matter how you look at it, and there's the same amount of sex appeal to Logan whether I stare at his perfect pecs and that delicious tattoo on his rib cage or if I fixate on the bulge beneath the cotton.

There is no decent place for my eye line in this kitchen.

"Well," I slap my hands on my skirt. "I need to get to work."

"You can take my office."

I don't want to face him so I go to the fridge to grab an apple I don't need. I don't even like apples. They're the

211

most boring fruit in the world. "That's your space. I'm cool here at the kitchen table."

"I'm not in my office much," he insists, sauntering up next to me, dick swinging.

Or at least I imagine it does. I bet it's long and heavy and hanging down in there, rubbing lightly against the gray seams of his sweatpants.

I rush with my apple toward the kitchen table. "I'm fine here." I point to my open laptop. "There's plenty of space, and it's quiet. Thanks, though. For the offer."

"Okay. It's fair game anytime." He opens the fridge and dips his head in, stretching his torso and giving me a better view of the tattoo he got while we were apart.

I didn't think he could get any hotter than back then.

I take a seat in front of my laptop so I have something else to look at. Anything else will do. But I truly don't know what image could replace his steely body in my mind's eye. I'm staring right through my computer screen, and despite trying to blink it away, his abs and that shadowy trail of hair leading down into his pants are all I see.

A cool sensation overwhelms my breasts, and my nipples peak. Logan really does hit the spot. It's hard to believe there's a woman alive who wouldn't desire him because he has something for everyone. You like the boy next door? His dimples will do you in. You like bad boy? His hooded, amber eyes will mesmerize you like a wolf staring through the trees. You want sporty? Cowboy? Entrepreneur? Fun friend to go out with until you're the last man standing? He. Is. Everything. He's a ubiquitous fantasy and right behind me he fulfills one that's timeless in those loose pants clinging desperately to that V between his hips.

I can't help but laugh inwardly at the irony. The only thing Logan is *not* is husband material. And yet, he's mine.

My body simmers with electricity. He is absolutely clueless I'm at my boiling point. Do men know about the sweatpants thing? Did he do that on purpose? Surely not. No. Because if he wanted me turned on, he would have taken a second kiss at the arena. I knew it was for the best, stepping away and not touching each other if unnecessary. Even so, part of me wanted him to tap into that reckless side of himself and ease his lips onto mine again. Maybe even dive his tongue into my mouth.

Metal cutlery clinks on a plate behind me, waking me up from this daydream. I try to ignore him putting something together for breakfast. The noise doesn't bother me. As a mother, I've learned to work through a two hundred decibel typhoon if required, so a tiny clank of silverware, the fridge, a toaster... that's not a bother. What's bothering me is that being with Logan was supposed to allow me more focus. Not worrying about the money for a short period of time was to give me freedom from that one distraction. It's only given me another.

I mean, put on a t-shirt already.

I click on my graphics creator and get to work designing images to schedule for the week. When, next thing I know, he's standing by me and his hip height is face-level. As if teasing me visually wasn't enough, Logan's fresh shower smell is as attractive as the woodsy musky one he'll spray on later.

"Whatcha doing?" he asks, leaning over slightly.

I need to work. And I'd like to do it alone.

"Trying to work," I say with the voice I learned as a mom. It isn't mean, but a sort of exasperation that contains a message to leave me alone.

"I was thinking," he says, and apparently takes a bite out of his breakfast because his next words are muffled. "I should go through the contacts list with you this morning and tell you who I've already talked to."

I am going to call some of these people today. And that would help. "Sure." I move my cursor but over what, I don't know. "Why don't you get dressed first?"

He sets a plate with a peanut butter bagel on the table then slides a chair next to me. He sits close. Too close. Enveloped-in-his-manly-body-wash-smell close. His leg bumps into mine, which he doesn't seem to notice, but I do. A shiver skates up my spine, and the image of his naked dick punches through my resolve again. I bet it's flopping right down his center. Maybe it's touching his thigh? Lord have mercy.

I reiterate. "Finish breakfast and get dressed. Do what you have to. I'll be here. Enjoy your breakfast."

"It won't take long." He takes another crunchy bite. "We can just do it now if that's okay?"

I am very grateful for Logan's *friendly* help. I just wish he felt more like one right now instead of someone ensnaring me in dirty thoughts. But I need the help, and Logan's time is precious, so if now works, now it is.

"Okay."

I pull up the spreadsheet Tom sent me that matches the one he printed.

Logan leans closer into my space to see the screen. He points to a contact, and his forearm grazes mine. Logan's arm is weighty and masculine against me, even in that subtle, quick moment. Thank God I'm wearing a bra because the impact of his inadvertent touch is embarrassing.

"This guy here. Lambert? He's having a renewal of his vows after this season."

I make a new column on the Excel sheet with a heading called *notes*. Logan adjusts in his seat; his rock-hard thigh brushes my bare leg, my skirt hiked up when I sat down. I tug at the sides of the fabric to push it down further, but it's only a knee-length one anyway.

But Logan isn't noticing any of the things I am. He's all business. I should be, too.

He points again. "Rosario is on my team. He saw you yesterday at the rink, and I talked about what you do. His sister is having her *quinceañera*. Would you make a cake for a birthday?"

"Guess I could do that." I type in the notes.

"You should stick to your guns if it's not your brand." He puts his arm across the back of my chair, his wide rib cage threatening, or promising, to swallow me whole. Logan has the kind of skin that looks like it tastes nice.

"Uh..." I flick my gaze to the spreadsheet again. "It's good. I'd love to do a birthday party."

He insists. "But is it your brand? Or did you want to do wedding cakes only?"

He is way too close. I want notes on these people, but equally my underarms are prickling now with his arm on the back of my chair. The memory of his lips on mine creeps back up my spine. His morning scent is intoxicating. His tattoo is intriguing, and my mouth is dry. All these physical symptoms, and he sits there completely unaffected.

"Logan... please." I sound annoyed. I'm not. More... bothered. Hot and goddamn bothered. I reel myself in. "Don't worry about my business. Just give me the notes. You need to get ready for your trip."

The sooner we get through what he knows about these people, the sooner he gets away from me and I can dig my heels in and stop slipping down this sexual landslide.

Logan takes a bite of his bagel and chews pensively. His jaw flexes with as much muscle as there is everywhere else on his body. He wipes his hands on his pants, right next to that thick dick lurking somewhere beneath, and points to another contact.

"This one here. Hughes actually called me to say congrats on our marriage. He's one of Ashton's friends from Los Angeles. He's getting married next week."

"Too late for me to pitch."

"Maybe not. Ashton told me his wedding planner took the money and ran. You never know. They might need a cake. Or even a 'just in cake.'"

It's corny, but it makes me laugh. "You did not just make that joke."

"Yeah. It was bad. Just trying to make you smile. You're all serious this morning. Still worried about Nino?"

Men are so damn clueless. "I'm serious all the time. I haven't changed." The words slip from underneath me. "Unlike you."

"*I've* changed?" he asks. "Funny how I don't see it that way."

"Never mind."

"You can't make a comment like that and think I'm going to let it go. What do you mean I've changed?"

My gaze meets his. "Honestly, forget I said it."

He traces his top lip with his finger, considering me, his light-brown eyes pouring questions into the small space between us. He wants to know what I meant, and it wasn't fair for me to ding-dong ditch him with this. It's just... I need to remind myself.

This Logan sitting next to me isn't the one from college. This Logan is a playboy. The NHL's very own rake. The Logan I knew from college, well, he wasn't like that. He had a small trusted group of friends and family, not a wide circle of famous celebrities and social climbers.

He used to take relationships seriously. Was he always destined to become this man? Probably. Maybe. Maybe not. Any which way, I can't let myself glorify the past. We're where we are now, and there's nothing but today. And today, he's the guy who is currently being written about in tabloids with disbelief at being married to me. At being married at all. It's as big as the fascination over any famous man, once perceived as a lifelong bachelor.

The silence between us isn't uncomfortable, but it hums with unanswered questions. In the end, he asks the last one I expect.

"What happened to Antonio's dad?"

My mouth goes dry. The answer isn't something I like talking about. It's mixed with shame, anger, and frustration.

Logan reads me immediately. "You don't have to talk about it. But I'd like to know."

I appreciate Logan giving me an out. This story is such an intimate part of my past. It's such a huge source of my mistrust in men. I consider not telling him, but when Logan and I began this whole thing, I knew it was a chance for Antonio to have a Hunter in his corner. Maybe Logan should know more about Nino, if not me.

"His dad left town after he heard I was pregnant."

"He was from Starlight Canyon?" Logan sounds surprised.

"No, if he was, you'd already know the story, right?"

"Probably."

"He was from California. I visited my brothers a lot when they moved. Once I stayed with them for a three-week vacation and had a thing. Nino's dad was a bad guy, who I knew was a bad guy, because he told me he'd been to

217

jail before. So trust me when I say I wasn't surprised he skipped out on me, on us. Nino's never met him."

As soon as I say it, I brace for the judgment. It's borderline flattering that some people think I'm too good a girl to make a mistake with a bad boy. But I was chasing Logan's replacement so hard in my twenties, I made some overly optimistic choices. Well, to be fair to me, some of them were good boys in the beginning. But it seems I attract cheaters.

But Nino's father was a bad boy right from the start. By that point, I was nearly thirty and I wasn't chasing love anymore. By then, I'd already decided there were no good ones left. So why not a summer fling with someone I knew I'd never love? Someone a little wild and wrong from the very start. It was the last youthful, stupid thing I ever did.

I managed to keep Nino's dad a secret from everyone but my family who, in light of my pregnancy, were on a need-to-know basis. The news spread all the way to Oaxaca, and every single one of my relatives asked:

Shay, how could you have been senseless enough to get with a criminal?

But Logan doesn't ask that.

Instead, he asks, "Are you two safe?"

His concern shocks me; every inch of my skin is still. Nobody has ever asked me that. They always want to know how I could be so dumb. Hell, sometimes I still ask myself that question, but then it doesn't take me long to stop asking. All I need is one look at Antonio with his eyes closed, sleeping like an angel, to know it was a detour to where I belong.

Logan seems all of a sudden two sizes bigger, hackles up, fire in his eyes, as if he doesn't get the answer he needs about Nino's dad, he's ready to rage.

I've never seen him like this before. It's both terrifying and sexy at the same time.

"Last thing I heard, Antonio's father is in prison, so I'm pretty sure we're fine. And anyway, my brothers will likely kill him before you do if that's what you're thinking. Calm down." I bump into his arm. "You're so transparent."

I mimic his words from the hall at the arena, hoping to lighten the moment, but it comes off as teasing flirtation, and with his skin so close to mine, it might not have been a good idea.

Logan's jaw tics. The venom is still in his eyes, his gaze still full of protection. "I promise you Shay, you can't see the half of what I'd do if that man ever came around."

I offer a grateful smile.

He contemplates me and my confession. "You might think I changed, but you haven't."

"Yeah? What does that mean? I still don't have my shit together?" I say it like a throwaway joke, but humor always borrows from truth. I don't have my shit together. Look at me now.

Logan doesn't correct me and tell me I'm doing great. I respect his answer more than vapid reassurance.

"Success is a very personal concept and can't be measured by anyone else. People can tell you you're doing great and you still know you haven't reached your potential. It seems to me you're not satisfied yet."

His aim hits the bullseye in my heart.

He tilts his head. "What I'm referring to is that you're still bold as fuck."

It's a compliment that sizzles through my veins, the kind I would pay for. But also one that's not true. Because if I was bold, I would lean over and let my hand trace that goddamn bulge between his thighs.

Instead, I'm relieved he'll be gone.

Chapter Twenty-Two

Shay

SIXTEEN YEARS AGO

I sit on the bed in my dorm room, tapping my foot. We likely only have a few more weeks together, less if I include the time he's away for games in between, so my patience is thin. Five minutes less with Logan is like losing an eternity.

Logan is now a free agent, and negotiations for what NHL team will sign him are all underway. He's told me one of the teams is the Scorpions. I don't pray for anything else anymore but for him to sign in-state. I can't think of anything else, and every moment without him feels like a waste of my time now.

The red numbers on my alarm clock read two-thirty. Why is my boyfriend always late? The women's march sets off at three, and the start line is at least twenty minutes away.

Just then, there's a rhythmic rapping on my door.

Finally.

"Come in."

Not one gorgeous hockey player, but two, enter my room. I'm surprised Logan fits in my small dorm room here, but it suddenly feels two sizes smaller with the giant that is Ashton.

"I brought another supporter," Logan announces.

I lift an eyebrow at Ashton. "Did he tell you what the march is about?"

"Yeah. I have a mom. Jolie is practically my sister. And I love women." He makes a fist and raises it. "The patriarchy is bullshit."

I really have a soft spot for Logan's best friend. On the outside, he's one of the most intimidating men you'll ever meet. Six foot five, stacked, lethal to watch on the ice, and the defenseman is lucky to still have all his teeth; he knows how to throw a punch and takes one like a man, too. And all the times we've hung out, he's been incredibly down to earth despite his stature on campus.

He took me in immediately when Logan and I started dating, being happy for us and completely at ease even when he's been a third wheel. I suppose when you're the third wheel by choice and not because you're nobody else's, it's not quite as upsetting.

Ashton could have anyone he wants but sure is picky. He's a home-grown, apple pie kind of guy who wants someone interested in the simple life, and a lot of the women who approach him seem engrossed in the status.

I hope he never gives in to that.

"All right, boys. If we don't hurry we won't make it, and I hate being at the end of the march. Especially when I made wicked signs."

"One sec." Logan rushes to my bed and throws down a plastic bag then rustles inside. "I got us all t-shirts." He pulls one out and holds it up against his broad torso.

It reads: *The Patriarchy Won't Smash Itself.*

"This is mine," he beams.

"You had to get one with the word *smash* in it, huh?" I cock my eyebrow.

He yanks me against his steely body and plants a kiss on my lips. He murmurs into my mouth. "It's a very versatile word."

He opens his mouth, and much as I want to invite his tongue inside, we're going to be late, so I push him back playfully. "We have to go."

"Hold on." He swishes his hand around in the bag and pulls another out. "For you."

I take the shirt and smooth it. Mine reads:

I'm not doing one more thing for a man today.

Not much makes me smile full tilt, but this does it.

Logan is that guy. On the surface, to anyone who doesn't know him, he might seem like he's in his own world. But he isn't. He's the best listener I've ever met and the most thoughtful person, and lucky for me, his love language is gift-giving. He leaves me notes, flowers, and stuffed animals.

And, of course, there's the gift he gives me every single night.

He points to the shirt. "Good for today but also very useful when you go back to the Canyon for breaks. You can wear it around the house."

As a woman with four brothers and a dad, this couldn't be more spot-on.

I slip it over my head and smooth down my static hair. It's a little tight, which he may have done on purpose, or maybe he hasn't noticed I've put on relationship weight. All I know is that at night, when we're rubbing up against each other, he always wants the lights on.

"I love it, Lo. Thanks."

"And last but not least..." He tosses a t-shirt against Ashton's chest.

Ashton doesn't even look at it before sliding it on. He glances down at his chest where he, too, has a size that stretches to the limit over his wide frame. He reads aloud, *"Real men are feminists.* Aw, bro, that's sweet. You think I'm a *real* man? *And* a feminist? I've never felt so seen."

Logan throws the plastic bag in the garbage can.

Ashton glances at his watch. "You said this thing starts at three? We better go."

An hour later, we're nearing the end of the parade, a sea of women, and men, shouting for equal pay. Logan shouts louder than anyone. He never tires of chanting, and when I glance over at my boyfriend, a wave of overwhelming gratitude pours through me. Ashton has made his way between us, mostly because both he and Logan have had a lot of women come up to us. These girls lose their sense of purpose to flirt and say hello.

It shocks me how audacious women are. It's both a good

and a bad thing, I suppose. Audacity is either being bold and willing to take risks or it's disrespectful behavior.

Thankfully, Logan is good at blowing off the attention. Even though he is, the attention never fails to make me painfully insecure. After all, I was the geeky, introverted baker girl in high school, and my body showed many signs of loving my craft. Nobody here at Golden Sierra quite understands this is something of a Cinderella story. I've never been a popular girl. I never won the award for best hair, best smile, or best dressed. I didn't even get most creative, the title I thought I'd most likely be given in the yearbook. No. I was by all measures invisible. But I'm uncomfortable in the spotlight anyway.

I liked it that way, though, until being with Logan. Now, I wish some of these women would notice I'm here and step off my boyfriend. It doesn't escape me that many of them are prettier than I am and have better bodies, more charisma. I just hope Logan never notices, too. Even though I think he'd be loyal, I don't know that much about men. Only that my brothers always told me never to trust them and my mom once explained they're all out for one thing.

I steal another glance at my boyfriend who has a sign in the air and still chants. "Equal pay! Equal pay!" He'll be hoarse by this evening.

Ashton skirts out of the way of a young woman who's been eyeing him and slides in next to me.

"Hey," I ask. "Mind giving my shoulders a break and holding my sign?"

"Course." He takes it, and with his reach becomes a walking billboard.

Just then, the one I thought was chasing Ashton actually goes up to Logan.

"Can you sign my sign?" Her sharp, high-pitched voice pushes through the chanting.

"I'm just here for the march today." He hitches a thumb behind him toward me. "Supporting my girlfriend and all the other women here as a servant to the cause."

Never once has Logan done anything but ensure every woman who comes up to him knows about me and understands he isn't available for any shenanigans. At least in front of me, he's never made me doubt. But it's a hard thing to deal with all the same. Jealousy works in mysterious ways. It's a powerful force whether its victim is deserving or not.

Ashton tilts his head in Logan's direction where the girl insists again on the autograph despite my boyfriend blowing her off politely.

"Just so you know, you have nothing to worry about with Logan when he leaves. He's as loyal as they come."

My heart drops into my shoes and throbs along with my feet. "I know." I keep hoping, foolishly, that he won't leave. *Santa Fe isn't so far away.*

Ashton means well, but this conversation is acid down my windpipe.

And the "fan" just won't step off my man.

But thankfully Logan flicks a weak wave of his hand in way of goodbye to the woman, turns his back on her, and strides over to me. The march has reached the end, and the crowd around us disperses.

Ashton lowers his arms and my poster along with them. "Damn. Crusading gives me an appetite. You two want to grab some grub?"

Logan's fingers lace with mine. "I was hoping we'd be alone for the nights we have left. Unless you want to go?" He checks with me but he should already know the answer.

"Let's walk?" I'm not ready to really face him over a two-top table with worry and sadness still whirling inside me at the thought of him leaving so soon.

Ashton takes the hint. "All right. Catch y'all later." He hands me the sign. "Let me know if there's anything else I can do. Sign a petition. Kick somebody's ass at the White House."

I laugh. "I wish it was that easy. Thanks for coming."

He fist bumps Logan and heads off.

Logan drapes his arm over my shoulders. I wrap mine around his waist. I love this man's waist. It's firm and ungiving. Solid. Secure. I hang on to him as we walk instinctively toward the same place we always do.

The riverside bench where it all began.

We're silent down the street splitting the north and south sides of campus. Logan kicks a small pile of red leaves fallen from the maple trees planted to line the main road. "I hope I can fly you out to see me before the autumn leaves are gone in New England. It seems like Boston's offers are getting heavy." His gaze is soft on mine. "You'd visit, right?"

I don't know where my head is at with the thought of long distance. It's not something I ever thought I could do at the best of times. And now, my dad has been so desperately down lately. My aunt has to go back home soon, and he'll be totally alone. Am I really going to be galivanting from one side of the country to the next and skip weekends at home for my boyfriend?

"You won't always have days off on the weekends." I hate being a downer, but it has to be said.

"True."

"And I need to see my dad."

"True."

We walk in silence again and reach the end of the tiny,

quaint Main Street in Golden Sierra. We come to the boathouse where there's a small gate. Logan opens it to let me through. We've been here what feels like a million times, but it's probably only been twenty.

I'm hit by how deeply I love this man and how hard I've fallen in such a short amount of time. We've shown each other our rawest parts, our pain, our vulnerability. But I do hide one thing... I'm terrified of losing him.

Since Logan became eligible as a free agent, I've been waging an internal battle—both sides are equally powerful.

He leads me by the hand to a bench to the side of the docks behind the college boathouse. The San Theodora River flows gently. We sit.

He smooths hair off my cheek and over my ear. Kisses me. "Tell me what's on your mind, *pastelito*."

"You already know."

"Yeah." A rough sigh leaves his lips. "That's all I can think about, too."

"I am happy for you, Logan. I really, really am. This is a one-in-a-million shot. I'm proud of you."

"Thank you."

I try to lighten the mood. "Don't forget all of us little people in the Canyon." I laugh, but it's not funny, and the lie comes out of my throat feeling like a dry cough.

I have to swallow.

Logan takes my head in his hands and kisses me like we're forever. His lips calm me in a way nothing else can.

Ever since hearing about Logan's departure, I've been sick with anxiety. I don't know if I can handle it. Can I really deal with what's to come, really? Any decision I make is riddled with shameful thinking.

The uncertainty over us is a parasite that eats me from the inside out every day.

Logan has brought me out of my shell with his soul that's like a safe haven. But sometimes, even with his arm wrapped warm around me and in the shelter of his chest, I berate myself for needing someone so much. For wanting him the way I do. It's embarrassing sometimes when the wanting shows.

When he's not with me, I'm yearning to call him in the middle of the day asking him to do impossible things like skip class or ravage me in the library bathroom. With him, I cling to his body like a lifeline. I'm too needy. Too dependent now. Sometimes, during a boring lecture, I'll catch myself staring into space, wondering if my heart would stop beating if we can't be together. Would my lungs fail, too?

He kisses my forehead. "Stop worrying. We'll make it work."

Isn't that what everyone says?

"Shay, it's only a short time until you're out of school. I can fly you to me any time you can come and I'll come home when I'm off."

It's the silliest thing I've said since he's about to be a millionaire, but my other line of thinking is more terrifying. "It will be expensive."

"Trust me when I say there is nothing I'd rather spend my money on."

Though I speak volumes in my head, I can't seem to make any of this come out. It would be good to talk it out and be honest about my concerns, but the dark thoughts I have tell me the end is coming.

"Shay." He hugs me tightly. "Stop. I can practically feel your brain buzzing. I promise. I promise it will be okay. I'm committed. This is it for me."

His words cleanse my body momentarily. *This is it.* Who wouldn't want to hear that?

I really can't talk about this too much. "I'll miss you."

"I'll miss you, too. But no matter how difficult it gets, or how desperately the world tries to tear us apart, I'll be yours. Remember that. Always, Shay. Yours. And only yours."

The sincerity in his eyes makes mine water. The bridge of my nose stings. Until now, I have believed every single word that's come out of this man's mouth. But, I'm sure he's being naive. We both are.

When we met we had everything in common.

All too soon, we won't.

Chapter Twenty-Three

Logan

I LIE DOWN on the hotel bed and toe off my shoes, letting them fall with a thud at the base. I cross my arms behind my head and stare at the ceiling. If we'd stayed together, would I have just had years in hotel rooms, with nonstop thoughts of what Shay got up to that day? Did she get stuck in traffic? What did she eat for lunch? Dinner? Did she dream up a new cake design?

The questions could be the same now as they would have been sixteen years ago, because Shay hasn't changed. Not even being a mom has changed her, but it was the steady in her I fell for, and the steady in her I still find attractive now. As well as those womanly thighs she had hanging out of her skirt this morning.

Being the kind of man who can't stop moving, a person like me is attracted to her nature. I remember as a kid, out on the open range with the horses, you could only feel confident galloping into the distance, miles away from home, if you had a landmark. I haven't been able to figure out how to stop moving, not even to go to sleep, and Shay's reliability of spirit is like a lighthouse to a sailor.

Not that the woman is easy or boring or does anything short of keeping me on my toes. Because as much as she's predictable, she's feisty, too. She can look me in the face and tell me I'm a dick if I'm being one. You never have to guess where you stand with an independent woman like that. Unfortunately, feisty women pick their men, their men don't pick them.

I'll never know for sure how it would have gone if Shay and I had worked out. Would we have had those kids? Built a house on our ranch? Though I used to wonder every once in a while when I'd see a cupcake or brownie in a coffee shop and get reminded of her, our present life together has made any remnants of wishing for a different path disappear. Without us being apart, Nino wouldn't be here. I have to admit, the kid wiggled into my soul almost immediately.

It's not hard for any child to win me over. I'm easy that way when it comes to the little ones. But Nino is special. There's no use denying Shay had to go down that path in order to fetch him, and that required things to be exactly as they are. It's the ultimate paradox. A catch-twenty-two.

I let out a long breath and stare at the black TV. The room is dimly lit apart from one lamplight jutting out from the wall next to the bed. This mattress is too soft. They're always too soft. I hate it when I sink too far into a mattress.

Some things never change. The hotel rooms are always too dim, and the beds are nothing like home.

And that reminds me of how Shay said I've changed. I know, in some ways, it appears I have, which was why I didn't carry on challenging her at that moment. I didn't want to hear about how to the outside world I'm some playboy. To hear her actually utter those words wouldn't feel good when it's the last thing I want her to think I am.

But what's done is done, and I can't apologize for doing my best to live life. I stayed celibate for a while, and made sure to knock on her door as much as I could in the months that followed, but the obstacle we faced was impossible to overcome.

I slide my cell from my back pocket, spin it around in my hand. It's eleven at night. I'm sure she's sleeping but I want to hear how her day was. I want the answers to the mundane questions which is how I know I'm in the danger zone. I'm falling all over again.

It's the first piece of evidence it's happening—wanting to know about her dinner, and the traffic and work calls should not be on my mind when I'm exhausted after a game and needing some rest. But when you fall, the ordinary becomes extraordinary. I know what a magical thing this transformation is. It makes your life something special, you're so present, so alive with love that the most common little things light you up.

Fuck it.

Hopefully she'll have her phone off if she's sleeping.

> How did the calls go today?

My phone beeps. She's up.

PASTELITO

Good and bad.

Why?

PASTELITO

I booked the job for the "just in cake" haha

Maybe it was a better joke than I first thought.

PASTELITO

It's still terrible.

Why was your day bad then? That's a high profile job. Exactly what you need.

PASTELITO

I need to deliver the cake to LA on Antonio's first day at Longbrook.

Mom guilt. A force so powerful even men can feel it in play. It seeps through the phone with a radioactive force. I know there's not much I can do to help. But I am off Friday so I'm ready to stand in.

I know it's not any consolation but I'll take him. I can stay in Longbrook all day so if anything goes wrong, I'll be there.

A long pause. I imagine Shay in my bed... *our* bed, staring across at the opposite wall at the sliver of moonlight that always makes its way into even the darkest nights. She doesn't have to be alone anymore, talking to the moon. She has me.

It takes such a long time for her to text back, I almost think she won't. But then...

PASTELITO

I can ask my dad.

No way... Luis can't be off the ranch all day. Work backs up fast.

Don't I know. I grew up on a ranch. You don't do chores for one single day, and the place is a shitstorm. Quite literally. It's why I was raised to think hard work is a virtue and there's no such thing as a holiday.

PASTELITO

Dad will be happy to...

I don't read the rest of her text, just swipe over to Face-Time and call.

She picks up right away, the low light of her cell making her look like an angel. God, I wish I was in that bed with her.

She whispers, "Hey..."

Antonio is sleeping across the hall. Hell, maybe he's right there in bed with her.

I keep my voice low. "Shay, don't put your dad out. I know he'd want to help, but if you ask he'll for sure say yes and then he'll get all stressed when the work backs up. Just let me do it. I'm off. The little man and I are good. We're buds. If anything goes wrong, I'm sure he'll be okay with me."

Only now do I reflect on just how good things are between Nino and me. It's all so natural. I'm slightly worried he'll only want comfort from Shay if shit hits the fan at Longbrook, but my gut actually tells me he's mostly excited. People with as much curiosity as that boy don't have a lot of room for anxiety to creep in among the constant new discoveries.

Shay's eyes are big and beautiful in this lighting. But pretty as they are, they're still full of doubt, just like they always are nowadays.

"I don't know," she says, "just..."

"Just trust me, Shay." The words come out harder than I mean. But whatever it is holding her back is starting to piss me off. "Sorry. Long day."

"It's fine. It's been a long one for me, too." She sighs. "I do trust you, Logan."

My heart is lighter until the caveat comes.

"With Nino."

It's a consolation. And it does feel good. But it isn't what I really want. I want *her* to trust me, like she used to.

"Good. It's settled then. I'll see you Thursday night when I get back. It's going to be all good," I reassure her.

"Okay. You better get some sleep."

Good luck with that. Now that I've seen her face, and her braless cleavage spilling out between those spaghetti strap pajamas, I won't.

She teases. "You need the rest. Especially after getting your asses kicked."

"You watched the game, huh?"

"Logan..." She rolls her eyes. "Of course I watched the game."

"I did pretty well, though. Right?" Both goals were scored by me, even if we did lose.

Her cheeks round with that smile-no-smile thing she does. It's more of a glow. "You would have looked better winning. Don't forget why you're there. You're there to win. With Ashton. I believe in you."

Damn does that make my heart thunder.

"Night, Logan." And there it is, that Mona Lisa smile.

"Night."

I throw my phone down on the bed beside and strip off. I already showered leaving the changing rooms at our away game but now I need a cold one. Every fucking time I talk to Shay, my dick thickens. She can give me shit. Shoot me down. Tease me... I gobble it all up.

The waterfall is cold on my back. I suck in a breath, and my abs flex. My skin tightens everywhere, and opposite to all my intentions, my dick is red-hot and standing tall with thoughts of those spaghetti straps. I imagine myself peeling them down off her shoulder, sucking her luscious tit into my mouth, as much of it as I could because that woman is blessed.

I swirl my tongue around her nipple. Suck it, and she groans for me... Now in my grip, my dick swells. I pump, wishing I could remember exactly how she feels inside. Her walls tensing around my cock. Her pussy wet and dripping down my balls.

I pump harder, grip myself tightly with the freezing shower almost painful on my back. I can still see her in college. The way her back would arch. The first time I made her come and she moaned.

Fuck... I want her. I want to be inside her... back in bed with her, legs splayed across my hips, tits bouncing, pussy lips spread around my...

The release is powerful, and I have to brace myself when I spill onto the glass of the shower. Spurt after spurt explodes out of me.

Fucking nobody makes me feel this way.

Nobody.

I wash off my dick, give the glass a spray with the hand shower, and towel off, cock still full and heavy with some sort of swagger as if it actually had her.

That was reckless.

I head to bed and loosen the stupid, Army-tucked bedspread and crawl inside the smooth, cool envelope of white sheets. Only then do I release a breath I've been holding since I first decided to text her tonight.

She's at home right now, in bed. I want to be in bed with her, and that thought is more worrisome than the ones I had in the shower. The reason Shay broke up with me the first time hasn't changed one bit. Here I am, away in my hotel room. There she is, the same woman as sixteen years ago. And now she seems to have an all-new reason to not pursue this chemistry we still so clearly have.

She's never said it, but it doesn't take a genius to read into her.

Shay hates my reputation.

The stories, the sold photos, the attention it drew to me is what made me more wealthy than hockey alone ever could have made me. People wanted to see my face on bill-boards for underwear and perfume because I was the George Clooney of hockey. There's something intriguing about a forever bachelor. People imagine they know just who you are. To them, I could be a bad boy. I could be a risk-taker. I could be a challenge. Women love playboys because they're adventurous, have great sex, they're fun and will get you high.

These are all the reasons Reggie gave me after I was first papped near a famous model and associated with her in some junk magazines. The speculation over us having a relationship (I only just learned her name that night) got a huge amount of shares and buzz online, too. I was in a bad place then. More than a year on at least, and I was still convinced I'd never get over Shay. That was when Reggie said if I was going to be miserable I might as well profit from it. He said we could stage it all. He curated my new image and put a shiny veneer on my inner country boy.

At first, I was a fish out of water going on date after date, night after night with the new woman Reggie set me up with. It really wasn't me at all. In high school and early college I was completely aloof with women; Shay was my only serious girlfriend.

Every night off and between seasons especially, I was a busy boy. Sometimes Reggie would manage to make it easier and set me up with a model I was already shooting with for a campaign. Eventually, I went out on the town with some and brought some home for the night. Others turned into friends. Some I never spoke to ever again.

One day, it all seemed normal to only have these lightning-strike moments with women. I tried dating one of them for a few months. Reggie arranged a date with a friend of Ashton's ex-wife, so I tried harder that time to be into her. I thought it would have been nice to do couples things with Ashton, but seeing as his then wife was vile, and my then girlfriend cut from the same cloth, I'm impressed I lasted three months.

I might have gotten around a little but I never lied, never led anyone on, and therefore, never cheated. Still, and it pains me to admit it, maybe that's why Shay is keeping her distance.

Fuck if that thought isn't torture.

Chapter Twenty-Four

Logan

SIXTEEN YEARS AGO

I'VE BEEN on the road for the past couple of days with the team. Fuck do I miss Shay. As if the news of my signing didn't make things bad enough for us, yesterday, I received her enigmatic text that cast an eerie veil over me I can't break through.

> PASTELITO
>
> My dad isn't doing well. Is there any way you can give him a call? You always seem to make him smile. I'll ping his details over.

> Baby what's up? Should I be worried? Of course I'll find a minute. Can I call you, too after the game?

PASTELITO

It's better we talk in person.

When I called Luis in the few minutes I have without the team around, he didn't answer. I tried again later that night, again, no answer. My guts were already twisted with how the contract negotiations ended, and now, Luis isn't well? I care about the man, and he means the world to Shay.

To say I didn't play my best the second day is an understatement. Little did I know, losing a game would be the least of my troubles.

Though I wanted to race directly to Shay's dorm, before the text exchange, I'd already planned to pick up a present for her from the jewelry shop, so as soon as the bus lands at Golden Sierra, I rush to the Main Street and with a fancy red, waxed bag in my hand, race to Shay's dorm. I know something is wrong. Maybe this gift will cheer her up.

I bound up the stairs at Slichter Hall, my heart pounds with so many conflicting feelings. I missed Shay and am hungry for her touch. I'm worried sick that Luis didn't answer my calls. And today, I have to deliver the news that I'm not staying in state. I'm nearly sick with it bolting up the stairs, but when I push open Shay's door, a new shock replaces all the others.

241

Shay is here, and along with my girlfriend, I greet three brown cardboard moving boxes and a suitcase.

She stands abruptly from her desk chair, throws a crumpled tissue in the garbage can, and rushes to me, throwing her arms around my neck. She doesn't say anything, face buried. I wrap my arms around her torso; her rib cage stutters, and I know she's working hard not to stain my sweatshirt with tears.

I crush her into me tightly, wanting so badly to absorb her pain and take it away. "Shay..."

I hardly get her name out, my voice is weak seeing her like this.

She speaks into my chest, words muffled and nasal, the sound of a person who's been crying. "Logan..."

We embrace so long I start to wonder if I'm in a dream. It's surreal, my woman aching in my arms with these boxes all around. I don't know which way is up. What the hell is going on?

She peels her arms from around my neck and backs away a few steps. Her eyes are bloodshot, her lips swollen, and I shatter seeing her like this. She throws her hands into her back pockets, her signature stance, but this time, she's not sexy. It makes her look vulnerable with her heart on full display.

I put the small bag on the bed and take her hand, leading her to her roommate's bed. The edge sags underneath our weight.

"Shay... what's..." I can't even finish my sentence. The words stop somewhere underneath the enormous stone in my throat.

She's leaving college?

She starts, "I'm sorry this is a blindside but could I really have told you on the phone?"

"I'm not worried about me right now and the surprise, I'm worried about you and why you're doing this."

She shakes her head, and tears stream down her face. She's trying to be brave, but whatever it is, it stabs at her over and over again right in front of me.

Finally, she clears her throat. "I need to move home and be with Dad. He's..." She breathes as though she might hyperventilate. "He's... I think..." She shakes her head. "Fuck, I don't know how to say it..."

"It's me, Shay. Just say it. Any words will do..."

"He's thought about killing himself."

Her words steal my breath. Imagining Luis at home in emotional agony, seeing my beautiful woman's anguish... pain crushes my heart and turns my bones to dust. I'm overcome with helplessness. I'm speechless.

But somehow, I rub her back, manage to soothe her the best I can. "Talk to me... I'm here for you."

She breathes deeply and tries to center herself. "One of the ranch hands called me because Dad wasn't out, even though he was supposed to be. So I called him to see if he was sick. I called. And called. And called again, and he didn't pick up. Fuck, Logan, I was worried sick, pacing, thinking maybe he choked on something or... then finally he called me back. We had a talk, and he said he was just down. I said: *How down are you, Dad? You've weren't at work.* He said: *I just don't think I can do this anymore.*"

If Luis' words fracture my heart. I can only imagine how splintered her insides are. But it gets worse.

"I don't know, Logan, I know it sounds dramatic..."

I rub her hand. "You're not dramatic. You can talk to me straight."

She shakes her head hard. "I just thought he's been so depressed, and he wasn't at work, and he says he can't do

243

this anymore and avoided my calls, and my intuition just had me going to dark places..." She sucks back a sob that threatens to drown the space. "I thought about what Fiona told us, about what to say if someone says something like *that*..."

I remember that day in our grief counseling. It was heavy but taught us an important skill I hoped none of us would ever have to use.

"She told us to ask if they have a plan. So I asked if he ever thought about actually not living and how he'd make that happen. He said..." Tears flow down her cheeks. "Once or twice... But he could never do that to us kids..."

I grab her hand that's as clammy as my own. I can't believe she had to talk to Luis like this. It must have taken every ounce of strength to ask that question. Her soul erupts with a new kind of pain I've never experienced before myself, and I hate she's doing it before me. A harrowing fear fills her eyes. Is there a more gut-wrenching conversation than asking your dad if he still wants to live?

Just hearing Fiona talk about suicide that day in our session twisted my guts. In the mere hypothetical form I could hardly imagine myself being as strong as this situation demands of Shay.

She sobs before me, my tough woman breaking down into floods of tears. She crunches over, face in her palms, and pours out her soul. Her body stutters with every excruciating sob, and she breaks down right in front of me.

"Come here..." I gather her onto my lap and hold her, smooth her hair and kiss the top of her head, giving her space to unravel. I give her space to not be the strong one. I let her vulnerability and pain pour out of her within my secure arms, giving her refuge.

The boxes. I know what they mean now without her

saying, and they represent her agony even better than her words. She would never leave Luis alone no matter the cost to her.

Finally, she chokes on her tears a few last times. I place her back on the bed and reach over to her roommate's desk to grab a tissue and hand it to my girl. Shay is so far gone she doesn't even bother being ladylike blowing her nose, but it's still clogged when she speaks.

"I have to go back, Logan. I waited to talk about this in person, but you know this call happened yesterday. I only waited so you and I could... I texted him a thousand times today but... I have to be there for him. My brothers are gone, and they can't move back right now. Anyway, the plan is for us to all join them in California eventually. Going home is the right thing to do. Family first."

"I get you and support you a thousand percent," I say, thinking of my own mom and how she's turned to drinking since Dad died. "If Colt and Dash weren't around, I don't think I'd feel confident leaving Mom on her own. Even though I hate to see you give up your education, you can always come back to it."

She sighs. "Honestly, Logan, I don't even care about that. I never really did. I've never been that great at school, I barely scraped into this place. I only did college away because I knew I'd never live away from family as an adult so I thought I'd give it four years to satisfy curiosity, you know? Even if my mom hadn't died, I wouldn't ever move away from my parents permanently."

Now, it's my turn to lose my shit because we both have news. I consider holding on to it. I consider giving her one day as a breather, giving us both a breather, but then what?

For the first time in my life, my mind has turned to freezing as a stress response. My body is rigid; my lungs turn into iron. I'm absolutely frozen thinking of where this might go, where the next conversation might end up.

"Logan?" She explores my face with concern. "Are you mad at me for moving back?"

"God no, baby. No... I'd never be mad about that. That you're a wonderful daughter and care about your family is something I fucking adore about you."

Her gaze flicks back and forth quickly from one of my eyes to the other; she reads me. "Something is wrong."

I avert my gaze, but it only snags on the tiny fancy bag at the end of her bed. Fuck, I never could have expected things to go down like this.

"Please tell me, Logan...."

"I got signed to Boston."

She stares at me, eyes welling up with more heartbreak.

Her word is a mere whisper. "Congratulations."

Her lip trembles, and rivers of sadness streak her features again. I swipe my thumb along the beautiful apple of her cheek to dry one, but another one comes in its stead. She bites her lip, looks to the ceiling for strength, but I don't know if she wants it for herself or for me.

My voice is thin. "I'm sorry, *pastelito*. I wanted the Scorpions so bad..."

"I know. Me, too."

She sniffles in until she has her tears under control again, but I swear to God she only passed them over to me. I'm choked up and ready to burst, and my stomach is sour with anticipation of what's to come.

And then, she says what neither of us has dared in any of these conversations, not ever since our once-in-a-lifetime love affair started.

"I guess this is it."

At the sound of the end, I come completely unhinged. "No, Shay. Don't say that."

"We've both known... we've been ignoring the obvious for too long..."

"Shay, I'll wait for you."

"You'll wait for me for ten years? Maybe more if you keep your health. Logan, we were foolish. Even if you were signed by the Scorpions, what were the chances of you staying on that team...?"

"I would have made myself indispensable."

"Logan..."

"I would have *begged* to stay if that's what it came to..." I'm unraveling.

And, as always, she anchors me by taking my hand in hers. "You need to live your best life."

"My best life is with you..."

"Logan." She hangs her head. A teardrop falls on her lap before she faces me again, eyes misted over. "You're the right person for me, I know that in my soul." She clutches her shirt right over that gorgeous heart of hers. "You are right for me, in that, there is zero doubt. But it's the wrong time...one of us has to say what we both know. You have a long career ahead of you with more uncertainty than we've wanted to accept. You'll be moved around, hell, maybe even out of the States..."

I know she's right, we've both avoided that detail. Even if I got signed to the Scorpions, the NHL is a volatile place. Trading is common, especially for rookies.

"Logan, I dreamed up all sorts of scenarios, trust me. I thought of all different what-ifs that might make this work. But if leaving my dad was hard before, it's impossible now. I won't leave him. It's not how we do it. Even my brothers have a plan to one day reunite us. Families aren't meant to be apart."

I just don't understand how after all we are and all we've been through together, this is it. "You're breaking up with me?"

"No." She puts her tiny hands gently to my cheeks. "We *both* know this is what has to happen."

I imagined a scenario where I flew back every time I could to see Shay and flew her to see me. I imagined us having fun with it for some time in our twenties and eventually, maybe when I was more established, I could even take less pay and beg for a spot in Santa Fe. Not that I even knew if it would work. It was wishful thinking.

Shay isn't some happy-go-lucky new adult with traveling the country on her mind. She's a young woman whose mother just died and her dad is alone at home. I know that. I've always known that. Even if Shay was in a different spot emotionally, I know her culture. Hell, I respect it so much I want to be a part of it.

But I'm not. And maybe I'll never be, because the situation of me being in any new city at any given time is, my health willing, a very long era indeed.

Breaking up isn't my choice, but it's selfish as hell to pin this on her. I refuse to let her feel guilty for sticking to her morals. I gather my ass up off the floor... for her, I need to set her free, too.

My head tips in a somber nod because I can't bring myself to actually say yes. But the little bag I brought along catches my eye again, and that's when the sting in the bridge of my nose shoots to my eyeballs and they glass over. I dig my fingers into my sockets to stop myself from bursting and making this worse than it is.

Despite my best efforts to be strong, my voice cracks. "What happens now?"

"I don't know. I guess it's like grief. It's not about getting over us. It's about learning to live without us." She blinks hard over glistening eyes. "I love you, Logan."

"I love you so much, *pastelito*."

Reluctantly, so, so very carefully, I place her hand back down on her lap and stand. My feet weigh a thousand pounds, and my body is made of rock. It takes all my energy to make my way to the door, and to pick up that little bag that held the promise I was never able to make.

Chapter Twenty-Five

Shay

I AM STRESSED the hell out because the "just in cake" is an absolute nightmare.

The couple requested the design be wedding vibes in Santorini. It was where they had their first vacation together and where he proposed. I thought it was both a great idea and an easy task. My sketch was gorgeous. I designed a four-tiered cake. My plan is to paint over a hundred Greek tiles and plaster them to the sides of the cake to represent the whimsical Mediterranean town. Fuchsia flowers will crawl up the sides and drop over the top.

On the surface, it seemed like a relatively easy task. Santorini is predominately white, and though my plan has fifty bougainvillea flowers in addition to the tiles, I am adept at making flowers now. What I didn't plan on was just how long it would take to paint the patterned tiles.

So now, as I wipe the fallen strands of hair off my forehead, even my ponytail feels like giving up. But finally I have a system. I have my white frostings and fondants, edible paint base over on the island. In front of me on the kitchen table are several pots of edible blue paint, each a subtle shade different from the next to give depth and texture to the design.

When I'm sick of painting, I mold a flower. Flower, tile. Flower, tile. I've been doing this for hours, and when I glance at the clock and do the math, based on my output for the last hour, I realize now this design is a time management nightmare.

Each tile is taking too long to paint, but it's too late to rethink it. I'm not going to be done until two a.m. or three a.m. at this rate and then I need to drive out first thing in the morning?

Quit complaining, Shay. Buck up. This is a twenty-five thousand dollar cake. It's a real stepping stone into the luxury cake business.

I nearly wet myself when the couple told me their budget. Who are these people with money like that? Friends of Logan's, that's who.

It's ungrateful to focus on the knot in my neck and the way my fingers cramp around the paintbrush. I'm fortunate to have a deal like this so early in my Shino Cakes days. But it isn't only the work that's causing my tension headache. Tomorrow, my little boy goes off to big kid school, and I can't even spend tonight with him because I have to drive this cake to Los Angeles.

To top that off, there was no use Nino being here

tonight when I can barely look up from the kitchen table, so he's at my dad's. My stomach entangles with thousands of competing thoughts, knots to match the ones in my neck.

Just then, I hear the beeping of the front door keypad, seconds later, the door closing. Logan's home.

"Hey, hey..." he says, coming into the kitchen. "Wow. A lot going on here... for tomorrow?"

"Yes," I say, crunched over my current pattern. I don't glance up, hoping I can stay focused now that my biggest distraction is here. I barely think about anything apart from my son and Logan these days.

He wanders over to the kitchen area, his footsteps casual and laid-back, which is the total opposite of how I'm feeling right now. For some reason, it riles me up that he's all relaxed.

It doesn't make sense to be annoyed with Logan at all. But on top of all the work I have to do, I'm low on sleep anyway. Our call last night had me tossing and turning until the moon that filters in through the crack in the curtains was replaced by the sun.

I adored the way he was last night. He's giving me way too many glimpses of the man I convinced myself no longer existed. That, coupled with still smelling his cologne on his pillow right next to me, got me hot and bothered. I should have just rubbed one off, released it all, but I refused to fantasize about him *again* with my fingers under the covers. But now, I'm tense. Sexually tense. *And* work tense. *And* mom tense, so to say I'm tightly wound is an understatement.

Logan comes over next to me at the table, close enough to me to smell his scent of the day—*fuck-me musk and cedarwood.*

"Wow." He's genuinely impressed. "You really went for it. Are all these squares going to be tiles?"

"Mm-hm." *Go away and take your ravage-me-now smell with you.* If I don't make eye contact he'll eventually get bored of asking me questions I don't have time to answer.

He saunters back behind the island, clanks around in a cupboard for a glass, then goes to the fridge to use the water dispenser. The fridge buzzes more loudly than usual, and water splashes like a monsoon behind me in the cup.

I sigh out a breath to relax and remind myself Logan has been nothing but helpful. He helped get me this job. He's taking Nino to school tomorrow. But it seems his help is something of a Trojan horse. It comes with a whole lot of consequences, namely me wanting to throw myself into his arms as haphazardly as I did back in college, and it really irritates me. I grit my teeth and continue to will him out of this room.

Instead, he sheds his jacket onto the back of the chair right next to me. I can't help but dart my eyes over to where he's slung it. He's now towering over me, inspecting my work, his bulging biceps and forearms with veins of a virile beast peeking out of the short sleeves of his black tee. Just under that fabric is that damn tattoo.

I glance up. As if he couldn't get any hotter, he has on a backward baseball cap.

It's nature's most cruel joke. Why do men get to maintain their looks for years and years and not women? I'm about the same age as him, but with a diminishing metabolism (which hardly worked before), and popping out a baby, has left my body looking like it's been in the trenches. Logan looks, well, maybe even better. He's more man than he was before but with the same coy, boyish dimple that makes women swoon over country boys.

I drop my gaze back to the work at hand but can't seem to figure out where I left off.

His meddling continues. "So what's the inspiration for the cake?"

I clench my jaw, again, and don't glance up. "Santorini."

"Wow. It's going to be insane when you're done."

"*If* I get done, Logan." *Take the hint.*

I can't concentrate with him this close; his energy pours down on me, landing over me like a cloak of lust.

I clear my throat loudly, but he refuses to pick up on my cues and leans on his hand right up next to me. Even his fingernails are sexy.

"Why did Hughes want this cake?" he asks breezily.

"They got engaged in Greece."

"Ah."

He lingers. *Please don't sit.*

He sits next to me with legs wide, his knee hitting my thigh under the table with a delightful sensitive pressure.

"Where's Nino?"

My heart drops all over again hearing my boy's name. Missing his first day at Longbrook is gut-wrenching. I want to be there for the memory. I want to be there if he struggles. Selfishness claws at my insides, but I can't do anything to fight it off. I need a career to help my little family, but my career at the same time takes me away from it. A woman's paradox. Why the hell don't men feel this way?

I need to give Logan a shove or I'll be absolutely screwed for tomorrow, and this means too much to me and Antonio to be polite any longer. I stand, the chair scraping the floor and nearly falling over.

I can't be next to Logan like this. I don't know why I got up, I need to be at the table, but I'm edgy now. My skin is on fire with Logan in here, and I'm determined to keep a wedge between us.

I lean my back against the island and grip the cool marble. Words race from my mouth at a hundred miles an hour. "He's at my dad's. I needed time to sort out this cake which, to be honest, I'm not sure I can even get done. I'm stressed as hell right now and have a million and one things on my mind, so if you *puh-leeease*, get what you need from the kitchen and find somewhere else to be."

He stands and comes near again. "Why don't you let me help?"

"Help?" My energy takes a turn. Or maybe the dam just broke because my voice is husky and the question comes out more like an accusation.

He pauses to read me. There's a beat of silence long enough to tell me he gets my drift. I'm not the only one who feels the storm coming.

He reiterates his offer, but this time, it's not so friendly, there's a sarcasm in his words. "Yeah. Help. As in assistance..."

"I know what *help* means, Logan." I cross my arms.

Festering, confused feelings bubble inside me. Not being at Nino's school tomorrow. Wanting to have Logan and push him away at the same time. How much I like being around Logan even though I know it's just killing me softly... I burst at the seams with uncertainty about what kind of mess I've gotten myself into.

The words come too easily because anger is the perfect protection. "I don't want your help. Your help is what got me all stressed out in the first place."

My statement is so unfair; my heart crinkles as soon as I say it, but I can't take it back. I have to put my guard back up.

He saunters brazenly toward me, stopping his toes at the tips of mine. "Me? All this is *my* fault, is it?" A rough laugh escapes his lips. "Yeah. Go ahead and blame this *all* on me. I know you do. Only problem is I don't know why."

"What's that supposed to mean?"

He steps his feet on either side of mine, anchors his hands on the countertop with his hands aligning along mine. Heat rises between us, and his voice is all gravel.

"You know *exactly* what it means." His gaze darkens. "Why are you pushing me away, Shay?"

Oh God. I knew we wouldn't last forever without talking about the past. It's not Logan's style to beat around the bush. He tolerated my barbed comments and took them on the chin. Unfortunately, they did nothing to deter that steely, hungry look in his eyes when our gazes lock, and now, I'm deeper than I ever thought I'd be. Desire has built, and it's time to knock it down.

Still, I have this cake to do, and the truth is too ugly and complicated for a night like this.

"Let's just forget it." My words are testy.

He leans in closer. "Let's not."

I grit my teeth. "Now's not the time."

"Well, I think it is."

"Why can't you just forget it, Logan?" I raise my voice.

He raises his more and comes undone. "Because I *can't* forget it, Shay!"

My breath hitches.

"I tried to let it go and I can't forget it, all right? It's time to spell it out because this push-pull shit is done. We hash it out now. I've always cared about you..."

"Oh yeah, I've seen what heartbreak looks like on you. You wear it like a devil in an Armani suit," I hiss.

"Oh, do I?" He lowers his face inches from mine, his hot

breath tumbles over my mouth. "It's a thousand times better than indifference, Shay, which is what you're giving me now."

"Indifference?" I almost let myself succumb to the truth he thinks he wants to hear but sure as hell doesn't. If only he knew how many times I thought about him. How I chastise myself every time I think about who he once was, how I worship the myth of a guy that doesn't even exist.

I choke up slightly, part in anger, part because allowing that deep, hidden sadness to escape burns my lungs. "Yeah, indifference is *so* much worse than watching the love of your life escort a new woman on his arm every night. If you're waiting for me to approve of the man you've become, don't hold your breath, because I promise, you'll pass out."

"Goddamn it, Shay..." He takes off his hat and throws it on a nearby counter. His sexy brown locks fall down over his forehead, drawn in with frustration. Then, he cages me in again, staring at me more seriously than ever. "It was just an act."

Raw emotion rises from inside us both.

"It was PR." He places his foot between my legs and presses into me. His muscular thigh brushes against the apex of my thighs.

The heat of his body is hypnotic. My body melts. Relents. My nipples peak. Why is he this close? His forearms flex as he holds on to the counter on either side of me. He's emotional and bracing himself like a man who's on the edge. But I'm on the edge, too, totally derailed by my own confession... and his.

I swallow thickly. "PR, huh? What happened to your integrity?"

He leans over me, and I have to arch my back so our

chests don't collide. "I lost it somewhere in the time I was waiting to get over you."

Angry tears burn at the backs of my eyes. "You didn't wait long."

"I fucking did." His large hand wraps around my rib cage. "I couldn't eat. I couldn't sleep. I wondered how on earth I'd even keep on playing, and Shay? I'm not even afraid to admit it. I cried into my pillow some nights. Without you, I went back to being a man on the run, only this time it was like I chased absolutely nothing."

I suck in a sharp breath but don't pull away, allowing the distance to close between us. His hand slides up my torso, and he grazes my pebbled nipple with his thumb. He stares down at me with wild amber eyes; near enough for me to taste his cologne.

"I did the best I could with what I had."

I devour his vulnerability.

"And now, you push me away..."

His touch is so familiar. His hands on my body make me forget for just a moment, but somewhere inside, rumination from so many years returns and reminds me why we can't be. "I missed that man for so many years, Logan. I blame you for taking him away from me."

He swipes his thumb tenderly along my bottom lip, igniting every cell of my being. "I'm still here." He drops his lips to mine. "And I never got over you."

He slips his hand up over my breast and pulls my dress off my shoulder. My pulse rages underneath my panties, and a rush of heat has me heavy in all the wrong places.

I swallow hard, tell myself to stop this even though I want his hands all over me exactly as they are. And more than that, I never want him to stop looking at me the way he does right now. Like he did when he told me he loved me.

I mutter, quietly, almost as if I don't want him to hear, "What are you doing?"

"I'm touching my wife."

He makes circles with his fingertips over the bare sensitive skin. It feels so good that it even feels right. He grinds his leg between mine, and the much-needed touch has me letting out an audible breath. My head falls back, as if allowing him access to more. My hips rock against him, my body is so immediately hot for this man, but I still have a few more words of resistance.

He lowers his mouth toward my neck, and I ease away from it; like a dance I float back, arching away from his lips until my shoulders hit the cold surface. I'm breathless. "I can't do this..."

But when I gaze into his electric brown eyes my heart hammers. I don't mean a damn word I said.

In an instant, I take the sides of his face in my hands and crush my lips against his. In no time at all, I part my lips and let him sink his minty tongue inside my mouth. Our tongues twirl, searching the moment and at the same time reclaiming the past.

I moan softly into his mouth. "Logan..."

"Fuck, Shay... I fucking need you..."

Haste possesses our mouths, our hands, our fingers as the tension splits like an atom. We burst with wanting, yearning; pent-up desire consumes our thoughts, obliterates our self-control.

He ravages my neck while I pant in his ear and somehow hoists me up onto the island until I'm lying down fully, his tall frame bent over me, devouring my skin, kneading my breast with his greedy palm.

His kiss sinks into not only my mouth but my soul. Just like when he kissed me all those years ago, his lips make me feel wanted. Desired for everything I am. Damn, this man knows exactly what a kiss is about.

But in this present-past collision, somewhere inside, a voice warns me... I'm not that college girl anymore. I'm a mom and a brand-new entrepreneur. I don't need the only man I truly loved, especially who he's become, sauntering back into my life and under the bedsheets... Is *my* Logan really still here?

His tongue dives in my mouth, owning me. My questions are drowned out by my panting and the dull, thrumming sound of my pulse in my ears. He holds himself up but presses the hard bulge in his pants against me, and it does nothing for my resolve to pull away. My hips start to ache and call out for relief.

As if reading my mind, he slides his hands down and massages his thumbs deep and hard into the crease of my hip bones, following the gorge right down, and the pressure causes an absolute ache for his touch between my legs.

"Fuck Shay, your body makes me weak..." he growls.

Still kissing him with manic need, I hoist my leg around him, securing him against me, willing him to rub harder, urging some sweet relief for the ache I've had there since last night, seeing his soulful eyes in the dim light of the hotel room.

Now he's here. He's taking me and I'm taking him. Electricity sparks in the air all around us. When he swipes his shirt overhead, and that dewy skin of his glows in the lights of the kitchen. My senses are numb.

He inches his hand up my thigh, under the flowing fabric of my loose dress, continuing up the back, then unclasps my bra, and next thing I know, my entire dress is on the floor. He stands to unbutton his pants, still staring at me completely fearless, as if I'm the last woman in the world and he's hellbent on taking me.

When I bring my hand back down on the island to brace myself, it lands in one of my bowls of frosting.

I try to keep my sticky hand off him, but when his teeth take my nipple, I gasp and grab his shoulder involuntarily. He must feel the smear of whipped sugar because it stills him. He raises his eyes from my chest like a starving animal and then looks at his shoulder.

He swipes a finger where there's a dab of frosting, licks it, then raises his finger to my mouth, putting it inside. "Everything about you is delicious, *pastelito.*"

He keeps his finger inside my mouth. "Suck."

I do as I'm told, high on momentum. I'd suck anything he told me right now. When I've cleaned him clear of all sweetness, he pulls his finger out and traces my lips.

"You're so fucking beautiful..."

I should stop now. Just because Logan's women were PR stunts doesn't mean he didn't do it. I told myself not to get with men like Logan Hunter. But his words...

I'm still here.

Is he really still here? Is the man I hoped to follow for the rest of my life still in there?

I survived our demise by a thread and stitched myself together with my distaste of who he'd become. But now, he just told me that man wasn't even real?

He waited for me?

He slows himself right down, nibbles my earlobe; perhaps my questions are tangible.

"Shay?" His voice is low. "Do you want this?"

"I..."

If any hesitation is going through Logan's mind, it's not there in his mischievous, ravenous gaze.

In one provocative, filthy dip, Logan plunges two fingers into my bowl of white frosting. His gaze is demanding, unwavering as he brings his fingers to the top of my neck and slowly draws a thick line of icing from the column of my throat, down my heaving sternum and over my tender, soft belly, stopping only at the seam of my panties.

His sticky hand finds my neck again, his thumb smooths the frosting on my throat. His touch is a firm, controlling sensation that brings every ounce of blood to the surface of my skin. He owns me.

But he doesn't know that yet.

He wraps his hand gently around my throat. "I'm going to start here..." His thumb presses down possessively at the top of my neck.

I swallow; his hold makes it a little harder, but it's turning me on, taking me to a point of no return. My lips part impatiently, my core throbs, and I don't know if this is truth or dare, or my opportunity to run from this mess I'm in.

"...If I get to the end of the trail..."

He traces his gaze down the silky white path straight to the seam of my panties, and I swear the cotton sets alight.

"I win."

A strangled whimper leaves my lips. "Win what?"

"You."

Before his lips lower to my body, we share one last gaze. In it, I see that flicker of vulnerability. He doesn't trust me either. He has no idea where my head is at.

After all, back then, I know we both took a bullet, but it's me who pulled the trigger.

"You have about sixty seconds to call it quits."

Chapter Twenty-Six

Logan

HER SKIN BUZZES, her nipples stand tall, but it's part fear, part desire. I know Shay better than she thinks I do. She let me take her clothes off, slide my tongue inside her mouth and even unbutton my pants. Though I've kept my cock covered, it pushes out the top indecently. I'm so hard my heart beats in my shaft. And this goddess is spread out like a goddamn buffet.

It was tempting to keep pleasing her, to make her feel good and see if she stops me. I could have kept touching her exactly how I know she likes it, and likely, neither of us would have stopped this momentum.

I've wanted to be buried in Shay again since I woke up

in Vegas. And the way her body responds right now, the way she's all edgy and annoyed with me all the time, tells me she's not any less sexually tense being around me than I am around her.

At any point, she could stop me, but if we keep going, if I dive inside her and feel her pussy wrapped warm around me, I can't let myself wonder for weeks to come if this was some lapse in judgment for her. If this is some one-off mistake. If this is just relenting to physical attraction which is still so overwhelming, the mere sight of her makes me weep. No, the wonder would destroy me, and I'm certain there would be no coming back from it.

I'd be a shell of a man.

This is far from an accident for me. It's reckless, perhaps, but one hundred percent deliberate. I need her to know what I'm asking when I pull down her panties and lap her up like the starving man I've been.

I'm asking to be chosen.

Her onyx eyes are wide, her rosy lips parted, her voluptuous breasts heave. This is a big deal for her as it is for me. It could be the end of the potential friendship we've begun. It could be the end of *me* forever. This woman has the power to be my complete undoing. If I hardly lived through the aftermath of our college breakup, how will I survive her now in all she's become?

I gaze at her one last time, and it's painful to see the hesitation in her eyes. I hate that my playboy charade has filled her with disgust, and if she lets me, I'll tear down that idol one brick at a time. I wish I could have her certainty, her trust... I wish she'd say yes before I even start down her sweet skin. But that's not Shay. It's never been her way. She'd never come to me first, but that worked between us because God knows I love the chase.

Our gaze connects almost tangibly. Her eyes flutter shut. I soak in her beauty again, remarking on how time has changed her for the better, something I couldn't have imagined possible. Her tummy is soft and womanly, covered with signs of her making a miracle inside it. I can't help myself from tracing her marks lovingly before lowering myself over her. This woman is magic.

Licking the column of Shay's throat and taking in the sugar rush along with her silky skin is enough to do a man in, even without the racing nerves of her stopping me at any given point. Shay will say no if she wants to, and I'm giving her plenty of time to reconsider what I'm about to do to her.

Her jaw clenches, and I just know it, inside that gorgeous head of hers is a clusterfuck as big as mine, but I dare myself onward, down between her breasts. I lick off the frosting, slowly, until she's clean in every spot, and ravaging her tawny skin beneath becomes a new temptation. I make slow progress, appreciating every single time she allows my tongue to trace down with my intentions.

When I reach her breasts, her dusky nipples are peaked, and I rub my cock into her thigh at the sight. It's painful, my dick is stretched to the limit, ready to burst right through my goddamn boxers, but still, I won't hurry. I allow every sensation to become a memory—the feel of her full breast in my hand, the way her nipple tightens ever harder when I bite it between my teeth. All of it. They're all new memories etched in my mind forever, because I know all too well I might need them.

I suck her nipple along with a generous portion of flesh into my mouth and devour her, and she mewls. She raises and circles her hips against my abdomen, writhing with pleasure. Fingernails scratch trails in my back...

It takes all my strength not to rip her soaked panties off

and tell her how it's going to be, not to drop my face between her legs and breathe in that womanly musk only found between her legs... cotton candy and lust.

My words roll heavy over her skin. "You smell like you want me... so wet for me..."

Her body says she's mine, but I need the rest. I need her mind. Her soul... I need that fucking *yes* to leave her panting lips and to know, for absolute certain, she chooses this.

I am two more licks from the waist of her panties.

Lick.

This woman is everything.

Lick.

I have to have her.

Lick.

I kiss her core through her moist panties. She's swollen under the fabric, her pussy lips are puffy. Just when I think I've made it, she drops my name like a bomb.

"Logan?" Her voice is husky.

"Mmm," I hum against her panties, rubbing the tip of my nose along the subtle crease. My dick fills painfully being so close to her. I sink my fingers into the flesh of her thighs, bracing myself for her answer.

My lungs are two boulders in my chest. All my optimism evaporates. Will she say we can't? Will she stop me from diving headfirst into us all over again?

She squirms her core, writhes it around my nose, deliberately making contact.

"Logan, I..."

Fuck Shay. Don't stop this. Don't stop us.

She reaches down and combs her fingers through my hair. "I..."

The buzz of uncertainty kills me... and then her answer comes.

"Yes."

With that, I slide my fingers under that goddamn cotton and rip them off. The flimsy fabric gives way, and my woman jerks with surprise, no doubt her hips burning.

I shove my pants and boxer briefs down in one go, kicking them quickly off from around my feet. I yank her bare body down to the edge of the counter. Her legs are spread to either side of my hips, and with her thighs unfolded, her pussy lips whisper open like a fucking invitation. I smooth my thumbs along her soft, swollen lips; they're silky, moist. The pink fucking calls my name.

And a part of me still can't believe this.

"Say yes again, Shay."

I glide two fingers up and down her slit, and they're covered in her wetness. I slip them into her dripping pussy.

Her back arches, and her ass clenches underneath her. She opens her eyes, and there she is. My girl. She bites her lip and pushes against my palm for more. "Yes."

My fingers slip in and out, thrusting possessively. Long gone is my patience. Hers is nowhere to be found either as she presses her hand against mine, urging my fingers in faster, deeper. Her head moves wildly from side to side, and her eyebrows furrow above tightly clenched eyes.

I drop to my knees and spread her wide, pulling her pussy lips open so I can admire every bit of it. I plunge my fingers back inside and bury my face in her warmth, tongue-fuck her folds, flatten my tongue and drag it from her entrance all the way up to her nub and lap up the taste of her. Fuck, she makes me hungry. Insane with lust. I'm savage. The floor is hard on my knees but I'd fucking bleed to stay down here all night.

I lick and suck, working my fingers in and out, circling her nub and, dirtier than ever, she reaches down and laces her fingers through my hair, pulls my head deeper toward her, and I feast on what she gives me. Her nails dig into my shoulder.

"You like that? Say it, baby."

"Mmmm..." is all she can manage, but it's enough to spur me on.

Patience is for another day. I've waited fucking long enough. I remember just how she likes it, flat tongue and then a hard suck on her tall, hard clit.

"Ah..." Her walls clench around my fingers, and her pussy bursts with the hot energy of her release.

I keep a steady rhythm. Her body undulates like a wave, and her hips force into me, asking my fingers to fuck her deeper.

I maintain contact with her throbbing clit. Her release pulses on my tongue, and I keep it going for as long as I can until she grasps a tuft of my hair.

"I need you inside me."

Fuck... a condom...

She pants. "I have an IUD. So just... are you clean?"

"I'm clean."

"Fucking take me, Logan."

Her desperation for me almost does me in then and there. The skin of my cock is stretched so thin I think it's going to break until the wetness of her soaked, warm pussy soothes its surface like a balm. Inch by inch I sink into her, watching her gorgeous pussy take me. I bite my lip to stop myself careening forward and pounding into her to the hilt.

I stare at the spot where she's stretched around my girth, enjoying my dick sliding in and out of her pink folds. "Fuck, Shay, you were made for me."

Her dainty hands knead her breasts. She licks her lips and rolls her nipples. I think I might explode on the spot. It makes me drive in harder; I'm struggling to hold back with the sight of her curves before me. I spread her pussy lips wider and drop my thumb to her clit, circling while plunging into her.

"Mmmm..." she whimpers and lets her head fall to the side, eyes pinched shut.

I need more contact. I want every inch of her skin on mine. I yank her hand up to sit, secure my arms around her and pull her in tightly. My mouth crashes against hers, our tongues thrash. I gobble up every tiny mewl and groan she releases in my mouth.

She secures her strong arms around me, wriggles her ass closer to the edge, allowing me deeper access. It's like I have a thousand hands and I'm grabbing her everywhere. I clutch her ass hard, steadying her, giving her what she's asked for and driving to the end of her, bottoming out with each thrust.

Her mouth disconnects from mine, and she lets out a scream. "Yes..."

"Is this what you wanted? You want it harder?" I growl.

"Yes," she breathes.

Ecstasy rises inside me like a wild roar waiting to release. I'm filled to the brim, plunging deep inside, riding her bare with no abandon. I need to be deeper, I'm insatiable now that I have her.

I slide her off the edge of the counter, and she braces herself with her hands behind her. I drive into her, my hips making contact with the cradle of her thighs. Her tits bounce, and tendrils of hair fall over her forehead with my every thrust. There's a lusty sheen of perspiration right over her heart.

"Come on my cock, Shay."

"Logan..." She unravels.

I drive in hard until my balls tighten and my ass clenches, trying to last longer, but I can't hold back the ecstasy. I spill myself inside her, a surge so powerful it's blinding. I'm fucking seeing stars.

When my dick finally stops pulsing, I place her curvy ass back down on the counter.

Eventually, her breathing calms, and she opens her eyes. She blows a piece of her fallen hair off her forehead. "Wow."

"That's just what a man wants to hear."

She laughs from her chest. Her eyes are wide. None of the same questions that were there before we started this are there. But I can't quite read her either.

But that doesn't matter.

She said yes.

I slip my slick dick out of her, kiss her warm, balmy forehead, her nose, her soft, swollen lips. I find my shirt to wipe us both off.

I grab her dress on the floor and shake it to straighten it out the best I can and I hand it to her. "We have work to do, Mendez."

"We?" She slides her dress over her head.

"Always we. I told you I got you."

She rewards me with rosy cheeks rounding, her eyes softening. "You're good with a paintbrush?"

"I'm shockingly talented at everything," I tease.

She searches the ceiling for that person up there who always agrees I'm cocky. She comes back to me.

"I can't have my wife doing a road trip without sleeping tonight. I'll be worried sick about you," I insist.

She catches her smile between thinned lips. "Fine, you can help."

"So you trust me?" I press.

She smirks. "I said you can help."

We spend the next few hours with our heads down, me forcing myself to concentrate and not fuck up her tiles. It takes more energy to not touch her than it does to keep painting after what has already been a long day of work and travel.

But it pays off when she gazes with hands on her hips, satisfied with the hundreds of pieces that will make up her edible work of art. Her genius astounds me, and my mind wanders to what she'd create for *our* wedding cake.

It's just turned one in the morning. We walk down the hallway, her in her dress and no bra, me in my boxer briefs, and it hits me. Last night, all I wanted was to be in bed with her. And now, I'll get what I wanted. *Everything* I've ever wanted.

After a chase scene with the cat, which Shay couldn't seem to keep out of the room until she placed him in Nino's teepee, we shed our clothes and climb into bed naked.

She needs sleep and I know it, but our hands still find each other. Her leg hugs over mine; the length of her body and every inch of her silky skin hugs me until she falls asleep breathing calm waves of breath over my cheek. I'm in heaven.

It's rare people are given an opportunity like this, one to turn around their biggest regret.

Shay is mine once again. And I'm never going to let her go.

Chapter Twenty-Seven

Shay

I WAKE UP WITH A SECURE, strong manly body spooning me from behind.

I said yes. What does that even mean? Did I say yes to sex? Or something else? I don't even know, but uncertainty doesn't stop the sense of warmth and calm that consumes me. Logan breathes deeply and soundly, spooning me from behind, and I don't want to stir him, I know he's always suffered from insomnia and it's beautiful to hear him rest.

But the clock on the side of the bed blares it's five thirty-eight, so it will go off in seven minutes anyway. I need to shower, pack the cakes, and then Nino will be back at seven so I can kiss him before I leave.

I need a shower first but I don't want one. I love the way Logan and I smell together. I'm sure if anyone else came in here, they'd just smell dirty sex, but I smell something different. A second chance.

Still, there's no way I could withstand the scent of Logan on me and concentrate on the road for nearly twelve hours all the way to LA.

I spin myself around to kiss him good morning but I'm not greeted by his handsome face. Cayenne lies on Logan like his head is the most comfy bed he's ever had.

"Oh my God..." I try not to laugh.

Logan's voice is muffled. "He's only been here the last hour."

"Why don't you shoo him off?"

"I'm trying to make friends."

I sit up and pull my cat upward off Logan's face, then place him on the other side of the bed next to me. Cayenne paces up and down and gives Logan the evil eye.

We both stare at the cat.

"I'm sorry to say, Lo, I'm not sure your olive branch worked."

"It's not a good sign, is it?" He scoops me into his arms, laying my head on his chest. "Your cake is amazing. They're going to be happy with it for sure."

"Yeah." I'm not thinking of my cake. Still, I say, "I hope so."

"I *know* so."

"Mmm."

As Nino's special day approaches, the cake and even Logan fade subtly in the background of my mind. My thoughts are on campus at Longbrook where I envision my son getting lost on one of the many trails. I know they said he'd have peers helping and a dedicated mentor, but it was

273

so hard to leave him at the school gates in my own home town, in a school full of children whose parents I know and who know me. Everyone looks out for one another, for better or worse, here in the Canyon. But Longbrook...

Logan smooths hair behind my ear. "Talk to me."

"This is nothing talking will solve."

"Nino?"

The sound of my little boy's name draws a whimper up my throat and a sting to the bridge of my nose. "Yeah," I wheeze. I try to hold it back but I can't.

Reality strikes hard and hot and drips out of my eyeballs in wet trickles of guilt. They splat on Logan's chest. I don't usually cry in front of other people. I try not to. But I'm emotional from last night and also sleep-deprived. There's no time to take myself off to a corner and let it out in private, so here we are.

Feeling the wetness, he pulls me up to look at him.

"Hey." Logan swipes a tear off my cheek. "You can talk about it with me."

I scrunch my face, annoyed with myself for not holding it together, but I just can't. "I want to have a successful business but not at the expense of my son. I'm sorry. It's just... I feel like such a bad mom not being there for him today."

I expect Logan to tell me not to feel that way. So many other times I felt guilty about something or other, my dad would say not to let myself feel that way. As always, men just can't understand.

Logan nods reassuringly and refrains, giving me space to work it out.

"I just feel so guilty and I can't get over it. I never want Nino to feel alone. Never. I don't know why I feel this way."

"Do you think I won't be able to support Antonio today as well as you can?"

My weak laugh is nasal through the snot of sadness. "I actually think Nino might like you more than he does me now."

He laughs lightly. "I'll never let you two down."

"It's about me, not you."

He hugs me close. "Mmm."

His energy is pensive as he holds me, and my sadness drains away slightly in the security of his embrace, but my guilt seems here to stay.

"Do you remember when we went to smash the patriarchy?"

I breathe deeply, and my voice sounds more like my own again. "Yeah."

"Women want equal pay. Equal rights. Equal representation in government. But I've watched my friends and teammates get married and have kids, and every time I watch the woman give in to the goddamn patriarchy when those babies come."

"What do you mean? That's not happened to me," I say, defensive. "I've done the last five and a bit years without a man at all."

"Yeah, but you still succumb to an ideology of what it means to be a good mom, and that keeps you in your place. Every mom I ever talked to seems to think that being a good one means always having a smooth running house, doing bake sales, throwing birthday parties. You have to always be giving and present. Motherhood must surpass all other identities or else you're a shit one. The patriarchy says the more time you spend with your child, the better mom you are. It's unrealistic and it keeps women down as much as the rest of the stuff we marched for."

"Yeah but..." He makes sense and at the same time... "I *want* to spend time with my son."

He kisses the back of my hand. "Listen, you don't need to tell me twice how impossible it is to have enough time with someone you love."

Love.

He kisses me again and plays with my fingers. "But quality over quantity. And sometimes we have to show, not tell. You started Shino Cakes because you want to show Nino how to live a full life. Staying here and telling him with your words to go off and live a full life will never teach him a lesson as much as showing him with your actions."

"I know but..."

He interrupts me. "Smash the patriarchy, Shay. Start by destroying the foundation that's still inside you. You are warm, sensitive, responsive, and even stayed married to this lunatic to give your son what he wants. How much more can you ask of yourself?"

"I guess." My guilt fades a little, though it hardly evaporates. Logan's words are food for thought.

He reflects. "My mom couldn't be around for us all the time. She had a ranch with tons of animals, a big house, and had to spread her time over four kids. She wasn't with me every second or even for every pivotal moment. But Joy Hunter is a hell of a mother. She's a huge influence on me. A good mom makes the most of what she has and teaches her kid to do the same."

I settle back under his arm, and he hugs me close. I'd love to be half the woman Joy is. She's a force to be reckoned with, for sure.

He runs his fingertips along my arm. "It might sound unromantic, but life is full of trade-offs. The biggest myth of the twenty-first century is we can have it all." He laughs lightly. "I swear the patriarchy made up that shit, too."

His statement surprises me. "You don't think you can

have it all?" Logan has never been a simple man. He lives life fully, in an almost grandiose way. What on earth could he be lacking?

"This conversation is about you, not me."

A beat passes, and I realize how shallow I've been to think just because Logan is talented, rich, and handsome that he has it all. He entered this agreement with a problem, too, after all. I know from years of my own toxic relationships, there is no lonelier place than by the side of people who don't get you.

"Well, thanks for the wisdom. I'll consider it." I say the words but go back to lamenting my absence today.

Logan doesn't miss a beat, just like back in college. "You don't believe me that a mom doesn't have to be around all the time to be a good one?"

I shrug. "I'm not sure."

"Is yours good?"

"Well, she *was* good," I say.

"No, Shay, she *is* good. She's still alive in everything you do. She *is* good, Shay, and she's not even here at all."

His words still me. He's right. I see her life in all the best things I do. Her life and influence is in my cakes. Her life is in the way I sing to Nino when I give him a bath. The amazing mom who she was is very much here even though she isn't.

Logan's depth never ceases to amaze me, but equally, his words are profound for this time in the morning. Though I'm sure nothing could conquer something as powerful as mom guilt with a few words, I do feel better. Better that he cares enough to listen. Better that he considers words that would actually make a difference to the person that I am instead of telling me to forget about it for the sake of his own comfort.

It's what I fell in love with. It's what makes me fall now.

I shake off the depth of that feeling with some humor because I don't think I can take dreaming about what this all means today. "Do you always give TED talks in the morning?"

I don't wait for the answer; I get up to head to the shower because Antonio will be home shortly and I need to pack the cakes. I feel Logan's eyes on the back of my body and wonder if he can see the cellulite in the dawn haze filling the room. My insecurities are drowned out by a high-pitched wolf whistle.

"Mighty fine ass, *pastelito*."

His words cheer me up, and I know there's no way over this but through this, so I let the good things shine on me. I smile to myself, satisfied that Logan likes the view, and give him a little wiggle before entering the bathroom. I peek at my man through the crack in the door until the sliver is all gone, and that's when all my cool crumbles. My heart races, my knees melt, and my back falls against the door.

He wants me.

And I said yes.

Chapter Twenty-Eight

Logan

SHAY SUCKED down her tears while hugging Antonio goodbye this morning, but he didn't notice a thing. She didn't wish him luck but rather asked him what he looked forward to most then spoke about that, putting him in an optimistic frame of mind. I watched them intensely. I marvel at the sight of unconditional love. Now, knowing Shay's feelings of guilt makes her warm, strong embrace of encouragement all the more meaningful to watch. I don't know how she could ever doubt what a great mom she is, because that child is a testament to her.

Antonio buzzes in the car the entire drive, not a worry

in sight. I sit in a café most of the day catching up on emails and give my big brother, Colt, a call to see how the wind farm investment is doing. I should know. But until now, part of me didn't care. It was where I put my money from the inheritance, but with my hockey salary, I never thought it would matter. Something about it matters now. Building a safe future suddenly feels like a good plan.

When I can't sit on my ass anymore and it's nearing pick-up time, I wander the town of Longbrook. It's quaint and historical, a smaller version of Santa Fe. Crooked streets trace through adobe landmarks, and the people walking around have that artsy tree-hugging look about them. It's calm, quiet. I feel at ease, and not a single person recognizes me. I hope Nino's day is the same, but it's unlikely to be. A five-year-old in sixth grade will certainly stand out more than I do here.

I check my watch, and it reads two-fifteen, so I let my feet carry me to Longbrook campus. The grounds are sprawling, taking up what I guess is at least twenty-five acres, maybe more. I imagine what a tiring task it will be for Nino just to get to and from his classes every day until he gets bigger.

I head into the building where I am set to meet Antonio. I'm a few minutes early, but when I reach the top of the stairs, he's sitting on a bench with a woman I haven't met.

Nino notices me right away, pops his little legs off his seat, and comes running up to me. "Logan!"

The only way to stop him from having a collision with my legs is to pull him up into my arms, so I whisk him into a hug. "Hey, bud. Why are you here already?"

The woman he was with comes over. "Hi. I'm Mrs. Hansen. Nino's mentor."

"The child psychologist?"

She nods but says, "I prefer being called his mentor."

I bounce Nino in my arm. "Is everything okay?"

Nino shrugs. "I got tired. But Mrs. Hansen took me to sit on a bench under this really cool tree that's like a hundred years old, and we just chilled."

She folds her hands in front of her. "We can ease in, Antonio, take it at your own pace. You lead the way, right?" She speaks to me now. "I discussed getting some lifts in the golf carts with campus security when Antonio has long walks between classes. We have a few cars and golf carts on patrol, so it shouldn't be a problem."

"It's like you read my mind. I was just thinking how huge the campus is. Thanks for your help." I gaze into Nino's eyes, so dark and beautiful, just like his mama's. "Is that something that would work for you?"

By the look on his face he'd more than like zooming around in the golf carts. "Who wouldn't like that?" He turns and waves to Mrs. Hansen. "See you next week for chemistry."

I carry him in my arms out of the building then place him down. He takes my hand as we walk. It's so small in mine, and him hanging on to me causes a squeezing sensation in my chest. I glance down at him next to me; he's not nearly as affected by this moment as I am. Nino probably holds hands with people more often than I do. He would have held hands with other students when crossing the road at his old primary school. He has his grandfather and uncles and Shay. Maybe even Mrs. Hansen held his hand today. It's likely.

But not only do I rarely hold hands, hell, I probably haven't regularly held someone's hand since Eve was eleven, twelve, and my niece told me she didn't need to hold it anymore when crossing the road or really, ever. It was a good thing, my niece feeling independent. But I miss it.

There's a stone sign on the side of the path, and Nino jumps up on it. His hand grips my palm to give him extra leverage and power in his leap. I help him balance on the rock until he decides to jump off. It's ordinary kid stuff, a bit of parkour for our walk to the car, but every bit of pressure on my palm pumps a burst of good feelings through my veins. It's meaningless to Antonio, I'm sure. But this hand in mine? I'm reminded how much I always wanted to be a dad.

I'm not prone to pessimism, though can't help but think about how old Shay and I are now. We're in our mid-thirties. Does she want more kids? Are we past the point of it being healthy and in the risky zone now? Thank God we're already married, because I know she wouldn't do it again out of wedlock, and we probably shouldn't wait a year for this discussion.

I help Nino climb into the passenger seat and lock him in his raised seat. We share a smile, and I wonder what he'd think about a baby sister or brother. His mind isn't on such matters, of course. As soon as I start up the car, he revs up conversation about his day.

"Mr. Alabaster was telling us about Shakespeare, and he put a glass eye inside his eyeball socket and he pretended to be a witch. It was funny."

I can't help but wonder if Mr. Alabaster might one day get himself into the same kind of trouble that old Finchley did with his *Lord of the Flies* experience.

"It sounds like a fun day."

"So fun. I wasn't bored once."

"Well, that's probably the best thing of all. I hate being bored."

"Me, too, but Mom says boredom is good for me. It feeds creativity."

I don't refute Shay, but boredom only ever caused trouble in my life.

My cell beeps, and a message pops up on my screen. It's Colt.

BIG C

> Hey come on over tonight for the last BBQ of the season. Everyone will be here. Plus we want to spend some time with Antonio and get to know him better.

And gosh do I want them to get to know this spirited kid better, too.

"Hey, little man, are you feeling up to some grub? A barbecue at my brother's house? We can see your cousin?"

"I have a cousin?"

Antonio is smart, but equally, there's no need to complicate things, so I just say, "Yes. Her name is Eve. She's fourteen and she has guinea pigs and dogs. And lots of games to play, so it should be fun."

The thought of introducing Nino to my family has my heart pinching again. I can't believe we haven't been able to make time for this.

"Yes!" he says enthusiastically.

They're going to dote on him to no end. Including Eve. She's always wanted a cousin and in recent years has been getting very vocal, joining forces with my mother who demands to grow the family daily.

I use hands-free commands to send Colt an affirmative, then glance over at Nino who bounces in his seat, and think about Shay, her family... I voice command a text back to Colt.

Can I have a plus two?

An hour later, I'm loaded in the car with not one Mendez man but two.

"Logan, you really didn't have to invite me to Colt's. Are you sure?" Luis says in the passenger seat.

"We're family. *Mi casa es su casa.*"

"But it's Colton's *casa.*"

"What have you been eating since Shay left?"

"Hey, I eat my veggies."

My eyebrow cocks.

"I do. Salsa. And the Mexican grocery store has freshly pounded guacamole. Healthy."

"Tonight's about protein, Luis."

I feel his shoulders drop like the thought of a steak is orgasmic. "I couldn't say no to a barbecue."

"Exactly. So stop being polite and be hungry instead. All you have to do is bring an appetite and eat."

He chuckles a dry, soft laugh from his belly. "That I can do." He turns to glance at Nino in the backseat. "*Hijo, Dia de los Muertos* starts Thursday."

His raspy voice answers. "Mom said we would do *abuela's ofrenda* when she gets back on Sunday."

"Ah, good." Luis turns again, satisfied. He says to me, "I don't suppose you have off on Thursday, Logan? It's been a long time since you joined us at San Fernando for Day of the Dead. It would be nice to have you. And honor your dad."

I've only ever celebrated Day of the Dead once with the

Mendez family. Though the occasion was full of heartache and resurrected pain, the celebration was a beautiful one. The two-day holiday honors the deceased with *ofrenda* or offerings. In Luis' home he built several altars, and on them were favorite things from this world for loved ones passed to welcome them back.

I remember the altars having some odd things on them. Yes, there were Virgin Guadalupe candles and incense and lace-like paper decorations that all felt appropriate for an altar. But there were also specific items like a pack of cigarettes and a Snickers bar on the one for her grandfather. On her mother's, there was a shot glass of peach schnapps, a decidedly non-Mexican drink but apparently one her mom would have every Friday when the kids got home from school to mark the weekend. Shay explained her mom's tooth was too sweet for tequila.

There were the in-home altars surrounded by golden clouds of marigolds but also the small boxes we made, mini *ofrenda*. I remember her helping me make one for my dad to take to San Fernando cemetery where the nearest big Mexican celebrations took place and where her mom was buried. Thinking about that time, that night, it was at this time I decided for certain Shay and I would be together until death do us part.

"I should be able to make it. I'd love to anyway."

Luis claps his hands together. "Ah, it would be wonderful. My boys will be back home for it." He taps my arm. "All four of them."

I barely have a moment to absorb his affection. I have yet to look those beasts in the eye. There were three of us boys in the Hunter house, and it was like a gladiator ring at our ranch most of the time. The Mendez house was even more masculine than ours. And it showed. Though the

Mendez boys, now very much men, didn't become ranchers, they made their way out to California with some business venture. But back in the day, they rarely lost a roping competition and were known for not needing the rope to win. Bare-handed wrestling of a calf is harder than it sounds. When I saw them do it once, I tried and got kicked in the nuts.

Living in a house among men explains why my sister, Jolie, can be volatile. Why she's tough. Shit, Ashton and I put her through the paces when we were younger, bombarding her with hockey pucks, covered in pads and pillows. Women with lots of brothers are a different breed. It explains why Shay, while still feminine and gentle in so many ways, isn't fragile like a flower. She's fragile like a bomb.

I can only imagine what ruthless, intimidating businessman the Mendez brothers are now. They take no prisoners and will definitely scrutinize me. But it's a test I'm prepared to pass. No man on this earth will ever be able to love that woman more than I do. I'll show them until they see it.

"Thursday works," I say. "I get back late, but it's an evening celebration anyway."

"Fantastic." Luis slaps his hands on his thighs.

I'm so glad I brought him here. It must be lonely in his home now. Five children and a grandchild, all gone. No wife. Just him, the cows, and a few ranch hands. I know what shitty conversationalists a lot of them can be.

We get out of the car and walk up the few stairs to the front door. Luis and Nino belong here with us. One enormous family. United.

It's my sister-in-law, Sam, who opens the door, but every

single Hunter face crowds behind her, excited for a peep at the newest family members.

"Luis!" Sam exclaims and leans in for a hug. "So glad you could make it!" She squeezes him then bends down to Nino's level. "And you must be Antonio. I'm Sam. Can I hug you, too?"

"I love hugs." Nino shrugs almost as though it's a silly question.

They embrace, and we enter the house for the rest of the pleasantries. Everyone is here—my younger brother, Dash, and his fiancée, Molly; big brother, Colt, and of course, Sam. Mom is here, and a glowing, round Jolie with Ashton holding her from behind. Eve is here, and her boyfriend, Kieran.

It's sweet but also a bit intense, like being animals in a zoo. Luis beams from ear to ear, though, as if the familiar feeling of being surrounded by a zillion bodies is exactly what he always wanted. Nino, however, isn't quite used to all the buzz.

But my niece, Eve, can relax anybody. It's a misconception that all people with Down syndrome are happy all the time. I've seen her annoyed before. It happens more now that she's in her teens, but I swear people with DS have some sort of sixth sense when it comes to knowing someone needs support. When they need a hug, a smile. Or even to be peeled away from a forest of strange adult legs.

She and her boyfriend, Kieran, who also has DS, come straight for Antonio.

"We're cousins." She waves at Nino with a smile.

"Hi," Nino says, his shoulders releasing lower in her presence, but he reaches up for my hand.

Eve points to her boyfriend. "This is Kieran. But he's not your cousin. He's my boyfriend."

"Okay," Nino says. "Hi, Kieran."

Kieran waves. "Do you want to go in the backyard and see the obstacle course we set up for the guinea pigs?"

Antonio's eyes go wide. "Yeah."

He glances up at me. "Can I go outside?"

"Course. We'll all be out there around the grill in a minute. Don't touch it."

"I know. It's hot..." he says but he's already running away from me with Kieran and Eve.

Colt, Sam, and Ashton are in the kitchen getting marinated meats on a plate to go outside. And the rest of the adults circle Luis to make him feel at home.

Everyone knows Luis on a superficial level. Jolie is his vet, though she's not doing certain large animal or cat calls anymore now that she's pregnant. My mom and Luis have known each other since Luis' family immigrated forty-odd years ago. It's a small town, so everyone knows everyone in some way, but while Luis is happy to be here, I know he's unsure of his place.

Still, my mom won't let people be uncomfortable for long. But she doesn't take the easy-does-it approach, making light conversation and talking about the weather.

She goes for the jugular, lets you know she's ready for the real stuff. "So, Luis, how is it with Shay and Nino all moved out? You okay over there?"

Luis looks at the floor and tries to brush it off his shoulders by lifting them casually. "Yes. Fine. Fine."

"Don't you lie to me, Flash."

The corner of his mouth raises at the apparent nickname I vaguely heard he earned when he was on the bronc riding scene in his younger years. "It'll certainly take some getting used to."

"You need two things," my mom says authoritatively.

"Food. And a new hobby. I'm already making meals for Jolie and Ashton, to stuff their freezer for when the baby comes..."

"About that," Jolie interjects. "We still have six months till little Fletch arrives. We might need another freezer."

"Or," Mom gazes over her eyebrows, "I might just have a new fridge to put them in. Luis, what do you like? Lasagna? Chili?"

"Joy. I can cook..."

"Nonsense. I know what ranchers eat when they come in from a long day. Let me guess. Potato chips and some sort of cheese dip?"

He chuckles low. "Nearly got me. Tortillas and salsa."

"You need real food, Luis." She takes a drink of her soda. "And a hobby. I got that covered for you, too."

"Mom." I scratch my jaw. "No."

"Why not? If anything would take Luis' mind off his empty nest it'll be my book club."

A pensive look overcomes Luis' face. "You know, that sounds all right. I like reading."

My mom tosses me a devilish expression and raises her eyebrow. "See? He likes reading."

"Luis, I'm not sure you'll be up for *this* kind of reading." Or maybe he will. I sure as hell enjoyed the spicy romance book Mom gave me one Christmas. It was about a hockey player who wouldn't settle down and eventually found love. And he also somehow gave double orgasms with his ten-inch dick and tattooed lines on his body every day he was apart from his childhood love, like being apart was a prison sentence.

I thought it was a little extreme but then reflected on how I haven't etched lines onto my body just to lament Shay, but I could tell a person near enough to the date how many days passed between Shay breaking up with me and Vegas. I have some sort of internal ticker. So maybe it wasn't that wild.

"Logan." My mom places her hand on my arm. "Let Luis decide for himself." She swallows a mischievous laugh. "Flash, if you aren't into the book club, I can also offer jewelry making. There are some nice men at my classes in Santa Fe who do metalwork." She turns to my brother, Dash. "Maybe you and Molly could help Luis out with some staff a couple times a month and give him a break for a change of scenery?"

Dash raises his beer bottle. "Can do. Happy to come over anytime with some of the guys."

"Me, too," Molly offers, threading her arm through Dash's. She's never one to shy away from ranch work.

I didn't think our girl, Chicago, would stay for the long haul but, man, I'm happy she has. Dash actually cracks a smile once in a while now, and though my brother will always be introverted, now at least I know he won't be alone.

"Thanks, Joy." Luis smiles at her like he knows exactly what kind of mischief my mom can get up to. "I'll consider it."

Colt announces, "Let's move this party outside, people."

We follow into the backyard where Kieran, Eve, and Nino have set up long rows of tunnels using logs, making a big maze for her guinea pigs.

Nino sees me and runs over. "Logan! Did you know guinea pigs can't really jump and climb? Eve told me. She's like a guinea pig expert. Their legs are so short, and they look like they're crawling all the time. Can we have one?"

"Little man, I'd love some pigs but I'm not so sure about Cayenne and guinea pigs together."

"Hm. You're probably right."

Eve calls over, "Come on, Antonio. We're going to start the next race!"

"See you!" Nino runs back to join the pair.

I've always loved my family. It's why I wanted to be on the Scorpions even though until now they haven't been a top seed. It's why I kept a house in Starlight Canyon even though I'm not in it much. I can't let go of this place. But I was a family man without a family of my own.

Now, I have it all.

The only thing missing here is Shay.

I pull out my cell and, knowing she's likely still on the road, I snap a photo of me with everyone milling about in the background. She can look at it when she has a chance.

> Your boys are doing just fine. Papá Luis is here, too. Hope you're having a smooth ride, pastelito.

I send it off and realize how much I do miss her. So fucking much. Now that we've crossed the line, I haven't stopped thinking of her, and the thirst has reached new heights.

Thank God she texts back.

PASTELITO

> Will you be home tonight at 8:30? I'll be at my hotel room around then and want to video call Nino.

> I'll make sure we're back. Don't know about your dad though. He seems down for a bender.

291

PASTELITO

LOL Love that for him. Thank you so much for getting him out of the house. I'll thank you properly for all your kindness when I'm back.

Not until I thank you first.

PASTELITO

Oh yeah? For what?

For giving me a reason to breathe.

Chapter Twenty-Nine

Shay

"Mom!" Nino exclaims, and his lips come toward the camera on Logan's end until they turn into a blurry blob on my screen.

A kissing sound squeaks out of the speaker.

He pulls back, and my sweet angel's face is there again. "Today was so much fun!"

"Tell me about it." I'm so relieved his day was wonderful, and at the same time, I ache to hug him and feel it vibrate through his little body for myself. I wish I could reach inside the phone and gather him up in my arms.

"I had English and math... it's so funny. My math

teacher is from England, and he calls math *maths*. With an s."

"Really?" I sound amazed because I truly am. I gobble up every morsel of these ten minutes we'll have together. I know Nino won't have more in him than that.

"Yeah. His accent is hard to understand. And Mrs. Hansen took me to a tree."

"A tree?"

Logan's face appears in the background. My heart sighs with relief seeing these two together. "He was tired so she let him chill. Right, bud?"

"Yeah. The campus is really big! And after school we took Papá Luis to see my cousin and the guinea pigs."

My son is so excited his day pours out of him like a whizzing kaleidoscope, and he ends it all with an abrupt few words. "Okay, Mom. Gotta go. I love you!"

I want to keep him on the phone but I know five-year olds don't have the attention span.

But Logan is there. My brown-eyed, gorgeous husband is there. Is he really my husband now? Or are we at boyfriend status? It's all confusing now, though the gaze coming back at me from hundreds of miles away comes from a man who knows exactly what he wants.

I feel beautiful for the first time in years just being at the receiving end of his amber stare.

"So the cake made it?" he asks.

"Thank God. Well, and thanks to you for running out to get all that ice in the morning. My air-con isn't the best."

"Hence me getting the ice."

"You're so thoughtful."

"For you I am..."

His words have me buckling at the knees.

"Well, all the cake parts are in the hotel room now, so

from here on out I should be good to go. I miss Nino," I admit. "And you."

The corners of his lips dance; that meant something to him.

"Just smash it. Okay?"

I giggle. *Giggle.* I'm so far gone. But knowing what he means touches me like that. "I will."

I've never been supported quite like this before. My brothers were definitely protective growing up. They're protective now. But shielding someone and nurturing them are two very different things. With Logan, I feel both. I feel it all. I feel everything *from* him. *For* him. I'm in trouble. It's kind of scary. But I'm pushing myself to believe it will last, that really he isn't that guy in the media. My heart squeezes with a wish that this is the man I truly fell for, that he's returned to me in the most beautiful twist of fate.

I want to tell him I love him. But I settle for something else. "I can't wait to see you Sunday."

He glances over his shoulder, presumably to check if Nino is there. His voice is low like thunder. "I am going to devour every inch of you when you're back."

Geez, this man gives me immediate pussy flutters. "Oh, are you?"

He checks for small ears again then comes back to me, gaze even darker. "I'm going to show you just how much I missed my wife. When you get back here, I'll make your legs shake. Eat you until you melt all over my face."

My chest heaves with the mere thought of it. I'm deep down the path of thinking how good it will be to have Logan between my legs again, when my phone pings with another message, nearly making me jump.

I clutch my chest.

Logan releases a naughty laugh. "You're in trouble. Who's the text from?"

"Santi and Rio are meeting me now. I need to go downstairs."

He sighs as though trying to allow his passion to go away with his exhale. "All right, there's one more thing I want to show you."

He walks over to the couch in the living room and shows me Cayenne lying there. In the frame, I see Logan's hand with a cat treat in it. My cat takes it but makes sure to swat Logan's hand afterward.

Logan puts the camera back on him. "How about it? No claws anymore."

I nod. "Impressive progress."

"I think so."

There's a beat of silence, but it isn't empty, it's full with anticipation. Will he say I love you?

"See you tomorrow, Logan."

"All right, *pastelito*. See you tomorrow."

Despite my exhaustion, there's only one thing that could put me back on my feet.

There, in the lobby of the hotel, are Rio and Santi, my brothers I don't get to see enough these days. Many years ago, they moved out of Starlight Canyon and to California with a business plan and every penny of their savings. It's a vigilante business they're in, monitoring software that's so powerful it's even proven successful on the dark web. It's tech that is as controversial as it is titillating, and it took years for them to perfect it, working on patents, and finally, after years of figuring out how to best use their tool, they're pursuing the private sector.

Somehow, all us Mendez kids turned out to be entrepreneurs. Our parents owned their own business. It's all we've known. But my brothers' ambition eclipses the total sum of mine and my parents'. They'll be billionaires at some point, and I'm not even sure it's so far away. They're going to be the most rugged, salt-of-the-earth, intimidating-as-fuck billionaires. And then, we'll all be together again at the compound they're building in California. We'll be the Mexican Kennedys.

Would Logan be up for that?

"*Nena...*" Santi calls me by the name that has stuck since I was little. My brothers don't call me Shay. They call me "baby girl." And they still treat me like one despite my gray hair starting to push through.

Santi, the most charismatic of the otherwise broody bunch of brothers, walks toward me with his arms wide open. I fall into his embrace, and he squeezes me in a bear hug.

My voice is muffled against his chest. "Sorry if I stink. The Mojave is hot as hell, and my air-con is crap."

He lets go and plants a sharp kiss in my hair. "Better stinky than far away."

My eldest brother by five minutes, Rio, wraps his arm around me and pulls me close. "Good to see you."

"Thanks for driving down to meet me."

"Wouldn't miss it. Gabriel and Enzo wanted to come, but they drew the short straws. We have contracts to get through. There's a private investor coming through the final stages."

297

"Seriously?" I can't think of four men who deserve this more.

Rio walks toward the hotel restaurant, and I follow.

Santi cocks an eyebrow and tilts his head like he's the man.

This investment will be massive, but Rio wears the news like he expected it. He displays pride on his broad shoulders but never brags with a smile. My twin older brothers, Rio and Enzo, couldn't be two more confident men. I wonder if my brothers ever fight about business like they used to fight about the best horses and hardest bulls to ride.

Rio moves me along. "We figured you'd be starving and thirsty so we already ordered."

He cuts through the hotel, and Santi and I trail his broad back, tracing the wake he leaves behind.

My brothers have always intimidated people with their presence. Even though they are docile as lambs with me and dote on me like I'm still a baby, I've seen what they're like when they're determined. They're relentless and all have our dad's hooded eyes. When they concentrate or stare, it's a lot to handle, and weakness and uncertainty becomes very clear to them because it doesn't last long in their gaze.

Rio pulls out my chair. We all sit and, as usual, my brothers have outdone themselves. Every bit of real estate on the white tablecloth is taken up by a tapas dish. They've already gotten me a beer. Water. Everything I'm gasping for after that drive.

"Guys, I really needed this."

"We figured," Santi says. "You've been through some life-changing things lately. And, this high-profile wedding? It's a big deal. Proud of you."

I don't even want to take the credit, and it's not all mine

anyway. I owe some of this to Logan. "Logan hooked me up with some warm introductions. He's very supportive."

"Mmm," Rio hums. There's more than a one-syllable sentence working behind his eyes.

Santi stabs a piece of chorizo on one of the small plates, and the motion somehow feels like foreshadowing for the conversation ahead. "This whole marriage has been quite sudden. You and Logan."

I've spoken with my brothers multiple times since that morning in Vegas. "I told you we were seeing each other for a while, so it wasn't sudden for us."

Rio eyes an olive, picks it up, and when his gaze meets mine, his eyes are subtly narrowed. "It's fast by anyone's measure. Even seeing each other for a few months before."

I shrug. "It's not like we were strangers. Hell, even if we didn't date in college we wouldn't be. Anyway, we're not kids anymore. At our age, it's easier to know what you want and what you don't."

If only that was true.

Rio doesn't smile, simply chews his olive as though with every bite he's solving a crime. He's a little like me. In fact, Santi is the only one of us kids who isn't too serious for his own good. My brothers aren't assholes, more that they're competitive and driven and just don't have time for bullshit. Santi had time for the bullshit and then some. Good thing he's had our family for guidance.

Rio finishes his food, and his Adam's apple bobs up and down his muscular neck. Normally, his shirt is buttoned right to the top, but he has one undone, and his tattoos hang out, a reminder that he's tougher than I've ever been.

"Have you changed your name?" he asks. "Are you going to change Nino's name?"

I know we're *together* but I still can't get over how backward it all is. Will we get unmarried and then at some point married again? Will he adopt Antonio and we all share a last name? Surely a person can't go from fake husband and downgrade to boyfriend? Never before have I preferred to tell a lie to the truth but I do now.

I work a swallow past a lump in my throat, then reach for my beer and try to wash it down, but the stone sticks.

"Why are you nervous?" Rio looks at me like an interrogation suspect.

Shit.

"I'm not nervous."

"So are you changing your name?" he repeats.

My brain moves quickly in the moment of panic. "We're still talking about it."

"See," he says, the way he always did as the bossy eldest when we were growing up. "This is why you date for longer to sort this shit out."

"Me changing my last name is something I need to think about. I like our name. It doesn't change whether I would have married Logan or not. It's just a name, guys, get over it."

Now even Santi pulls his lips into a thin line. "Is Logan cool with that? You keeping your name?"

It's like a game of tennis is playing out in my mind. Would my brothers like it better if I stayed a Mendez? Or if I went traditional and took my husband's name because that will make Logan seem more manly? Fuck, I hate chasing an answer that's the one someone else wants to hear. It's not my style to people please.

I blow it off. "You're too hung up on stupid shit, guys. I'm happy. Nino is ecstatic and has been totally in love with Logan from day one. We're secure. Safe. Isn't that all you've ever wanted for me?"

Rio and Santi share a glance as though they need to confer before answering. My brothers are like the goddamn mob.

Santi is the first to soften. "We just don't want you hurt again."

I wish I could say their grudge is extreme, but I've been through some rough times with men. I'm sure they'd never choose for me to marry the man Logan portrayed in the media.

"I know you guys are suspicious of Logan, but it's not what you think it is."

Santi leans back and folds his hands behind his head. "You have to admit it, he's not exactly the kind of guy we'd pick for you. You gave enough cheaters a chance."

That aches. "Logan isn't a cheater."

I don't think so. No, he's just never committed. What was he, even? He's not like the other men who screwed me over, right? It raises the hairs of intuition. Am I being wise believing Logan isn't some womanizer? Or is it wishful thinking?

I shake it off the best I can. He told me the old Logan is still there. I have to believe that. I want to *believe* that. "Let's start fresh, guys. He's wonderful with me. And wonderful with Nino."

"Okay..." Rio leans on his tattooed forearms, exposed with his starched shirtsleeves rolled up.

It occurs to me they may have used their tech to check Logan out. I know it's spying by proxy, and I shouldn't ask them what they dug up, but I want to know. Did they see anything really bad about Logan?

I blurt, "I'm sure you checked Logan out. So just spill the beans."

"Of course we checked him out. He's a liar, Shay," Rio informs me.

My heart drops, and the world stands still. Lying about what? Did he get with someone during his last away game?

Rio leans in closer. "He's not who he says he is."

My heart beats in my shoes now. The walls of the restaurant crumble, and I'm losing gravity. I don't know if I'm going to pass out or float away.

"Most of Logan's women were setups. Of course he's not a saint."

Rio and Santiago glance at each other, deciding to keep some details to themselves.

"But it's mostly a PR stunt, his image. The guy's a liar," Rio says.

I could piss myself right now with relief, even though a part of me cringes thinking about Logan having sex with other women, which is the detail that clearly possessed my brothers' shared gaze. But they only found out what I already know.

"He told me that already. I don't care if he lies to everyone else to build a brand as long as he's honest with me."

"You don't?" Rio says, like I'm being stupid.

"No. Not really."

We all wear different faces. The one you show the world. The one you show family. And the one you never show anyone.

It's the last we all want so badly to be seen. When someone stares into the eyes of the third face and still loves you, it's true. It's forever. It's real. And it's what I think I can have with Logan.

Somehow, no matter how much I push him away or

play the tough-girl act, he sees me for my vulnerable, genuine self. And he never lets me fall.

They are practical men, so I play on that. "Guys, I'm married to Logan. So it's pretty black and white as far as I see it. You either accept him and we all build something bigger from it, or you continue to be suspicious and annoy the hell out of me every time I see you."

I eat some food, more to quell my nerves than to satiate hunger. The rise in defensiveness over Logan shows just how much I care. I've fallen for that man all over again.

Rio hums pensively. I hate it when he does that. Truly, truly hate it. He's such a know-it-all, but the scary thing is he's often been right in my life.

Rio tilts his head and stares at me. "That's true."

He dips a piece of pita bread into a Mediterranean dip. "Well then, we have to roll with it. All four of us are back next week. As far as you're concerned, we got you. But don't blame us for giving a little evil eye. It's good to keep Logan on his toes."

"You guys can't help yourselves. I know. Your resting expressions are... well, I just bet Mom was scared when your mugs arrived in this world."

Santi tips his beer toward me. "Hey, these mugs got your back every day of the week, *nena*. You'll always be our little sister." He finally gives me a smile I really need right now.

I trace the rim of my water glass. "I know. Thanks for your concern, but I'm happy. He's good to me. Really, really treats me and Antonio like his number one priority."

It's true. Since the moment Logan and I embarked on this crazy agreement, I've wanted for nothing. I can go grocery shopping with his credit card and for once say yes to all Antonio's requests. Logan stocks the house with cheese-less treats, and when he's away, sends Tom over to check all the windows and locks. All I need is more time with his body.

Santi reassures me. "We're happy for you. We really are. And happy for Nino, too. He needs a dad."

Thinking of Logan as Nino's father only deepens how I feel about him. Logan really does fit every one of his edges into my puzzle except for one thing. He's still playing a strong game, and I'm reminded of why we couldn't be together in the first place. And why we're together now—to keep Logan on the Scorpions.

I wish I had that romantic feeling inside people usually have when they find their other half, their missing piece. Instead, fear pools inside and I wonder if God has other plans for me like the first time around.

Chapter Thirty

Logan

Luis picked up Antonio an hour before I had to leave for my game, and every minute ticked down in goddamn agony. Shay hit traffic on the way home, but I held out hope, not touching my aching cock in hopes of burying it inside her and giving her a dose of what it means to be missed by me.

Her text came in to go on ahead without her and that she'd meet me at the arena came through, I thought I was going to die. My balls were fucking hanging to the floor by the time I got to the arena. But worse than that, my attention was still firmly glued to my cell. I worried about her getting back all right and about getting to the game.

Unfortunately, I have to be at the arena hours before a

game and all I can hope is that I get to see her for a few damn minutes. I don't think I'll be able to play tonight if I don't hear from her beforehand. Or at least see her rink side.

I get back into the locker rooms after a kick around with a soccer ball, keeping warmed up, when my cell beeps in my pocket.

PASTELITO

We're here!

> Leave Nino with your dad and come to the locker room entrance.

PASTELITO

Will they let me?

> They'll let you or else they'll have a goddamn lunatic on their hands.

Moments later, I'm in the hall waiting next to Marlon, one of the security guards who keeps fans from entering our private domain. I'm waiting with zero fucking patience and have to tell myself a thousand times it takes at least five minutes to walk from where she is rink side to me.

Marlon is the kind of security guard who has a constant expression of disinterest and boredom going on. But he sure notices me because I'm fidgeting like a hungry animal.

"You all right, Mr. Hunter?"

Just then, the double doors at the far end of the hallway burst open, and a flash of long, dark locks appear.

"I am now."

She comes toward me, her steps at first normal—mine are, too, until I ask myself why I'm fucking around walking —and I quicken the pace to a jog until I whisk her up in my arms and crash my lips onto hers. She kisses me back like she's missed me just as much. I secure her tiny frame in my arms, shuffling us up against a wall, and I press her back into it, harder than I want to, but carnal urges rush through my body. How could I have missed her this much in just a few days?

She moans into my mouth. "There's a guy watching."

I smile, my lips smooth against hers, and I flick my eyes to where Marlon is at the end of the hall. He isn't looking at us but of course he knows we're here.

I let her feet drop to the floor and take her by the hand, leading her down the hall to the changing room double doors Marlon guards.

"Marlon, this is my wife."

"Ma'am." He tips his head politely.

"I'm going to need to take her on the other side of these doors."

"Mr. Hunter, you know only authorized personnel go through."

I gaze at him hard in that way that lets him know I want him to read between the lines. "I'm *authorizing* my wife to visit the closet on the other side of these doors. A ten-minute pass is all I'm giving her."

He furrows his brows for a moment then releases them wide and high when he gets the drift. His eyes flicker as he considers allowing us through. "All right." He opens the door for us. "Ten-minute pass."

I whisk Shay through and find the janitor's closet just on the other side of the door, shoving us both inside. It's dark, and we clang about until I'm able to somehow brace her against a solid wall without supplies on it. We kiss hard, groaning, moaning... I'm trying not to make so much noise but I'm absolutely feral after not seeing her for days.

Ten minutes is all I have. Every inch of her skin feels incredible in my hands. She kisses me, but I feel her arms reaching and fumbling along the wall until she pulls the string to the light and a soft glow illuminates the space.

"I missed you..." I say, pushing her dress up the sides and off her body. "Did you wear this just for me? Were you just waiting for me to slide my hands up your thighs and my fingers between your legs?"

"Fuck, Logan," she sighs.

I unclasp her bra and toss it to the floor.

"I never stop thinking about you ever. I need you..."

We're breathless, rushed, needy. My hand smooths down her panties and I run my fingers along her slick slit. I kiss down her neck, nibbling along the way. She throws her head back, offering herself to me. I flick her nipple with my tongue, and when her fingernails rake through my hair, my back breaks out in chills.

I kiss right down her stomach and peel her panties down her thighs, letting them join the pile with her dress. Then I press my thumbs to the folds of her pussy and open it wide. I kiss it gently and glance up to see her eyes fluttered shut and her eyebrows tight in sensual concentration.

The sight of her makes me lose my shit, and I dive in. I devour her, every part of my mouth feasts on her core.

"Logan..." she breathes.

"Fuck, Shay. The only thing better than my name in your mouth is my cock."

"Ahhh..."

"Mmm... you like it when I talk dirty?" I give her a long, languid stroke with my tongue. "I can taste how much you missed me."

She's absolutely soaked. She groans and tugs at my hair. There's an upside-down bucket, and she props her leg up on it to give me better access, melting against the wall.

"Greedy girl," I hum against her core. "Touch yourself."

She pinches her nipples, and I insert two fingers inside her. She's so tight. So warm. So mine.

Did she want this every second we were apart like I did?

I scissor my fingers in and out. "How many times did you think of my fingers inside you while you were gone?"

"None." She scratches her nails through my hair again and tugs at my shoulder like she wants me to come back up to her. "I want your dick."

I run my flat tongue from her entrance all the way up. "Yeah? You want me? You want my cock, Shay? Let me taste how much you want it."

I don't have long to bring my woman full tilt, but her nub is hard and tall. I circle slow then fast, hard then soft, until her hips grind into me and she cups the back of my head, pulling me deeper into her core.

"More."

I suck her clit into my mouth, gently, but I know it will feel anything but to her. I reach my fingers up and inside to that special spot that drives her wild, and as soon as I do, her pussy tightens in my mouth, her clit pulses under my tongue, and her hand lashes to the side, sending something clattering to the floor.

"Fuck me..." she groans, high-pitched, wild, but at the same time trying not to be loud, but someone is bound to hear. Marlon at least.

I don't care if he does. This is my wife. She is mine.

She claws my arms to come up to her, and I press a dirty kiss onto her mouth. How the hell am I going to play after this? Fuck. Maybe I'll play better. Knowing she's there. Knowing I'm going home to more of this goddess.

"Fuck me, Logan," she demands, swallowing like she's still thirsty, her eyes still closed.

I undo my pants, and she immediately grabs my dick

and gives it a hard jerk. She rolls a bead of pre-cum around the tip, and I nearly buckle at the knees from her touch.

She's breathless. "I want you..."

"Your wish is my command."

With our height difference, standing isn't going to work easily in this tiny closet, so I turn her around to face the wall and hitch her hips up toward me, bending her over. Her tits hang full and womanly, her ass is round in my face. I spread her cheeks wide to have a look at her glistening pussy before plunging myself inside.

"God, I wanted you," she murmurs.

It's just what I needed to hear. Being away from her was torture. I know Shay doesn't show her emotion with ease. Knowing she missed me, knowing she thought about me and wanted me as much as I did her is everything. And it makes my cock rock-hard. Blood surges. I'm already so close to exploding inside her tight little cunt.

Her insides clench me. I spread her ass cheeks open again and massage her backside gently with my thumb.

"Shit..." she hisses.

"You like that? I can't get enough of you, Shay. I want to touch you everywhere. Not a morsel of skin is off limits to my hands, my mouth..." Another surge of lust has me close to the edge. I have to clench my jaw to stop myself from releasing.

"I like it. So much..." she whimpers.

"My dirty little wife." With me caressing her backside, she's dripping right down my balls.

My hands grip her ass firmly, knowing I need to hang on for dear life to stretch these last few thrusts out before I spill inside her. She bucks her hips back into me every time I drive in. I completely bottom out, and she braces herself against the wall, her strong shoulders flexing. She slams her hips back into me, and her beautiful round ass dances with her movement. I love her skin. I love her curves...

I love her. I fucking love her...

I bury myself deeper inside her, and she reaches down, sinking her claws into my thigh.

"*Yes...*"

She doesn't even have to utter another word, and I'm a fucking goner. My dick spurts and surges, spilling hot cum deep inside her. We come at the same time, our bodies taut with intense orgasms, me holding her hips, her the wall, to stop ourselves from totally collapsing on the floor.

We finally slow our pace, panting, and eventually I have no choice but to slide out. She comes up to standing, and I spin her immediately, needing more contact. I press my lips against hers.

That was everything. Shay isn't a woman for a sensitive man. She doesn't wear her heart on her sleeve and shower you with words of affirmation. This showed me what I needed to know. She missed me, too.

I hold her against my chest. "I wish I didn't have to go."

She gives me one of her famous one-syllable laughs. "Come on, Hunter you know what you have to do."

"What's that?"

"Smash it."

I'm somehow more focused than ever, even though my gaze constantly slips to Shay, Nino, and Luis rink side, just behind the plexiglass. Though glimpses of Shay nearly crush my heart, I'm in so deep with that girl, Nino and Luis aren't without impact. I want to win for them, too. Nino stands on his chair occasionally, secured by Shay. I can't make out Luis' cries from where I am, but his mouth has been open for so much of the game I can't imagine he'll have a voice left after this.

So even though we're one up, when the coach sends me on for what is my last two minutes of the game, I want to make it count, make my little family proud. I want to see them scream until their cheeks are red.

This isn't just a game anymore. I want Shay to be proud of me. I want her to be proud to be my wife.

Every one of my teammates is in good form, and none of us are complacent. But I have two minutes. The opposition piles toward our defense, and Ashton intercepts a shit attempt on our goal. He deftly glides away from me, but I know this play. It's a fake. As expected, he sends it in a straight line right across the ice and straight to my stick.

As I glide across the ice, every heartbeat echoes in my ears, every breath rushes in and out, sharp and deliberate. My blades dig deep into the surface below in what will be my last chance to prove my worth today.

My focus narrows to a pinprick of light at the end of the rink. The goalie stands tall, an intimidating wall of determination, but when I close the gap between us, I see the chink in his armor. A split second of doubt flickers in his eyes, and as long as my aim is on, he's fucking mine.

With a burst of speed, I barrel forward. The cold air bites my cheeks. Their defenders converge, their sticks slashing across the ice, but I'm in my own world now, a world where time slows and every move is muscle memory. Every move is a lifetime of passion, hard work, and destiny.

I feel the weight of the puck on my stick, an extension of my will. The tension in the air is palpable as I wind up, muscles coiling like springs. At this moment, it's just me, the goalie, and the net.

With a thunderous crack, I release the shot. The puck screams through the air, a blur of black against the white ice. Time stands still as it sails past the goalie's outstretched glove, a perfect arc toward its destination.

And then it happens. The net bulges, the red light flashes, and the crowd erupts into a deafening roar of cheers and applause.

But amidst the chaos, there's only one sound that matters to me—the heartbeat in my ears, the gentle hum of my second chance.

The buzzer goes, and my teammates flood onto the ice, all heading right toward me, but I'm already flat up on the plexiglass, glove thrown down, hand splayed with Antonio's mirroring mine on the other side. The little boy might stare at me, but I only have eyes for his mom.

Until Shay, hockey was the only thing I thought I was put on this earth to do. The approval I get from Shay Mendez right now makes even the mayhem in this arena totally disappear.

I finally know what it means to be content. I'm done. I couldn't have found a better place for my feet to stop moving.

Chapter Thirty-One

Shay

LOGAN HAS BEEN HOME for the past few days, as home as a professional sportsman can be with games and practices. With Antonio in school further away, we needed to miss the games in the evening, it's too much for him.

Though I miss Logan, I'm not that college girl anymore. Him being gone sometimes helps me focus on my business, it gives me time with Antonio alone, time to make sure my dad is still okay, although since my weekend away, it seems as though Joy Hunter is trying to take over that role.

It's a blissful week and goes by in a blur until *Dia de los Muertos*. In between the moments of work and my son, my time was filled with thoughts of Logan, so much so, I forgot to prepare for the arrival of my brothers.

It will be a moment of truth. They were pretty nice to me in Los Angeles, but I know they haven't fully accepted anything, and two of them weren't even here. They're a veritable gang en mass.

Antonio is already over with my dad and brothers who arrived earlier this afternoon. I'm in the bathroom and have put the final touches on my sugar skull makeup and rhinestones. I slick back my hair and don my headpiece—a large, tall colorful crown of flowers. The dress I wear was my mom's. Only five years ago did I finally decide to alter it for my size. In some ways, I'm her image: our eyes are dark as night, our hair to match, and she too had lengths of silver weaving through while only in her thirties. Our noses are feline. But unlike me, she was tall and slender, and thanks to my stature, it fits okay over my much more ample bust, but it was always too big or too tight. Now, it fits like a glove.

Today, I'm allowed to transform her death into a joyous celebration. With her spirit's return, it might be Thursday, but for her it will be the weekend when she throws back her shot of schnapps. Today when I think of her, she isn't sick. She is happy. She is smiling.

And my gosh is she staring back at me in the mirror. I almost laugh out loud. If I look like my mom, I must be old now. I learned through her what a gift, honor, and strength that is. I hope age has made me stronger. More bold. More powerful.

Mom used to say the ocean is old but it will still drown you with vigor. So even though my makeup has settled a little into my fine lines and crow's feet, I rise to my full height and own it.

Just then, footsteps approach, soft thuds on the wood

floor. Logan appears in the room and heads for me. He kisses me like he never plans to come up for air. But he eventually does with a little white makeup on his lips.

I wipe it off for him. "That's the last kiss for a while. I saved my lips for last but I won't have myself walking around looking like a drunk clown tonight. No smears."

He scoops me in. "How about you don't do your lips tonight?" He kisses me again.

I press him off playfully and turn back to the mirror to pat on some white cream. "Not a chance." I glance at him, and our eyes connect in the mirror. "Okay, I'll wipe it off after family photos."

He pulls me against him from behind and sniffs my hair. "You always smell so damn sweet..." His gaze traps mine in our reflections. "You're stunning. Absolutely breathtaking."

I dip my eyes bashfully. "Thank you."

I check the time on my cell and finish my makeup quickly. "We have to get going soon. Are you sure you want to come tonight? You're not too tired?"

"Wouldn't miss it for the world."

"Sorry you didn't have time to make an *ofrenda* for your dad." I've been thinking of it all week. Should I have made one for him? They're such personal expressions, it didn't feel right.

He takes my hand. "Follow me."

He walks us into the enormous closet where there is a beautiful wooden seat along one wall, which I never quite noticed is actually a trunk.

He opens it. "I still have it."

"What?"

"I still have the *ofrenda* I made with you in college."

He lifts the shoebox out of the trunk, and my heart

floods with memories. We painted that box black on the floor of my dorm room with my poster paints.

He closes the trunk and sits on it. Staring at the object transports me back in time. Before the fancy clothes in backlit wardrobes were hanging around us. Before he went to the pros. Before I became a mom.

A shiver skates up my spine thinking of how our lives are full of sliding doors. Only a week after that night, Logan was out of mine for what I thought would be forever. Now, here we are.

He runs his fingers along the top and opens it, peering in. The breath of the room slows and stills, making way for the whisper of his father's soul, still to be seen, heard, and felt inside this very box.

Logan pulls out a bag of Doritos. "These might be a little gross now."

"We can replace them." I laugh. "That flavor is Antonio's favorite, too."

"Yeah?"

I nod.

He fingers through the rest of the contents. A horseshoe. A small black comb, because even though his dad wore a cowboy hat all the time, he never let his hair be mussed underneath. Marigolds, completely dried up, and two candy sugar skulls in plastic wrap, shedding a white dust from their age. A guitar pick. A photo of Logan and his dad.

I pick the photo up gingerly. "You look so young."

"So does he."

"He was."

"Yeah. Your mom, too."

"Mmm."

Something similar to sadness but more like mutual

knowing passes between us. It's been a long time since our loved ones were young and then all of a sudden weren't. We'll always want them back, yet it's an impossible wish.

Logan mirrors my thoughts exactly. "I want him back, but that's the paradox of death, isn't it? I want everything I have now, but I wish I didn't have to take the path that brought me here. You know?"

"I know." I take his hand and kiss him. "I deeply, deeply know."

He puts the photo back in the box. A seriousness fills the room with intense meaning. "Now we're where we are, and I've stopped wishing we ever broke up, too. We have Nino because of it."

We.

Chapter Thirty-Two

Logan

Luis has been hosting this celebration for years, and the altar, though still familiar to the one I remember from years ago, has new decorations. Candles glow, bunches of marigolds are dotted about in every container he probably has that can hold water. Candles are on every shelf and mantelpiece. Traditional mariachi music plays, and there are at least thirty people here.

Everyone is dressed to the nines in skull motifs or simply wearing colorful dresses, charro suits, tunics... the display is a celebration of culture for those to which it belongs, and the Mendez invitation to be part of what and who they are, even if you're not.

Ranch hands and their families fill the living room. Nino sits with another boy on the couch, both playing with Rubix Cubes. Diana, who owns the café in town, is here with her girlfriend, and other neighbors I vaguely recognize mill about, drinking, doing the two-step while chatting.

Luis is inviting, inclusive, and sentimental.

But his sons are not.

And there they are. Standing on the far end of the living room. All four of them in a menacing line of black suits, ties, and shirts. Their eyes are black circles painted as skull sockets, their faces bearing bone-like designs drawn to commemorate the celebration, or perhaps to test my mettle.

Shay already warned me they might not go easy on me. I'd expect nothing less. If Jolie didn't marry my best friend, I'm not sure what kind of man it would take to jump over the hurdles us Hunter men would erect.

Shay leans in to speak quietly, "They typically wear all black to this. And that face paint. Don't be vain. It's not just for your benefit."

A smile dances on my eyebrows. "Got it."

She sucks in a deep breath and lets it out.

I thread my fingers through hers. "Hey. I'm not nervous."

"I am."

"You don't have to join me, but I'm going in." I dart my eyes over to the row of men standing there, expressionless skulls but exuding some kind of dare despite it. They're ominous and still, like they're someone's tombstones. But I've always had confidence in my ability to win people over. Being a brother myself, I know what's going through their heads.

Just then, Nino slides between our legs. He's dressed to the nines in a suit like his uncles, though his shirt is white and he wears a matching bow tie. A white flower adorns his lapel, and Shay outdid herself with his Day of the Dead face paint

"Logan! Where's your skull mask? I picked out a skull for you with Mom."

I lift it in my hand. "Got it here, bud. I'll put it on soon."

"Then let's take a selfie!"

"Definitely. I'm just going to talk to your uncles and then I'll find you."

It's unlike Shay to shy away from conflict, but she takes the opportunity to split. "*Mijo*, let's get you a drink."

"I'm not thirsty. *Tío* Santi got me one."

"Okay, then Mama is thirsty." She steps away with Nino toward the kitchen and mouths over her shoulder: "Good luck."

I spin on my heels and head straight for the brothers. It's a little hard to make each one out as I approach, since they all look like reapers, but they become clearer the closer I get. Santi is definitely on the end. I recognize him best because we were in the same year and his eyes are brightest in the frames of his black sockets. He has Luis' eyes, a lighter amber shade of brown, a bit like mine. The others stare at me, onyx irises almost invisible if not for slivers of white semicircles lining their lower eyelids.

Rio and Enzo, the eldest twins, who must be nearly forty now, lean against the wall at the end, arms crossed, and watch me approach as predators watch prey. Gabriel, the middle brother, who was a year ahead of me back in the day, lifts a finger in way of greeting.

But as expected, Santi is the first to speak. It would be messed up to ignore me. "Logan," he says, like he's been expecting me.

I suppose they have.

"Long time no see." I extend my hand.

He reaches out with his own, also painted with a skull design.

I lift my mask toward the others to say hi. "Gabriel, Enzo, Rio."

The men offer me almost imperceptible nods.

I use a classic male conversation opener because it's clear they aren't going to give me an in. "How's the tech business going?"

Her brothers were all sportsmen in high school. They are built like fucking brick walls after all, and when they weren't studying or in football practice, they were on the ranch wrangling calves, riding horses. There can't be an ounce of fat on these boys. But there were brains going with the brawn. All the guys but Santi got scholarships to college, but earned surprisingly un-sporty degrees. They went into computer science.

I already know a good amount about their business, but in the Starlight Canyon world, man's friendly conversation is typically about sports or work. So I begin with work.

I look directly at Santi who's most likely to talk. He was always charismatic compared to the others.

"Tell me about it. It's crime? Security? I'm not sure I understand."

I totally understood Shay when she explained, but if I can't get these guys talking, I can't get to the part where I tell them how I feel about Shay.

"Yeah," Santi offers. "We built tools that can penetrate the dark web. They counteract anonymizing software."

"So is that the software people use to make themselves anonymous for criminal purposes?"

Rio finally acknowledges my existence by glancing over but doesn't say a word.

Santi answers, "That's it. But we aren't giving this to the general public. Shit, there's enough track and trace in fucking cookies and social media data. People would go mental."

I can sense this conversation could go well beyond my understanding quite quickly.

"Shay tells me you were talking to a philanthropic investor."

"Yeah," he says. "Our tech in the right hands can fight crime. In the wrong hands, it will just make it easier for criminals to create new ways to hide. We didn't want to sell our playbook to the devil, you know? It's actually been hard to find the right person, but we're partnered up with Thaddeus Getty. Just signed this week."

"You're serious? Shay didn't say who it was."

She really didn't, and that man is... well, he's a loose cannon kind of man who chases space and at the same time wants to save the planet. And a man who is stinking rich with a name known to nearly everyone on Earth. Aligning with Thad Getty is going to be an overnight game changer.

"Don't tell anyone," Rio finally speaks. His words are somewhere between a command and a threat. "It's not public yet, but apparently we're family now."

And there it is. The segue we've all been waiting for.

Rio doesn't look at me, just takes a pull from his beer. He talks while staring out into the sea of people. "We can trace anybody, anytime, anywhere."

He doesn't finish his sentence, but I can do it for him. *So don't tell a goddamn soul because we'll know it's you.*

Shit. I'm glad I've kept my nose clean enough over the years.

Rio pushes his back off the wall and steps toward me. Faces me. We're twin towers.

"So what about *you*, Logan? What have you been up to all these years besides hockey?" He asks as if he thinks hockey is a disguise and I'm actually a serial killer.

"Family and hockey was it. I'm a simple man."

At that, his black-lined mouth twitches up at the corner. "Oh yeah. You don't seem so simple to me." He flicks his eyes down. "Nice watch by the way." Accusation is still thick in his words, as if I stole my Rolex or something.

If Rio thinks he can goad me, I've been through just as much on the rink over the years and had to keep my cool. It's one of my skills to come across unbothered, casual and in control, even when my heart thunders and a snarky locker room response dangles on the tip of my tongue.

They don't need to like me, though I'd rather they did. But what I need is for them to believe I have Shay through thick and thin. That she's safe with me.

Rio's identical copy, Enzo, still gazes at me from behind his twin's back. He wraps his black skull lips around the neck of his beer and doesn't take his death stare off me when he drinks. Come to think of it, I'm not sure I even know what that brother's voice sounds like.

Santi lifts his wrist, revealing his own bling, giving me a break. "It's a reliable place to store cash. Independent of inflation or deflation."

I got mine because I thought it looked good, but he's not wrong. Luxury watches hold their worth. But him having his own makes me wonder.

How did these guys manage to live in one of the most expensive small towns in California, invest in their tech for years? The few times I've seen one of them around, their shoes always appeared to be luxurious Italian leather and their suits tailored to their every angle. Once I saw Santi at a rodeo when I was out with Dash, and

Santi had on crocodile skin boots. I swear he was wearing a Stetson, those cowboy hats cost at least five grand. They had impeccable style whether in jeans or the tuxes they wear now, and I bet the G Wagon in the drive is theirs, too.

Where did they get their money? Like Santi says, it must be all locked up in goods, because if they had cash flow, there's no way Shay would have taken my offer in Vegas. I don't think she would have felt any shame asking her brothers to help with Antonio's school. She wouldn't have to ask. Once they knew the situation, they would have paid.

But for some reason they can't. Or couldn't. Or like me, she has subconscious ulterior motives.

Santi lowers his arm and tucks his watch back up into his black shirtsleeve, and finally, I think I get a friendly smile, but it's hard to read what kind it is because each one of these men is painted with dark lips, eyes, and cheekbones of the underworld.

I'm standing with a group of ironically muscly skeletons, dark eyes threatening a showdown and working to make sure I know I'm not in their inner circle.

But I will be. Maybe not today, but at some point it will happen, because this is it for me.

Just then, Nino rushes into our space, and the little ghoul grabs my hand. "Mom told me to come and get you. She wrote you a *calaverita* in the book Papa Luis bought."

"What's a cala...?"

Rio explains. "A funny epitaph for someone who's still alive. Funny or... a chance to display cutting truths."

I don't really understand, but probably will soon enough, because Nino tugs at my hand.

I don't miss eight eyes dropping to where Antonio holds

me, and when the dark eyes rise again, the mood of aggression fades a decibel.

"I'll be there in one minute, Nino. I just have one more thing to say to your uncles."

"Okay. Hurry!" He puts his hands on his hips. "And wear your mask!" He spins and runs off toward his mom, bumping into a few people along the way.

I missed Nino and am heading out for a string of away games. So if I can't make headway quickly tonight with these guys, I want to spend the time with him and Shay.

But not before I give them something to think about.

I rub my hands together. "Should we just finish this brilliant conversation off, gentleman?"

Black painted eyebrows rise.

"Listen, I know it's hard to accept one day Shay is single and then the next, she's married to me. But she is. Shay is my wife." I lift my left hand in the air. "I'm taking this ring six feet under; that choice has been made. But when it comes to us." I flick my finger between me and the wall of skeletons. "I can be Shay's husband. Or I can be your brother. I'll leave that up to you."

They say nothing. I didn't expect them to. You don't convince a man like a Mendez to trust you overnight, especially when Shay explained they found out about my publicity stunts and considered me a liar because of it. I never thought of it that way exactly, but I guess they're right on some level. I did lie to the public about who I was. Maybe that makes me one to watch. All I can do now is slowly bleed out their suspicion by treating Shay and Nino the way they deserve.

We'll get there. One day.

I put on my mask and make my way to the kitchen where I find my woman bent over the pine table, writing in some kind of book. Her ass stretches the beautiful pattern of her vintage Mexican dress, and her waist nips in, revealing a perfect spot for my hands. God, I want to take her again. No doubt our time in the broom closet will be added to my spank bank when I'm away. Which is all too soon.

The first time I left for the road when I knew Shay and I were actually doing this, it didn't sit right. Now, thinking of leaving tomorrow when I've hardly been with her this week makes my stomach brittle. Ready to shatter. I've never wanted to skip hockey. Even when Shay and I were in college, I wanted to play; of course, then I didn't know the pros would be our demise. I wanted it then, because I wanted the dream. It created financial stability doing the thing I love most.

But now? I have the money. I have the lower back pain and nightly shoulder ache to go along with years of playing the game. And for the first time in my life, I just want to stay home because I actually have one.

I slip my hand around Shay's lower back and tug her in. Nino is on her other side, looking at what she's writing.

"This is the *calaverita* book my dad got a few years back," she says, finishing with a blunt-dotted period. "People are invited to write in it every year. It's just for fun."

"Great mask!" Antonio slides the book toward him. "I want to find you a really good one." He sticks his pink tongue through his black lipstick and thumbs through the book. "Here's the one someone wrote about Mom."

On the page is an outline of a tombstone, black-inked flowers and grass along the bottom. The tombstone is left blank for people to write. On the gravestone, someone has written Shay's fake obituary.

I read:

. . .

Here lies Baker Shay, master of dough,
Her bakery bustling, her cakes a show.
With flour in clouds, she'd sneeze and bake,
Until one day, a sneeze she couldn't shake.
Into the flour, her sneeze did land,
A dusty explosion, oh so grand!
But alas, poor Shay, couldn't catch her breath,
And sneezed her way to floury death.
Now she rests, with a sprinkle of white,
In doughy heaven, she'll bake through the night.
To Baker Shay, whose sneezes were her doom,
Rest in peace, sister, in your floury tomb!

I chuckle. "Okay. I get it."

Shit. I hope they haven't called me over to write one. I'm crap with rhymes but might manage a nice scathing limerick about her brothers dying from their assholes being too tight if given enough time.

"It doesn't have to rhyme," Nino says. "A lot do, but they don't have to."

Shay stares down at the book, her body language morphing into something less confident. "Most of the rhyming ones people prepare before coming to the party."

I flip through and read a couple more. There's one for Luis. One for Aunt Rita who I met years ago. It's cute. Light-hearted. She died from a broken stiletto. It's all part of making peace with death.

Shay turns the page and points. "I wrote you one," she says, not looking up at me.

328

"All right, let me see it." I read.

> *Here lies our Logan, hockey's bright star,*
> *On the ice, he'd shine near to far.*
> *With stick in hand, he'd glide and strive,*
> *But one fateful moment took his drive.*
> *Caught in the net, tangled and tight,*
> *He fought and struggled with all his might.*
> *Alas, poor Logan, trapped in the mesh,*
> *No more slap shots or victory's fresh.*
> *Now he rests in the rink's embrace,*
> *Forever frozen in his hockey grace.*
> *To Logan, whose passion never ceased,*
> *And who will be loved eternally.*

My heart swells as I read it again. And again. And especially the last line. Once. Twice. Three times I read it, then I glance up at Shay, peering at her through the holes in my skeleton mask.

But her gaze is low, and she wraps her arm around Nino as if she's anchoring herself, stopping her from floating away on a cloud of bashfulness that totally overcomes her. Because she's, in her own Shay way, showing her cards. My heart batters my rib cage looking over at my two little skeletons. We're in it till the end.

I drape my arm around her. "I love you, too, Shay."

Chapter Thirty-Three

Logan

Leaving my favorite people behind wasn't easy. I had to force myself off Shay and when I grabbed my protein shake to head off to the airport, I wanted nothing more than to stay and make Nino pancakes before school. He'd probably laughed and said his mom's were better, but these were the urges I was having now. Every day. Multiple times a day.

Three days have passed. The Scorpions have managed to climb the leaderboard thanks to more goals than I've ever scored in back-to-back games. Maybe Coach was right. Maybe I needed sleep. Maybe I needed less drinking, party-ing, and distraction. But I *am* distracted. It's just that this one feeds intense focus, too. I'm doing it for all of us now. Not just me.

I'm almost back on my home stretch again. We showered, listened to coaches' debriefs, and even Rosario has turned off his celebration beats in the locker room. I'm tying my laces on my sneakers, so fucking ready to get back on that plane, when Coach sticks his head through the locker room doors.

"Hunter."

It's Coach.

"Give me a minute?"

I tap Ashton's side and follow him into a barren hallway. Fluorescent lights beat down. Coach leans his back against one of the walls, his head dropped.

This doesn't feel good. I don't know why or how I could have gotten myself into trouble, but trouble is coming.

He lets out a sigh and raises his head, lifts his cap off, scratches his bald dome, and replaces the cap. "I normally don't override the processes around here..." He struggles with his words. "But I wanted to be the one to tell you instead of Reggie, and he'll be getting word tomorrow."

An ominous shadow looms between us and makes me shudder.

"Out of respect to you, and you have a brand-new wife and kid who I know can't move school..." He draws his lips into a thin line. "I wanted you to know from me... I actually changed my mind about you. You've been playing stronger than ever since settling down. It's not your performance. It's not you at all, Hunter. With Dane retiring we've had a chance to bid for Greason..."

Greason. One of the top defenders in the NHL. A very *expensive* top player.

"Salary caps. It's the goddamn salary caps that fuck us over every time," he grumbles.

"Coach. Just spit it out." I think better of my tone, that's not the kind of cowboy my mom raised. "Respectfully, of course. Sir."

Coach's bloodshot blue eyes lock with mine, but he doesn't say what I know he needs to.

I do it for him. "I'm getting traded."

I'm met with a somber nod.

My head falls. *"Traded..."* I say more to myself than to him.

I can't believe this. Everything has been perfect. I bought my dream home in Starlight Canyon. I filled it with my dream wife and a perfect son. Even the cat nearly likes me now. And I can't move them. I can't. I know Shay won't leave her dad, and Antonio's situation is unique and not something we can cart around the country hoping every school can cater to.

"It's not this season, though," he explains, "so you'll be able to play out with Dane. I know that's important to you boys."

"End of season?" My words are grim.

"End of season." He nods.

My stomach crumbles down my legs, and they go all tingly. I've got till April, maybe May in Starlight Canyon. It will go too fast. It's not enough time.

"I'm sorry, Hunter. I really, really am. Honestly, my preference would be to have you and Greason play together, but we can't spend on you both. We got goddamn money coming out of our ears spending it on stupid bullshit instead of players. I know the caps are for the good of the league and to encourage better competition, but you're not the first player I had to reluctantly trade because the budget couldn't expand."

A whirlwind of thoughts swirl in my head, but none of the words are worth saying. Not even the whole alphabet could change my situation. And I can't take it personally. People are traded all the time, especially because of the salary caps. Reggie wouldn't want me taking less. No player wants to devalue themselves, so when a hotshot player comes in, a lot of times, someone else has to go.

It is the life we live in the NHL.

It's just not the life I thought I was living in anymore. Somewhere along the way, I started thinking I was going to go off to work and come home to Shay and Nino and suffer in that pattern a bit until my off-season break. Then do it all over again until my abnormal schedule becomes normal. I've been protected by this halo of love. I forgot to brace myself for change.

Coach scrubs a hand down his sullen, remorseful face. He might have been pissed at me a million times over but he's a mentor. And mentors always have trouble letting go.

I know it's not him. He's given me so many approving nods and tips in the past few weeks. I know it's not him.

"It is what it is," I say bluntly.

"Maybe there are schools where you go for your son?"

I shrug, because refuting him takes more energy than I have.

He gazes at me intently and leaves me with three final words. "You have choices."

I didn't say a word in the car to the airport. I'm not sure I even blinked. My body was so numb transporting myself from that moment in that hallway lit up like some deathbed tunnel.

Traded. After all this. Fucking traded.

I hardly notice any of my teammates around me. My feet drag around automatically. I've been through this drill a thousand times. I don't need conscious thought to get me from point A to point B.

But when I finally nestle into my seat on the plane, Ashton places his hand on my arm, stopping me from putting in my earbuds.

"You gonna talk to me?" he asks.

"I don't know if I'm ready."

A silent laugh jerks his chest. "That means you'll never be ready so you might as well talk."

He's right. This news will never get any easier. Not after listening to a Nate Smith album. Not after eating. Not after even a glass of fucking wine. This will never get better.

I spill it. "I'm getting traded at the end of the season."

Ashton is as frozen as I've been for the past hour.

"Yup. And you know my deal. Shay and Nino can't move."

"*Shiiit.*" His sympathies are present in every letter of that word.

"But what the fuck am I going to do?" I throw my hand up. "I'm too fucking old to fly somewhere after practice, then there are away games even if I wanted to try it, just... It's fucked. I honestly can't say fuck enough times to express how I'm feeling right now."

Ashton lets me sit with my feelings.

A beat of silence passes, and just when I think we might let it drop, another wave of frustration spits out of me.

"I finally get my shit together. I finally have a reason not to be..." I pause, and the realization hits. All those years of running from loneliness. From feeling like I didn't do life the way I should. I finally course correct with the woman I love, and life fucking steals it away. "I finally stopped being afraid of getting old."

Ashton's eyebrows lift. Getting old is something all sportspeople understand. We're well aware of our mortality before many other people our same age are. My non-pro sports friends who are thirty-seven like me don't have a hip in need of resurfacing and fingers that don't straighten out anymore. We're knobby by the time we're forty in this profession, and it makes you consider what life will be when you're seventy. Eighty. You want light in it because your bones aren't going to be the thing making you happy the way they did when they attacked a goal at twenty.

It's why having Shay and Nino is everything. When I'm old and gray and my arthritis is going off on my rocker swing on the porch, I want other thrills around me besides hockey. I want the thrill of staring into Shay's face when the sun is setting. Of watching Nino grow up. Of more kids and even grandkids.

I can't have it all. I was right when I said it's the biggest fallacy of our age.

"Fuck," I hiss out, venting more frustration.

"Yup," Ashton agrees. "But..." He sighs. "It sounds like you're having a pity party to me."

My head whips up. My eyes narrow because I recognize those words. And I'll recognize the advice to come. It was mine to him not so long ago.

"Yeah, bro," he continues. "It's your decision to make. There's no right or wrong answer, just a series of possibilities." He smiles smugly, referring to the time we were on the pond and I made his tough decision with my sister out to be, well, a little simpler than it might have been.

I punch his arm. "Fuck off."

"Seriously, though, Lo, you do have choices here. You might not like them. I know how hard some of them are to make. But you aren't trapped. Figure it out."

"It's not that easy."

"Well, let me help you by using your own logic. First, you figure out if you want the girl."

I run my fingers through my hair. "I fucking want the girl, Dane."

"Then take her and screw the rest."

"You make it sound so simple."

He cocks his eyebrow, brown eyes glazed with satisfaction at being able to repeat my own advice back to my face. "You make a decision, you work around that decision."

"Fine, dickhead. You win. I get it. What you went through with Jolie was hard."

"Damn hard. But worth every second."

The flight attendant comes over and offers us drinks. I choose the wine because I really need it now. Ashton, a bottle of water. We drink for a moment. Let the gravity of what he's saying sink in. He doesn't need to explain himself. What he's suggesting is clear as day.

I do have options.

But am I ready for that permanency? Am I ready for that level of identity shift?

I pop in one earbud. "Thanks."

He nods.

I put the other earbud in. It goes without saying that if I have more questions I can talk to him. But I don't need to talk. I need to think. I need to listen to my heart. Because the decision on the line will forever change life as I know it.

Chapter Thirty-Four

Shay

WHEN I BECAME A MOM, I lost my ability to deep sleep. Logan gets home late. It's one-thirteen in the morning. I'm groggy when the door clicks open and shuts.

I told him not to change what he likes to do when we moved in and to just be natural, so he makes his way to the bathroom. I can tell the difference in the sound of his regular footsteps from his quiet ones. He's considerate, so he tries not to wake me.

But when he goes into the bathroom, he closes the door without shutting it by the handle, hoping to not make more noise. Only thing is, it creaks open one millimeter at a time until it's wide open and I see the reflection of him in the shower. Steam rises off his back. His muscles are lean and strong. I make out the sharp edges and angles of a body so capable, so honed to perfection through the pursuit of passion.

He braces his arms on either side of the temperature dial and hangs his head, his posture wilting from the strong stance he usually has to something more... defeated? I know they won tonight. I know his performance was insane. He scored six goals, and I don't think the world record is more than seven or maybe eight by one player alone. He was off the charts.

Maybe he's tired.

I'd be tired.

He doesn't stay there long. I know he showered thoroughly before leaving his venue, but Logan explained he can't climb into bed naked and think he's dirty. I like that about him. He towels off his firm chest, sliding the towel down to his groin and rumbling his thick, long hanging shaft.

He switches off the light and pads quietly to the bed, crossing the sliver of moonlight his window coverings never quite blot out. In the moment of spotlight, I peek from under the covers, glimpsing a rugged god.

He slides under the sheets, and despite having made an effort to be quiet, slips his body in perfect sync with mine. He breathes one last slow exhale, as if it's the very last time he'll breathe today.

I reach behind, grab his hand, and wrap it around my middle. "You had an amazing game."

"You're awake."

"Mmm."

His body isn't the same. His skin usually melts into mine when our bare bodies touch. His hips press into my naked ass, his belly rests somewhere around my shoulder blades. Heat radiates off his body, but softness does not.

"Are you okay?" I ask.

He doesn't answer, so I flip around, aligning ourselves, face to face. His features are shadowed. "What's up, Logan?"

He snuggles his body as close as it can be to mine. "You know I love you, right?"

Something about his words makes my heart whimper. They read like a preface. Like he's paving the way for some other conversation.

"Do you know that, Shay?" he asks again.

"Yes. I know that." My voice is weak; it feels like there's a *but* coming.

He swipes his fingers through my hair. "You're my priority. You. And Nino." He lowers his lips to mine, pressing a kiss against my mouth I very much need.

It's a reassuring kiss. An *I'll never hurt you* kiss. Yes, his lips are present. But his mind isn't. Still, his hands wander around my hips and pull my ass against his body. His dick surges slightly when it makes contact with my thigh.

Our kiss is deep, and he moans into my mouth, "Shay..."

It's romantic. Sensual. And my name on his lips comes out with such a wanting.

It's different the way he is tonight. The same desire is there. The same feathery fingers and expert touch is there, but it's... different. Better?

He cups both sides of my face and kisses the corner of my mouth. Easing me onto my back, he peppers delicate kisses along my jaw, and my head falls to the pillow, my eyes close, my heart rate slows. His mouth infuses some kind of drug into me. I'm floating on a high. My mind is lighter than ever.

His kiss is slow, needy but not greedy. He takes his time making his way down the column of my throat, patient even in the darkness of the night that races to morning. He stops briefly in between my breasts, dotting my sternum, kneading my breasts in his hands but not rolling my nipples like he might do. No, this moment might be sexy but it's... romantic. It's gentle. It's... loving.

His mouth tastes the trail of skin like a delicacy not to be rushed; he's savoring me. No haste. He swipes his thigh between my own to pry them open but still doesn't change the slow pace with which he worships my skin. My core must be burning his pec that touches it; between my legs is such an outpouring of lust, but still, he's not tempted to race ahead.

He reaches my belly. His hands rest on the cradle of my hips, and he raises his mouth briefly to say, "I love your skin."

I caress my fingertips along his bare back. "I love yours, too."

It's not easy for me to say these things, but he deserves to know. I need to try harder to open up. To trust and to let go of the ties that hold me back from a love that's truly special.

His tongue reaches my pussy, and he uses two thumbs. The first touch on my folds has my breath hitching, and he pulls me apart to swipe his flat tongue from my entrance to my clit. The motion is so slow, so deliberate, and blood fills my core, swelling it with wanting, sending an inviting wetness for my man.

He climbs back up the length of me. His strong arms brace him; he hovers but allows his now thick shaft to rest along the seam of my pussy. He pushes against me subtly, but it sends a jolt of burning electricity through my bones.

He drops his forehead to mine. "I love you..."

How many times will he use those word? How many times will he steal my breath with that emotion, with his generous heart, with his courage to take me as I am?

He needs to hear it, too. I know he does. He wouldn't tell me that, though, because Logan wouldn't want it if it wasn't given freely. But the words strangle my throat. Something about those three words just feels like my undoing. It feels like a total loss of control. Like opening Pandora's box.

But I can show him. I might not be able to say it aloud, but I can show him with my body. I love him, too. I do. So much, it hurts.

I grab either side of his face. "I want you inside me. Take me." I kiss his lips. "I'm yours."

With that, he reaches down and runs his cock along my slit. The sensation sends shivers up my spine and a rush of ecstasy through my body. I just want him inside me. I don't even care if I come.

He sinks himself inside, stretching me to the limit is a full, almost burning sensation so hot I want to buck and writhe. But even though my clit is already full to the limit, ready to burst with just one more flick, I rock my hips ever so gently.

We aren't having sex now.

We're making love.

In this moment, my body is his, and that's as precious as any three words. He has my vessel. He has my heart. It's the only place my soul can live, and inviting him in is the best I can do.

I want to work through my fears and trust issues, I want to erase years of seeing Logan as the NHL playboy and find my way back to the worship I had for the college boy he once was. I'll get there...

For now, I show him.

His dick is so hard I feel his every vein and ridge rumble along my insides. I'm so stretched its ecstasy. It's a slow, steady rhythm. My hands enjoy the flex of his ass when he dips inside me, bottoming out.

In and out. In and...

"Ahhh..." I sigh. The feeling is overwhelming.

With that, he quickens the pace slightly. I urge my hips against his bones harder, too. His thumb swipes in a faster, more deliberate motion.

And then, I can't hold back anymore.

"You want to come for me, *pastelito*?"

"Yes."

"You want me to take you there?"

"Yes," I whimper.

"I'm taking you everywhere. I'll never leave without you..."

His words sharpen my senses slightly, but little blood remains in my brain to process anything. I just spread my legs wider, as wide as I can while he rails into me, thrusting harder, our hips colliding in a powerful feeling so different from the times before.

I love this man.

"Come with me, Logan..."

His powerful glutes ride me hard. We slap together with passion. Loud, balmy skin connects as he penetrates me deep, soul deep.

Finally, my clit explodes and pulses under his thumb.

"Mmmm..." I bite my lip.

He thrusts three more times, and while my entire body quivers, burning-hot desire spills inside me. His body brings me to the next level, blinding me. I throw my hands to the sides and grasp the sheets to stop myself completely disappearing in this moment.

Finally, his thrusts slow and his face drops to my neck. He kisses me. I kiss his salty skin in return and open my eyes to the darkness of the room, but flickers of blinking light dance in my eyes.

That was *everything*.

He slips off to the side of me. We snuggle as though our bodies are one. His breathing slows, and his arm grows heavy around me, a veil of security.

But I can't shake the change tonight, not just for me, but for him, too.

I only fall asleep just before dawn, demons chattering in my head telling me something is very, very wrong.

Chapter Thirty-Five

Shay

To say I'm not a morning person is an understatement. And having had zero sleep, on top of not being the most cheerful person at this time of day, has me standing in front of the coffee machine ready to throw it out the window for being so damn slow. I need a steady flow of caffeine to be human, and the only other thing that makes me feel that way is my son.

He bounces into the kitchen in his pajamas. *"Buenos días."*

"Buenos días, mijo." My voice croaks. "Did you have a nice sleep?"

"I had a weird dream," he says matter-of-factly and sits,

placing his worn and tattered oven mitts blankie on the table. "I was a hockey coach. And I took my team to the finals with my super-amazing plays."

My cup of coffee finally fills, but it's Nino who makes me cheerful. He always has the most vivid, cutest dreams. "You should tell Logan. Who knows, maybe one of your plays from the dream really is for the pros."

"It's true that math is all around us. Even in sports."

I sit opposite him with two toasted bagels. Butter for me. Peanut butter for Nino. I swipe the spread on his. "Maybe even especially in sports. Think about it. The arc of a basketball. The angles on a pool table."

"I know! It really is the most useful subject."

I slide his bagel on a plate across the table, and he munches.

Logan walks in with those glorious gray sweatpants on. "Morning."

He looks rough. He *never* looks rough.

"Logan! I had a dream about math and hockey!" Nino exclaims.

Logan pops a pod into the coffee machine, and it whirrs. "That sounds like you went to heaven for a little while. Nino heaven."

"I know, right?" He bites into his bagel again.

Logan quietly waits for his coffee. Logan is never quiet. It's the second *never* of the morning, which makes my ears prick up. And then, the third comes.

"Are you having breakfast?" I ask.

"Uh..." He scratches his head, pausing as though it's some complicated decision. "Not today."

He *never* skips a meal.

Something is wrong. Really wrong. I knew it last night.

I knew something changed. Something was different. It seemed different in a good way then, but now?

Logan has a game and needs to get to the arena. I planned to meet his teammate, Rosario's, mother to plan the *quinceañera* cake, and she lives an hour north of Longbrook. So I'll need to drop Nino, head to the meeting, and Logan won't be back until it's too late to talk.

I've never been good at sitting with bad news. It's both a strength and a weakness of mine. It's always opened the door to conversations others might avoid, but it's closed some doors, too, because I'm a hopeless type who has always chosen to end things instead of sit and wait it out.

There isn't much time for Logan and I to chat before I leave. He stirs his coffee with a spoon, even though he doesn't add any milk or sugar.

My laugh is hollow and half-hearted, my comment just to see if I can make him smile. "You're stirring what exactly?"

I see his cheeks lift a bit, but he doesn't lift his head.

"The metal is supposed to cool the coffee down faster."

"There's temperature control on your fancy machine. Or like most men you didn't read the manual?" I tease.

I hope my little prod makes him come alive like it usually would, but he still stares at his mug.

"I actually didn't know that. Maybe you can show me sometime."

Oh God. Logan is not himself this morning. Should I ask him what's the matter? But what if it's me? Then I have to think about it all day, and we can't resolve it, and I might mess up my meeting because one thing that stresses me the hell out is love. It's what's going on with Logan. It's wanting him to be okay.

Nino finishes his bagel.

"Baby, I set your clothes over the chair in your room. Why don't you get dressed and I'll come help you brush your teeth in a minute."

"Okay." He grabs his mitts from the table and heads back down the hall.

I swallow thickly and make my way next to Logan. I slide my arms around his waist and hug him from behind, laying my head on his broad back. "Are you okay?"

"Not really."

"Want to talk about it?"

"Well, we need to talk about it."

"We do?"

He hangs his head and nods.

I turn his body around to face me. "You're freaking me out, Logan."

"Sorry, I don't mean to. We need to talk, but it'll take some time to iron shit out. But unfortunately, I've never been good at hiding my feelings, and it's just a tough one, you know?"

My heart nearly explodes with anxiety. "No. I don't know. You should tell me."

"There's not enough time now."

"Don't do this to me, Logan. Now I know something is wrong, it will eat me alive today."

"Honestly, Shay…"

"Tell me…"

"I'm getting traded," he blurts. "At the end of the season, they're trading me. I don't know where, but come April, May, I'm done here with the Scorpions."

His words are a sucker punch, a hard, ruthless blow, and with my defenses down, tears instantly threaten behind my eyes. I have to look away. What the hell? He's being traded? I didn't plan for this. We didn't talk about this. I clear my throat and push away the devastating sadness the only way I know how.

I summon anger in its place. "So our plan didn't work. It's over?"

My words have more force than I intend, and Logan's defeated energy stiffens into something else. Something hard. Like he's immediately erected a fortress. "Over? What exactly do you mean by *over*, Shay?"

I don't know what I mean by *over*. But as usual, I choose the words that make me appear invincible, though I'm very far from it. His words sucked the strength and soul right from my body. And when I don't feel strong, I self-destruct. It's happening now, but the words come out like second nature. "Our agreement. I can't give you my end of the bargain anymore so I guess it's over."

He laughs maniacally, and I know I hit a nerve. Logan is one of those calm, collected men, suave and classy, put together and unshakeable, so when he does shake, it's like tectonic plates shifting. He's not loud but he rumbles strong like an earthquake.

"You are my wife, Shay. You think I give a shit about that agreement anymore?" He cages me in against the counter. "Is that all it is to you?"

Say no, Shay, Say no. Tell him he's so much more.

But even if I tell him I love him, that he means so much to me it will only make the trade that much harder. I couldn't do it back in college. How can I do it now when I love him a million times more and he means the world to not just me but Nino? I haven't completely forgotten how much Logan's reputation hurt me, especially when I experienced it amongst a string of lying, cheating men.

With Logan here, coming home regularly, we can work on it.

My jaw clenches. Fear stabs at my insides. In just six months he'll be gone. Not just during the day and a few nights a week. Gone. There is no way I can move. There is absolutely no chance of Logan coming home after regular practice or a home game.

Despite fear plucking my every last nerve, it's not what I see in Logan's gaze. It's not what his hands on my hips are telling me.

"Do you trust me?"

I wish I said nothing. But instead, my words would haunt me for the hours to follow when Logan leaves for Santa Fe.

"I'm not sure."

"You're not sure?" he asks. "Are you serious?"

He's halfway between shock and pain. I hate seeing him this way. I hate that I'm hurting him, but my shadow follows me still, and she's hellbent on putting me back behind my wall.

I choke on my words. "I haven't thought about it."

"You don't need to think about whether you trust someone or not. It's a feeling, Shay."

"Well, I don't know."

He rubs his temples. "I said you were mine." He throws his hands back to the counter and grips it, white-knuckled. "What the hell more do you want from me? How many more times do I need to fall at your feet and worship you before you love me back enough to say it?"

I'm hurting him. I've hurt him so much and I know it. I hurt *us*. Finally, a single truth falls from my lips. "I'm afraid, Logan."

He softens almost immediately at my confession. He of all people knows I don't do vulnerability. He pulls me against his warm chest, wraps his strong arms around me, and I press my ear to where his heart beats wildly.

I admitted it. Now he knows.

"I'm afraid of getting hurt like I have been for years since college. And I'm even more afraid of being hurt now than I was back then."

He smooths my hair and kisses the top of my head. "I can't undo all the things I've done between now and then that have made you doubt me. But I promise you this... I'm prepared to earn your trust. I will fucking beg for it until my hands and knees are bleeding. I'm not asking you to be unafraid. I'm just asking you to love me anyway."

Chapter Thirty-Six

Logan

I STROKE HER HAIR. I can palm her entire little head. I know how much it took out of her to admit she's scared. I am, too. I'm about to make decisions I knew would always come, but still it's such a surprise.

I'm facing choices that are so permanent I don't know how I can make them without knowing she's going to stay. Until now, I didn't realize how much Shay leaving me back in college left a permanent scar. How so much of the distance I created between me and other women was the same distance Shay creates to protect herself.

Maybe I should tell her about my plan. But I want to be chosen.

"Shay, you are the person my soul cries out for. You're so undeniable there are no other options. And I'm scared, too, because I felt this way before, I was ready to do anything to make it work, and all you found were reasons it wouldn't."

A tear trickles down her cheek. She does love me. Somewhere inside there, there is love. But I need more. I need trust. I want her to follow me. To believe me. To promise me she won't give up, to think I'm the man to protect her and Nino for the rest of my life. I want her to commit to me. I know better than to ask for all that now, but this is it. I have a couple of moments left before our bodies are torn apart by my demanding schedule.

I have a game tonight.

I'll be in Santa Fe without her today with the biggest decision of my life weighing in the balance. Does it depend on what she says? Maybe. If it doesn't, I sure as hell won't leave her with any doubt about what I want or the way I feel.

I grip her arms firmly and make sure she hears every word I utter. "I know you still think of the past. I do, too. It didn't go to plan. It all fell apart. It was one magnificent fucking display of heartache. But the way I see it, the pieces are still here between us, Shay, and I want to put them back together in a new way, with you and that beautiful boy down the hall. I'm all in."

Her eyes brim with tears, and the bridge of my nose stings admitting it. Admitting that I held on to my first love the way I have. But it's the truth. And if I'm about to destroy my other world, I need to believe I can build another.

Shay doesn't get to respond because Antonio enters the room.

"Mom, I'm ready to brush my teeth."

She sniffles and tries to sound normal. "Be right there."

"Thanks." He skips back down the hall.

A heavy silence hangs between us, not the kind where there's nothing to say, but rather far too much.

"Where does this leave us?" she asks.

"I told you what I want. Take your time but... I need to know what *you* want."

The one good thing to come from my years of Vegas fuck-ups is that I'm still halfway decent at playing on even only a few hours of sleep. That day on the ice, I am distracted, though. I miss way too many drill shots and nearly took one to the mask, too.

What I'm contemplating wasn't supposed to happen so soon. Something about the decision ahead of me feels all too familiar to the emotions I had when my dad died.

Not yet.

Not now.

Too soon.

Just like then, I have to accept the end of things is part of life. I'm willing to do anything for Shay now. But I know what happens in that woman when fear takes hold. And making a decision so permanent and of such enormity for... *almost?* Almost having her. Almost forever. Almost a family. Almost a husband.

Almost would tear the fucking skin from my bones.

She hasn't said it yet. She hasn't told me she loves me.

She hasn't told me she thinks this will last. But I *feel* it. It's not just in my intuition but in her every touch. It's in the way she stares at me, pretending not to smile at my jokes, but her lips quirk up like I'm the most delightful person in the world. It's the way she cooks for me and puts extra spice in my portion just how I like it, even though it's more work. It was in her *calaverita*. In her always knowing the score for my games and being so pissed at the players that check me she swears in Spanish. Her love is in how she rubs my shoulder in the exact place it hurts, without having to ask where it aches. Shay shares her son with me, quite possibly the ultimate display of love.

Do I need her words to make this decision?

We get on our gear. I slug some energy drink in hopes of getting a second wind.

Ashton comes into the locker room from kicking the soccer ball with some teammates. He takes out his earbuds and packs them into their case. "So you have a call with Reggie?"

"Yeah."

"Have you made up your mind?"

"I think so."

He contemplates me.

I chew my lip. "Were you sure? When you did it for Jolie, were you a hundred percent sure?"

He glances around to check if anyone listens. He sits next to me and asks discreetly, "You want to know if I was sure when I decided to retire?"

I nod.

He scratches his head. "I wasn't sure exactly. I tried to justify it as a good move even if I *didn't* have her." He blows a laugh out of his nose. "With women like Shay and Jolie, I don't think you'll ever be sure about anything."

My sister and Shay are both feisty and independent. They don't need men to complete them, and even though Jolie is much more open with her feelings than Shay, she sometimes makes choices that seem so illogical you could never guess them.

He continues. "It happens for all of us. I knew I was getting gnarly and going to end up useless to anyone or anything if I played another season more with my ankle. The thing that cropped up for me over and over, though, was what to do after. You at least have the wind farm."

"I'm sure the turbines will be stimulating conversation," I deadpan.

"And you already have a kid, which was something I worried about at the time." He slaps my arm. "You're going to be a great stay-at-home dad."

"I have a kid if Shay stays with me."

"She will."

"Why do you say that?"

"You won't give her any choice."

"I let her leave last time."

"That clearly had to be. And it had to happen to bring Antonio here."

It's uncanny. "I said the same thing."

"But this time? No, this time you won't let her leave. You're gonna retire, bro, because it's the only way. And you know what they say about the right thing?" He throws his sneakers into his locker space. "The right thing isn't reactive. It's proactive."

"Who said that?"

He whips his shirt off overhead. "Your dad."

Ashton grabs his water bottle and squirts some drink into his mouth. "Bro, you do what you have to do." He throws a towel over his shoulder, preparing to head over to the massage therapists. "We're lucky we have this season. Let's make it count." He points at me. "Then we can join the golf club."

Chapter Thirty-Seven

Shay

I MADE it through the car ride to Longbrook just listening to Nino talk and sing to songs on the radio. I made it to my meeting by numbing myself completely. I turned into a whole other person to get through that. But as I drove away from Rosario's family's house and to the restaurant near Longbrook where I agreed to pick up my brother, Santi, the energy I've used to prop myself up was nearly completely deflated. When he gets in the car, I have to hold my jaw tight not to burst into tears.

I don't even glance at Santiago. He stayed in New Mexico after the Day of the Dead celebrations in order to see some old friends. Being that we were both in Santa Fe today, I offered to pick him up and take him to get Nino. Santi wanted to see his new school.

My brother doesn't notice I'm a zombie. "Hey. Thanks for the ride. Can't wait to see the place. Nino made it sound like paradise."

"Mmm." If I open my mouth enough to form a word, it might allow a sob to creep out.

He stares out the windshield, unaware, and tells me about the meeting with his friend. "I can't believe how much Gaspar's life has changed. It's hard to believe that old gigolo has a family now. Cute kids, too. Twins." He pauses. "What's with all the twins these days? Is it something in the water? I swear there are twins everywhere you look in California."

I grip the steering wheel. Stare at the road ahead, but know I need to answer or he'll ask what's wrong. "Maybe it's all the older parents there. IVF maybe?"

"Hm. That makes twins more likely?"

"I think so."

His gaze seems to strip off my cheek and find another place out the window. "Well, he's doing great. He's still an artist, and I have to say I'm impressed he didn't give up on his dream to do that." His hand lands on my arm. "It's not easy to keep going. I know about that…" He taps my arm. "Proud of you, too, *nena*. You got this cake business on lock…"

With his touch, with his pride, I burst. Tears well up and I have to blink fast to keep watching the road. I wipe my burning cheeks, but as soon as I dry them, the tears wet them all over again.

"Oh no. I made you cry. Shit. What did I say?"

"It's not you."

"Did you not book the cake?"

I booked the cake. In fact, it was another mind-blowing budget the Rosarios had. So much so it made me wonder if Logan was actually subsidizing these deals and making contributions.

"I booked the cake."

"Is it Nino?"

I've almost completely stopped crying now. "No. Antonio kicks ass. He's so damn cool."

I sense his mind searching for any other reason in the world that could bring me to tears.

I admit what's on my mind. "It's Logan."

The energy shifts quickly in my passenger seat. "Fucking..." Santi speaks through gritted teeth. "I actually started to think he was all right."

"No. He didn't do anything wrong...." I say past a stone in my throat, and then when my next words come out, they force more tears. "The problem is he's done everything right."

The last word is high-pitched and accompanied by another set of pitiful sobs. I grip the steering wheel and head for straight but I'm sniffing and crying...

"Pull over..." Santi commands.

We only just pulled off the freeway and into Longbrook, so I find a small side road not a mile from campus.

I quickly regret letting one of my brothers in on this. If any men have been reluctant to love, it's these guys. Family. Their business. Horses. Tamales. That is all they really care about and not necessarily in that order. Santi will just tell me to forget about it.

"Ooof..." I hurry to clear away my outburst. "I don't know what got into me there."

"You said it was Logan."

"Yeah. I don't know why I said that." I can't talk to Santi. "Must be that time of the month." *That will work.*

"Come on, Shay, that might have worked when we were younger, but periods don't scare grown men."

My brother's glossy dark brows are pulled inward. His lips form a thin, concerned line.

"You can talk to me," he reassures. "I've changed a little since doing this business. I'm more sensitive now. Try me."

"You? Sensitive?"

"*Nena*, for you I'm always sensitive."

"Which is exactly why you're the wrong person to talk to."

He's exasperated but keeps pressing. "Well, as far as I see I'm the *only* person to talk to. Come on." He glances at his watch. "We have about ten minutes before we need to get up the road."

"You'd be a great shrink. *Your hour is up*," I say sarcastically with air quotes.

"Deflecting," he deadpans. "And by the way, I learned that term *from* my shrink, and it's a job I promise you I'm really not equipped to do. But I can be your brother. And if you don't tell me to get it off your chest then tell me to spare me, and Logan, because I'll ask him why his name came out of your mouth while you cried."

I have no idea why but I try to play it cool. "I love him. That's all."

He pushes his fingers into his eye sockets. "Jesus, Shay, I hope you fucking love him since you're married."

Shit. In my moment of weakness, I almost slipped.

"Yeah. I mean... it's really hard to explain. But it's not normal love. It's like..." I dance my arms around in front of me, hoping to catch some way of explaining. "It's like a kind of love that makes me..."

"Scared?" He finishes my sentence.

His gaze is that of a kindred spirit, and it disarms me.

"Yeah," I admit quietly. "Scared. I'm scared. And because I feel scared it's sending smoke signals. Like maybe that means it's wrong."

"I hate to break it to you, but I'm pretty sure that doesn't mean it's wrong but more that it's real."

"Surely love isn't scary."

"It sure as hell is. Fuck, just look at the four of us. We've ridden bulls, broken wild stallions, faced being ruined and risking our entire savings on a ten-page business plan. Us Mendez boys are brave, but love? It's been too frightening for even us. Yeah, I'm pretty sure love is scary. Well, real love is anyway."

"I don't know."

"Think about it. This Logan thing aside, have you ever been more worried about anything in your life than Nino?"

I bite the inside of my cheek. "No."

"See? Case in point." He shakes a finger. "Love. Love in all forms is scary."

"I don't love Logan the way I love Nino, though. It's totally different."

"Yeah, but both require the same thing. Trust. With Nino, you have to trust yourself. With Logan... you need to trust *him*. Both situations are scary."

"And therein lies my problem."

"You and me both." He gets a faraway look in his light-brown eyes. "You have two choices with this one. You either get brave. Or you get regret."

I've never known Santi with anyone serious before, but he's clearly referring to losing someone. A forbidden love? A fling? Who is this mystery woman who enters my brother's mind on a cold autumn day? I don't know. I *want* to know.

But for now I only have a few more minutes to pull it all together before we need to pick up Nino. And to digest this unexpected advice.

It's so obvious now Logan is one of the best things in my life, and me going through these growing pains shows it. But I worry I'll never change. Can I really trust him? I don't know how many years he has left in the NHL but we won't be physically together for much of them. I still can't move, so the best we'd have is long distance. His reputation creeps back up on me every time I think of it.

I look to the sky and flap my lips with exasperation. "I just wish I had a sign how to, I don't know, just be more trusting and show him how I love him without having to say it out loud. I mean, maybe it's growing up around you hard-asses, but saying I love you all the time just seems cringe."

Santi laughs like what I've said genuinely amuses him. "Yeah. Maybe."

I sigh. "It's just laughable, though."

"What?"

"God giving *me*, a person with trust issues, one of the hardest, most difficult trust tasks around."

"And what's that?"

"A long-distance relationship." I swallow down the stone that's back. "Logan is getting traded at the end of the season."

"Ooooh," he says like the penny has dropped. "Shiiiiit. I'm sorry." He waits a beat. "But he's kind of old so is he really going to be away for long?"

I smack my brother's arm, but he's at least made me smile again. "He's not old. He's *your* age."

"I mean, for hockey he kind of is, though. Right?"

I turn the car back on. "We need to go."

We drive in silence, and my brother's aura disappears

for a while. Has the memory of that woman come back to visit? One day I'll ask, but right now, I try to be present, focus on the road, and consider booking myself in for therapy when we get home.

Santi wants to see the campus, so I park in the visitor's lot and check my emails on my cell while he's gone. Every single one of Logan's contacts has gotten back to me. Weddings, parties... anything to celebrate with a my cake. My social media posts with the Santorini cake blew up. This really is just the beginning. It occurs to me in some way, being financially set to pay for Nino's school would be within my reach within a short span of time.

Only a while ago in Vegas I would have been ecstatic with this situation. I'm quickly closing in on not needing this marriage for money, but all I want to do is run into Logan's arms and hear how proud he is of me. All I want is for him to witness me growing, to thank him for being a part of it.

Thinking of him that way brings the ache back. I try not to be confused by it and consider that maybe Santi is right. This ache is real love.

Just then, the doors open. Santi helps Nino into his car seat in the back, then straps himself into the front.

Before setting off, I turn and reach back to grab my baby's hand. "How was your day?"

He beams. "Mom, my mind is blown."

Gosh, this boy makes my chest beam.

"Why's that?"

"One word." He spreads his hand as if across the sky. "Tessellations."

Oh, God help me now. I don't even remember what that is so I'm either old or I didn't pay nearly enough attention in middle school.

Nino reaches next to him, snatches his backpack, and rummages around. "Oh, and there's something I have for you. Logan put a note in my lunch."

My heart winces. God, he's so thoughtful.

Nino digs around in his bag. "I read the one he gave me, and he left one in there for you today, too."

"Really?" I'm confused.

Nino hands me a folded-up piece of paper. "It says," he reads the outside, *"Give this to your mom."*

I take the paper, and sure enough, there is Logan's surprisingly neat handwriting that blasts me back to college when he scribbled notes and left them tucked into my own backpack, under my pillow, in my toiletry bag. Everywhere.

I open the note, and there, in no more than four simple words, is the sign I've been waiting for. He doesn't write that he loves me. That, I've heard before. These four words are far more profound.

Ask me to stay.

I stare at the note for what feels like an eternity. It's like some epiphany makes the rest of the world fade away for a moment. And when I come to, I know what to do.

"Hey, are you boys up for going to a hockey game tonight?"

My brother offers one of his million-dollar smiles. "Always down."

He turns. "What about you, *gordito*? You like hockey?"

"If we're seeing Logan, the answer is yes."

An optimistic desperation grips me, but before I put the pedal to the metal, I take out my phone and text Logan.

I need to see you.

Chapter Thirty-Eight

Shay

IT'S HARD NOT to speed all the way to Santa Fe. I have to get there before Logan starts pregame prep. Not that I have any clue what I'm going to say or do to get in the building, but I hope like hell I can get there before Logan has to warm up. I should have told him I was coming tonight before the game. Before I let him play with his head as mussed up as mine is.

He thinks I'll be watching from home. Hell, he probably thinks I won't watch at all. I've been such a hard-ass with him; the guy is a hero for fighting through my shadows. Geez, even my text was lame. I should have just written *I love you.*

I check the clock on my dashboard. Shit. We got caught in so much rush-hour traffic, it's five-thirty. Even if I wanted to illegally pick up my phone now to write something a hell of a lot better and more romantic, I can't. He'll be warming up off ice or having a briefing. Whatever they do pregame, all I know is that Logan told me for two hours before puck drop and for an hour after the game, if I ever had an emergency, I needed to call Colt or Dash. Meaning, he cannot pick up his phone.

When we finally arrive at six, there are already fans littered around, tailgating. My brother hasn't stopped searching online and coming up short for tickets. When I finally dish out fifty bucks for parking, I turn off the ignition.

"Tell me you found tickets."

"No luck. But in my searches I did find out why. They're playing the Huskies tonight for the first time this season."

"Dang," I say under my breath.

He adds. "I guess everyone is thirsty for more knuckles after last season when Ashton beat the C-R-A-P out of Jolie's ex and the story broke that those two were together."

Then a lightbulb goes off. Jolie. The box. A Dane or a Hunter or both will surely be in the box tonight.

I text Jolie.

> Hi can I ask a massive favor? Are there any box seats left for tonight? If I'm being really greedy three tickets would be amazing.

I wait, biting my lip the whole time as an ellipsis from Jolie's end comes and goes. Comes and goes.

Finally...

JOLIE HUNTER

Sorry babe. I actually has a couple extra but I was having Braxton-hicks contractions so we gave them to Ashton's brother. Fletcher and some of his teammates are there tonight. Maybe ask Logan?

His phone will be off.

JOLIE HUNTER

Damn. That's true. I guess that means I can't text Ashton either. Sorry. You know I would have!

I came all this way and now I'm starting to feel like I overreacted. But I don't want to ruin Logan's mindset. I don't want to wait another second to commit to this man. It's unfair. To both of us.

Nino has had a long day and been in the car for hours. I turn around and reach into the backseat to unclip him. "Come on, baby. Let's stretch your legs."

The parking lot is massive. Dusk descends, but headlights illuminate the space in equal measure as the sun sets. The smell of barbecue fills my senses. Someone not far from us turns on some sort of sound system booming out energetic music.

I hold Nino's hand. "I'm not sure we'll make it to the game tonight." I try to mask my defeat with my stoic mom tone, but it doesn't work.

"Are you okay, Mom?"

"I just... really want to see Logan tonight. That's all."

"Will you ask him?"

I bend down to Nino's eye level and rub his arms. "Ask him what?"

"To stay."

Nino must have read the note. And now Santi knows its contents as well. I feel him stiffen behind me.

"Please ask him to stay, Mom. You're really happy when he's around. If he stays you'll be even more happy."

My heart whimpers. Kids notice nothing when you want them to and everything when you don't.

Asking Logan to stay in college wasn't an option. I would have never stopped him from achieving his dreams. I couldn't leave. That note... it changes everything. Logan isn't at the beginning of his career. I'm sure he doesn't want to think he's at the end either, but that's the only thing that note suggests. Retirement. But do I really want to be the reason Logan ends his career just because I struggle to keep my demons at bay and to trust? Not at all. No fucking chance.

It's time for me to step up. For both of us.

Tonight, I'm going to tell Logan something else. Something more meaningful. That I believe we can make it. That I'll be here no matter how long he's gone. But I can't tell him if I can't get in that damn building and then he's gone for days again on the road. This can't wait. I'm desperate, not only because he deserves to hear how much I adore him, but also...

Ashton.

I can't be the reason Logan doesn't play a single moment of this season to his best ability. This is Ashton and Logan's last chance at a Stanley Cup. I need to be the reason Logan is lifted, not knocked down. One game could make all the difference at the end.

So damn it. I need in that building.

I look over at the lit-up arena. And then, I have an idea. "Come on."

I drag Santi by the arm, Nino by the hand.

We sweep around the side of the building to the players' entrance. With a game on, all the security is out front, but now, we face a locked door. Santi and I gaze at each other, not sure what to do.

I pull my brother close so I can whisper in his ear, "Can you still pick a lock?"

His eyes dart down to Nino who he really doesn't want to know he can do it—heck, I don't want Nino to know his uncle used to be a bad boy either—but Nino isn't paying attention to us.

"Yes," he says through gritted teeth. He flicks another glance at the door and whispers, "But there's no lock."

What? "There's no..."

By the time I really settle my gaze on the high-tech, no-key door, Nino is on his tiptoes making the backlit green keypad sing.

"I remember the code. From when we came to meet the coach."

The door releases with a click, and I bend down to give Nino a mega kiss. "You really are my hero, *mijo.*"

Once in, all I can do is hope like hell Marlon is still at the door to the locker rooms. He is. Time is ticking, so we walk quickly down the hallway, so fast Nino struggles to keep up and Santi sweeps him up into his arms.

We get to the tall, imposing block of muscle with an earpiece outside the locker room doors, and only now do I realize I'm asking a huge favor. He already said nobody is allowed on the other side of the doors when Logan wanted me in.

"Hi. Marlon. I'm not sure if you remember me..."

He gives me a look as though he couldn't forget. *Gosh. I wonder if he heard us...*

"Please. I need to see Logan. It's an emergency." I try to

look distraught, but Marlon's face is full of dubious deep lines.

His response is polite. "I'm sorry, Mrs. Hunter."

My God do I love the sound of that.

"I can't let you on the other side of the doors."

"Yes. I know. But could you maybe see if Logan could come out?"

His expression tells me it's not his first rodeo. His eyebrows lift to the ceiling, eyes close, and he shakes his head.

He opens his eyes again, and I must have such a horrified expression from hearing *no* that the man does take a little pity. "Listen, if he has his four player tickets available, you might catch him on the ice for warm-ups. I'll radio over." He presses his finger to his ear and asks about the tickets.

The few minutes it takes to receive a response is agonizing.

But it's affirmative. Before too long, a staff member comes into the hall through a mystery door with no handle. "Hi, Mrs. Hunter?"

"Yes. And our son. And my brother."

"Great. I have your tickets. I just need some ID."

Crap. My ID doesn't even say Hunter. But surely Logan put my name down somewhere? I hesitate, but Marlon comes to the rescue.

"Trust me, Pat. This is Logan's wife. I can vouch for that."

He cocks an eyebrow at me, and for the first time since I entered this hallway, I'm grateful Marlon did hear us in that closet.

"If you say." She waves her hand. "Come with me."

We follow her through winding corridors and up tons of

steps. By the time we reach the seats we're being given, we're what feels like a million miles away and a stadium of bodies away from my husband.

But there he is. On the ice.

We're not exactly rink side this time. It's a myth that players always have the best seats. Truly, we have a great view in the second tier, right in the front row, with an excellent bird's-eye view, but we're hardly rink side. We're not close enough for me to get his attention.

"You guys want to weave down and see Logan up close?"

"Yeah!" Nino exclaims.

We leave our seats to make our way down, winding and dodging. Fans are pouring in like sand into an hourglass, fast and thick. Santi hangs on to Nino's hand while I stand on my tiptoes to see which entrance is the least full. Everyone wants to see the guys warm up now.

We pass stands selling fries, hot dogs, beer, and then a merchandise shop. I have an idea. Something Logan will love. "Let's get some jerseys."

I practically shove my way to the front of the line and buy us all tops, find a marker in my purse to sort mine out. I toss my brother one and yank the other over Nino's head so fast his hair rises with static.

Santi slips his on more casually and then eyes me. By now, I suppose my desperation has raised his suspicions. "You sure do need to see your husband."

"Yup." I take Nino's hand. "Let's go."

"*Stay,*" he says. "Are you sure there's not more going on than you told me? The way you're acting has me thinking this is a red alert."

I play innocent. "What do you mean?"

"I mean, I'm happy to be here, but why the urgency?

You know I'm always up for a little mischief, desk life isn't necessarily my thing, but..." He leans over closer and says quietly as if Nino might hear, "*Stay?* Are you two okay?"

"It's about the trade. I swear. I just don't want him making any decisions without hearing from me."

"You sure?" His light-brown eyes bore holes right through me. "Because the way you're acting is, how do I put this? Out of character."

I nod and smile, but more to myself than to him. "That's a sign right along with the fear, Santi. You're scared and acting crazy and you know... you know you're in love. Now let's go."

Unfortunately, my cute idea at the merch shop was a big mistake.

When we enter the bottom level of the arena, there are people everywhere. I worry about losing Nino in the huge crowd. But this is where Santi excels.

He takes my hand, I have Nino's, and he somehow cuts a rude trail right through the fans, not giving a crap if anyone minds his budging. He's right, though. Now is no time for manners. Finally, we reach the plexiglass, and there he is. Number nine. My husband. All the women around me are giddy and jumping up and down in low-cut tops, hoping to get some attention. Just then, someone plasters a cardboard sign right in front of my face.

I wiggle to the side of it with what floor space I have. I shout his name. But this is never going to work. The players are so used to ignoring fans on the sides.

Santi has an idea. "Shay, you need to make your way near the player benches. I'll get his attention." He pops Nino on his shoulders and makes his way up some of the stairs to higher ground, then lets out the loudest country boy, cowboy wolf whistle you've ever heard. It's the one he used to blow to bring the dogs back to heel.

It works. A few of the players glance over, including Logan. With Nino on Santi's shoulders, I really hope they're recognizable. They must be, because even behind his mask I notice Logan's gaze widen with concern. Santi and Nino both point wildly in my direction, and Logan traces it right to me.

Confusion and concern overcome him. I shove through the fans, working my way over to the player pit, and he skates over with more fury than I've ever seen. He shoves his way off the ice through a door into the stands. Tons of people have noticed he's come out of formation and is heading for the stands. Crowds ram in behind me to get a glimpse.

An elbow hits me in the shoulder blade, nearly knocking me off my feet. Logan's hand comes out just in time to catch me.

His teeth are gritted and he glares at the guy who shoved me. "Get the fuck off my wife." The rush of fury in his eyes has security guards coming over to hold back the crowd, and Logan.

Logan takes off his mask and gloves and throws them down. He's more worried than I've ever seen him. "Are you okay? Is Nino okay? What are you doing here?"

I'm more worried, too. This is it. It's my moment of truth. "I had to talk to you. I don't want you playing and thinking... me and you..."

"I don't want you worrying about me..."

"Well, I do. I worry about you all the time. I think about you all the time. Every dream I have includes you now, Logan..."

He pulls me closer, and I'm met with a wall of man and hockey gear.

"I love you, Shay. It's going to be all right."

I don't have much time. I need to get this out. He needs to play his best tonight. He needs to win this Stanley Cup, and then... we'll make another plan. "I know you do. And I love you, too. I loved you then. I love you now. I'll love you always."

With that, his lips crash into mine. By now, thousands of eyeballs are on us. His embrace is warm and firm, and I want to stay in it forever. I'll do everything in my power to never be away from this man again. The crowd cheers, a few people whistle, and a lifetime of passion is shared in this moment.

Unfortunately, there's a game to play, so he pulls back, puts his helmet halfway on, and flashes me that *jump me* dimple. "That's all I needed to know, *pastelito*."

He turns to leave.

I catch him with one word. "But..."

He spins. "Shit, there's a but?"

I have to say this now. I know these things will move fast. He'll talk to his agent soon, and I can't let him give it all up because I can't put my big-girl pants on. "But I don't want to ask you to stay."

He comes back over to me and swipes his hand around my hips. This time, his gaze is darker. "You sure know how to confuse a man..."

"You needed me to tell you I'm yours. I am. I'm all yours, and this is it for me, just like it is for you. But if you stay, I know what that means for you, and that decision needs to come from within. Whatever you need to do to live your life to the fullest, like what you want for me, I want it for you, too, Logan. I want you to achieve your dreams. We'll make it work. I'll be strong for you. I promise."

He presses one last kiss onto my lips and whispers against them so no one else can hear, "I already told Reggie I'm done."

Something between a gasp and a sigh leaves my lips. "Really?"

"Really."

"What if you don't..." I don't finish my sentence. I don't want to be negative or jinx it, but what if he doesn't win a Cup?

He reads my mind. "Oh, we will now, baby."

He takes a step away.

"Wait!" I call.

He grabs his gloves from the floor and stares at me.

"I wrote you a note, too."

I turn around, slip my hair from my back to front and show him my jersey. Of course it says Hunter. But there, above his name, I scribbled something else.

M. R. S.

Mrs. Hunter.

Butterflies fill my belly. I peek over my shoulder, wondering what he'll think.

He pulls at his shirt, giving himself air as if he's hot. His gaze licks up and down my body. "That's my wife right there."

I wobble my head, sassy.

"You are in so much trouble." He doesn't even care that everyone is watching us. "You better be wearing that jersey with nothing under it when I get home."

Chapter Thirty-Nine

Logan

I KICKED ABSOLUTE HUSKY ASS. It was like taking candy from a baby. Ashton, of course, was on his best form ever to humiliate Jolie's ex, and I seemed to have an out-of-body experience. I had wings. I took flight.

And I just have a feeling. When I arrive home late that night, I recognize it. My intuition. My heavy gut. It's telling me this is the season. And it's telling me the time is right. Not only because I'm retiring and so is Ashton, but because this Cup win would matter. It would matter more than any other time because I have Nino and Shay now.

I can already see them jumping up and down like maniacs, celebrating, and the thought of it makes me smile to myself in the darkness of our house.

I still can't believe she came to the game. I can't believe she mooched her way in, got tickets... Santi helped. What was going through her mind? I have to know and I only have about ten hours before I leave for the East Coast tomorrow.

Thank God I'm here tonight.

I walk quietly through the house, and though I'm desperate to see Shay, I can't help myself. I crack open Antonio's door and see him sound asleep. He's actually in bed this time, oven mitts crushed tightly against his chest. His night light illuminates his thick glossy eyelashes, and his lips are all soft and mushed open in that cute way lips do when a person is in deep sleep. He's probably drooling a little, but I even find that adorable

I can't believe how lucky I am to have found Shay again, but to have her come with such an incredible child is more than I'd ever dare to dream. Just a couple months ago I was lost, and frankly, self-destructive, and now I'm building a real foundation.

I close the door gently and make my way into our bedroom.

Shay is still up in bed, reading with a singular lamp on. She puts down her sticker-backed Kindle. "Hey. I couldn't sleep."

I take myself to the bedside and kneel next to her. Grab her hand and kiss the back of it. "I'm surprised you aren't exhausted from that night."

She throws her face into her other hand. "I must have looked like a lunatic."

"No." I tip her chin up with my finger. "You looked like my wife." She's more beautiful than ever right now. "Thank you for coming." I hesitate to say it but I want her to know. "I needed that."

She laughs lightly. "Did you? You already made the decision to retire, though?"

"True. For the same reason you didn't want to ask me to do it, I didn't want you to feel guilty or hold it in the back of your mind that it was your fault I stopped playing or anything like that. So I did it before you answered. It's my offering to our future. This is what I want. I'm done being famous and playing hard. I want you. Nino. This is where I hang up my skates. Where I hang my hat and where my boots come off."

"But you still wanted me to ask you to stay?" She cocks an eyebrow.

"Of course I did. I'm not needy but I need a bone once in a while."

"You do, huh?" She rakes her fingers through my hair. "I need a bone, too, but what we both really need is sleep."

We lie down alongside each other, and she flicks off her bedside light, the only one that was still on. She rolls onto her side, and I roll onto mine, finding my way to her body. I reach around her warmth and take her hand. Even in our sleep I know there will be an uncontrollable attraction.

Will I even sleep?

She whispers, "Logan?"

I breathe in the honey scent of her hair. "Mmm?"

"Why do you love me?"

"Fuck, baby, there's a list till morning."

"Just give me one. One to remember until you get back home from your next away games."

I could tell her how caring she is. I could say she's talented. She's a good mother and sister, and I find her family values admirable. She asks this question now because when we leave, her insecurities will all flood back in. Over time, they'll fade.

"I love that you don't let me get away with anything. You're a tough-ass woman who's hard to please."

"You love that I'm hard to please?"

"I do. It makes me better."

She pulls my hand up to her mouth and kisses it. She sighs, and the room stills for the first time since I arrived in it. But she has a few more words, ones I'll remember for a lifetime.

"I don't know much about love," she says. "But I'm pretty sure the best kind is the one that makes you a better person, without ever changing you into someone other than yourself."

Chapter Forty

Shay

SIX MONTHS LATER

Over the months that followed, Logan was more determined than ever to stay fit and get rest in light of his retirement.

It helped me not miss him so much to throw myself into work, and come the new year, I booked in and had meetings with over thirty potential couples all able to get a cake in my new Shino Cakes price range. Of course, I still gave friends and family discounts to anyone in Starlight Canyon.

Funnily enough, none of these high-end, well-to-do brides had such bridezilla tendencies as my very own father.

The good thing about Logan not being around is it gave time for Dad to plan that wedding reception he promised and for family from Mexico to get visas. Because my dad insisted upon paying for everything from his own coffers, it would be a humble reception, but when I walked in the marquee he rented and had placed to the side of our home on the scrubby patch of land where nothing ever grew, I couldn't help but suck in a breath.

If I were to have gotten married, this is exactly how I thought it would be.

Not Vegas.

Not something grand in a fancy hotel.

I imagined a marquee to the side of my childhood home, decorated by my dad and some ranch hands with a cake by my mom. My uncle's mariachi band would play, and some Canyon high school kid with dreams of making it in New York would DJ later in the night. That was what I thought might happen, and this is close enough to make my heart stutter and my eyes mist over.

The space is simple and festive. It's funny how things just feel right. Logan belongs in this dream as much as the rest. He might wear flashy clothes and have his shoes shined the old-fashioned way, but he's a simple country boy underneath it all. He's the small town's teenage crush. He's the best first date that didn't cost a dime, just staring at a river, talking. He's home grown, as I am, and I just know he'll love this marquee.

Waves of reminiscence overcome me, and I start to choke up.

But my old man bridezilla interrupts with another second-guess. Or is it his third? Or fourth? I don't know, the man lost his ability to make decisions when he started planning his daughter's wedding reception.

"I'm not sure there are enough decorations up. This marquee is huge. It looks empty."

"It's perfect, Dad. Remember I told you bodies will be in here, too. They'll make the space full. Stop worrying. Logan and I don't need anything lavish anyway."

His lips form a thin line. "And the cake? Maybe..."

I shoot him a daring gaze. "Don't go there with the cake. I take no requests or criticism. It's *my* cake. It will be perfect."

He pulls an imaginary zipper across his lips.

I wrap my arm around him. "Did you ever think you'd be able to get rid of me?"

It was meant to be a joke, but my comment sends instant tears to my dad's eyes. His sentimental words are garbled through a tight throat. "*Mija*... I wish your mom could see how wonderful you have become. To meet Nino. To see you in white..." His worn workman's hands wipe tears from his sun-kissed cheeks.

My eyes sting, and I give my dad a big hug. "Me, too."

He clears his throat. "She would have approved. She always thought the Hunters were good people."

I laugh lightly at a memory bubbling up. "Once, at a bake sale, Logan bought one of my brownies, and she pointed at him. She said, 'He's going to be very handsome one day.'"

My dad chuckles. "He's a good man."

"I'm very lucky."

"Hold on to him." My dad's words are far away. "Enjoy every moment."

I've been pushing myself to be more vulnerable and allow myself grace for wanting things like fairy tales. This is why I told Logan I wanted to wear a wedding dress tonight. It's also why I kept it in a no-go zone in our closet.

I sit in my childhood bedroom, glancing at my hair in the mirror on the wall, waiting for my husband to come. He's five minutes late. So maybe five more. Impressively being on time is something he's improved upon, but I still have to give him leeway.

Then, there's a light knock on the door.

I stand, smooth the front of my satin dress, suddenly feeling so nervous. I didn't have time to go to a bigger city or look online or go anywhere but Buffy's Boutique on Main Street. So my dress is simple. Spaghetti straps, a little cleavage, but Buffy tailored it perfectly along the curves of my childbearing hips and mummy tummy, and frankly, I don't think I would have liked the way I looked better if I was still twenty.

I hope Logan agrees, because as much as I feel beautiful right now, I want him to think so, too.

"Come in," I spread out my veil behind me.

The door creaks open, and there is my six-foot three handsome husband in a tux fitted to his every angle. He's dapper. Sexy... and his jaw is totally slack. He throws his hands in front of his mouth, surprised, and by his wide eyes, it's pleasantly so.

It's the first time in a long time he's been speechless, and the empty space conjures up butterflies.

I smooth the sides of my dress with nervous hands. "You like? I know it's not all rhinestones and lace."

He still hasn't blinked. "You, my love, have literally taken my breath away." He comes in and closes the door. His jaw works in concentration as he beholds me like this is a fairy tale. He takes me by the hands. "I've never seen anything more beautiful."

"I hoped you'd like it. I didn't have much time to..."

"Stop that. It's not your style to apologize. You. Are. Stunning. And the words you're looking for are..."

"Thank you?"

"More like... yes, I am stunning." He lightly traces the bare skin over my collarbone, down over my peaked nipple that unabashedly makes a show, and wraps his hand firmly around my waist. "Do we have to go out there now? People expect me to be late." His gaze is full of mischief.

"Ten minutes late is all you get with the Mendez family before you're expelled. I'm sure we'll get back to doing forever and everything else going through that dirty little mind of yours soon enough."

He kisses me gently. "How will I keep my hands off you tonight?" He lets his forehead fall to mine. "Later, baby, I'll fall to my feet and slither up this dress so fast, you won't know what bit you."

I'm so damn happy I could explode. And it only gets sweeter.

"Before we go out there..." He pulls a ring box out of his inner jacket pocket. "I got you a present."

"Logan..." I take the small velvet box from him; one of its edges is worn down. It doesn't appear new, nor from one of the many luxury jewelry stores Logan has insisted on taking me to when it was Christmas and Valentine's Day.

"What is this for? We have rings."

"Open it."

Inside are two basic silver rings. They match, one with a sun and one with a moon. They're beautiful... but I don't get it.

"They're promise rings. I bought them for us the day you left Golden Sierra." He points to them. "They go together. The sun and the moon. I thought you'd be the moon back then, but I'm not so sure anymore."

I'm stunned. I drop my gaze back to these rings, now nearly twenty years old.

He carries on like he's nervous about what I'm going to say. "You probably don't remember the little bag I brought with me that afternoon."

I do. It was small, fancy-looking for us back then, but I was far too gone to think about what was inside. "You bought us promise rings?"

Just like Logan said, there I was preparing for the worst, and Logan was preparing for the best. It's just the most heart-wrenching example of how our most essential qualities, how our boundaries, defenses, fears, and even strengths can be the worst of us.

My eyes sting.

He kept them.

I love this man. He is everything I thought he was then and more. "Should we wear them?"

He glances up at me. "That's the plan. But you don't have to put it on now. It just felt like the perfect time to give it to you."

"Let's wear them now." I take his hand in mine. "Since neither of us remember our vows from Vegas, let me just say, Logan, I promise you sarcastic laughter, truth you never asked for, to push myself to grow with you, and of course... a lifetime of cake." I slide the ring on his right ring finger. "Forever."

He processes what I said with the kind of joy that beams straight from the chest. Then, he takes my right hand and professes his own promise. "Shana Guadalupe Hunter..."

Ever since I changed my name is can't stop using it. "You just love saying that, don't you?"

He raises his eyebrows. "I do. And I promise you riotous fun, to push your boundaries and your buttons, to put you and Nino first for the rest of my life. I promise to support your true potential, and last but not least... I promise gray sweatpants."

I gasp and slap his chest lightly. "Shut up. You knew..." I purse my lips.

He kisses my cheek. "You're so transparent."

Chapter Forty-One

Logan

AFTER DINNER and a heartfelt and very tearful thank-you speech by Luis, Shay and I have our first dance. The hundreds of eyes on us are tangible, but they soon fade, and there's nothing but me and my perfect wife.

Our song plays, but it sounds so distant because even in this tent full of bodies, there's a silence between me and Shay. It's calm, it's a moment where we're alone in the presence of all these people.

I kiss her gently. "I'm so glad I chased you."

She kisses me back. "I'm so glad you finally caught up."

I rub her back. We sway to the romantic melody, and her cheek rests on my chest. I pull her in tightly and run my hands over the small of her back. It's satin and smooth to the touch, but I also feel the curves and dents and worn edges of our past. Shay and I are complex, and the strange thing is, I'm not patient with anyone else. I'm not still, or calm. But this woman stops my world from spinning.

Our dance comes to an end, and it's hard to let go of her tiny hands, to peel her body from my chest. But we're not just here for ourselves. In fact, I'm pretty sure this is Luis' party. He spins a finger in the air as if he pre-planned this moment with the DJ and rushes on the dance floor as soon as we're finished. He takes Shay by the hand to the edge and starts to encourage a conga line to form behind her.

My entire family is here, loads of people from the Canyon, and many of Shay's relatives from afar. All her brothers are here, and the space is filled with laughter. The dance floor is rocking as a long conga line with nearly every person I love snakes around the room. Music blares into the darkness around the Mendez ranch nestled between cozy mountains.

My eyes scan the space where friends and family swirl in a kaleidoscope of colors and emotions. My grumpy brother, Dash, holds on to the waist of his wife, Molly. Colt's gaze dry humps his wife, Sam. Ashton and Jolie are absolutely jamming, neither one being able to resist a party, and my mom and Eve shimmy their shoulders in unison.

The uplifting beats of the music beckons to them, and they surrender willingly, letting the melodies guide their movements. There, at the helm of the whirlwind, is my bride—radiant, beautiful, somehow able to look offbeat in a conga line. A laugh rises up into my throat. I love seeing how the wine lets down her guard. Her mouth sings to the lyrics of a song we used to hear at the bars in college.

At the tail end of the line is Luis who wrangles her

brothers as they trail behind. Those men are as hard to read as Shay. None of the Mendez siblings seem to have inherited Luis' vulnerability, though Santi is the most like me, and he furrows his eyebrows, wobbling his head to the music, enjoying it a lot more than the others as he hangs on to his dad's hips. Gabriel, Rio, and Enzo follow behind, and their expressions are more like professional dancers deeply concentrating on their steps.

Those men are my brothers now. Though they haven't exactly embraced me with open arms, everyone knows I can get along with a hard-ass, so I'm sure we'll get close over the years, if they ever come up for air and away from their desks.

The conga snake weaves around the marquee, and I'm filled with a sensation I've never felt before. The dance floor is a canvas, each step paints a story of connection, joy... shared history. This town is its own little universe, one I might have left for a while to swashbuckle and gallivant but... *this* is who I am.

It's no surprise I ended up back here. We all need gravity to stop us floating away into the great expanse, into some sort of existential crisis where we can't figure out what the hell life is about. Starlight Canyon is a familiarity of decades of companionship, neighbors, and friends. And now, Shay is the star around which I revolve. She can make my life shine just as sure as she can burn me, and my heart rises and sets with her.

I don't know how I ever lived without her all those years.

When 'Girls Just Wanna Have Fun' comes on, a lot of the men on the dance floor head for the bar, including my brothers and the Dane boys. Colt pulls in next to me and lifts his finger, then orders a round of beers for us.

"Just have to say again, Logan," my older brother puts a hand on my shoulder, "Dad... well, he would have been..."

"Proud?" I finish his sentence.

"I was going to say surprised, but you might be right about that, too." He smiles devilishly and slaps my back affectionately.

We drink for a moment and stare at the large group of women with their hands in the air like they just don't care singing to Cyndi Lauper's timeless girl-power anthem.

Dash can't take his eyes off Molly who has a slip. He nearly drops his beer to rush off and help her, but two of Shay's cousins catch her by the arms and prop her back up, Molly giggling all the way back to her feet.

When did we all become so smitten? Normally, we'd all be talking about horses and calves and bull riding. Hockey. Football. Man stuff. But instead we silently nurse beers, glued to the beauty radiating from that dance floor.

Finally, four men bring the testosterone back to life inside us. Shay's brothers join us at the bar. We all shake hands like country boys do, and I get four more beers for the men I'm still not sure are sure about me.

Colt is an even better conversationalist than I am, and as the eldest who took on the job of man of the house in his early twenties, a natural host, too.

"I read in the *Financial Post* you gentlemen signed a pretty mighty deal."

Rio nods once. "That we have. It's been a long time coming."

Colt lifts his beer. "Congrats. I know how hard it is to get the attention of investors. Especially with controversial tech."

I add, "We even had a tough time with the wind farm."

Colt nods. "That we did."

Santi grabs my shoulder. "Not sure securing that investment was as hard as winning a Stanley Cup."

Though I offer a humble shrug, it's hard not to go on about it. Ashton and I share a knowing gaze... we can talk shit about this to the grandkids for all eternity. Now's not the time to gloat, but it's nice to be able to impress Shay's brothers with something.

Enzo, who is almost impossible to decipher from Rio apart from his Clark Kent glasses, chimes in. "In part we have you to thank." He glances between Colt and Dash. "If you two didn't help with sending over ranch hands and help to Dad, we wouldn't have been able to stay in California." He peers over at his sister who sings along with her girl gang.

"And Shay moving back..." his gaze meets mine now, "we never really realized what a sacrifice it was till now."

Rio reaches inside his jacket pocket and pulls out a velvet ring box. "We brought you this as a gift. It's for Shay actually. We figure now you have our sister and nephew, *you* don't need anything else."

If he means it as a joke, I can't tell. But he's right anyway. I take the box and open it to see a vintage gold engagement ring with a simple small diamond.

Santi points to it. "It was our mother's."

Rio adds, "It was given to me, the eldest..."

Enzo interrupts, "By five minutes."

"Older still," Rio says, rushing over his brother. "The point is, it was supposed to go to the first to get married. Mom guessed wrong about us. We're married to our work," he says, with an almost melancholy tone. "It will be happier on Shay than in that box."

Sometimes I wonder about men like these guys. What holds them back from diving in? Why haven't such good-looking, intelligent and fit men found love? But we all have our reasons. I never found it either in sixteen years.

I know what Shay would say to this gift. She's confessed to me how much she wished her brothers would settle down. I close the lid of the box. "She'll be the placeholder until one of you falls."

Rio's laugh is dismissive, but he's somehow grateful for the words at the same time. Somewhere inside there, just like was hidden underneath layers of Shay's outward tough appearance, is likely someone sentimental. All humans are the same on the inside.

The conversation turns back to the thing we all have in common: ranch life, farming, and it all falls into place like it's always been with the men of Starlight Canyon.

When the party dies down and we tuck up Nino at Luis' house to take our honeymoon, which now as a parent basically means a night on our own, we get home, back to our bed, back to our little life that means everything to me.

I lead my wife by the hand to the bedroom. Even though earlier when I first saw her in this dress I was hasty to take it off, by the time I press her back into the wall of our room and kiss her, I do it with a heightened awareness. I touch her body like I'm retracing my steps to the purest place in my heart. I enjoy this day, the one that will become our official anniversary, the one where I'll give her gifts of paper and silk, silver, gold, and platinum... if we're blessed with so many years together. But we never know how long we have.

So I kiss her for today. I'll never have a day like it again. I stare into her mesmerizing dark-brown eyes, and love fucking overwhelms me. Tendrils of ebony silk frame her face, and I'm in awe of how much soul is in her gaze.

I'm not a super religious man, but looking into Shay's

eyes is a spiritual experience. It makes me think about my mom, my dad, Luis, and Shay's mother. I think about how people so close to us once stood here like this, romantically pressed against the wall, behind a closed door in a wedding dress and a tux. I think about how fragile it all is, how blessed I've been to even get Shay back. I don't want to be greedy but I sure as hell hope we're given more years than our parents.

"Logan?" She cups my jaw. "What are you thinking?"

I'm making a wish, wishing harder than ever before in my life. "I'm praying to God."

"For what?"

"To let me keep you for the rest of my life."

Epilogue

Logan

FIVE MONTHS LATER

It's Labor Day weekend, and it's a scorcher in San Juan Diego, California. After what the Mendez boys have said was a cool August, the sun comes back from its vacation. We are all flapping our t-shirts for air and swiping sweat from under our cowboy hats when we finally tumble into the cool air in Santiago's house on the Mendez compound, known to their family simply as The Compound.

"No need to take boots off, the cleaner is coming tomorrow," Santi says, strolling into a gorgeous home of oak-beamed ceilings, boots clicking on travertine tiles.

We all follow him through the cavernous open-plan living room that's more like an entertainment area with a bar off to one side, huge wraparound sofas, and a pool table. It's not decorated like a bachelor pad but it has all the toys of one. I remember Santi being quite the wild bad boy, but the place displays no sign of debauchery. Still, I imagine I might find a bra tucked into the crevasses of the couch. Even if he didn't want them, I saw girls throw more intimate things than panties at him when he used to get in the ring.

But we all grow up, I guess. He seems to have replaced rodeo broncs for thoroughbreds. I can say, after touring The Compound, it's mighty inspiring what they've accomplished, not least of which Santi's stud stallions.

I lead Shay in by her lower back toward the kitchen. "This place has exceeded my imagination, gentlemen. It's an impressive plot you have."

Gabriel leans against the counter in a kitchen that looks as untouched as mine did before Shay moved in.

"Yeah, our first company wasn't a hit, but we made just enough to get The Compound started. First ten acres was scrubland, but we saw potential."

"We had the opportunity to bolt on acreage twice over," Santiago adds. "Luck was definitely involved in being able to stick together the land we have now. It's a patchwork quilt."

I mean every word I say. "Well, you had the vision and balls to invest. It was the first time it paid off of many."

Here, her brothers have over the years created something similar to what my dad set out to do at our ranch, only on our land, it never went further than two houses. The intention of The Compound is akin to the Kennedys'. The guys have five houses here now and more than enough space for the sixth, should we choose to move here when Nino leaves Longbrook.

Time will tell if we'll move. It might be an even harder decision if more children are involved. We've been trying for a while, and I'm not sure my mom could cope with Nino *and* a baby being so far away from her. And, of course, now that Ashton and I both have families, it feels right to be dads together.

But it's all too much thinking ahead of myself. After the wedding reception, Shay got the birth control removed, and contrary to how I figured it would be, it hasn't been the one-and-done situation I imagined. Shay had a miscarriage, and I was forever grateful to Sam for helping her talk through it. I understood the pain, hell, I still wonder what could have become of that creation, but I'm not a woman.

We should be beyond it now, but I still worry about what happened a few months back. Was it our age? Could it happen again? Should Shay be working so much? She's been on fire with her career with features in bridal magazines and delivering multiple cakes every month because she still can't seem to let go of the control over delivery.

I'm so damn proud of her I could fucking pop, but I do worry about her health.

Luis pulls out a stool at the breakfast bar and plops down. "It's hotter than a dragon's ass out there. You told me the summers here would be the same as back home, but it must be triple digits today."

Shay and Rio share a wary glance.

Luis has weathered almost ten years of arthritis, continuing to work on an unhealthy dose of anti-inflammatories to get by and perform his duties on his ranch. With Shay being set financially now and his sons, too, it's time he sells up the ranch, and even though nobody has brought that up directly, every comment Luis makes is a reminder somehow.

Luis will move to The Compound, but even though he agreed willingly, he still finds reasons this small town southeast of Silicon Valley is going to be so much worse than Starlight Canyon. The heat wasn't his first knock of the day.

Santi grabs a six-pack of beer and another of soda from the fridge and sets them on the counter. I could pour all six of them on my tongue and it still wouldn't quench my thirst. I open a soda for Nino and hand it to him.

I give Shay a soda, too, before slugging half a bottle of Chimayo with my arm loosely wrapped around my woman's shoulders.

Santi flicks the top of a beer bottle open with a satisfying sizzle and hands it over to Luis. "There are Indian summers in the Canyon, too. It's not like you've never felt heat before."

"Yeah," Luis takes a slug of his beer, "but the mountains cast shade at all the right times."

Santi is the first to become bored of the criticisms. "We're not forcing you to move here."

"I know. I'm just saying..." Luis puts his hands in the air.

I don't know Rio well yet, but if I have to guess, he's the kind of man who doesn't take long for a decision to be made, and when it is, he never looks back.

"Dad, make a list of what you need here, we'll sort it. You'll be happy here. The town is friendly, we know people already, and you'll have the horses, but actual stable hands to do the hard stuff. Isn't that your dream retirement?"

He flaps his hand, as if swatting off the word retirement.

I get it. People only like that word if they're leaving work behind. But when your work is your identity, that's another thing. I'm lucky to have jumped into something even more significant than hockey with Shay and Nino. I have something bigger than my career, but Luis just has a million question marks before him. And frankly, I hope the boys do give him some time. They all seem like workaholics.

Earlier this year, nearly two decades after setting off with a hundred bucks between them, they finally secured the investment with a world-renowned multibillionaire, Thaddeus Getty. In the little time since working with him, Thad has secured further investment, and their company already has a valuation of three hundred and seventy-eight million.

Nearly every day I think about how, if they'd signed that deal with Thad only a month or two sooner, Shay and I might have never made ours.

"Well, you know what..." Luis hoists Nino up on the stool next to him and ruffles his hair, still staring at Rio. "I do have a request."

"Shoot," Rio says.

He points in the air, serious as ever. "It's that silly..."

Santi interrupts him. "Do *not* say the gate."

"What?" Luis shrugs and glances at Shay as if she's about to agree with him. "What are you protecting around here with that thing? Fort Knox?" Now Luis turns to me. "Sorry, not that I think gates are bad. The one at Starlight Ranch is, you know... fit for purpose."

Enzo, who's probably used up his patience for people for the day, takes his glasses off to see if there's something on them, then replaces them on a face identical to Rio's.

"Should we have the cake now?" he asks in his low, tempered tone.

Shay slides out from under my arm and claps. "Yes. Cake. Let's do it. I'll be right back, just grabbing it." She disappears around the corner to where she left the cake box in Santiago's study.

Nino reads the side of his can of soda. "Uncle Enzo?"

Enzo, who is quiet, brooding, and even a little distracted from the present, now peers at Nino from behind his Clark Kent glasses and lifts his eyebrows.

Nino still considers the can. "Did you know you can use soda as a cleaning product?"

"Yes. I do."

"How come if it can dissolve rust, it doesn't burn our insides?"

Enzo crosses his arms and leans against a wall. "Stomach acid pH is higher than Coke."

Nino's mouth forms an 'O'. "That makes sense." He immediately puts two and two together.

I know Enzo doesn't have Nino's aptitude, but he's the closest person I know to having it. The pair simply nod at each other, almost having an invisible conversation about the chemistry of soda pop.

Just then, Shay comes into the room, and quickly, her brothers rush to take the cake off of her.

"I got it," she says, still not wanting anyone handling her masterpiece. She places it on the counter.

Rio shoves in between her and the cake and shoos her off.

"It's bad enough you insist on baking your own cake. Don't you want a day off for your birthday?" he asks.

"I am *not* eating someone else's cake," she says, as though he asked her something far worse.

"Well, get out of here and at least let us put the candles on," Gabriel says.

Luis lifts Nino off the stool and carries him on his hip to the dining room.

I sweep my arms under Shay and cradle her in my embrace. "Come on. You need to sit down. It was way too hot out there."

She laughs. I carry her a few steps around the corner into the dining room and set her down at the head of an Italian design twelve-person table. I pull out the chair for her to sit on her birthday throne.

Just then, Santiago's surround sound comes on with the song Luis prepped me to learn when it was Nino's birthday a few months ago and Shay and I were to wake him at an ungodly hour with this tune. In my family, we got to sleep in on our birthdays. Turns out Mexicans have to get up at the crack of dawn.

I take out my phone with the lyrics I typed in.

Four deep male voices come from behind, singing, "*Estas son las mañanitas...*"

I try my best to sing the melody of this Mexican birthday song. I must have listened to it a hundred times to get it right for today. I didn't do the best version at Nino's birthday and felt like a dancer behind by one step at every word. I fare better this time.

Luis sings his lungs out. "*Despierta, mi bien Shaylita...*"

Enzo carries the cake, singing, approaching slowly so the candles don't go out.

I can't get over how self-conscious Shay's become. Her cheeks brighten with heat, and Enzo is now next to her, the candles illuminating her every bashful feature.

Nino stands on his chair for the last line, serenading his mother. "*Levántate de mañana, mira que ya amanecióooooo.*"

Enzo places the cake in front of my wife. Shay's face twists with a sort of adorable shy quality I've never seen on her before. Not even when I'm telling her how much I like being between her legs. Well, it is a big moment.

She gazes up at me, and I swear her eyes are glassy.

"You okay?" I mouth.

She nods quickly.

Nino jumps down from his chair to run around and take back his mom's hair. "Make a wish!"

With only three blows, she snuffs out all thirty-seven candles.

Santi hands the knife to Shay who, given her reverence for her creations, would normally be the only one to cut it.

She smooths her hair behind one ear, and I swear the tip of it is rosy. "I've never made a cake like this before. I hope it's good."

Luis rubs his hands together expectantly. He barely ate lunch earlier, saying he was saving room for extra cake. "I'm sure it will be delicious."

She hands me the knife. "Will you cut it?"

"I got you."

I slide the knife down through the cake, feeling the weight of every layer under the hilt while Shay grabs the sides of her chair next to me.

I slide out a piece, laying it on its side on a plate. It's four layers of pink in ever lighter shades.

"Is it strawberry?" Nino asks.

"No..." My wife is all out blushing now and takes our son's hand. "It's a girl."

"Huh?" Nino scrunches his nose.

Shay lets out a sharp breath. "It's a girl cake."

Luis gasps so loudly he could steal the entire room's oxygen. "Oh my..." He stands and rushes to our sides. "Are you...?

Nino's voice squeaks. "Holy moly, holy moly!" He throws himself on Shay. "A girl! I can read to her!"

Good God, this boy of ours. *I could weep.*

Shay stands and hugs her father who is desperate to hold her tightly.

His voice is muffled in her hair. "You know it's a girl? My goodness, this family needs some women."

She laughs into his shoulder, and the nasal sound of it tells me tears of joy wet her father's shirt.

We've been waiting for ages to announce this. In light of the miscarriage, we wanted to be more sure, closer to the safety zone. Closer to feeling like this time, it will be okay.

Her brothers wrap their arms around her, and I hardly even know who is where anymore as the celebrations collide in a flurry of excitement.

Shay quickly pulls back, looking for Nino, and crouches. "What do you think? Can you handle being a big brother?"

Rio puts his hand on his nephew's shoulder. "I'll teach you everything I know."

Enzo, constantly reminded he's younger by five minutes, refrains from correcting him this time.

Nino is beaming. We didn't leave it until now to talk about having a sibling with him. I already know he wants this, too.

He pushes his glasses up his nose. "Can I name her?"

Shay and I glance at each other, scanning each other's gazes for the consequences of saying yes. Nino has an eclectic vocabulary, and *Cayenne* is the least of it. We could end up with a daughter called Pythagoras or Khartoum, his newest favorite capital city name.

Finally, Shay offers up some of that diplomacy she's so

good at. "Maybe you could. What kind of name did you have in mind?"

"Carmen."

The room goes still. Shay's lips drop open with this unexpected answer, and I imagine her heart swells instantly with a sense of longing for her mother. It's sad my father won't ever meet my son, my wife, and my soon-to-be daughter. Shay carried one child and now carries another without the support of her mom. Maybe she's not thinking about these things. But I am.

I dart my gaze to Luis; he wears one of those smiles where the lips turn down instead of up, but I catch sight of a glimmer of hope we actually say yes.

I bend down next to Shay and take Nino's hand in mine. "I can't think of a more beautiful name."

Shay glances up at her dad, and I know in her gaze is an ask for approval. He nods, subtly.

My wife puts her hands on her belly and speaks to our unborn daughter. "Baby Carmen, you better put your chaps on, because with these men, you're in for a wild ride."

THANKS SO MUCH FOR READING MY STORY!

If you're not ready to let go, join my newsletter to receive a deleted scene from Perfect Playbook. You can get that here...
https://dl.bookfunnel.com/2xubtvtysg

And maybe you guessed right about the next series and feel ready for more Mendez? Check out my next series all about those handsome broody brothers of Shay's. Echo Valley will be full of intrigue, suspense and fabulous tension and angst. Got your chaps ready?

First up in the series is Enzo and Ava...
Enzo Mendez is a broody and elusive entrepreneur hiding a secret behind Clark Kent glasses. When he hires hacker Ava Morris to help unearth his past, she discovers what he least expected - his heart.

Preorder now!
https://geni.us/lkdYe

Acknowledgments

This novel started as hours of voice notes with my alpha reader and PA, Char. Your help in plotting and bringing characters to life, and keeping them on track, is next to none. You are a talented critique partner and I look forward to many more books with you! I don't know what I'd do without you.

I also had some fabulous editors and helpers involved in this manuscript. Julia from Entirely Bonkerz is responsible for the late release, but also the much better execution! I love your honest criticism. My trusted editor Emmy Ellis always delivers on time and Isabella Bauer drilled into the Mexican culture for me as a sensitivity reader, making sure my intention to infuse the book with it was respectful. I'd also like to thank Valeria Noda for her input in this area with reference to the language in particular. Thank you to my editing team!

My beta readers came into play when I was already editing, due to the release change it was a bit all over the place but your notes and love for Shay and Logan really kept me going! Thank you so much to Caroline, Tabitha, Tori Ann and Amila for taking on this task!

To my ARC readers... how could this be possible without you? I'm in awe of your generosity. Do you have any clue just how important you are to keeping the indie community pumping? Irreplaceable.

Last but not least, I want to thank my children, who may never even read this acknowledgment, but to whom I owe such a credit for this book.

I somehow managed to come back to my dreams after many years of prioritizing everything but myself. Did I sacrifice? Or was this aspiration merely a case of delayed gratification? My children, instead of feeling hard done by when I need to work, give me so much encouragement and love on this journey of mine. It's so much more fun to celebrate *with* someone than without.

Thank you, my loves, for the words I hear so often- *"I never want you to stop writing, Mummy. You look so happy when you do it."*

Upon reflection, sometimes it seems I've sacrificed nothing and gained everything. It just took a long time to see it.

Also by Sienna Judd

About the Author

Sienna Judd is a small town, contemporary romance author who lives for all the spice and book boyfriends who are book husband material.

Sienna is an American girl married to her Prince Charming. She lives with her husband, three children, pony, dogs, guinea pigs and countless other animals on a small farm in England. She thinks kitchens are for dancing, is everybody's hype girl and might be known for talking too loudly.

Like every respectable woman she also loves drinking champagne and eating half of every chocolate in a truffles box.

Her spirit animal is a butterfly.

Made in the USA
Monee, IL
03 January 2025

76004845R00246